VICTOR EROFEYEV

GOOD STALIN

Glagoslav Publications

Good Stalin
By Victor Erofeyev

Glagoslav Publications Ltd
88-90 Hatton Garden
EC1N 8PN London
United Kingdom

www.glagoslav.com

A catalogue record for this book is available
from the British Library.

ISBN: 978-1-78267-111-4

CONTENTS

A mon père

All the characters in this book are fictional,
including actual historical figures
and the author himself.

I

In the final analysis, I killed my father. The solitary golden arrow on the dark-blue dial on the tower of Moscow University, in the Lenin Hills, showed minus forty degrees Celsius. The cars weren't starting. The birds were too scared to fly. The city had frozen like aspic with a human filling. In the morning, when I glanced at my reflection in the oval mirror in the bathroom, I noticed that the hair on my temples had turned gray overnight. I was thirty-one years old. It was the coldest January of my life.

In fact, my father is still going strong, and only recently gave up playing tennis on the weekend. Even now, although he has aged greatly, he still mows the lawn at the dacha with the electric lawn mower, between the hydrangeas and the rose bushes, among the gooseberry thickets he has loved since he was a child. He still drives, stubbornly refusing to wear glasses — a habit which drives my mother crazy and spells trouble for pedestrians. Retiring to his study on the second floor of the dacha, he sits by the window which is scraped by the branches of a tall oak tree, and sluggishly rubs his strong-willed chin and types something on the typewriter (perhaps he's writing his memoirs), but all this is mere detail. The murder I committed was not physical but political — and in my country, that was as true a death as any.

•

Do our parents really count as people? I have always been unsure about this. Our parents are undeveloped negatives. Of all the people we meet in life, the ones we are least familiar with are our parents, for the very reason that we never meet them: the initiative has been seized right from the outset by our 'folks' — in other words, they meet us. The umbilical cord is never really severed: we consist of them to exactly the same degree that we find them impossible to understand. The collapse of our knowledge of them is ensured. The rest is all conjecture. We're afraid to catch sight of their bodies or peer into their souls. For us, therefore, they never turn into people, forever remaining a series of impressions of which the origin is unknown, unstable puppet-mirages.

They are untouchable beings. There is nothing we can do about our opinions of them, which are sucked out of our fingers and founded on prejudice, lingering childhood fears, the struggle of idealism against reality, justification of the unjustifiable. But equally there is nothing our parents can do in the face of our appraisal of them. Our mutual love belongs neither to us nor to them, but to an instinct lost in a mother's womb and in the womb of civilization. In this instinct we actively seek an uplifting human beginning, and we cannot help but take vengeance on this instinct for its blindness by engaging in profound speculation. The love that goes by the name 'fathers and sons' lacks the common denominator of gratitude and is full of endless insults and misunderstandings, which give rise to the bitterness of regret that comes too late.

Parents are a buffer between us and death. Like great artists, they are not entitled to age; our inevitable revolt against them is as much biologically predetermined as it is morally irreproachable. Parents are the most intimate thing we have. But when family intimacy reaches the proportions of an international scandal, which puts the family on the brink of destruction, as happened in my household, you can't help but begin to think things over, reminisce and analyze things. It is only now that I have at last made up my mind to write a book about all this.

ANONYMOUS LETTER

To the Minister for Foreign Affairs of the USSR, Comrade A.A. Gromyko.

cc: Austria. Vienna. Representative Office of the Soviet Union at the United Nations. To Ambassador V.I. Erofeyev.

Airmail; on the envelope — the names of three pilots: P. Osipenko, V. Grizodubov, and M. Raskov, Heroes of the Soviet Union all. The 40th anniversary of the first non-stop flight from Moscow to the Far East. Stamp # 31-1791840 (sent on January 31, 1979 at 6:40 pm) Moscow, Post Office, Unit #9.

Second copy (to me): MOSCOW. 27-29 Gorky Street, Apt. 30. To: V. Erofeyev.

Airmail; on the envelope — the Baikal Seal. From the series: contemporary animal fauna of the USSR. Stamp # 31-1791840. Moscow, Post Office, Unit #9.

The return address and last name on the envelope were made up. The writing and punctuation of the anonymous author have been left unchanged.

RESPECTED COMRADE MINISTER!

It seems to me that the localized scandal currently taking place in literary circles ought to prompt certain other institutions involved in the struggle between two social systems to draw certain conclusions. Specifically, I have in mind the Ministry of Foreign Affairs.

To think: in the family of one of our most loyal diplomats, whose reputation is flawless from an ideological point of view, there grew up a real scum-bag, who writes obscene, sexually-pathological short stories, and who has now helped to write and edit an underground almanac with a clear anti-Soviet stance. And Victor Erofeyev's story, which is set in a public bathroom which we are supposed to understand as representing Russian society, is simply unprecedented!

<...> And whilst they try to work out, in literary circles, how a young man without a single book to his name came to be chosen as a member of the Union of Soviet Writers, oughtn't we to be wondering whether he picked up these strange ideas of his abroad, where he used to live, and now spends a lot of his time, because of his parents' official duties? It does not seem likely that he was actually recruited by anyone, but one thing is almost certain: the ideology of the enemy went straight to his head!

<...> There is much talk at the moment about how his parents' connections will help this class dropout extricate himself from a situation in which, up till now, he has behaved extremely impudently, without the faintest trace of repentance. It would be deeply regrettable if his parents' seniority were to put the brakes on this political matter, which looks very much like a rehearsed diversion. On the contrary it seems vital that we introduce an educational campaign at the Ministry of Foreign Affairs using this regrettable incident as an example, so that all the others can contemplate the potential consequences of liberal parental views, and the lack of constant vigilance with regard to issues of...(the second page of the letter is missing, in both copies).

•

I might just be the individual with the most freedom in all Russia. In essence this is a pretty meaningless achievement: there isn't much competition in this field. People are too busy competing against one another in other ways. I don't know what to do with my freedom, but it was given to me like the gift of clairvoyance. It somehow came about that I was left outside all the various ranks, regalia, faiths and awards. I suppose I got lucky. I have neither bosses nor underlings. I'm dependent neither on bastards nor on the Red Army. I don't give a shit about critics, fashion or fans. Being the freest man alive in the world's most ridiculous country is an absolute riot. In other countries there are serious people who carry the burden of responsibility like a full pail of water, but here — here there's nothing but a ridiculous, untranslatable assortment of common folk, policemen, intellectuals, collective farmers, political prisoners, half-wits, managers and other mindless idiots. Ridiculous people have no need of freedom.

What brilliant ideas Russians have come up with — all of them brilliantly absurd. We created the Third Rome, resurrected our forefathers, built Communism. We believed in everything! The Tsar, white angels, Europe, America, Orthodoxy, the NKVD, the rule of council, the communes, revolution, the 10-ruble bank note, national exclusivity — we believed in anything and anyone, except in ourselves. But the most absurd idea of all was to call the Russian people toward self-knowledge, to bang the gong and ring the little Buddhist bell:

"Arise, Brothers! Let's embrace one another! Let's drink!"

Sure enough the brothers will get to their feet, and they will certainly have a drink. You will find yourself sitting down among the intelligentsia all night long, talking of God, death, women, author song, fate…your veins will expand, the number of concepts in your mind will multiply. The horizon will expand on all sides: one minute you're having a smoke with Byron, the next you're playing pool with Che Guevara. But when you wake up in the morning, the intelligentsia is no more. Bohemia is going out of fashion. And then all you can do is sit and get dumbed down by big business, TV, politics and the oligarchs. Or you head down to the nearest nightclub with the young people of today: and in the toilet you'll find out all there is to know about the cosmic wars between good and evil, the etymology of Japanese curse words, forty-four ways to be disagreeable to top-models, and the mythical abyss of Armageddon; and you'll be able to dance a few ethnic dances while you're at it.

Russian writers are ridiculous, too. Some of them laugh through their tears, while others simply laugh. They freak out about morality in this ridiculous country. But, like the Aztecs, they are bloodthirsty, and have a penchant for human sacrifice. They cut off the heads of their women and their enemies. Their novels are peopled with ridiculous fathers and ridiculous children. Turgenev and Dostoyevsky were not alone in talking this subject to death: the Silver Age in Andrei Bely's *Petersburg* did so too. The revolutionary son and the reactionary father. A book, a bomb, terror. Had my mother only known back then — when, as she tried to foster in me a love of literature, she felt pained by my childhood indifference to the printed word — that I would go on to reflect this subject in my life, and harm my entire family by doing so, she would probably have taken all the books from our family library and burnt them.

•

From a letter from my mother to my father, sent from Vienna to Moscow, dated February 17, 1979:

> *My Dear Vov,*
>
> *As of tomorrow I will have been living without you for two weeks. And it seems to have been raining almost non-stop, night and day. The rain is hot and cool, by turns…*
> *I already wrote and told you that I'm trying to keep myself busy all the time, to the max, and to be among other people, in order to rid myself of gnawing thoughts. But now, it seems, I have exhausted all opportunities forget-togethers of any kind. And after all, how many such get-togethers could I expect to enjoy anyway, given the secluded life we lead?*

For the third day running it is pouring with rain, and when the rain stops a thick fog descends, so that you can't even go out for a stroll in the street. <...>

For the umpteenth time I find myself worrying about you! What on earth have you got to do with literary experiments? Victor behaved like an absolute idiot, opening himself up to criticism from all sides, at a time when he was yet to achieve anything, when he hadn't yet 'made it', as they say. How irresponsible he was! He screwed up badly, and has ruined so much in his life for a long time to come.

But as for you! What do you have to do with it? Irreproachable service, at the expense of your health and your nerves. A colossal responsibility. An entire life-time given over to work. Staying up working until midnight, when others are (illegible) or drinking vodka.

I must stop now, for I can't bring myself to write about this any longer. <...>

I'm sending you something.

The socks are for Andryusha, and the jar of caviar is for Olezhka. The wine is for all of you.

Kisses,

Galya.

•

Like a wild animal, time is quick to uproot itself and change its place of habitation. In dusty, crocodile-skin suitcases, expensive briefcases with torn handles, and *Stolichnaya* vodka crates I find the business cards of the deceased, invitations to parties for government officials who have long since retired, menus for lunches and dinners with non-existent people, and special editions of newspapers (mainly containing obituaries). Bureaucratic existentialism, a yearning for immortality, a hunger to leave a mark. My father was a real hoarder.

MAMA: What do you need all this for?

My father never gives an answer to this question. In the main drawer of his desk is a copy of *Pravda*: it contains an obituary,an apotheosis unprecedented in the history of journalism, contained inside the black lines of newsprint. The style in which the report on the leader's post mortem is written is so excellent that one can't help thinking: this is a work of literature.

In those days, all life was literature. On March 5th, 1953, all of the characters were divided into two camps: those who wept and those who were happy. But there was one individual who didn't notice that Stalin had died; who didn't notice the mourning music playing on the radio, nor the red flags with the black ribbons, hung up by the road-sweepers on the streets. That individual lived in Moscow, right in the city center, at 27/29 Gorky Street, near Mayakovsky Square, and his neighbors, in that huge Stalinist building with an intricate stucco façade, reliably constructed by German POWs, were the most prominent Stalinist writer, Fadeyev, and the wonderful socialist-realist artist Laktionov, by whom, as a matter of principle, my mother refused to have her portrait painted: she was in love with the Impressionists, but Laktionov's reputation had been sullied by that time. Mother therefore did herself out of a portrait which might have fetched a lot of money nowadays. As well as the Impressionists, mother later fell in love with the songs of Okudzhava, and one day, Galina Fyodorovna, who chain-smoked *Java* cigarettes, pulling them out of a soft, crumpled pack and ritually smoothing them out before she lit them, brought him to our house. And there he stood, Okudzhava: slender, young and arrogant (perhaps out of shyness); he was drawn to the collection of Georges Brassens records — my father had once known Brassens — and it seemed to me then that as soon as Brassens started singing, Okudzhava completely forgot we were there;when, out of politeness, he remembered, the conversation around the table had turned to the subject of Stalin's death, and mother said that on that day everyone had cried because they couldn't understand what had happened, and Okudzhava said quietly:

OKUDZHAVA: That was the happiest day of my life.

And it was an incredibly awkward moment.

The individual who didn't notice Stalin's death was five and-a-half years old, but that was no excuse. Children back then went about life, walked around, sang songs, and knew what was going on in the country. Moreover, this particular boy's father worked at the Kremlin as an aide to Molotov and as Stalin's official French interpreter. It may be that I am just a very forgetful person, but no matter how hard I strain my memory, I simply cannot remember that day of mourning. How is that possible?

I asked my parents this question for years. First of all I found out that my mother had cried that day, with her friends. They all worked together at the Soviet Union's Ministry of Foreign Affairs, and they cried for two reasons. Firstly, they loved Stalin. Secondly, they were scared that without him the country would collapse. My mother later admitted as much.

MAMA: I regret crying, because Stalin was a monster.

As for the second point, history showed that that group of friends was right. Stalin died; the Soviet Union began to fall apart the very next day, and our neighbor Fadeyev shot himself a short while later. And try as we might to embalm the country, it continued to disintegrate until it eventually fell into putrid pieces.

But what about papa? Did papa cry?

PAPA: I was too busy that day to cry.

How about that! When papa didn't want to talk about something, he didn't give evasive answers but kept his answers brief and to the point. But of course, there was so much to do — ordering the coffin, the wreathes and the hearse, buying up bundles of flowers from all over the Soviet Union, to the extent that there was nothing left to put on the grave of the composer Prokofiev, who died on the same day as Stalin. Then he and his comrades had to find a suitable spot in the cemetery, and over the next few days tried to bring order to the funeral stampede on Trubnaya Street, and evacuated those who didn't make it to the requiem service. And only recently did father confess.

FATHER: I sighed with relief that day.

But is there really any truth in this confession, or is it just that time, like the wild animal that it is, had moved on to pastures new?

From an article by Daniel Vernet — in *Le Monde* — dated January 25, 1979:

DES ÉCRIVAINS SOVIÉTIQUES NON-DISSIDENTS
REFUSENT LA CENSURE ET ÉDITENT UNE REVUE
DACTYLOGRAPHIÉE

Moscou. — Un café dans une petite rue de Moscou. Un group d'écrivains a retenu la salle, mardi 23 janvier, pour présenter à quelques amis soviétiques, écrivains et artistes, une nouvelle publication. La jour prévu, pourtant, le café est fermé. La veille, des médecins ont décidé que le lendemain serait "jour sanitaire", que le café avait absolument besoin d'être désinfecté de tout urgence.

Cinq écrivains: Vassili Axionov (dont les œuvres sont connues en France, telles que *Billets pour les élolies* ou *Notre ferrailleen or*); Andrei Bitov, Viktor Erofeyev (critique et homonyme de l'auteur de *Moscou sur vodka*); Fasyl Iskander (écrivain installé en Abhazie) et Eugène Popov (jeune poète sibirien) ont publié une revue en dehors des circuits officiels, en refusant de se soumettre à une quelconque censure.<...>

Ce recueil, qualifié d'almanach par ses auteurs, selon la tradition russe du dix-neuvième siècle, se présent sous la forme d'un grand cahier de format quatre fois 21-29. Avec plus de cent vingts pages, il représent l'équivalent

d'un livre de sept cent pages. Vingt-trois auteures
soviétiques y sont publiés. <…>

L'almanach s'intitule *Métropole*, aux trois sens du
terme: métropole comme capitale, comme métropolitain
(underground), et comme célèbre hôtel de Moscou, car
les auteurs "cherchent un toit". <…>

NON-DISSIDENT SOVIET WRITERS REJECT CENSORSHIP
AND PUBLISH JOURNAL

Moscow. A café in a small street in Moscow. A group
of writers had booked the room inside for Tuesday, January
23rd, in order to present a new publication to a few Soviet
friends, writers and artists. When the day came, however,
the café was closed. The day before, some sanitary experts
had decided that the next day was going to be "cleaning
day" and that the café urgently needed to be disinfected.

Five writers: Vasily Aksyonov (whose works, such
as *Ticket to the stars* and *Our Golden Piece of Iron* were
well-known in France); Andrei Bitov, Victor Erofeyev
(a critic and the namesake of the author of *Moscow-
Petushki*, Fazil Iskander (a writer from Abkhazia) and
Yevgeny Popov (a young Siberian poet) have published
a journal without official permission, refusing to submit
to any form of censorship whatsoever.

This collection, described by the authors
themselves, using 19th century terminology as an
'almanac', is a huge folder, four times the size of A4. It
contains 120 pages, the equivalent of a 700 page book.
Twenty-three Soviet authors contributed to it <…>.

The almanac is called *Metropol*, and the word
has three meanings: metropolis, as in the capital;
metropolitan, as in the subway system (the underground);
and the famous hotel in Moscow, because the authors
are "looking for a roof over their heads" <…>.

•

My father was one of the most brilliant Soviet diplomats of his day. He was noted for his quick and ready wit, his unbelievable capacity for work, his optimism, charm, enduring good looks and modesty. He loved to tell jokes. His jokes were like the play of sunlight in the tree-tops. They stayed with me, not in verbal form, but as a mood: they had their own special, warm microclimate, which became the microclimate of my childhood. It sometimes seems to me that my yearning for the south (the only trait of mine which I also detect in Bunin), the fact that I think of the pyramidal poplars and white acacias,which one doesn't see in the Russian North, as my trees, and my 'recognition' of Parisian sycamores as the matriarchs of Russian flora can be attributed directly to the jokes my father used to tell.

My father was a *decent* person, capable of holding his own alongside senior figures in the party, even in the Stalinist era, and generally speaking, unlike many of his tin colleagues with the protruding eyes of toadies, lackeys and 'dimwits', he liked to stand with his legs shoulder-width apart, almost in the American way, in the wide pants that were fashionable back then, screwing up his eyes a bit — at least that's what I heard from Maya Koneva, the daughter of the famous marshal, who had known my father well in the early 1950s. There is a color photo of them from that time, in front of a white ZIS limousine with its doors open and a Sochi oleander, tennis rackets in their bronzed arms, which I consider to represent the ideal of the sweet life under Stalin. I had occasion to hear praise of my father from such varied figures as the great physicist Pyotr Kapitsa (over lunch at his summer house on Nikolina Mountain), Rostropovich, Gilels and Yevtushenko.

I couldn't help but be proud of my father. He never brought back expensive gifts from abroad 'for his seniors', never courted his bosses' wives. The speculating that had become standard practice among other diplomats — they bought expensive Western items overseas (cameras, tape recorders, Rolexes and record players) that had not yet reached the pitiful Soviet market, and sold them on through Moscow consignment stores for personal gain — was not for him. In his view — that of a committed Communist, a 'Stalinist falcon' with steely eyes who had been directly involved in the development of the Soviet concept of the 'Cold War', my father genuinely believed in the advantages of the Soviet system over capitalism, and used to dream of world revolution.

•

I was born in September 1947. I enjoyed a happy childhood under Stalin. I lived in a clean, cloudless paradise. In that sense, I can hold my own with the suspiciously sporty Nabokov. I too was a little baron, but whereas he was aristocratic, I came from the *nomenklatura*. I was born into happiness. Many years passed before I realized that. As Russians would have it, those who are born with a silver spoon in their mouths are happy people, those who are lucky. Mama seems to have believed for a long time that I was born happy as a result of some absurd mistake. When she gave birth to me, she had a dream in which she was paid a visit by Dostoyevsky, whom she did not often see in her dreams.

DOSTOYEVSKY: Well, are you content?

MAMA: I have only been this happy once before in my life. When the war ended, I celebrated victory in Tokyo. I was working at the Soviet Embassy, in the military attaché's department. The staff drank up all the wine we had, first the ordinary wines then the rare vintages. By the end two triumphant diplomats were fighting over a woman.

DOSTOYEVSKY: That woman was you.

MAMA: It's obvious who you are — you're Dostoyevsky.

Dostoyevsky frowned.

DOSTOYEVSKY: Drown him.

My mama pondered the great writer's suggestion.

•

From a letter from me, in Moscow, to my parents in Vienna, mistakenly dated with the preceding year (a mistake people often make in January): 1/27/78 instead of 1/27/79. The letter's tone is soothing,whilst its content amounts to a 'filial' mixture of truths and half-truths. It is quite a cunning letter:

Dear mama and papa,

an opportunity has arisen to write you a little letter, and fill you in on what's been going on. Olezhka — the biggest optimist in our family — is beginning to babble more and more; he pronounces words in a funny way, almost managing not to get them mixed up, and can string a few simple sentences together, and on top of this he is now going to kindergarten, which he seems to enjoy and where he has picked up all sorts of knowledge, particularly of the musical variety (he walks around singing). Vescha is overworked just like before, and looks skinny and see-through. I've been engrossed in my affairs too. One of these projects is worth discussing in more detail. Throughout the course of the year, a few Moscow–based writers (including Bitov, Aksyonov, Iskander and myself) have been working on a literary almanac, which contains experimental prose and poetry. Recently we took it to the Writers' Union and asked them to publish it. To our surprise, our initiative was greeted with much suspicion, and this soon developed into a full-blown scandal. They started dragging us to the Writers' Union to rewrite it, and be made to see sense; people got angry, and stamped their feet. For the household names (the almanac contained works by Akhmadulina, Voznesensky, Vysotsky and others), the scandal — about the revisions — took on Moscow–wide dimensions: the Western printed media and radio jumped on the bandwagon and pandemonium ensued. An enlarged secretariat of the Union gathered (attended by nearly 70 members), at which people like Gribachev, Y. Zhukov and other — 'savages' — spent four hours threatening us. I don't know what's going to happen next, but if you ask me 'they' simply lost their minds. I too took a lot of personal blame (at the Union and at the Institute). Our literary affair (for that was all it was)grew into God knows what (thanks to the idiocy of a few zealous preservers of stagnation). I'm writing to you about this in the hope that you will relate to what's happening with a sense of calm, appreciate my good intentions (and not just mine, but those of my friends as well). Unfortunately, as can be seen from the way the matter has progressed, the dark forces are currently in the ascendancy, but if they take extreme practical measures, the scandal will be transformed from one that is limited to Moscow into something seriously big (what's going on now is somewhat reminiscent of what it was like in 1963, according to the people who were there). I am refusing to give up hope that the matter will reach a more-or-less tolerable conclusion. In any case, don't take any steps without first consulting me. I understand that all this worries you, but not saying anything is simply not an option now. I feel alright, but my nerves are pretty shot, and there's more to come. Andryushka and Veshcha are terribly worried too, poor things… Thank you for the fishing pants… although I've got other things on my mind right now. Hugs and kisses, I'll let you know about any developments as soon as I can.

Veshcha sends her kisses too.

Yours, Victor.

•

In postwar, half-starved Moscow, grandma called mama at work with a gleeful account of what I had had for breakfast:

"Vityusha ate an entire jar of black caviar!"

My mother had an interesting job. She read things which no one else was allowed to read, the sort of things for which you could be executed on the spot. A modest chosen one, a young Goddess, who had been let in on the secret of the universe in a skyscraper in Smolensk Square, she read American newspapers and magazines searching for slander against the Soviet Union and summarized it for the directors of the press department.

The Americans were acting shamefully, piling slander upon slander and shitting all over the Russian people. The Americans wrote that the Russians were a self-destructive people who had driven themselves to Siberian death camps, and that Stalin was the most tyrannous dictator in the world, a cannibal who had swallowed up the Baltic states, Poland and the rest of Eastern Europe. He was no longer good old Uncle Joe, their ally in time of war. Others, less hardened to all this, might have suffered diarrhea or paralysis on reading such pronouncements, but as for mama, this slander from the Americans washed over her like water off a duck's back. She understood that the building sites of Communism, out in Siberia, weren't death camps. She genuinely hated the Americans, with the exception of Theodore Dreiser, whom she translated into Russian in her free time: she used to dream of being a translator. Mama knew that American women had crooked, hairy legs, which they made a great show of shaving. Images from an alien, foreign way of life were before her eyes every day. A winking camel offered a cigarette to her, as well as to the whole of America. But if she couldn't stand America, there was one person for whom she reserved an extra special hatred: my grandmother, Anastasia Nikandrovna.

Whereas the Americans were merely drawing up plans to land troops in Red Square, to give the Communists and the white bears a fright, grandma had already landed in Moscow and taken over our apartment. She had an apartment on Mokhovaya Street, in a two-storey building adjoining the Kalinin museum, directly across from the arched entrance of the shallow Lenin Library Metro Station, with stove heating, the unique smell of Russian provincial widowhood, and plumbing but no sewage (there was always a bucket of soapy water under the sink in the hall; I used to pee in it); we had a gas stove in the apartment, however, and grandma soon became queen of it, relegating Marusya to the background. On the stove she would fry sausages and boil the laundry in a gurgling zinc tank big enough to boil a large child in. She pulled out the sodden laundry, buttons and all, with huge wooden tongs like giant lobsters made of rags, rubbed it against a ribbed washboard, rinsed it, dripping huge drops of sweat on it all the while, and hung it up to dry in the kitchen on gray wooden clothespins with prodigiously strong springs. Our kitchen would be transformed into a campsite, in which, to my childish delight, you could easily get lost and then spend days trying to find one another. She used to heat up the heavy cast-iron irons until they were ominously red; the tips of the irons glowed like mystical implements of torture from the Middle Ages, with which, after grabbing them with a rag, she would frenziedly set about ironing my father's suits, which hissed and let out hot steam from under a wet old sheet with red burn marks on it; the sheet had been reincarnated as an ironing rag. As I sit at my Macintosh typewriter, I now realize that in my head, grandma's bath and laundry shop was transformed into stylish work. Grandma overturned a tub of energy on me. I am her grandson.

She used to run around the kitchen excitedly, burnt and half-naked in a pink bra, complaining about her heart, and then off she went, either to take a bath that was so hot that it caused the mirror to weep with moisture, or to the hospital, in an ambulance. Mama considered her a hypochondriac. Whenever heated rows erupted, grandma would start slamming doors so hard that the window panes flew out. My nanny, Marusya Pushkina, who had the face of a rural maid from outside Volokolamka, and who was eternally happy as a result of the surprises life threw up, grew adept at lying to me: she said it was just a draft. Mama lived under grandma's occupation, locked herself in the bathroom whenever there were rifts, swallowed her tears, and sat hunched in the corner; but she simply didn't have the strength to force grandma (papa's protector) out of the apartment.

"Feed the child kasha," mama said quietly from the Soviet skyscraper, as she flipped through *Life* magazine.

•

Papa used to bring home from work, with a shy expression on his face, blue packages from the Kremlin's product distributor containing delicious food: crunchy dairy sausages, thin *Doctor's* smoked sausage, boiled salted pork, salmon, smoked sturgeon and crabs.

> *Crabs are tender, crabs taste great,*
> *Come and try them now — why wait?*

proclaimed one of the rare billboard advertisements of the day, at the entrance to a quarter-garden, where there were two huge, aristocratic vases depicting marble goats grazing on vine leaves (there is now a casino at the site, which gleams with Vegas-style lights). For dessert they used to give papa ridiculously priced *halva*, pale-pink fruit *pastila*, rum-flavored *zefir* covered in chocolate, Clumsy Bear candies, multi-colored Kievan candied fruits, Turkish delights, gingerbread cookies with honey and other treats. Sometimes there were dark-red spots on the packaging: this was a fresh cut of beef soaked in blood. The sharp smell of small dimpled gherkins, with the yellow center of a flower in deepest winter, with a window decorated with frost ferns, permeated the kitchen. The Stalin-era cookbook *On Delicious and Healthy Food*, with its elegant sepia photographs of tables laden with food, sturgeon, suckling pigs and vintage Georgian wines, certainly didn't seem out of place in our home.

I was a skinny boy and didn't enjoy eating. In the struggle to win back my appetite, grandma soon resorted to torturing me with cod liver oil. A day came when her dream of turning me into a fat kid came true, and, seizing the moment, we rushed over to the photographer's place to get our photo taken, hugging one another, cheek-to-cheek. Privileges, billowing up tenderly like smoke, enveloped every aspect of our lives: the fashionable new suit made of imported English cloth that was tailored for papa each year, for free, by the store on Kuznetsky Bridge; medical centers at Sivtsev Vrazhek, with carpeted corridors, the outstretched palm leaves of pot-plants and affectionate doctors right out of children's fairytales; the clean entrance to our apartment block, which was manned by guards because Comrade Vlasik, the all-powerful head of Stalin's personal guard, lived on our floor; the New Year's trees at the Kremlin, smelling of Adzharian mandarins bringing expensive gifts; film-books to be used for trips to the cinema, so that we could watch films, which were few and far between; special expeditions to get books (applying for subscriptions to collected works, and volumes that couldn't be found in regular bookstores); and theater tickets to every kind of show, right down to reservations for places at the Novodevichy Cemetery.

One summer, we moved to a Soviet Ministry summer house outside Moscow, on Trudovaya Street, in a long black ZIM that looked like the 'sharp-toothed' American cars of the late 1940s. There, in the endless June twilight, with a giddiness brought on by my bicycle and the bird cherries, and a trace of fresh milk on my sensual adult lips, I played chess on the wooden porch with Marusya Pushkina, whom Sasha, my father's black-capped chauffeur, was courting.

•

A born winner (my parents named me after the victory over Germany), I won my first ever game of chess against Marusya. The world was full of sturdy, dependable things: street-lights, skyscrapers, metro stations and white park benches with curved backs, on one of which, at Sokolniki one winter, we continued our eternal tournament,in spite of the snowstorms. The chess pieces moved around the board with snow up to their waists. I was coughing non-stop as a result of my whooping cough; she was wiping her nose playfully with a mitten that had a hole in it. We were well-matched, both losing pieces as a result of lapses in concentration, mixing up our bishops and our kings, and both reckless by disposition.

Learning to accept defeat was something I found hard. I would throw my knights and pawns at Marusya, with tears in my eyes. Once we had made friends again, we would rescue the pieces from the thawed snow together. Spring always came suddenly, catching us unawares on the way back to the metro, with streams, flower beds around the linden trees, soaked boots, and fresh air reinvigorated by the sun. A family consisting of servants, relatives, our closest friends, and mama's girlfriends had turned into a dependable clan. I lived in bliss.

•

From an article by the first secretary of the Moscow branch of the Soviet Writers' Union: Felix Kuznetsov. The scandal involving *Metropol*, *The Moscow Writer*, February 9, 1979:

<...> and the shame, which demands what appears to be a cover-up, in this collection of all manner of material, is greater than one can imagine. Here there is ample evidence of literary tastelessness and helplessness, backwardness and vulgarity, covered with just a thin veneer of eternal 'absurdism' or a newly emergent search for God. Practically all those present at the joint meeting of the Secretariat and Party Committee of the Moscow's writers' organization, where *Metropol* was discussed, spoke about the extremely poor quality of this collection.

And it is quite a paradox: here, strained conversations about the soul are found right next to the immoral dirtiness in which the budding writer V. Erofeyev is engaged — for example, in the story *Edrena Fenya*, the protagonist of which studies the inscriptions and images on the walls of the men's bathroom, then moves into the women's bathroom with the same goal in mind. To say nothing of the title of the second story, *The Half-mast Orgasm of the Century!*<...>

·

Every Russian wants to be tsar, but not all of them get the opportunity. The Russian tsars were always very democratic. My grandmother, Anastasia Nikandrovna, who was born in the Kostroma Region and had the maiden name Ruvimova, once saw the last Russian tsar in St. Petersburg. He was buying buttons in Gostiny Dvor on Nevsky Prospect, without any guards in attendance. Apparently he had lost some button from his overcoat, tired of asking his servants to buy him replacements, and decided to go out and buy one himself. Not out of spite, without wanting to offend anyone. He wasn't trying to prove to anyone that he was just like everyone else: that he too could stand around choosing buttons, but that was how it appeared, and grandma never forgot the day she saw the tsar; it became a key part of her modest collection of her greatest reminiscences about her life. If Nikolai II had not been buying buttons in Gostiny Dvor, it's entirely possible her life would have been far poorer in the matter of recollections, but lo and behold, along came an incident like that.

"Was the tsar really alone, without any guards?" I used to ask her when I was a child, at a time when it was advisable not to talk about the tsar at all.

And she would answer as if she had not merely seen the tsar buying buttons in Gostiny Dvor, but as if she and the tsar had been close — as close as it was possible to get.

"I didn't notice anyone else."

"You didn't see any guards?"

"None whatsoever."

"And he didn't have his daughters with him?"

"What sort of man," grandma would utter in surprise, "takes his daughters with him when he goes to Gostiny Dvor to buy buttons?"

"Then perhaps he was with his son?" I insisted, just like a child.

"Wait," she would say, "I'll tell you exactly how it happened. I had gone to Gostiny Dvor to buy myself some white lace gloves…"

"Perhaps it wasn't the tsar, you just thought it was?" it suddenly dawned on me.

Grandma was speechless. She gazed at me with uncomprehending eyes, as if I had stolen the watch from her wrist. Then, when she had come to her senses, she turned away from me and refused to talk to me the whole day.

The next day — at the dacha — I asked her:

"But how did you figure out that it was the tsar? By his epaulettes?"

"Tsars didn't have labels on their epaulettes, saying who they were," — grandma said, enlightening me.

"By his mustache, then?"

"All the men in Russia had mustaches back then," grandma answered, "and a lot of them had beards too."

"Then by the way he walked?"

"He wasn't walking at all, he was standing there rolling buttons in his fingers."

"And did everyone recognize him, or just you?"

"There was no-one else there. Just him."

"And were you buying your gloves far away from him? How many feet away from him were you?"

"I hadn't bought them yet, I was just comparing prices."

"Were you right next to him?"

"Buttons and gloves were sold in the same department at Gostiny Dvor."

"And he didn't say anything to you? He didn't help you choose your white lace gloves?"

"He was otherwise engaged, with his buttons."

"And how long were you standing there like that next to one another, he with his buttons and you with your white lace gloves?"

"You idiot," grandma said, "people don't ask daft questions like that."

And once again she refused to speak to me for a whole day and was silent all through dinner, although it was a delicious dinner because she was a good cook. Her meat pies were particularly good. Whenever she made meat pies, grandma's cheeks would turn rosy. It was with the same rosy cheeks that she talked about the tsar.

"Perhaps the tsar was with his wife?" I had asked her that winter, at our apartment on Gorky Street.

"You mind your own business," grandma said, "and concentrate on your homework."

"So why did you call me an idiot that time?"

"I didn't call you an idiot."

"Oh yes you did."

"You're fibbing."

"I'm not fibbing."

"He was on his own," said grandma, "He was standing in Gostiny Dvor and taking an age to choose some buttons."

"What about the tsarina, was she there?"

"Only don't tell anyone."

"I won't."

"That I saw the tsar."

"Why not?"

"Promise?"

"Promise."

"No-one at all?"

"Not even mama?"

"Not even mama."

"But I'm supposed to tell mama everything."

"But you're allowed not to tell her about the tsar."

"He's more important than mama?"

Grandma thought about it. She was my paternal grandmother.

"Are you aware that your papa wants to leave your mother?"

"And go where?"

I imagined papa leaving mama on as now-covered track through the woods and going off on his own, and I felt very scared and cold on his behalf.

Ever since then, and even today, whenever I find myself buying buttons — especially if I'm at Gostiny Dvor in St. Petersburg — I feel as if I am a Russian tsar.

•

In the chaos of the post-war spike in the birth-rate, it seems as though, by some mistake, I was given someone else's fate. In the accompanying document, which set out in rough outline the matrix of my earthly existence, there were actions and occurrences for which I was decidedly unprepared. A black-and-gold panther with rabid energy had taken root in me, though there was only room for a quiet, trusting animal. I was sluggish. I would spend hours trying to tie the laces on my shoes; I never learned how to do it the right way. My laces are forever coming undone, much to the annoyance of any women who happen to be walking alongside me. I hop down the street on one leg, looking for something on which to rest my shoe so that I can do up the lace. At first they like this, it is my party trick, and they laugh at my clumsiness, but before long these bitches start showing their satanic side.

On the other hand, I was never at rest. I was a whirlwind of desires, whipping up everything around me. This wild incongruity can be seen in photographs of me as a child. The wild stare of my black eyes, which drilled into the world in an attempt to drill a totally new, unheard of law out of it, was the stare of a shy, stooping child with a tender, charming smile, which played over the lips of a cannibal. The huge nostrils are ready to breathe in a whole carpet of smells, take off its grass cover, and make off with the aroma of food and drink. This nose, with its trembling wings, was particularly aggressive and inhumane. My huge head, for which we could never find a cap that was the right size, nor the right size of the hat that was part of the Soviet school uniform, and which had the dimensions of the skull of a pre-historic ape — a fact not lost on my classmates,who poked fun at me by calling me "ape" — rested on slender shoulders, and when I took hold of it with my slender hands (which have remained slender to this day), there were shades of Munch's painting *The Scream*.

•

From Kevin Clouse's article *THE SOVIET UNION IS HARASSING THE FOUNDERS OF THE NEW JOURNAL, International Herald Tribune, February 7, 1979*:

Moscow (WP) — The Soviet authorities have begun a campaign of harassment, persecution and threats to intimidate the founders of a new unofficial literary magazine that seeks to challenge state control of the arts.

The five editors of *Metropol* have been upbraided by the Moscow Writers' Union and several have been threatened with expulsion from the Union.

The State publishing watchdogs, in the two weeks since the journal was announced, have been withdrawing films, plays, novels and even magazines, containing articles by any of the editors, from circulation. <...>

Vasily Aksyonov, one of the Soviet Union's most popular writers and the principal editor of *Metropol*, said he had been accused of seeking notoriety in the West so that it would be easier for him to emigrate.

Mr. Aksyonov, who has made several official trips to Western countries in recent years and whose stories have been officially translated into English, said he had no intention of emigrating. <...>

•

I am standing in front of a black wooden telegraph pole. It's summer. There is discord in the air. I'm not sure how old I was. I've got a straight, short fringe and an extremely short haircut. There may have been a white hat covering it, I'm not sure. One thing I am sure of, though: there is an iron tablet nailed to the pole. There is a skull and crossbones on it. There is a jagged red arrow going through the skull and crossbones. I'm standing in front of this pole in a state of holy terror I get the feeling that if I reach out and touch this wooden pole, I'll be killed. I don't know what this means, but something tells me that is what's going to happen. Every subsequent thing that happens to me in life has this arrow superimposed over it, running through it. I came into life through the horror of death. Death woke me up. The first impression life made on me was the wild fear of death. It made me what I am. I never recovered from the shock. Whenever I see a skull and cross-bones, the electricians' sign, I shudder, as if I am being reminded of my *raison d'être*.

Among the tall pines, some goats are wandering around. They are considered personal property to a lesser degree than cows, which are practically forbidden. Death and goats are in an idyllic field. I want to pet the goats, but am scared to do so because of their horns, some of which have been sawn off. I pick some grass and hold it in my outstretched hand for the goats. They bleat and shit little round pellets of dung. I feed the goats grass. Goats are the first animals to appear in my life. The goat's song is the musical genre of my childhood. I stretch out my hand as if to touch the pole, then pull it back. I'm playing with death. The horror of death envelopes everything. Then everything grows dark. But that summer my consciousness will be awoken once again — and once again it will be because of death.

We're driving along the highway in papa's chocolate-colored Victory. There are fields all around us. Suddenly a thunderstorm breaks out. We hear a horrible hissing sound, and then there is a terrible clap of thunder. Lightning strikes an electric pole right next to the car. The base of the pole turns into a fiery palm tree. Sparks fly off in every direction. Death puts on a show more powerful than anything I ever saw, either at the theater or at the movies. I have been given my assignment and now I must deal with it. The God-thunderer, whoever he might be, has prodded me with his finger.

The God-thunderer brought order to my life. This was the first time I had experienced order. Later I often lost my way in the whirligig of happenstance, but death became the guiding light of my life, it beat out its own rhythm, and eventually I took heed of it. The powerful mechanism of the fear of death, instilled in me from birth, began to operate. I personally have nothing to do with this mechanism — it is my personal matrix. I knew neither the icon lamp nor the icon. I was never christened by my parents. I was never secretly taken to church by my grandma. In the Soviet Union, death was seen as non-existent. Death was seen as wilful. Marxist philosophy neatly sidestepped death, holding its nose. The deceased were treated with disdain, like deserters. Undertakers did an exceptionally lousy job. The stink of corpses that had not been properly buried hung around the cemeteries for many years after the revolution. Stray dogs, including fine hounds and Borzoi,would eat them. Then a quick way of disposing of the corpses was discovered: cremation. The musical boxes of crematories sprang up throughout the country. Only alcoholics got jobs as grave diggers. I had to deal with death on my own, without any middle-men. The absence of priests close at hand turned me into a serial killer of death.

•

When I felt my face lit up by holiday fireworks, and when papa's chauffeur Sasha (who had talked Marusya Pushkina into living with him by promising to marry her, but proved to be a scoundrel, for he had already been married in a former life) brought a New Year tree into our apartment, and we started decorating it, standing on chairs and trying to reach the top, to hang a red star on it, and putting baubles and fish on the branches, and at the bottom, my first childhood god, with the rosy face of a coachman, snub-nosed in the Russian way, it felt like a breather. This Frost-God had been cut out of world mythology using crude scissors and left alone for two weeks, until the pine needles fell off the tree, until the old-style New Year, but even this small shard from the global pantheon warmed me up with its gifts. He spoke to me about the secret of the world, he was my ally.

Early on the morning of January 1st, while my parents were still sleeping, I jumped out of my bed, which at the time was in my parents' bedroom near a window with a hot radiator, and ran into the dining room, which smelled of pine needles, so that I could crawl under the tree. Santa Clause, with his coachman's face, was surrounded by gifts.

The radiators were so hot that I often had nightmares about ominous mass demonstrations. My young life, wrapped up as it was in the arms of death, was given succour by holidays and gifts. Life consists of holidays and gifts; everything else is just misunderstandings. Life consists of distractions from death. I was never given a proper grounding in the moral code of misfortune, slavery or cowardice. I never suffered the humiliations of the communal apartment. My own spontaneous moral code consisted of boundless trust in the world, complete openness to it. I was that most open of souls, who was born to become a dancing god.

I don't understand how it's possible to work the whole day through, year after year, for an idiotic salary, with a short break for lunch, your bosses shouting at you and nothing but gloomy rudeness from your co-workers. I can guess why people have to work, but what I don't get is — what for? But I was aware, from my earliest childhood, that there are two kinds of gifts. There are your dream-gifts, which you daren't even think about, and if you do, then only before you go to bed. A model railroad for example, with a huge number of railroad cars, bridges and rails. Gifts like that ensure you will be lucky in your adult life, they turn you around and steer you onto the right path throughout your life's journey. And then mama quietly comes up behind you, and you don't even notice her coming, so absorbed are you in the gift, and she pats you on the head. That is a moment of pure, unadulterated happiness.

And then there are those "stop hassling me" gifts. They're bought without any real thought, out of necessity, and they emit a strange energy; they smell like cooked macaroni. Some game or other involving chips, or a fake fire engine with a ladder made of shoelaces. You sit down next to gifts like that and you feel sorry for yourself and your parents. You don't let it show, you force yourself to be happy, you give mama a hug, but you think to yourself: "Why are you being like this? I can see what's going on."

•

From a letter written by my brother Andrei to my parents in Vienna (he's eight-and-a-half years younger than me):

Moscow 5/8/79

Dear mama and papa,

One or two more letters, and our epistolary correspond-ence, which has lasted so many years — an entire epoch in my life — will be over. <...> These letters helped me learn to write, but I never really got the hang of it — my writing is forced and clumsy.

So now I'm in a very difficult situation, I am at a loss what to write in order to comfort you and cheer you up, because I myself am in complete disarray as a result of this horrible situation, which is scarcely even believable. I can see (or rather I can hear in your voices) frustration and sadness as a result of what happened, and I can also see what Vitya is going through, the consequences of the blow *to his psyche which, by so carelessly neglecting to consider the consequences of his actions, he has brought upon himself, and I'm scared, very scared that all this might prove to be fatal to the relationships within our family, that it might undermine them. <...>*

•

I disassemble my memory, like a tent, tying the string of remembrance into a series of bundles, and wait until I come climbing out — an artist 'from nothing'. A family album. I only know Ivan Petrovich Erofeyev from my unconscious memory, which I was never able to bring up to the surface, however hard I stared at the photos of us together — they show us repairing the primus stove on a sunny day at the dacha — however hard I tried to remember his pince-nez and his Turkish hat.

GRANDPA: It must be great to be a policeman. You stand at your post all day, swinging your stick from side to side — not a care in the world.

GRANDMA: What a joker! No-one could tell jokes like he could.

The joker-newcomer, whom I never did manage to remember, the primogenitor of humor in the Erofeyev line, became a little mound in the nineteenth sector of the Vagankovsky Cemetery, but grandma explained to me affectionately that at Razdory grandpa used to spend hours playing at toy cars with me.

I was a passionate toy-lover from my earliest childhood. In my sandbox I built a whole city, with a highway, bridges and railroads, and then precision-bombed it with a red and brown striped children's soccer ball. Grandma said that grandpa used to play soccer with me too. I was a reckless football player in the fields near our dacha and in the forest clearings, where it seemed as though the trees only purpose was to be used as goalposts, and you always wished you could move them farther apart or closer together; but if I couldn't remember grandpa, who was the ghost standing between the birch tree and the asp as I fired goal after goal past him?

I was also mad about riding my tricycle. I used to pedal like crazy, shaken whenever I went over the wooden snakes — the roots of the pine trees, winding along the forest path; I would take off and my bell would ring in the air of its own accord. Most of all I loved to build up speed and then free-wheel through the puddles, stretching my legs as high and as far apart as they would go. I would often get stuck in the middle, turning my steering wheel and looking to either side for an age. I knew I was going to get stuck, but this bit of knowledge was stupid — surplus to requirements — and I drove straight into the puddles regardless. As I assemble the collage of my original creative influences, I begin to realize that it's hard to underestimate the role puddles played in my childhood. Not only were they obstacles, they were also temptations. I used to love beating them with sticks. They would splash in all directions. I would stand there all wet. I was a glutton for punishment. But more than that I loved to drag my stick through the puddle slowly and then poke it into the chomping bottom. That chomping sound cast a spell on me. I loved the tire tracks left by bicycles and cars in the dirt; the idea of leaving tracks leaving something behind, drove me wild. Grandma always scolded me for having dirty hands and dirt under my fingernails. I spent my whole childhood being sent to wash my hands and clean my nails. I was a sculptural composition like the famous 'girl with a pitcher' — I was the 'boy at the washstand nailed to the tree, at the dacha'. My love of women stemmed from those swirling puddles.

Ivan Petrovich, whom, try as I might, I simply couldn't remember, died of a heart attack at the Kremlin hospital on Granovsky Street. When I grew older, grandma, during an argument, accused me of causing grandpa's death. The blame was hung around my neck like a rope, and I looked at grandma in horror, with burning eyes.

GRANDMA: You were being silly and demanding that he gave

you a piggy-back. And he agreed to do it, the poor thing, and he never should have done.

I found this pretty convincing. Back then everyone had been doing a bit of killing. Some people had been killing Germans, others — their own kind. I had killed my grandpa.

GRANDMA: He died two weeks before he was due to collect his Lenin Medal.

It is all my fault. If you follow this family logic, then, since I had killed my grandfather, it made sense that I should kill my father as well.

•

From my last letter to my parents in Vienna, dated May 8, 1979.

Dear mama and papa,

This moral cross which events have put on me is heavy, very heavy. I don't even know what to say. They punished me exquisitely-through you, with your bitterness, and, of course, your disappointment in me. I could, of course, throw myself into explanations on paper and give free reign to my pent-up emotions — but what would that achieve? It is a cruel paradox: seeking to do something I felt had to be done, and was the right thing to do, I inflicted injury on the people closest to me, from whom I have experienced nothing but good — you. I pray to God for one thing only: that in these bad, sick days, we can maintain the unity of our family, and preserve our mutual understanding and trust. This is constantly on my mind...

•

I was as silent as a partisan until I reached the age of three-and-a-half. The only exception — "ai!" — occurred when I knocked on the kitchen door in our neighbor's endless apartment, where the giant Boris Fyodorovich lived, with his lively, attentive eyes, along with a whole rabble of relatives, spongers and meowing cats crawling out of various rooms, and their Polish maid, Zosya, asked me, through the door:

"Who's there?"

"Ai!" I replied, instead of "It's me!"

And everyone made fun of me. "Ai" became my nickname, my password, a byword for my sunny, reckless self. I burst my way into life with the clownish scream of "ai!" During my childhood dreams I was like a member of an African tribe: the cosmicization of humanity and the humanization of the cosmos — two parallel processes, defining a person's worldview. I searched for my reflection in all the mirrors of the anthropomorphous universe, in which grandma, Marusya Pushkina, a bug and ants are all preservers of the word. It was precisely by means of this prolonged muteness that the word made me its carrier, chose me, and rewrote the information it foretold on me.

In fact, a *child-word* was exactly what I was: someone who had been born into the world in order to pronounce the word. All the kids around me would speak — but I kept quiet. African mystics know of the many methods and means there are to make speech come more easily. The main ones were clearly unsuitable for someone like me, who lived in Moscow: smoking tobacco in a pipe, chewing a cola nut, sawing your teeth, rubbing them with coloring substances or tattooing your mouth. Something told me that the bringing on of speech was associated with considerable risk, because it broke up the harmony of silence. Silence and secrecy are highly significant as a form of initiation, since the world originally existed without words. I still have a slight speech impediment to this day, I am instinctively tongue-tied, and during my childhood this was a real problem for me (I used to blush with embarrassment when I spoke), my lips would be strained and would cramp up, I couldn't understand people who found that speech came easily, television newscasters and commentators; I feel the same way about chatterboxes as I do about traitors. The well-known Stalin-era poster in which an honest woman has a finger raised to her lips — don't spread idle chatter! — appeals to me on a metaphysical level. The thought of speaking horrifies me: I am afraid I might rip open the world, so that the guts of phenomena and consequences come pouring out, I know there is no sense in relationship between cause and effect. In my childhood dreams, at first, I never needed speech, because everything that existed in them understood the unspoken word, the endless rustle of the air.

The situation developed as follows. I saw a rough embodiment of a phallic deity in a tree. I saw a heavenly half-God pouring water from itself, as if from a fountain. They exchanged information without words. However, being Ai at the time, I was unaware that the phallic deity's wife, who had given birth not only to the plant-life but also to the animals, was jealous of all the other women created by the demigod, over her husband. I sensed that there was something wrong in that, I couldn't understand it at the time, but I now realize that he was sleeping with them. Then I noticed the tension in their relations. It's possible that the woman didn't stand for it, and was cheating on her husband, too: there she goes making her way home on the Moscow metro in her white blouse: next stop — Mayakovsky, it's time to get out onto the platform, and then the phallic deity, which looks like a tree, comes after her, grabs her by the throat and squeezes it. Between the unfaithful spouses, after such a furious row in the bedroom, in which a colorful Dagestani rug covers the whole of the wall behind the bed, pauses can be heard in the sound of their breathing — the pauses required in order to generate words and encourage speech. I begin to realize that the word is the result of betrayal, the form of its discourse, and I creep under the sofa.

Long-lost items, games, coins with very little face-value, and the wrappers of eaten candy are lying under the low, dusty sofa.

I remain silent, shocked by the truth that has been revealed to me. Crawling under the sofa after me, in her brown stockings, comes my third-cousin Lena, who is the same age as me, and who has come to Moscow from her hometown of Kerch. She wants to live with us, and register, but something is preventing her from doing so. The word 'Kerch' still crunches like sand in my teeth whenever I say it, and somehow sounds like the word 'heart'. Her father is a military pilot with the fitting surname Yelagin. In the summer she and I used to play on Trudovaya Street, in the thick raspberry bushes which scratched our hands at the dressing station: we showed one another our infantile bodies, our genitalia. I now understand that I myself consist in part of Lena, of her joints, her nipples, shocked not only by the secret of the word, but also by her vertical incision. I know now that we are here under the sofa, that I am destined to have a parallel life, but I don't know with whom, or when. Androgeny has been released in me. It is more powerful than insanity. Huge-headed, with thin, white, provincial braids, Lena appears to be the first embodiment of me-as-a-girl, the very closest thing to me, someone I can talk to throughout my whole life. I am not enough for myself. I need to start speaking, but I have neither cola, nor even tobacco at my disposal. I am about to be blown out of my silence, however. Lena, like a seasoned explorer, makes her way into my shorts. She pulls out my penis and creeps towards it with her mouth, coiling the iridescent snake. Wheezing, she starts to suck it. Our faces are distorted by the bliss of incest, three times removed. It grows with every second.

"Darling," I say to her, stroking Lena's head.

She can't stop herself, she crawls out from under the couch and runs into the dining room.

LENA: "Auntie Galya, Auntie Galya, Vitya said something!"

"Why are there so many policemen?!" I yell in an angry voice, crawling out from under the sofa after her.

I can see myself walking along Blagoveshchensky Lane by the commission store with its small display cases, as if they're embarrassed by their bourgeois goods, and a company of militiamen is marching toward me. Where are they going? To what end?

MAMA: "They're going to the bathhouse."

Sure enough, the militiamen have bath towels under their arms. They're marching off to have a bath.

"Vitya said something!" mama cries.

"He'll grow up to be a dissident," remarks Andrei Mikhailovich Alexandrov-Agentov, who would go on to be an aide to Brezhnev, shaking his head.

I find it hard to say exactly when it was that I lost my innocence: and that leads me to think I was born guilty. Somewhere far away, at the back of the dining room, I can see a blade of grass: the figure of grandma Lilya, Anastasia Nikandrovna's younger sister. She plays the role of a saint in the family: she never has any money. When she stays at grandma's, grandma checks that she doesn't turn over on the sofa too much during the night, and leave a hole in it, but grandma Lilya would always fold her arms and say:

"Nastenka, Nastenka…"

•

Memory is like a corpse being eaten by the dog it once loved. Left alone in the apartment, it howls with fear and hunger for hours, running around its master's body, but hunger eventually trumps its devotion: it eats its master, carefully at first, going for the bare hands first of all, but then it can't hold back, it loses its reason, it rips him to pieces, shaking its head from side to side and growling. The resurrection of the owner's chewed corpse is a miracle impossible to imagine, yet sometimes it happens. The owner shudders. The pieces of torn meat and skin wrap themselves back around his hands, legs, calves and genitalia, with a whistle. The innards are thrown back out from the dog's jowls and hasten back inside the master's open stomach. The bullet-wounds heal. The spots of blood disappear completely from the walls; the puddle of blood disappears from the floor. The eyes slip back into their sockets. The stomach draws itself back in and grows back the hair which women once stroked with such affection. The smell of decay disappears. The heart starts beating. The master gets up, and walks over to the cupboard; the dog, wagging its tail in delight, runs after him in anticipation of a walk. Its collar is put on. The door that leads onto the stairwell landing is open. The dog and its master scurry down, slam the door and go out into the street. While the dog does his business in the nearest square, its master takes a look around. He didn't come out for this walk seeking to get revenge or settle a few scores. He longs for the sweet taste of reconciliation not just with his enemies, but with himself. He smiles. He's content.

●

I drank a toast to Comrade Stalin only once in my life: on my fifth birthday. A load of kids had been brought round, including the two brilliant Podtserobov brothers: the preschooler Kirill, who would go on to become first a drunkard, throwing up in the bucket that was kept under his ascetic bed just in case, then a drug addict, who rode on his grandmother's shoulders around their huge apartment both in his dreams and while awake, and the schoolboy Lyosha, a dependable, determined young man, who for some reason fell hopelessly in love, at an early age, with the Near East, a huge map of which hung on his wall (looking at this map, I too felt a jealous desire to fall passionately in love with something, some bit of land or other — visually I liked Africa, but I didn't know what it was for; America was painted in a cold, hostile color; and it didn't occur to me to fall in love with Russia back then — so I ended up with nothing), and later sped, as though carried by an express train, straight to the destination of his purpose in life: he became the Soviet Ambassador to an Arab country. Lyosha knew far more about everything than anyone else, and certainly more than I did. With me he was condescending, and spoke so assuredly and in such an exact manner that I would lose my chain of thought, and, to keep the conversation going somehow, ask absurd, confused questions, shifting to a diametrically opposed view in a matter of seconds. Throughout my childhood mama had a mortal fear that I would grow up to be the village idiot — I didn't show the faintest trace of being a child prodigy — held up Lyosha and the beautiful young Milochka Vorozhtsova, with her black curls, as an example for me to follow. Not much hope was held out for me — practically none, if I'm honest — and I didn't even dare fall in love with Milochka, aware as I was of my defective brain. We had just sat down at the table, and poured some tomato juice into our glasses, and Marusya had just brought a steaming fish pie in from the kitchen, when Boris Fyodorovich's elder son, leaping up from his chair, puckered up his lips as if he was about to spit (he always spoke in the same way that he spat), but instead pronounced the first toast, which was not to me, but to Stalin.

LYOSHA: I propose a toast to Comrade Stalin!

We all stood up. Around the table there spread something that I wouldn't exactly describe as confusion, but my mother was surprised: we never drank to Stalin at our house, it wasn't the done thing: not out of political considerations, but because it simply didn't feel right. I sensed this confusion and, like a monkey, got up to clink glasses, so as to smooth things over. I loved toasts anyway, because the grown-ups were always making them, and up until that moment I had never gotten the chance to make a proper toast. Moreover, I was once again shocked by a feeling of delight in front of this boy, who was older and more mature than me.

The feast ended in bloodshed. As I ran around the table after the guests, chasing the inaccessible Milochka, the general's daughter, who was impossible to catch, I flew into the corner of the table and got the corner of my mouth torn off. It's still half-cut to this day. If you look carefully enough you can see that my mouth is asymmetrical.

Mama picked me up, covered in blood as I was, and took me to the clinic on Sivtsev Vrazhek, where there were a lot of palm trees and where the guard refused outright to let us in because mama had forgotten her pass. Scared, I bled a little bit more — but they still didn't let us in. They refused to let us in for such a long time that I was left with the impression that I had spent my entire childhood with blood pouring out of my mouth. Mama turned into a wild tiger and screamed at the guard, begging him and making threats, but the guard was immovable.

And he stayed that way.

•

I made up for the sick incongruity between the different parts of my 'ego' with my patricide. It was thanks to my patricide that I aligned myself with my intended purpose, the sense of which began to reveal itself over the course of the rest of my life. I jumped headlong into my destiny, although I often found myself having doubts about it all over again. The flashes of anger of my childhood, and my cut mouth, stayed with me forever. The resilience I had acquired didn't become my mandate in life. Human weaknesses would tempt me later in life, too, weakening my concentration, preventing me from overcoming challenges with the ease of a trained athlete. On the contrary, it used to hurt when I fell over, and I would spend a long time rubbing my wounds. But I somehow managed nonetheless to fake sense (what an apt typo) — to *make* sense of the cocktail of which I consisted, of its various ingredients. I didn't understand everything, and I am not destined to understand everything, but Russia certainly helped in that regard. I don't know whether I ought to thank her or not. I was sent there (here) with a secret mission of some kind. To live in Russia is to walk upside down on the ceiling. It is to have inverted vision. I don't know where my true homeland is. I suspect it doesn't exist. But Russia was the place of my childhood paradise.

2

I owe my birth to such an outrageous piling up of global circumstances that I can't help but see it as anything other than a pure, but in its own way meticulously intricate, accident. The fruit of an 'accidental family' *par excellence*, if I could have had my pick of all possible family crests, I would probably have chosen, not without the help of the poet Osip Mandelshtam, *a crooked cue, a pock-marked billiard ball and a holy billiard pocket*, if only because neither my father nor I were ever very good at billiards. Even our closest ancestors exist in my consciousness without names, identifiable at a glance by means of their half-forgotten professions — some of them genuine, like porter or priest, some very much fictitious — professional revolutionary, for example, which was the profession that my grandmother, not without a hidden agenda, ascribed, in my memory, to her father, Nikander, whom I never met. Grandma was prone to making things up. True, those of us on my mother's side have a faint link to the aristocracy through her grandfather, which is *personal* and therefore not very significant, but also, via a very complex system of brothers and sisters-in-law, and more specifically, via the rather colorful Kyandsky family, to Russian culture: to the man who invented national radio, Popov, for starters; from him we could be traced back to the family of the chemist Mendeleyev; and from him, eventually, to Alexander Blok. But these are by no means forty-second cousins, they're just…the family dregs. Without really knowing where to begin when it comes to the *private conspiracy* of circumstances which went against all honor and common sense, my choice would nevertheless fall on the little-known, unsuccessful Anglo-American intervention at Murmansk after the October Revolution. I once saw images on the TV of the collapsed, snow-covered graves in which *they*, the enemy, now lay. My grandma on my father's side, Anastasia Nikandrovna Ruvimova, who made up stories, was a very good-looking woman. She lived right on the border with Finland, in Sestroretska, where her father owned five dachas that he used to let. She used to cover about fifty *versts* a day on her skis, and a Finn named Yuho was fond of her. Not long before her death, while watching a hockey match between Russia and Finland, she said to me, with a touch of nostalgia for the quiet life on which she had missed out:

"If I'd married Yuho, I'd be cheering for Finland right now."

She was being courted by a tall man with beautiful black rings under his eyes, by the name of Ivan. In 1918, grandma, fleeing starvation, moved with her family from Sestroretsk to Petrograd, and from there to Karelia. Ivan made no secret of his desire to marry Anastasia, but it was at that very moment that the Americans attacked.

There was a *cunning* young guy in a pince-nez who worked for the Karelia railroad as a bookkeeper. The Bolsheviks had put him in charge of mobilization. Smitten by my grandmother's beauty, Ivan Petrovich Erofeyev made sure the tall Ivan was the first name on the mobilization list, although the latter had a white ticket exempting him from service. They shaved Ivan's head, packed him off to Murmansk and he went missing in action in a battle with the Americans.

What happened next was like something out of an opera. You can almost hear Tatiana's aria from the opera *Eugene Onegin*: *Another man has married me. And true to him I'll ever be…*' In 1920, after returning to Petrograd, Anastasia Nikandrovna bumped into her *first* Ivan in the street by chance.

"You're too late, Vanya," my grandmother said, already pregnant with my father. I don't think the Americans perished *in vain* at Murmansk.

Thereafter, in order to make life a bit happier, grandma painted her husband's genealogy in bright, somewhat garish colors. As a result, my great-grandfather, Pyotr Erofeyev, emerged from her stories looking like a sexual hero of the countryside in greased boots, a prosperous miller in a house with lace door jams, who had numerous wives and fathered nineteen sons, the last of whom was born when he was nearing eighty years of age. As for the man in the *pince-nez*, he wasn't painted in bright colors, but he was noted for his kindly nature and absent-mindedness, confirmed by with a story about an Eskimo who melted at his house while he was out strolling in his Sunday pants, and by the fact that he secretly referred to his grandmother as a 'commissar', which vaguely reflected how he felt after some torture at the hands of the Chekists on Gorokhovaya Street, where they took him for interrogation, on Felix Dzerzhinsky's orders, and demanded, holding a gun to his head, that he reveal the secret hiding place of some gold that grandpa didn't have.

IVAN PETROVICH: God be with you! What gold?!

DZERZHINSKY: God isn't with us. God is against us. But we'll finish him off.

Ivan Petrovich realized that Dzerzhinsky pronounced "God" the way they do in Poland, and this God seemed to him to be dark and distant. He took off his wedding ring and handed it to Dzerzhinsky.

IVAN PETROVICH: This is all I have.

DZERZHINSKY: Put that back on! No arguments. Jailer!

The Jailer came in; he had the face of a poet.

DZERZHINSKY: Send this citizen (he gave Ivan Petrovich's face, which was covered in flour, a quick once-over)… home!

Death had taken root so deeply in my genes that my earliest childhood memory was an electric telegraph pole with a skull and crossbones on it near our dacha; the pole of horror: touch it — and you'll die. When my grandmother, in her younger days, decided to join the Bolshevik Party so that she could take part in the food distribution programs, grandfather warned her:

"If you join the Party, I'll divorce you!"

"It's a shame," grandma told me when I was little. "I'd have been a Party veteran by now, and you'd be listening to me on the radio."

In the 1920s, the couple, along with half the country, joined the other discontented isolationists who were going through the torturous process of growing into socialism. And my father was born to them, and he lived happily to the age of eight and then drowned during a vacation on the Volga — it was a *miracle* that they managed to resuscitate him. My father, who never reminisced about his boring, sickly childhood, left school with straight A's, and applied to the Institute of Architecture, amazed by the feats of the Soviet Polar exploration heroes. But he didn't go on to become a polar explorer — he failed the entry test because of his health (he had weak lungs). Then, to the delight of my grandfather, the chief bookkeeper for the railroad union, he got into the railroad institute with the inhuman abbreviation LIIZHT, which sounded like the noise of a locomotive putting on the brakes, but at the last minute he enrolled instead at a third Institute of Higher Education, purely *by chance*: he had hit on the idea of taking himself off to fight in Spain, as a volunteer. With no talent for philology, and indifferent to 'artistic literature', which he always put in inverted commas, he enrolled to study philology at Leningrad State University, in order to learn Spanish.

•

Interpreters with gleaming new medals on their chests wandered the corridors of the university — my young father dreamed of sailing to the Spanish shores with them in a submarine. Thin, in his *only* brown velour coat, he was already a fully-formed Soviet man, a strong-willed Komsomolets through and through. But when Franco won the war, he stopped studying Spanish, and turned instead to French.

"Comrade Erofeyev," Stalin was to ask him ten years down the line, when they met face to face at his office in the Kremlin, where Lenin's death mask was in pride of place, "Where were you born?"

Stalin, according to my father, always spoke in "a very low tone and made a lot of grammatical errors." One got the distinct impression, he added recently, that he was a man of "Caucasian ethnicity". My father misheard the leader's question.

"At Leningrad State University, Josef Vissarionovich."

"You were born right there at the University?!"

Stalin found it incredibly funny. He started laughing, clutching his side, and seeming to say, with every fiber of his being: "Well, you really got me there! I can't take any more!"

At that very moment Beria and Molotov appeared at the doorway to Stalin's office, so that they could be present during the discussions with the foreign guests. They stood there, at a loss as to what was going on, their pince-nez gleaming symmetrically. How could this skinny young man have made the leader laugh so much? What was the secret here, and what were they talking about? They didn't make so bold as to ask — and Stalin saw no need to explain the joke to them.

"You really made me laugh there," he said to my father affably.

My father had been *noticed*.

"Let's get down to business," Stalin said in a serious tone, inviting everyone to sit down. "Now then, you just go about your work calmly, and don't be nervous," he nodded to my father. "I speak fairly softly, so if you wish you can ask me to repeat things. I speak slowly, though."

He summoned Poskrebyshev with a bell:

"Has our guest arrived? Show him in!"

Maurice Thorez, the head of the French Communists, stepped hurriedly into the room.

"Well, *Bonjour!*" Stalin greeted him warmly.

My father began interpreting. From time to time he felt Beria's attentive, unblinking eyes fixed on him from under his pince-nez. According to Molotov, Stalin used to refer to those eyes of his as snake-eyes.

•

My father's predecessor in the role of Stalin's French interpreter had been relieved of his duties after mixing up his aviation terminology during a visit by a military delegation from Paris.

"I get the feeling my grasp of French is better than yours," Stalin had said to him.

"Stalin held himself *modestly*," my father commented with regard to his first meeting with the leader. "His charm had a powerful effect on me."

However, my father was only able to make the Father of the People happy because, every year, during his youth, in the middle of March, he fell victim to mysterious bouts of tonsillitis, with abscesses in his throat and a temperature of 104°. Little did my father know, when he joined the Department of Philology, that Russian philology could be just as deadly as the Spanish Civil War.

"On March 12, 1939 I was lazing in bed again and having a terrible time of it, because due to my illness I was missing out on a party. Our group was celebrating the birthday of one of our classmates, the poet Sergei Klyshko.

Klyshko was a real live-wire. He didn't shy away from writing anti-Stalinist poems during lectures, letting his messy hair touch the paper. He and my father were friends, and used to see each other every day. The girls used to like both of them. My father tried to persuade him to be more careful, but he just waved him off. Once, after getting a little drunk in the dorm room, Sergei recited a little rhyme that was doing the rounds in the city to my father:

> *Stalin, Trotsky, Lenin, see —*
> *Hooligans they are, all three.*

My father laughed nervously. Everybody who was there that jolly evening at Klyshko's place was arrested the following day, as participants in an "anti-Soviet gathering".

"That really shook me. But I knew that Sergei wasn't embarrassed by his behavior, telling anecdotes and reading anti-Soviet poems aloud. Someone probably snitched on him. They soon let the girls go, but the guys were kept behind bars for a long time — some got their ribs broken. Kostya Ivanov had his kidneys kicked in — they beat him half to death, demanding information, but he had drunk some vodka that evening, and he passed out right there at the table and couldn't see or hear anything. Sergei was sentenced "to the maximum".

"'The maximum' — for poetry?" I asked, in a melancholy tone.

"It was clear to me that I oughtn't to read them."

It was hard to argue with this. Our conversation had gone full circle, and it quickly died out. In my father's family, it took a long time for the mass terror, which was all around, everywhere, somewhere close at hand, and about which thousands of books had been written, to be acknowledged. They didn't hide from it, or try to put in a corner: they simply ignored it. But so many were arrested that in the end it became too much to bear. Leningrad University, which was full of philological stars, was shaken to the core. The NKVD came into the lecture hall to take away the bearded Latin professor, right in front of my father. They arrested him so elegantly — the young officer even helped him on with his coat — and took him out of the auditorium so graciously, patting him on the back as they did so, that the Latin teacher left with a smile on his face — as if he was going to the staff room for a cup of tea. From among the close circle of family friends who used to gather at Ivan Petrovich and Anastasia Nikandrovna's on Zagorodny Prospect to play cards on Saturday evenings, they took Fedyakin, a railway worker who was a member of the Party and had been awarded a military medal. Fedyakin sometimes asked abstract questions:

"Is it possible, Ivan Petrovich, when it's raining, to walk along the street between the drops of water without getting wet?"

"Well, both of us would need to lose a little weight first," Ivan Petrovich said, laughing the question off.

When Fedyakin disappeared, the family shrugged their shoulders: whatever for? — but later came to the conclusion that "they know best".

·

My father's life changed in an instant. In his second year at university he was called up by a letter sent in September 1939 to Smolny — the cradle of the Revolution. My father's fate, in the shape of a man with the Communist rank of Secretary of the City Committee, affably thrust into his hands a copy of the newspaper *Leningrad Truth* containing a photo of Stalin, Molotov and Ribbentrop exchanging smiles. This was the wedding between the Soviets and the Nazis.

"Do you know who that young man next to Stalin is?"

"An interpreter," my father guessed.

"Would you like to be an interpreter, too?"

"Yes."

"Who are your parents?"

The non-Party member railway worker Ivan Petrovich didn't give rise to any objections. Anastasia Nikandrovna had already retired by that time. She had left her job as secretary of the Leningrad branch of Union Photo, where she supplied photos to the local newspapers. She took orders, and sent films off to be developed, and then to be printed. The advanced world of photos had turned her into an important, even somewhat capricious person. Throughout my childhood she kept telling me about her boss and his funny surname, which was something like Tyunkin-Ryumkin (I remember now: it was Tyutikov!), of whom she was particularly fond: to her, Tyutikov was more important than any of the clients in her photos, and certainly more important than the other photographers, who used to try and court her. Grandma used to meet various celebrities, too — the 'leading lights' among the Soviet writers. She always had an unkind comment at the ready about writers, and was very concerned when I became one.

GRANDMA: A writer? What are you thinking! All writers are drunks.

"It would come in, on occasion, and stand there rocking back and forth," she said, mixing up her Tvardovsky and her Simonov, her Katayev and her Fadeyev.

This was the age of the group photo. Everyone had their picture taken in rows, in groups; all the factory workers together, the whole school together, all the hospital staff together — and they were thereby turned into a Soviet nation. On one occasion Union Photo let through a group photo through the net that Pyatakov, an enemy of the people, had snuck into. The vigilant newspaper never published the photo, but there was quite a scandal.

"How was I supposed to know what he looked like!" Grandma said to her favorite boss, Tyunkin-Ryumkin, in her defense. Just to be on the safe side, she soon quit her job at Ivan Petrovich's request. Tyunkin-Ryumkin was thrown out of the Party. Ivan Petrovich got a cat, named it Zhmurik and started to spoil it. Whenever grandma wasn't there, the cat would sleep on the couch. On hearing her step on the staircase, Ivan Petrovich would shout out:

"Here comes the Commissar!"

Zhmurik would leap off the couch, rush around the apartment and hide behind the trash can.

"We're sending you to Moscow," Smolny said to my father.

My father made no objection. He later admitted to me with a chuckle that if he hadn't agreed, he would have ended up writing some graduate dissertation about the role of articles or prefixes in French in the seventeenth century. Philology didn't inspire any respect in him. It was depressing, like his childhood. At the appointed time my father arrived at the October Train Station with a wooden suitcase, in order to go study at the Higher School for translators of the Central Committee of the All-Union Communist Party. There was an emotional parting on the platform with his parents, Zhmurik (Ivan Petrovich was holding him in his hands) and his friends.

"Have a safe trip!" they said.

"See you soon," he replied.

•

My father managed to join the ranks of those blessed with an outlook that was special because it was not based on the individual. Gratitude to the regime for having been given a higher education, and being able to climb the ladder was *nothing* in and of itself. These people didn't *use* the system, as if they were just passing through, but fed off it until they became totally saturated with it, and saw exactly as much as it wanted them to see. They stopped *being*, and were subconsciously ready for death from the very outset. The system didn't so much kill off unfulfilled poets, as happens in any self-respecting dictatorship, as feed off non-existence. The sacrificial terror was no whim, but the logic of its survival, a brilliant mathematical conclusion based on the *difference* between the future that had been promised and the human material that was packed off for reprocessing. Stalin had declared war on human nature. No-one had done such a thing before (the Holy Inquisition was the stuff of *weaklings!*) in human history. The people were scoundrels, the Party comrades were shit. All of them, even Molotov, were drawn backwards, towards a right-wing leaning, towards the feeding trough of private property. Stalin cut them down, generation after generation.

STALIN: I want to grow lemons that can withstand the cold.

It was a metaphysical challenge worthy of a former seminarian. The success of the measure depended as much on Russian submission as on the continual renewal, the cleansing of society of those who kept that *difference* in mind. The future was like a joyful sigh following the removal of antinomy.

I was surprised at first, then realized my surprise was misplaced, when my father told me he never felt worried in Stalin's presence. Unlike the intelligentsia, who *worried* when they saw the leader, and who made jokes about Stalin that were born of this worry, my father existed as one of his *extensions*, an additional quantum of light. It was difficult to come back home from *this* situation.

•

The translation courses at the Central Committee of the All-Union Communist Party, on Miyuskaya Square, were the 1939 equivalent of the Tsarskoye Selo Lycée. For the one hundred students there are a hundred professors and administrators. The students are taught languages by foreigners, and during their free time they are fed well and even have their rooms cleaned. And studying in the English department here is my deeply-affected mama from Novgorod; papa had begun to court her, had even kissed her once during a date; there were letters too, proudly signed *Vladimir*; mama had been particularly excited by that signature, but the next date never came, though she sat waiting for it in a new orange sweater: he moved on to her friend, a real beauty and her roommate in the narrow room, Lyuba; and Lyuba, a red-head, started coming into the dormitory with a proud look on her face, and swaying her hips from side to side, after her rendezvous with my father in the dormitory. The poet Boris Smolensky, rejected by Lyuba after dedicating numerous poems to her, suffered no less than mama, but their shared sense of rejection did not trigger a romance between them. Mama concentrated on languages and became an intelligent girl who loved art. My father trod the boards at the student theater. He would jump onto the stage — a ship's deck — in his sailor's uniform, and shout out, his eyes bulging "May Day!" then hide in the wings. The theater was foretelling what was about to happen to him.

•

Who am I to judge the features of the 20th century? Had there been one shooting fewer, or one less gas chamber in Auschwitz,

I might never have come into being. Efforts at self-sacrifice cannot be post-dated.

At the beginning of the war, my father, who had graduated by then, after passing his exams at the translator's school, was at the special-forces division undergoing training in diversionary acts of sabotage behind enemy lines. His last parachute jump before being sent to the front line went wrong: he broke his leg after landing in a tall fir tree, and ended up in hospital. The surgeons decided to amputate his leg up to the knee, fearing lest it became gangrenous. They told him that if he objected he must write a refusal. My father wrote one. He lay in the corridor listening attentively to his burning leg. He had a high temperature — he was delirious. His chances of survival were practically non-existent. Some young doctor saved him *by chance*, after deciding to try out a new preparation on his leg — Vishnevsky's cream. Twice a day the doctor patiently rubbed the cream into my father's leg. Vishnevsky himself materialized from out of the cream in our home many years later: a larger-than-life man, who held himself like a general and drank French cognac. Compared to him, my parents were like little characters from Russian literature. There were loads of bread crumbs on the table, left over from dinner. He guided his finger along my spine — and wasn't happy. Once they had got to know him, he took mama's appendix out and performed what she herself described as some virtuoso stitching in front of his students. Every last member of the group that flew out without my father to blow up bridges in the Smolensk Region was killed.

"So, kid, consider yourself lucky," said the surgeon who suggested cutting off papa's leg, putting a different spin on things altogether.

After leaving hospital my father just *happened* to be tracked down by, and invited to work for, the People's Commissariat of Foreign Affairs, as the Ministry of Internal Affairs was then known, since most of its staff, thrown into the volunteer army to defend Moscow in October 1941, had perished after being surrounded.

"You've a life of red carpets to look forward to now — you'll soon forget about us," the commander said to him when they parted company.

•

The Germans fought well at sea! Just look at one of their courageous deeds,which made the world stand still when it became known: a U-47 submarine rammed into the British base at Scapa Flow (Lieutenant Captain Prien was the senior officer, and it happened in October 14, 1939) and sank the battleship *Royal Oak*. Hitler became a threat at sea. His struggle against shipping in the Arctic during the *blitzkrieg* against Russia was led by Grand Admiral Raeder, a religious man who would not tolerate dirtiness, either in the fleet or in naval military methods. However that may be, the German military fleet has Raeder to thank for the unique concept of 'a war without hatred'. Another of the enemies conspiring against my birth, along with Raeder and Rear-Admiral Doenitz, the German submarines and trans-polar aviation, was the battleship *Tirpitz*.

"We've decided to send you abroad, to Sweden," Dekanozov, the Deputy Minister of Personnel, told my father. "You will be given training in diplomacy when you get there. Kollontai is an experienced ambassador. Any questions?"

One of Beria's men, Dekanozov was shot in 1953 — though he was blissfully unaware of this at the time. The opportunity to work in neutral Sweden would, of course, make him happy. He would even try to find enough free time to get to know the daughter of the anti-fascist physicist Nils Bohr, but, in accordance with the law of the magic fairytale, in order to attain happiness, the hero must first be subjected to deadly trials.

"And what should I wear for the journey?" my father ventured to ask, as he stood before Dekanozov in his military shirt.

"You can change your clothes when you get there."

So my father became Odysseus. Sweden had been cut off from her allies. Norway and Denmark were under occupation. Finland was fighting on the side of the Germans. My father was ordered to go to Kuybyshev, from there — to Archangelsk, then on by naval caravan to England and, God alone knew how, to Stockholm.

If I were to write a script for Hollywood, I would begin with the bombing. Announcement: this is a film about the daring of the American and British naval officers — *Titanic* is taking a break. The Germans are bombing the wooden buildings of Archangelsk. Archangelsk is ablaze. Flames are sweeping around the brick building — a rarity in the city — of the Intourist hotel, where my father is staying. The allies don't dare let their fleet set off on the return trip. My father is not going to be able to leave Archangelsk any time soon.

"Comrade, are you going to Sweden too? A fellow traveler? What's your name? Vladimir, let's go get some stewed meat!"

In the foyer of the hotel, up to their ankles in ash, two young diplomatic couriers in black hats are throwing cans of stewed meat to each other, as if they are playing rugby.

"Vladimir, here's lend-lease for you!" the diplomatic couriers continue throwing the cans. The caravans of transport ships, escorted by a convoy of military ships, are bringing us strategic shipments, equipment and — heads-up! catch it! — stewed meat! from Britain and the US. In return they get our raw materials. Let's go and have a drink! Vodka — there's no better medicine for burnt cinders.

"This is the third time we've sailed to Sweden." The first diplomat throws his hat onto the bed, in a room for two.

"What's it like out there?" my father asks.

"There's no death! War, like human life itself, mostly consists of a series of transfers."

"Shut up, nameless one!" the second diplomat poured the vodka into cut glasses. "The more I fear death, the further it gets from me."

"Volodya, don't pay any attention! The Germans have put their biggest military fleet in the North, headed by the battleship *Tirpitz*."

"It has a displacement capacity of 52,600 tons and a compliment of 2,608 men," the second diplomat added. "It's like a whole city! No one else has a ship like it!"

My father looks at them with understanding.

"We have our own maid, Volodya!" The first man says, twisting his lip. "She's the spitting image of Lyubov Orlova. The crew are experienced. Why is it that actresses all sleep with their directors?"

"As well as the battleship," the second one continues, "there are some cruisers too beyond the Arctic Circle," he counts them off on his fingers."The *Scharnhorst* (in fact I don't think that one was there, I checked in a reference book — author's note),the *Admiral Scheer*, the *Lützow*, the *Köln* and the *Nurnberg*. Five!"

"After the war the *Nurnberg* will sail under our flag. We'll rename it the *Admiral Makarov*!" the first man laughed.

"Wait! They're escorting more than twenty state-of-the-art destroyers. 520 German planes are being put into action, along with the considerable might of a fleet of submarines under the command of…"

"Rear-Admiral Doenitz," my father added. "What's there to be pleased about?"

"It's a sledge hammer! Hitler has set Doenitz the task of completely shutting off access to our Northern ports."

STALIN: Soso lay with Istomina
        In a shameful naked state…

The diplomats look around.

"Volodya, did you hear anything just then?"

"No."

"Neither did we."

"If they don't blow us up, we'll power through!" the first

diplomat said, glancing happily at the stamped bags of diplomatic mail. "Volodya, let's drink to that!"

In July 1942 the Soviet submariner Lunin successfully attacks the *Tirpitz*. The battleship heads off for repairs to the fjords of Norway, although Western historians believe that Lunin, with his K-21 submarine, was no more than an advertising gimmick. However that may be, the path is now open for the allied ships. By the beginning of September the QP-14 convoy has been formed: a handful of Soviet and English dry-cargo ships and tankers, which are like little children, surrounded by the attentions of the English and American military vessels. There are no Soviet 'governess' ships in the escort at all. To look at the convoy, you would think it invincible: a group of cruisers, twenty destroyers, Air Defense ships, eleven corvettes, trawlers, submarines and minesweepers!

"Volodya, where are you going? Come and join us on the cargo ship!" The diplomats are waving at my father with their cans of stewed meat from the deck of the Soviet vessel.

"They sent me to join the English on a trawler."

"They sent you too far! Come and sail with us!"

"I have my orders."

"We'll see to it now. Our captain's a good guy!"

Vladimir climbs aboard the trawler *Lord Middleton* without any sense of pleasure at all. He knows almost no English. Who did he have to talk to? Diplomats got all the luck — they were given places next to fellow Russians, but Katya Varennikova, an extremely young pregnant woman, who is sailing to her see husband, who works in London, was put on a British cargo ship. As always, Russians love to change places, to swap seats. Before they set off the mother-to-be tearfully asked my father to take her with him:

"Volodya dear, I'm frightened of being among strangers."

No one had noticed that they had got to know one another pretty well while living at the hotel.

"How fortunate it is that there's no God," Katya continued. "If I die, I won't have to burn in hell."

"Why would you end up in hell, anyway?"

Katya shrugged her shoulders. My father ran around after her, courting her — to no avail.

"My Brits have gone sour," he told the pregnant beauty at the port. "The convoy's departure is set for the thirtieth. Besides, the presence of women on a military ship — as you're well aware — is a bad omen."

The Scots, who made up the majority of the trawler's crew, though they turned the woman down, were affable towards my father. The captain, whose teeth had been browned by tobacco, barked out orders.

CAPTAIN: Give him a yellow naval robe with a hood, some warm underwear, some boots and a weapon of his own — a Mauser!

The right clothes, in other words! For the first time in his life my father looks like a real man — in his yellow robe, and with his Mauser in his hand, he is fearless.

The QP-14 convoy had barely got out into the White Sea when the German reconnaissance aircraft got it in its sights. And it all kicked off! The convoy set up a heavy ring of defensive fire against the Germans. But the Germans know what they are doing, the bastards! They had been on course for Spitsbergen. The sky is teeming with airplanes. The war moves inside Vladimir's head, which is being subjected to incessant attacks by large squadrons of He-177 torpedo planes and Junker-88 dive-bombers.

To the rear of the trawler my father notices a series of fires burning in the sea.

GOD: War, like any other creative game, is clear proof of my existence.

People with wild, screaming voices are drowning in the icy water and the lakes of fuel oil. No one is going to come to their aid: the convoy has been ordered to go full steam ahead away from the enemy, without stopping to save the dying. The German planes push the caravan to the edge of the packed ice at Novaya Zemlya, and can reach it even there, although, due to the need to economize on fuel, they can't hang over the enemy for long.

Vladimir gradually grows accustomed to life under the bombs. His innate curiosity doesn't wane. I'm listening, Captain!

"Before the war *Lord Middleton* was a whaler ship. Whales, essentially, are like those Germans: they're milk-drinkers. I have a team of 52 men. Look what we have: two weapons — one at the bow and one at the aft, two large-caliber machine guns on the captain's bridge, and also a device for launching long-range bombs. There's some good news: Katya has had her baby."

"Really?"

"This morning. We'll have some champagne when we reach Iceland. The German aircraft are not really going after us, although we have to carry out endless maneuvers. Believe me, as soon as we get past Spitsbergen in the Atlantic, it'll be easier."

Vladimir has to admit that the saying 'plain sailing' certainly doesn't apply in this case. The passage between Spitsbergen and Norway proved to be the most dangerous section of all. The aircraft didn't let up. It would probably have destroyed the entire convoy, but Arctic fogs began to form. A sheet descended over the convoy. The German aircraft still didn't have radar. The main German ships hadn't got out to sea. Hitler had decided not to risk his fleet.

In the Medvezhy Island region, however, the German planes went on to sink several ships right away. Both those jolly card-playing diplomats were burned alive. They hadn't wanted to leave the bags of long-outdated mail on the burning cargo ship. Katya Varennikova drowned that same day along with her daughter, whom the British sailors had christened Marina because she was born at sea.

In the Atlantic the convoy is confronted with submarines marked with swastikas. They approach the convoy above the surface, insolently, then drop underwater and start firing torpedoes at it from all sides. My father, who is standing, as always, on the captain's bridge, is thrown back against the railings by a wave caused by a powerful explosion. Don't drown, papa! In the immediate vicinity of the trawler, the British destroyer HMS Somali — a brand new ship that has only just been put in the water, a real beauty — is struck. A torpedo hits the engine room.

The destroyer tilted to one side, but didn't sink. Two other destroyers and my father's trawler, as an aide vessel, were given orders to transport the damaged ship to Iceland. The crew of HMS Somali climb back on deck from the lifeboats. The rest of the convoy continues its journey. Several days later, during a storm in the night, HMS Somali is split in two. It rapidly sinks to the bottom with its entire crew. The sailors throw huge nets into the ocean. Their catch: fifteen (out of a total of six hundred) people, blackened from the cold, and a huge quantity of fish. They gave them a few mouthfuls of rum, wiped them down with spirits, and gave them hot water bottles. Two men survived. Their task complete, the destroyers rush on to catch up with the convoy. The trawler remains alone in the ocean.

•

Silence. Sunshine. The weeping polar nights (their season has already past, but we'll leave them in for added beauty). The weather is good for sailing. It sometimes seems to my father as though he — a fully-grown young man — is out on a pleasure cruise during a vacation. The ghosts of love come into being in the blue distance. The clouds are like wedding-night feather-beds. The only pity is that alongside him there is no… — whom does my father want to embrace? In the morning he sees some strange smoke that has appeared on the horizon beyond the ship's aft. It is the signal to be ready for battle: "the surface ships of the enemy".

"Full ahead!" the sea-wolf screams into the megaphone.

But the ship couldn't match the speed of the three unknown destroyers. The one at the front let out a volley from the guns on its deck, to demand that the trawler stop.

"Fuck you!!" the captain wheezes, winking at my father. "Spread out, prepare for battle!" he yells into the megaphone.

The trawler bristles with every last one of its worn-out weapons. My father squeezes the handle of the Mauser in his pocket. But he has forgotten where he put the bullets. He runs to his cabin, finds them under his pillow — the bullets — and runs back to the Captain's bridge. (I have inherited from him a lack of competence with anything technical, although as a child I once amazed everyone with my sharp-shooting at a shooting gallery.) A painful pause ensues. My father knows that the Germans won't get him alive. The destroyers, cutting through the water noisily, are getting close, standing tall — right up to the sky — over the trawler. My father throws his head back. And suddenly shouts are heard:

"The yanks! The yanks!"

The destroyers come right up, as close as they can get. After climbing aboard, sailors from Oklahoma, Minnesota, Mississippi and Alabama — white men and black, our allies, so much our own that it brings tears to the eyes — the yanks throw down onto the deck of the trawler bags bearing the eagle crest. Inside are preserves, cans of beer — everything that my father and the Scots have been deprived of for so long. A sumptuous feast was served up on the trawler. Everyone felt like a hero, and started walking around drunk, and shouting at my father:

"Stalingrad! Stalingrad!"

STALIN: Isn't it a little too early to be celebrating?

In the evening my father, horribly embarrassed, teaches the crew a few more, equally hard-hitting words from the Russian language.

•

Our Soviet Odysseus steps ashore in a foreign land for the first time. He feels like a real globetrotter. How nice it is to feel the firm soil beneath his feet, to pass quietly along the streets of

Reykjavik. It never gets dark in Iceland: the brightly painted houses are lit up by electric lights in the evenings. Vladimir admires the girls, who are reputed to be the most beautiful in Western Europe.

Iceland has always attracted Russians due to the way it goes beyond all limits. It was no accident that Dostoyevsky's most demonic hero, the handsome Stavrogin — who, incidentally, never talks about the place, since an imaginary country has no need of tourist impressions — spent some time there.

By some strange coincidence, not to say a provocative irony of fate, I too spent some time in Iceland at the same age as my father was when he was there, twenty-two, although, unlike him, I never actually set foot in the country. My own personal Iceland lived on the sixth floor. On Prospect Mira, near the Riga Train Station, in the diplomatic house, the courtyard of which was guarded by a Soviet policeman. I had to gather up all my *unsovietness* and *unrussianness*, in order to go into the courtyard on my own, in my unbuttoned red coat with its virgin white fur lining, without arousing suspicion. This was a test not only of my foreignness, but also of my impudence, for which I might have had to pay a heavy price in those days. Moreover, this was my first dissident breakthrough outside the orbit of the Soviet world: the experience was such a powerful and endless one that it knocked me out of the wheel of Russian literature for good. At a time when all I had was the desire to write, when I had endless doubts about myself, and didn't believe in myself, but had some stubborn presentiment, I experienced my Iceland like an entrance into a novel, as a transformation of my own life into a divine text.

On the numerous occasions when I ruined this text in later years, my thoughts would return to Iceland, as to its source, the concept behind it, its unattainable template. Iceland became the country of my descent into sin, my utterly illegal, forbidden love. My Iceland was a couple of years older than me, and worked as a diplomat at the smallest embassy of all the NATO countries, in an incredibly quiet alley near Vorovsky Street, and I was still in my fifth year of university, just recently happily married, a newlywed awaiting his young wife, who had got stuck in her Eastern-European country due to visa delays. And, on November 7, a group of intoxicated friends, after hanging out near the cinema, has brought Iceland back to my parents' apartment — they are out of town — and Iceland and I are standing on the small, unsteady balcony of my parents' bedroom, overlooking the courtyard, and watching the Soviet military salute, and she is watching it with such joy, such genuine happiness, that I realize something: it is a salute of happiness in our honor. And, as only happens when you are young, everyone gradually goes off their own way, in a rhythmical dispersion, and dissolves into thin air, as though it has been predetermined in advance that there would be no delays or obstacles, and that we were going to be left alone together, head-over-heels in love, connected by everything and forever, almost mute due to a lack of English vocabulary. If there is a matrix of earthly love, if there is a matrix of earthly bliss, then on that public holiday in honor of the revolution it materialized on the carpet of my parents' living room. We lost our heads. Love demands simple,kitsch words, it doesn't need the Ornamentalism found in Zamyatin, with its tendency for petty-bourgeois romance. It is best described as a parody of literature — if it really is love. And we began to live like that — mutely, not trusting English words, in her apartment on Prospekt Mira, in all the illegitimacy of our love, in a mute fairytale, on the periphery of which we could hear the roar of hostile forces. Her slow movements as she pours the tea; the heavenly way she turns her head when she glances back at me on the boulevard; the copy of Gorky's autobiographical novel in Icelandic in her slender, aristocratic hands; her blue couch, on which I set superhuman records of passion, so that I would never have to repeat them, and, perhaps most importantly, so as never to be jealous of anyone ever again. And those words *elska min*, which have remained in me forever, and her open white legs — to hell with Stravrogin, to hell with my father's military passions!

I go down into the Rizhskaya metro station, I'm twenty-two, it's late, I should be getting home, and I look at the spectral passengers, at this late hour, on the escalator — and I know that no one is ever going to be as happy as I am. She tells me that in Iceland there are folk songs but no folk dances. There are folk dances everywhere else, but not in Iceland — just as there are no last names. There are only patronymics that have come to life. We had no need to assert our existence in hot geysers — we had semen a plenty. She has a scar on her finger, and I have one too — on my left index finger. I got mine while peeling radishes in the seventh grade, using a long knife with a wooden handle. In the kitchen. Blood. Scars on my fingers. We are both marked. But according to her, the phalanx of her finger was cut off altogether, but she quickly put it back on — and it grew back. How did it grow back? Such things aren't possible. They aren't possible either with your finger, or with you yourself: it just doesn't happen.

I look at the unearthly way she turns her head, her beautiful black head, and at her eyes, ever so slightly moist with excitement — and this wintry Moscow boulevard — we have to make a decision — she's pregnant, I'm the father, and I simply can't believe my luck.

"Austa!" I think to myself now… "The Captain's daughter! How did you lead your life? Where are you now? With whom do you live? How many children do you have? The grandchildren have probably started popping out too, by now. How are your two sisters? What's new with them? And what became of us?"

•

After undergoing repairs in Iceland, HMS *Lord Middleton* sets a course for the British Isles. And once again — how much can a man take! — a mortal danger hung over my father. Late one evening, when the crew was already getting ready for bed, the alarm went off:

"An enemy submarine!"

My father jumped off his bunk and climbed quickly up the metal rungs to the deck. An experienced sailor, he listens carefully to the rhythm of the waves, as they roll across it. Seizing the moment, he pushes the heavy door open. There are six meters between him and the hatch on the captain's bridge. He has run most of the way there when he hears a shout from the captain, who is cursing my father through the megaphone: Vladimir had failed to slam shut the door of the hold. From inside the hold, a bright projector is lighting up the whole area with its beam — an ideal target for the Germans!

Father spins around without stopping. A heavy wave crashes over him, knocking him over, but he manages to catch hold of the handle on the door — and he clings on, dangling like a clown — until the next wave throws him inside. Drenched, his teeth chattering from the cold and the nervous shock, he nonetheless has one more try. This time he reaches the stairs on the captain's bridge. On the crooked surface of the ocean, he spots a flickering, greenish light. The trawler approaches it carefully. The Scots have the unidentified object in the sights of one of their guns. A naval duel is about to begin. Father clenches his teeth. He doesn't know how to pray.

Imagine his surprise when, after getting nearer to the mysterious fire, the sailors discover a drifting log, lit up by a malachite light! The log splinters when the bullets hit it. The crew has a good laugh over the watchman who raised the alarm because of a log floating in the ocean at night.

•

They polished the deck and buffed the handrails until they sparkled. And then they sailed in. The authorities in Edinburgh, who had thought HMT *Lord Middleton* lost, organized a gala reception for the crew. A military orchestra, blowing out the furs on their bag pipes, played triumphant marches in the wind. A guard of honor, consisting of tall Scotsmen in plaid kilts and colorful tartans,was lined up in front of the town hall. Inside, a grand banquet awaited the sailors: they were served haggis. It was grayish-brown in color. "Looks like shit," my father laughed, as he put a portion on his plate, smiling his first diplomatic smile. But when he tried it, he said to himself, without any diplomacy at all: "It would be better if it were shit!" Vladimir's stomach was hurting terribly. It was the first time father had appeared before such a large audience of foreigners. He looked odd in his shabby field shirt. No one paid any attention to that. All of Edinburgh stared intently at this real-life Soviet, who had arrived from Russia, where battle was raging.

"Where are you headed? We have to go back to sea again soon. Why not join us?"

Vladimir left in the old-fashioned compartment of the sleeper car. The captain and seven sailors saw him off at the station. They drank loads of whiskey, straight from the bottle. Father kissed the entire crew, and waved them off from the window for a long time. Mountains thick with forests, which had taken on pastel hues due to the whiskey, began to stream past the window. He stood in the corridor by the window for half a day — as was his wont on rail journeys. He arrived in London late in the evening.

The platform was dimly lit by some blue lamps. No one came to meet him. Vladimir caught a black cab. After climbing the steps of No. 13, Kensington Palace Gardens, he rang the doorbell. The old, heavy door was opened ajar. Father announced who he was. He was let in. The young diplomat on duty that night was delighted to have someone to talk to. They had some tea.

"Do you believe the number thirteen brings bad luck?"

"Why do you ask?"

"They bought the building under the embassy at a special discount because of the number. Since then the mansions on either side have either been destroyed or suffered serious damage because of the bombing. But the embassy's been left completely untouched — not a trace of damage.

"Have they been bombing heavily?"

The other member of staff had come in, yawning.

"Have you seen a cat anywhere?"

"What cat?"

"There's a cat that's gone missing."

The fellow who had lost his cat took my father to a nearby hotel.

"Those fascists! I'd grown fond of that cat. My wife stayed behind in Moscow."

"It'll turn up," father said.

He was ever the optimist. Feeling the pleasant warmth coming from the big hot-water bottle placed at his feet under the sheets, he fell asleep the moment his head hit the pillow. Father could sleep anywhere, in any situation, back then. He slept so well that a pistol going off next to his ear wouldn't have woken him. But in the middle of the night, Vladimir woke up. It was pitch-black outside. The blanket lay on him like a sandbag. Father thought the ceiling had caved in. Endeavoring to get up, he heard splinters of glass tinkling on the floor. A breeze was blowing into the room. Not a trace remained of the window-frames or the shutter. A heavy contact mine had clearly fallen somewhere close by. Deciding that things would be clearer in the morning, father went back to bed.

The German pilots fought well! Hitler was the thunder cloud of the skies. His aircraft did as they pleased in the sky above London. In the morning the dank air was acrid with smoke, just like in Archangelsk, but father saw no trace of despair on the tired faces of the people of London. The people looked composed and focused. The movie theaters were open as normal. In the big department store, where the embassy staff took father the next day, the efficient salespeople dressed father in civilian clothes in less than half an hour, putting his Soviet field shirt in a bag carefully. Although no one paid any attention to him on the street, father felt awkward in his narrow pants and a hat, an accessory that had never adorned his head before.

"You didn't come over with Katya Varennikova by any chance, did you?" the embassy staff suddenly asked him, out of the blue.

"She drowned," father said. "Along with her daughter."

The men laughed.

"What's the matter with you?"

"Do you know what she used to do?"

"What?"

A fresh peal of laughter rang out. Vladimir decided not to ask any more questions.

"I found the cat," said the embassy staff member whom he had met before.

"See, I knew you would," father smiled.

Father was able to find common ground with people quickly, but he lived his whole life without ever laughing once. Sweden was as far off as victory, at that stage. The Americans took it upon themselves to drop father off there. They finished their coffee and went out onto the landing area.

"Well then, let's go," said the military pilots, handing my father a Chesterfield. Three heavy bombers stood on the landing area in the evening light.

"Wonderful machines!" said father. "Why don't you open a second front?"

The Americans smiled.

"Ask Churchill!" A large black man stuck out his pink tongue with lazy contempt. "He's scared of the Germans."

They were always very proud of their technology. Technology is the soul of the West. To reach Sweden they had to fly over Norway, which was under German occupation.

"We're going to be in the shit!" the Americans assured father. We'll cross over the narrow section at night, gliding with the engines turned off."

"It's quick and painless that way," winked the black man, "like having a tooth pulled out."

That night the Germans spotted the American bombers over Norway and chased after them — they brought one down, the one with the big black man at the controls, in Swedish airspace, which was unfair in every sense. One out of three — odds like that made Russian roulette look tame. After sleeping right through the battle in the sky, my papa, the simple-hearted Odysseus, landed near Stockholm in early November 1942, on the eve of the 25th anniversary of the October Revolution, after a journey that lasted roughly two months in total.

•

The writer is the polar opposite of the diplomat. I've begun to catch myself thinking that, as I follow the advance of a young man toward the moment when he becomes my father, I am involuntarily lapsing into a semi-ironic tone, and I try to explain this to myself internally. Perhaps I fell out of love with diplomacy, which,at best, is nothing more than the outstanding subordination of one's being before the interests of the state. Perhaps the historical experience that has been accrued up to the present day has transformed my father's behavior into a series of, at the very least, simple-hearted acts (by a 'simple-hearted Odysseus'), and I cannot help but react to this with a certain degree of arrogance. It is more likely, though, that this has something to do with the incompatibility of the roles of father and son.

Children, however they turn out, turn our lives into a trap. A beautiful girl from a more senior grade (I saw this happen today next to an apartment block on Plyushchikha Street), smelling of the right *eau de toilette*, suddenly starts running away from her young, bespectacled companion, then turns to him with a laugh and says, lovingly:

"I'm so...*afraid* of you."

From her parents' point of view, this love is treachery. And as for her — she's a young slut. There was a good reason why, in traditional societies, parents used to choose brides or grooms for their children: we own our children, because we gave birth to them; they are a product which only we can sell, but they will never see it that way.

Children betray us with every aspect of their behavior: their fashion, their dances, their habits and their language, which serves as a way of poking fun at us. We have children as a continuation of ourselves in love — our children scream, stop us from sleeping, shit in their pampers and get sick. We go out to meet them at the metro at night, so as not to offend them, and they get embarrassed by us. When I went to the graduation evening at the school on Gorky Street, near Pushkin Square, I was embarrassed by the fact that mama (who was still young, and well-dressed) was walking alongside me. When we drew alongside the Museum of the Revolution, which was once the Museum of Gifts to Stalin, I even tried to pull away from her, and walk along on my own, but she didn't realize what the matter was, and muttered: "Why are you hurrying along like that?", and probably thought I was anxious about something.

To our children, we are a buffer against death. They, to us, are not only a continuation of the species, but also the promise of our own personal eternity, not as distinct as a religious eternity, perhaps, but an eternity nonetheless. If death is considered the highest criterion of reliability, then we are clearly not on an equal footing. The death of a child kills the child's parents, it is an attack on their immortality. The death of one's parents is merely a personal tragedy for each individual.

Parents are more important than literature. When he describes them, the writer's style begins to shudder. The writer tries in vain to turn his impression of them into a vivid description. But children are often more important than life. When, on my way back from a walk around Red Army Square one day, I was crossing the street with a fashionable denim stroller, in which my little son Oleg was sleeping, I realized that if a situation arose in which it was either him or me, I would sacrifice myself, and be hit by a car. This self-sacrifice opened up without a creak, like a well-oiled door. It was something in which there wasn't even a trace of magnanimity.

We are crafty, however, about our fate. We choose our children based on our affinity to them, and we frequently cast off for good accidental, collateral children — they are not suited to the particular type of eternity that we want.

On a winter's morning, returning to Moscow from the dacha where I'm writing this book, I see crowds of people, almost invisible in the morning gloom, standing at the bus stops in the Pavlov settlement, sleep-deprived and cursing life — they're heading into the city to work for the good of their children. I get the impression they all work at chemical factories. The smiles on the faces of parents as they leave the maternity ward is a vulgar thing, which must be paid for dearly. Children don't notice the efforts we make — and we are expected to live with this self-evident state of affairs. The outpouring of love around the table on our birthday is like the electric lightning of a burnt-out lamp. Parental affection — "dear son!" — comes up against a brick wall, its eroticism has nowhere to go. A great 'fucking over' is at work, in which we play the passive role of the continuation of a species which stopped being aware of itself a long, long time ago. Obsolescence is the formula for parental senile abandon, reduced to its purest form. We can't pay ourselves off with an inheritance, even if there is one. A few chairs thrown out with the trash — that's all that will remain after we've gone.

Children are inhuman. They are enveloped by a mortal fear on their behalf and by an absurd pride which bursts into the stories we tell about them, which always seem laughable from the outside. It's unpleasant if our children grow up to be dim-witted, and ugly, but children who are excessively smart and successful drive us into having complexes and become the judges of our failures. Parents mask their children's shortcomings; but children jump at the chance to discuss their parents' shortcomings. There are, of course, exceptions. Nabokov idolized his father, which partly accounts for his hatred of Freud. But his ideal father was a construct that he created in his own mind, well-suited to literature, but not to life. We make a great drama out of every trifle in our children's lives, whereas they make our dramas seem banal, if they notice them at all. Parents have already done the most important thing in their lives — they brought us into the world. The rest is all insignificant.

•

"My teacher in the art of diplomacy was Alexandra Mikhailovna Kollontai," my father said many times, with justifiable pride. In 1942 Sweden chose to remain neutral. Goebbels' propaganda campaign was very much in evidence. On the central street of Kungsgatan hung the huge reflective window-front of the German Information Bureau: photos from the Eastern Front had been put on display in it, glorifying the great victories of the Arian soldiers. The Germans were winning with smiles on their faces. The window kept getting smashed in by Norwegian students. The Germans had to put in new glass, only for it to be smashed in again. In response the Fascists smashed in the windows of the Soviet Information Bureau, in Railroad Square, in which there were multiple images of Vasily Terkin laughing with his teeth showing (laughter trumps smiles), but this window was made of ordinary window glass, and it was easier to replace.

It's a strange thing, diplomacy. The continuation of war by peaceful means? How brilliantly Kollontai conducted the negotiations regarding Finland's withdrawal from the war! Aware of the close ties between Marcus Vallenberg and the Finnish President Ryuti, she carefully but persistently set about planting the idea in his mind that there was a need for him to exert pressure on the Finns, and persuade them to cease their war with the Soviet Union. Vallenberg heeds her advice and leaves Helsinki — and Alexandra Mikhailovna promptly sends a telegram to Moscow recommending that the bombing of the Finnish capital be stepped up while he was away.

"She was a master at using her own personal connections in

the national interest of the USSR," father emphasized during a family chat with me.

"The Swedes," Kollontai explained to the embassy staff, as they crowded around her wheelchair, "with the exception of the Fascist groups among them, don't feed on sympathy… what are you doing over there, Petrov?"

"Nothing."

"Thought not…well look here, Petrov, remember this: the Swedes have no sympathy for Hitler's regime, and have no wish to find out what it's like to live under it."

Father often had occasion to witness Alexandra Mikhailovna scolding Swedish ministers in her office for giving up their neutrality.

"Whatever are you thinking, my friends!"

"Forgive us, comrade!" the cabinet ministers blushed.

Carried away by the admiration he felt for Kollontai, papa once told me that as the war raged she turned around a statue of Charles XII, pointing towards Russia as if at an enemy, so that he faced the Germans. The story was apocryphal, but it is one that has stayed in my soul. The embassy relied on the strong anti-war mood of the Swedish people. Vladimir spent almost the entire war working as an aide to the ambassador. Initially, on his arrival, he was put up in a hotel. He was awoken one night by an apparition: there was a girl standing in his room, and on her head she wore a crown with burning candles on it. Father rubbed his eyes: was it a dream? An act of provocation? The result of a long period of abstention? The girl came up to his bed, and with a smile handed him a tray on which there was a cup of coffee and some cookies. Father propped himself up on his pillow, drank the coffee and ate the cookies with a crunch. Still smiling, the girl walked out, closing the door behind her. On the walls of the embassy's main hall, in which they served lunches and held receptions, there hung some large plates which had been given to Kollontai by workers from the Leningrad porcelain factory,and which bore the inscriptions:

"He who won't work, won't eat!" and "Long may the workers and peasants reign!"

Kollontai had father help her out with the work she did in the evenings on her memoirs. In the midst of war, and with Stalinism in full swing, she was writing them in French for a Mexican publishing house. In her room was an iron-shod trunk. Pushing her wheelchair over to it with her long, elderly fingers, she lifted the heavy lid with father's help: on the inside were some labels with tsarist coats-of-arms. She put her hand deep inside,until she reached the archeological layer she was looking for — and took out some letters from Lenin, Martov and Rosa Luxemburg. Looking at some photos of Plekhanov which had been dedicated to her personally, she admitted:

"For a long time my closeness to him stopped me from joining the Bolsheviks."

Kollontai was a member of Lenin's first government, but spoke out against the Treaty of Brest-Litovsk, and, along with her friend Shlyapnikov, set up the liberal Workers' Opposition; when this movement was routed, she left the government. From time to time Alexandra Mikhailovna, leaning back in her wheelchair, would tell father about herself, trustingly. She said that she had lived several different lives, but that the common thread running through all of them was one of her basic character traits — rebelliousness.

KOLLONTAI: I was a young lady in Petersburg society, and my noble heritage serves me well in Sweden. The conservative Swedes, who are mad about the aristocracy, are able to overlook my bolshevism, and the fact that I am a Soviet envoy, because of my noble past.

Long before this, back in September 1914, the Swedish Minister of Internal Affairs had been instructed to arrest Kollontai for spreading revolutionary propaganda. King Gustav V signed an edict for her deportation from the country for good. With a cunning luster in her big blue eyes, raising her thick brows and shaking her fringe, Kollontai told father how awkward it had been for Gustav V when, in 1930, he had had to accept her credentials as the ambassador plenipotentiary of the Soviet Union in Sweden. The king secretly annulled his old edict. Ivan Petrovich continued to work on the railroad. Father's parents lived in Petersburg for the duration of the siege. Each day he plodded along to the October Train Station, after switching his own pants, which were now too loose around the waist, for his son's Komsomol pants. On the fast train that took father to southern Sweden, he met a blonde girl. Before leaving the station she put on an SS uniform. Suddenly there was a terrifying explosion. The head of the woman next door was ripped off, and flew through grandmother's open window. Grandmother didn't know what was the done thing in such situations. Ought she to give the head to her neighbor's husband? Call the police? Put it out with the trash?

"How did you cope with all that, Nina Vasiliyevna?"

Grandmother had been on good terms with her neighbor: she had just finished adjusting a dress for her. The neighbor had promised to pay her for the work. Was Communist sex something akin to drinking a glass of water? Fundamentally opposed to marital relations, Kollontai believed that the family encouraged and validated people's egotism, which hampered the building of Communism. Eventually she married Dybenko, however.

KOLLONTAI: I was 17 years older than Pavel, but that didn't bother me. As long as someone loves us, we remain young. But I began to feel burdened by being the wife of a division commander, and he grew bored of being the husband of an ambassador. And our love had died out, too.

Kollontai was not only a Bolshevik, but also a sexual revolutionary — a legend of the Silver age, a lover of chocolate candy, a bisexual advocate of free love between 'worker bees'. Lenin was shaken by Kollontai's theories. My father wasn't entirely convinced by her either. In 1905, on Bloody Sunday, Kollontai had gone to the Winter Palace; shots were fired and she started running; and by the time my father met her, many years later, she was already paralyzed and confined to a wheelchair. Kollontai had long had to abstain from the pleasures of the flesh, and had sublimated into a great politician. When Ivan Petrovich returned home, the couple had a long discussion about everything. Almost all their neighbors had died of starvation. Grandmother was a seamstress, and it was this that saved her. The corpses had to be transported on sleighs to Boris Erisman's medical institute. The rustle of the hair on the corpses, caused by the wind and the frost, gnawed away at them. Petrov came in. Petrov, the aide to the resident spy responsible for supervising the workforce in the Soviet colonies, said to father:

"Can't you see she's not one of us, she's surrounded herself with dubious characters: the maid's a Swede, the chauffeur's Swedish too."

Father refused to cooperate with Petrov.

"You'll come to regret it, but it'll be too late by then," Petrov said.

He tried to lean on father again, on more than one occasion.

"I'll tell Kollontai about this," father said.

Petrov called father every name under the sun. Later Petrov worked in Australia, and ran off with the embassy cashbox. Several of the young single men failed to cope with lengthy stints abroad. Arkady, one of my father's acquaintances, after sending numerous requests to be replaced, sent an anonymous denunciation of himself to Moscow. It contained detailed descriptions of his drinking bouts, his late-night rendezvous with prostitutes in parks (they even included the names of his favorite tipples, the names of the bars and parks he frequented and the names of the prostitutes). He was called home immediately. Suddenly, at the beginning of August 1944, a telegram came: father was to be sent on a business trip to Moscow. Kollontai was most perturbed. She sent a response to Moscow declining the invitation. She had already grown used to having father around. Moreover, she had grown attached to him. What men fail to appreciate is that a woman in a wheelchair still has a woman's needs. During those Swedish nights, when she took time off from the games she played with the Finns each day to try and get them to stop fighting, they would talk to one another in French.

"And how do you say 'relationship' in French?"

"Liaison."

"Say it again?"

My father is a fool. Moscow sent a second telegram. Kollontai said no again. Then a telegram came from Moscow, signed by Molotov. At that point Kollontai admitted defeat.

"It doesn't make any sense to me, but you're going to have to go."

The dark-browed advisor Ilya Chernyshev — my parents moved into his spacious Moscow apartment many years later, after he drowned whilst working as the Soviet Ambassador to Brazil; his aide, who had rushed in to try and save him, had his head bitten off by a shark, and the aide's mother, though she knew nothing about the accident, had a dream in which her son was sitting headless on the riverbank, fishing — the advisor Chernyshev, half tongue-in-cheek and half in earnest, asked father:

"What on earth did you do to make them so determined to call you back?"

Father said nothing. He was at a loss what to say.

•

"Did it ever cross your mind that they might arrest you when you got back to Moscow?"

"Why would they do that?"

"Not for anything in particular. Why did it take you so long to get back?"

"There was a war on," father chuckled.

The liberation of Europe was unfolding before father's eyes, in all its glory. He continued to play the role of a Soviet Candide. He flew out of Sweden in late August 1944 on the *Douglas*, a British military-transport plane. After flying over Norway without any difficulties, the plane crossed the North Sea, but as it approached Scotland — you guessed it! — a German fighter plane began to spray it with tracer fire. The right wing caught fire. The pilot tried to put out the flames by carrying out maneuvers, but to no avail. The cabin filled up with smoke. A rubber fuel tank hung along the length of the ceiling, above the passengers' heads. There were a lot of military air bases on the Scottish coast, and the pilot attempted to land at one of them. The moment the plane touched down, father, along with the other passengers, jumped out and ran as fast as his legs would carry him, to take cover behind the nearby hangar.

I can see my father running now, holding his hat on to stop it blowing away, and I suddenly realize that he is not afraid of losing his life: he has a charter of immunity, consisting of an almost puerile levity, recklessness and indifference to danger. His suitcase escaped intact as well: a team of firemen managed to get to the burning airplane straight away. They put out the flames with sand and foam, and father's Swedish suits went on to live an endless, aimless life in his dark-brown Swedish suitcase, with its solid silvery buckles, with the naphthalene in grandmother's apartment, until the day she died. Anastasia Nikandrovna's skin remained girlish, and her consciousness was unclouded until the very end, in spite of the fatal disease she had: inflammation of the spinal cord. It left her paralyzed from the waist down and had already reached her lungs, but grandmother won her own personal battle of Stalingrad, by casting off this misfortune, and for fifteen years (complaining of a constant burning sensation in her legs) she was living proof of the miracle that is the human body, for future physicians to study. Strangely, I wasn't given sufficient time to enjoy taking pride in my grandmother. She died at the age of 96 in the intensive care unit at Kuntsevsky

Hospital. During the silent funeral service, held in the local registry hall, the family awaited father's decision. Aesthetics must come first. He went into the next room, glanced into the coffin — and grandmother looked beautiful. He nodded: she must be brought out before the family. We began to say our farewells, with an even number of flowers. At the Vagankovsky Cemetery, mother, who had not seen her for ten years, made the sign of the cross over the old woman, bidding her adieu.

A new challenge awaited father in London: FAU-2 ballistic missiles. They flew to the city at high altitude, faster than the speed of sound, and landed in such a way that the first thing you heard was a colossal explosion, and only afterwards — the whistle they made on the way down. The Germans never told the British about this new weapon, and at first no-one could work out what it was that was falling on them. Everyone lived under the threat of a sudden and incomprehensible demise. By agreement with the Americans, father was sent to the US military air base in South Wales. From there he was supposed to be sent to Casablanca, then on to Cairo, and from there to Moscow. The American pilots, full of bravado, enjoyed themselves as they flew. A second front had been opened, despite Churchill's stalling. The worst, it seemed, was over. Early one morning father was put in a heavy bomber, which he recognized as the same one in which he had flown to Sweden. After settling in his metal-plated seat, father, covering himself with a blanket, dozed off: the journey to Morocco would take at least six hours. He had just drifted off to sleep when suddenly he felt the plane landing. Father went over to the co-pilot, to find out what had happened.

"We had been ordered to land in France."

Father peered through the window. Traces of furious fighting could be seen on all sides. Beneath the plane's wing was the huge, burnt-out city of Caen, in Normandy. The US high command in France were surprised to see my father, a Soviet. They suggested that instead of continuing his flight, he should join some officers who were going to travel through France in a jeep, to Toulon.

Vladimir joined them, bouncing along on the army suspension. What is the definition of good fortune? Turning an impossibility into a reality. His account had been opened. The points were beginning to pile up. France looked magnificent, despite all the collaborationism that had been exposed there. Plane trees, ever so slightly jaundiced, lined the roads. Palm trees poked out of the earth at the intersections. In Toulon he caught sight of the Mediterranean Sea. It lay there looking golden, in stark contrast to the Baltic Sea off the coast of Sweden, which was full of herring. The houses were yellow, with shutters on the south-facing walls, and the cafes were noisy. The people wandered the streets happily. Some French militants, wrapped in cartridge belts and weighed down by grenades and automatic weapons, were kissing a group of curly-haired girls who looked Italian. The curly-haired girls twisted their bodies under the effect of the kisses. Father went straight to a movie theater. They were showing some chronicles seized from the Germans. It was stuffy in the theater; people were smoking and making a racket. Hitler appeared on screen and raised his arm — and the screen was ripped apart by a blast of machine-gun fire. The audience roared with approval.

From Toulon the Americans took father to Rome. Instead of returning to Moscow, father began his Italian vacation. He didn't find the Soviet military unit in Rome, as it had left for Northern Italy, so the Americans took him to Naples,where they put him in the care of a British base. The British were suspicious of Vladimir, but allowed him to live in a tarpaulin tent inside the airport while he waited fora plane that could take him further. The problem was, however, that the British didn't give father any food, and he barely had enough money left to buy a box of matches. Father wandered along the road to Vesuvius in low spirits, and got lost. A young Italian was coming towards him. Delighted to discover that my father was Russian, the man invited him to join his communist cell. Vladimir politely declined, but the next day a cheerful band of sunburnt communists came up to his tent and began squeezing father in their embraces. They had brought with them a bag stuffed full of edibles, along with some red wine and cigarettes. Father began to live like a king. The British decided to get rid of this suspicious character. They put him on a plane bound for Cairo. But the plane never reached Egypt. It touched down at the decrepit airport in Bari. The Germans had bombed the city relentlessly: it was from Bari that the allies departed for Greece. Once again father was accommodated in a tent, but the bombing was so intense that he spent a lot of time in ditches and ravines. Vladimir got so dirty that he became unrecognizable: he never had time to take a shower. At dawn two British soldiers burst into the tent, pushed him out, grabbed his dark-brown Swedish suitcase (it was a real treasure, it must be said) and ordered him to run and catch a plane bound for Cairo. Father jumped up, got dressed and started running, but all he saw was the tail of the plane, as it gained altitude. His suitcase was on board. A few days later he was reunited with it in Egypt, where he looked around Cairo and went to see the pyramids. An old Arab led him around on the back of a camel and sold him an old signet ring with the inscription 'Everything passes'. Thereafter it was plain sailing. Father flew to Iran. At the Soviet embassy, located in a neglected park, he saw the hall in which the conference between the heads of the three Allied powers had taken place a year earlier. Father flew from Tehran to Moscow at the beginning of November, 1944. In Moscow the smell of victory was already in the air. It turned out that Molotov urgently needed a reviewer with a strong command of French — and father was the man chosen for the job.

•

Vyacheslav Mikhailovich Molotov had the habit of lying down for a half-hour nap during in the afternoon. There was always a vase of flowers and a dish of walnuts on the circular table in the relaxation room near his office. He was the second most important figure in the government. Cities, cars and collective farms were named after him, and likenesses of him hung on the streets and in museums. He used to play the violin in restaurants during his youth. He never laughed, and when he smiled it looked forced. Molotov was comprised of a suit and tie, an earthy complexion, a large forehead with deep, high temples, a pince-nez on a large, porous nose, and a bristly but carefully trimmed moustache.

Father saw in him neither an orator nor an ardent revolutionary. Molotov listened patiently to his favorable assessment of Kollontai, without interrupting his future colleague or expressing any support for his views. Kollontai, for her part, had not had many bad things to say about Molotov. She had played quite a significant role in his life: as the head of the Central Committee's women's section, which Molotov was in charge of, she had introduced him to his future wife, Polina Semyonovna Zhemchuzhina.

During his first few months working for Molotov, father couldn't shake off the sense that he was about to be fired at any moment, and that if they hadn't fired him yet it was only because they hadn't yet found a replacement. Molotov never slammed his fist down on the table like Kaganovich, whose aides used to die of heart attacks, but he used insulting nicknames like 'hat' or 'auntie'. Molotov ordered father to change his signature so that his whole surname could be seen, as was the case with his own. On one occasion, after coming back earlier than expected from a meeting with Stalin, whom he went to see every evening, he walked in on father playing a game of chess with one of Podtserob's senior aides, who was in the running to become a chess master.

"I used to play chess, too," Molotov said, after glancing at the players. "When I was in prison, in a dark cell, and it was impossible to read and there was absolutely nothing to do."

•

Father was already beginning to get itchy feet. Two days later, he flew to Paris for an open-ended trip, for a peace conference. On July 26th, 1946, he stopped in front of his office window in the People's Commissariat of Foreign Affairs.

In our family we have our own special short course on the official history of our parents' relations. They met in 1937 at the philological faculty of Leningrad University. The short course acknowledged that at this stage things went no further than a mere acquaintance. There was a passing reference to the fact that each of them had other things on their minds at the time.

According to the short course, my future parents moved to Moscow to start studying to be interpreters. They socialized with one another whilst they were there, too, but that was as far it went. Then they were apart for the duration of the war. Mama was evacuated to Fergana, in Central Asia. She was side-tracked by a different love interest whilst there. They didn't write to one another.

Then, in the short course about my family, comes an unexpectedly powerful — and in no way predetermined — moment of enlightenment. On July 26th, 1946,papa is standing at the window of the Ministry of Foreign Affairs (it was still known as the People's Commissariat at the time) when he catches sight of mama walking along Kuznetsky Bridge. And he suddenly realized that he was fated to be with her. He ran outside and proposed. His proposal was accepted. They ran to the Registry Office. Papa had to fly off somewhere immediately afterwards, either to San Francisco or to Paris, so there was no sense in waiting. The wedding was a modest affair.

The only slight problem with this story, as mama said one day (on one of their wedding anniversaries), was that the window of the Ministry didn't look out over Kuznetsky Bridge. Thereafter various ghostly characters began to appear in the story. They were clearly part of an apocryphal story. Mama suggested, in deliberately vague terms, that "there was someone else there" at the meeting on Kuznetsky Bridge. There was a lot more that remained unclear too, but one thing's for sure: whatever those windows looked out over, I was born the next year.

Picking up the thread of the story again, father spotted a familiar face: Galya Chechurina, walking down from the Lubyanka toward Kuznetsky Bridge with a female friend. Running out into the street, he caught up with them:

"Where are you heading?"

"To the gymnastics parade."

In actual fact the two friends were walking up toward the Lubyanka from Kuznetsky Bridge, and papa *couldn't* have seen them from his window. My atheist mother is convinced to this day that there was some element of mysticism at work here. Some random loose ends had become interlaced in a metaphysical rhythm, in order to send me flying into the world like a frightened parachutist from an aircraft.

The two friends, Galya and Lyuba (the same one who had enticed my father away from mama, so that all she could do was bitterly remember his letters, signed '*Vladimir*'),were on their way to the 'Dinamo' Stadium. Off the cuff, father proposed to Galya (and not to Lyuba, who had been with him at the commando school, where he broke his leg, after which they separated: she went to Algiers, to join De Gaulle, and he went to Sweden) and suggested that they go and sign their marriage papers. Galya was caught completely off guard, and he took her off to the nearest Civil Registry Office. The office refused to register their marriage, citing the fact that "they did not live locally." After wandering around Moscow to no avail (mama had already asked whether they could go home and had begun to get annoyed), my parents, using random passersby as witnesses, registered their marriage at a small registry office (deaths and marriages were registered in the same room) on Miussky Square, where, before the war, they had studied to be interpreters together, and had been interested in one another to varying degrees. There was no wedding ceremony.

So my papa now worked at the Kremlin. As for what he did there, I wasn't completely sure, but whenever my friends and I (in winter, wearing scarves pulled up to our eyes, in beaver-lamb coats, hats and felt boots, and carrying small shovels so that we could dig in the snow in Gorky Park) went past the Kremlin, I would tell them, in a voice that made it clear I knew what I was talking about:

"This is where my papa and Comrade Stalin work."

Marusya Pushkina, due to her innate sense of justice as a country girl, would try to correct the order in which I had named them. I wasn't having any of it.

Papa was invisible. He worked day and night: Stalin's colleagues used to head home when it was already light outside. Sometimes, in the morning, I felt like running up to my parents' bed, if only to look at him sleeping, but I wasn't allowed into their bedroom. On Sundays and public holidays, however, papa would *materialize* as a young, gray-eyed man with a slanted fringe, and I would be overcome with happiness.

I was especially fond of big revolutionary holidays. The songs would come pouring out of the loudspeaker in the street from the early morning. But I used to be woken up even earlier, before the music started, by the rumble of the tanks, which rushed past, together with the *Katyusha* rockets and other military technology like merry toys, puffing out smoke, along our central street in the direction of Red Square. Four pictures of leaders in profile, their cheeks pressed tenderly against one another like four fish singing in an aquarium, hung from the building opposite us, between some long, dark-red banners. Papa took me with him to the parade. He wore a light-gray diplomatic uniform with general's stars, and I enjoyed seeing the soldiers, stretched out like a string, salute him. The height of dear papa's greatness was something that took place somewhere else, however — and not on the Red Square, where I hadn't noticed Stalin standing on the mausoleum.

I don't know how it happened, but one day, to my great joy, papa accompanied me to the dacha on the suburban train we used to take, which had a red-wheeled locomotive which emitted particularly tasty-looking smoke. We went out onto the wooden platform at the station near the dacha one summer's morning, and papa, in his general's uniform, sat down, without leaving the platform, on a bench, to tie his laces, then leaned back for a second and promptly fell asleep. The station's duty policeman came up to us and stood near the bench without saying a word. I thought we were in serious trouble, and I started crying, quietly, so that he wouldn't notice. Papa's hat fell off his head, whereupon he woke up and looked at the policeman inquisitively.

"What are you up to?" he asked in annoyance.

"I'm watching over you while you sleep, Comrade General!" the policeman saluted him with bravado. That man was, without question, the best policeman I ever met in my life.

•

My papa never got sick. In Molotov's secretariat, being sick was considered a violation of party discipline, and papa was a disciplined Communist.

"A disciplined person," Molotov used to say to his colleagues, "never catches cold, and is responsible about his clothes and his behavior. You won't catch him sitting by the window or running around without a coat in cold weather."

I was therefore very surprised when I once saw papa with a bandage on his hand. He evaded my questions with ease. My childhood paradise was an additional story appended on top of the adult world, in which strange turns of events were liable to take place.

"Somehow we finished work unusually early, around 1am," papa said. "Feeling contented, I went home and slipped into the tub. I wasn't able to relax for long, however. My wife (*mama, when she was expecting me, ate pea soup all the time. To this day I hate pea soup, I can't even stand the smell of it*) began hammering at the door and announced (*the combination of these two very different verbs conveys, like in the movies, the prevailing atmosphere in the household at the time, but I won't do it again*) that I had been summoned to the Kremlin as a matter of urgency; a car was already on its way. With my hair still wet, I charged downstairs.

Stalin's private limousine took me along the 'axial' to the Spassky Gate in no time at all. After getting through security, I ran up to the second floor of the government building and rushed down the long, narrow corridor. As I turned a corner I slipped on the parquet floor, which was as slippery as ice, and broke my wrist — blood came spurting out. After getting to my feet, I quickly wrapped it up in my handkerchief. Stalin's top aide Poskrebyshev stood at the end of the corridor, cursing me at the top of his voice for my tardiness. Continuing to scream out curses, he literally grabbed me by the scruff of the neck and shoved me into Stalin's office through the chain-stitch door.

Two silent delegations were sitting at a long table, facing one another: ours, consisting of members of the Politburo, and a foreign one. The 'big boss' was standing in the middle of the office, his pipe in his mouth. Nodding his head in response to my greeting, he directed me toward *his* place at the table. I put my notebook on my lap, to hide my injured arm. Stalin paced back and forth behind me with inaudible steps, in soft shoes. I took notes and translated what was said, as usual.

Suddenly Stalin fell silent. He came up to me and, pointing his pipe in the direction of my handkerchief, asked suspiciously:

"What's wrong with your hand?"

"It's nothing, Josef Vissarionovich, I did myself a little injury, it's nothing serious," I muttered fairly indistinctly.

"Come on, tell me," he insisted.

"I fell over, it's nothing to worry about."

"You fell over? Where?"

At that moment the door flew open and a doctor carrying a

medical bag flew into the office with two assistants, all of them looking extremely worried. Poskrebyshev — came in after them. Whilst he had been talking to me, Stalin had pressed a button on the underside of the table to call for medical assistance, without anyone noticing. Jumping to the conclusion that something had happened to him, they had started to panic. Noticing the doctor's puzzled expression, Stalin said calmly:

"Find out what's wrong with his hand."

The doctor bounded over to me and, with the help of his assistants, quickly washed and re-dressed my swollen hand.

"You can go now," Stalin instructed, and the medics left the office as hastily as they had appeared. Those in attendance watched all this in silence. Then the conversation started up again."

There was a little epilogue to the story about the hand. After the reception, Stalin, holding father by the shoulder, asked Molotov:

"What's wrong, Vyacheslav, why don't you look after him? He's so lean and pale. Don't you feed him properly? You ought to."

"I keep him fed," Molotov blurted out, unsure where Stalin was going with this. Stalin's interest in the young man gave him the unpleasant sense that a change of generations might be on the way at the Kremlin.

"Why don't you ever put your employees forward for awards, Molotoshvili? I'm thinking of your interpreters in particular," Stalin insisted, giving father a playful look, as if he was an accomplice. "They sometimes face health risks in their line of work! Make some nominations — we won't turn them down!"

Soon father was presented with his first major medal, the Red Banner of Labor, at the Kremlin. In the stories he told, Stalin came across in a very different way from the various images there were of him, moving in a trajectory all of his own, full of a touching love for René Clair's film *Under the Rooftops of Paris* (father translated films for the leader, too), and of "modesty", "geniality" and "hospitable manners".

When the film ended, Stalin, rising from his chair, turned toward father and beckoned to him to come over with his finger. When father reached him, Stalin picked up a bottle of *Sovetskoye* champagne from the table in front of him, filled a glass and handed it to him.

"Thank you, Comrade Stalin. I don't drink at work," said father.

Stalin laughed and continued to insist.

"Come on, come on, drink," he said. "Molotov doesn't mind, you had to work pretty hard."

Molotov and the other members of the Politburo smiled. Father gratefully drained the glass of champagne in one gulp.

·

When I picture this scene, with Stalin treating my father to a glass of champagne, and smiling tenderly at the handsome young man, in admiration, I feel strangely affectionate. I can even feel a tickle in my nose. Why is that, exactly? For one thing, what about…and secondly, what about…and thirdly, and fourthly… the ever-righteous "*what about*". But it's so pleasing to me to know that at that moment, in the half-light of the auditorium, my father reached the very summit of his profession — his own personal Everest — and I'm eternally happy for him, and everyone who hears this story from me, regardless of their views, feels a sense of affection. The reason for this affection is insane. People write with exactly the same sense of delight in their memoirs about encounters with Hitler, Mao or Kim Il Sung.

Boundless power is intoxicating. To be noticed by the almighty — to become one of the chosen few, to join the exclusive club of historical figures. My head tells me that those cowardly vermin, those members of the Politburo who were smiling at father — all those Voroshilovs, Kaganoviches and Berias — were a pack of wolves, who, out in a field somewhere, in the snow and by the light of the moon, would be willing to tear my papa to shreds, given the opportunity. I can hear them howling. When they eat papa he'll become one of them, and will turn into a young wolf. Ignoramuses and criminals for whom the gallows weep. Father's boss, Molotov, was an ideologically twisted fruitcake with a pious expression. Stalin was a political serial killer. What would I have done with them all? I would have killed them. I wouldn't have had anything to say to them. Yet for some reason I still go weak at the knees, I find it a sweet sensation. It is the illusion of an orgasm.

The truth of power is not something that one can feel sympathy for. It lies behind murderers. Big politics begins with blood. The Russian take on power — a crude and vomit inducing thing, consisting of chauvinist jokes, offensive slang, rare beefsteaks, forgetfulness, muddy heads, long-term drunkenness, sadism, onion-breath, impunity and humiliation of everyone in succession — fills me with scorn and disgust. If they had drawn *me* in with their cynical familiarity — I'd have gone running to tell everyone what shits they were the very next morning. But if those in power had set themselves the goal of paying me off, I would have found myself in a quandary. I enjoy thinking about how Red Army soldiers raped and killed young women from the nobility. I lie in bed and picture it. I am a virtual tormentor, someone who in the real world loathes rape and can't stand even a friendly bit of pushing and shoving from some bastard. But why is it, after all, that I'm not indifferent, why does this subject bother me? Why am I so sympathetic to vanity, why do I get upset about such trifles? A writer's glory is the shadow of power. But sometimes one wants so much to come out of the shadows.

•

Stalin used to amaze father with his humanity. This could be seen in the way he used to come into his assistant's room at his dacha and make a great fuss, checking which bed-linen he had been given and pinching the pillows to see how soft they were; and it was evidenced in the way he showed understanding of things that seemed utterly unacceptable.

A colleague of my father's, Ivan Ivanovich Lapshov, after having too much to drink at dinner at Stalin's Sochi residence and losing his way in the corridors, was struggling to find the room he had been allocated. He sat down at a desk, opened one of the drawers…and sobered up rapidly at the sight of a collection of pipes. The voice of the 'big boss' boomed out from behind his back:

"What are you up to, rummaging around in my desk like that?"

The poor apparatchik got off with nothing worse than a *terrible* fright. Father maintained, incidentally, that Stalin couldn't stand the slightest trace of familiarity. By way of example he used to tell a story about something that had happened to Lebedev, the Soviet Ambassador to Poland, who often came to Moscow with Gomulka and other Polish leaders for talks, and was present at confidential talks in the Kremlin. In 1951, while in Warsaw, Lebedev took the liberty of sending Stalin a copy of his book about the construction of bases of socialism in countries with national democracies,inscribed: "To Comrade J.V. Stalin, for review." Over this inscription Stalin wrote the missive: "Pull him out".

•

But what father loved most of all was to reminisce about one particular lunch at the Kremlin palace, with a huge number of guests in attendance. He is sitting next to Stalin and interpreting an unhurried conversation with the guest of honor. The leader, in his ceremonial, cream-colored generalissimo's uniform,is in good spirits, sipping at his wine-glass from time to time. The disciplined young waiters are scurrying about, replacing the silverware with great care after each course and putting clean plates,embossed with large emblems of the Soviet Union, on the table. They are serving turkey. One of the waiters is pouring cranberry sauce onto the plate over Stalin's shoulder; his hand is shaking. Some red drops fall onto the generalissimo's tunic. A hush descends on the table. Beria frowns and leaves the table for a few moments. Stalin doesn't even bat an eyelid. The senior waiter runs over to him and feverishly wipes the stains with a damp cloth. Stalin stops him with a simple gesture. The young culprit has vanished, and does not reemerge. A restrained animation once again reigned around the table.

"There's self-control for you," father said.

"Did they shoot the waiter?" I asked.

"I don't know," father said, shrugging his shoulders.

We are bound together by the similarity of our smiles, our noses, our mouths, slightly opened due to absent-mindedness, the impatient twitching of our legs, a sluggishness that comes on suddenly, the way we fold our hands behind the back of our head, and our intonations, to such an extent that taken together we are like a time-machine. But even though I am able to take partial control of this situation, by resisting the similarity of our weaknesses, the fact remains that people sometimes mistake my father for me — they are horrified by how old I've grown — there is a disease like that, which makes you age overnight. In the past, everyone used to tell me how closely I resembled my father. Nowadays they tell him how closely he resembles his son. This is a little social victory I have achieved,from which I don't derive any joy. I'm getting increasingly fearful of resembling him. That's the way things are going. I already have a stoop. Father still has hair on his head to this day, he hasn't gone bald, but his memory loss, which he tries to mask with humor, to no avail, is getting increasingly scary. His speech contains more and more interjections, pauses and platitudes. As for his driving, as I've already said: it's apocalyptic. In this I see my own future, if indeed I am to have one — especially in the morning, after I've drunk champagne and vodka the night before. It would be nice to know, incidentally, where that time-machine is headed.

Time and again I exasperated my father with this question: did Stalin believe in Communism, or was he simply a Soviet imperialist and nothing more? Between the two poles of opinion about Stalin, as a sadist and maniacal murderer (the opinion of the Russian intelligentsia) and as a devotee-inquisitor, father leans toward the latter even today. He is untroubled by what the intelligentsia say — as if he is throwing down a challenge for me. The intelligentsia, by way of example, hated Andrei Alexandrovich Zhdanov — hated him mutely, on the quiet, with all its heart, for destroying even the appearance of freedoms, and for the public executions of Akhmatova and Zoshchenko; but in our family Stalin's chief ideologue was regarded as a savior. Father had received a letter of farewell from my grandmother from Leningrad, when it was under siege: she and my grandfather were no longer able to get out of bed, they had no more strength. He had written to Zhdanov requesting help. A few days later a military man had arrived at grandmother's apartment with a bag of food and even some wine. As he worked at the Kremlin, father was able to thank Zhdanov in person.

"What of it!" the latter waved him away, *modestly*.

Father remembers it even now:

"Zhdanov was active, and disciplined, and had quick reactions. I was very bitter when I found out how he had died."

Furthermore: Zhdanov, according to father, had been against the sovietization of post-war Finland, spoke in favor of our northern neighbor being neutral, and suffered a fatal heart-attack after being heavily criticized in the Politburo for his political liberalism. The circumstances surrounding Zhdanov's death are as mysterious as everything else that surrounds the fairytale of Russian power.

We are sitting at the table and drinking tea, in our apartment block on the renamed street of my childhood.

"In my view," my father says, "Stalin wasn't a political

murderer who derived pleasure from torture. I can't reconcile that with his outer appearance."

Father maintained the custom of drinking *weak* tea throughout his life. And grandmother never grew out of the habit of economizing on tea: I remember a microscopic aluminum teaspoon at home which was used only for tea leaves.

"Wasn't it you who told me about his "strong, yellow eyes?" I asked.

"He had a horrible stare," father admitted, patiently. "He knew that, and usually he hid his eyes. For something he held dear he was capable of killing everyone around him. His repression was based on faith. He managed to introduce communism into our people's consciousness. He was a smart man. Look at the pact he made with Hitler. No other leader of the Soviet Union would have taken such a well-chosen course of action. We pushed Hitler into a war with the West.

•

Farewell, Chagall! I notice an interesting thing about me: I'm drawn towards socialist realism, its style excites me. It's probably a bit like the craving a pregnant woman might have for "something salty". In other words, it is a physiological need, with no underlying political reason. The concept of my imaginary exhibition, within the framework of a book, consists of a comparison between socialist realism and the movement which made a complete mockery of it, Sots Art, which emerged during the final years of socialism as a harbinger of its end. Sots Art consisted of both fear and humor, both bitterness and retribution. But this dissident invention, which was intended to destroy socialist realism, proved in due course to be fairly lightweight. For all the importance of such artists as Ilya Kabakov and Bulatov, who found their metaphysical life-blood in Sots Art, and for all the wit of Komar and Melamida, who worked with the image of Stalin with false respect, it is becoming clear that socialist realism itself was the real national drama, in which the experience of utopia was played out as one of the ways in which it was possible to live.

Russia is a prisoner of cheap paradoxes. Akhmatova wrote that poems grow out of arguments. It was a phrase that stunned the intelligentsia with its revelatory power. But in my opinion, that skinny kitten which came back to the staffer at the Soviet Consulate in London after the air-raid, when everyone thought it was dead — that is a metaphor for creativity, which is growing more and more embarrassed by its own name.

What I find striking is not the conformity of Brodsky, Gerasimov, Yablonsky or Laktionov, who inspire pity in me for the inherent weakness of the artist's position, but the ideal Russian dream in which the state mirrors the people, which came banging into Stalin with a political correctness of Shakespearean proportions. The Russian avant-garde worked towards creating a Utopia too, and the presence of Malevich's black square (you'll find it if you look closely) in this book is no accident. Moreover, Petrov-Vodkin with his red horse, the cubist posters of the twenties, glorifying the Komsomol, the angular nature of my equally cubist parents when they were young, Filonov's dubious nonsense and, lastly, the stooped, almost embryonic posture that we all (papa, mama and I) share, point to a direct link between these two utopias. It's another matter altogether that the avant-garde utopia attempted to burn into the heart of the matter, to suck out the brain, whilst the naïve churchiness of socialist realism amounts to a national mysticism which was not put down on canvases at the command of politicians, but was commissioned by the Russian God himself. Some things are bought on the cheap out of sheer madness. In the painting *At Lenin's Grave*, painted by Brodsky immediately after the funeral service, the funeral hall looks like a tropical forest, full of palm trees with tall, splayed branches. Lenin's death was transformed into a funeral ceremony for an African rural chieftain: the Russian government, which had seen better days, was compressed into two-dimensional representations of the Politburo, and what looks like a statue of Krupskaya. In another painting, Stalin stands beside Zhdanov's coffin. Again, palm trees are used to highlight the solemnity of the occasion, and the disciplined liability and immortality of a Communist death. Zhdanov, the make-up artist's plaything, looks so lifelike in his coffin that he may as well have been alive. So I can find a justification for father's senile lack of sensibility. At a recent state funeral for one of his friends, an ambassador who used to play tennis, he asked me:

"It's a sad event, of course, but doesn't it make you wonder?"

En effet. Father had learnt the classical language of diplomacy — French. But as well as diplomatic receptions, there is also such a thing as diplomatic funerals. Addressing the deceased, who lay in an open coffin in accordance with Russian tradition, but was lying in it with a certain inherent *chic* and nobility which even death couldn't redress, the Ambassador of an island state in the Far East said, in the presence of the Russian Minister of Foreign Affairs:

"Dear Mr. Ambassador Extraordinary and Plenipotentiary, your efforts to strengthen relations between our two states must go down as an achievement."

It hadn't even occurred to me that the deceased, even though he wore an array of medals on his jacket (including two Orders of Lenin), could still be called an ambassador. But when the telegrams from the President of the Russian Federation and the General Secretary of the United Nations were read out, I realized that the cross, cassocks and prayers were irrelevant in this case. For a brief moment, diplomacy had conquered death.

The Socialist realists sought to depict the Russian soul, its inexhaustible reserves of enthusiasm, on which you could fly around the world forty times. In an early painting by Laktionov, some young Soviet tank operators show off their wall-newspaper to their heroic captain with such pride that the painting seems to be a mockery. What to do: shoot him? Give him a medal? He is a remarkably talented artist. Some Florentine landscapes can be seen in the windows. It is no worse than anything by Deinek, who moved from avant-garde painting towards socialist realism. But in the end the Russian God threw off his mask.

Once the utopia was over, in 1954, Plastov painted *Spring*. A nude woman with pink nipples and steep thighs, from between which there comes the smell of a vagina which has just been washed in the bath with that peculiar Russian passion, squatting in front of her child in the springtime snow — this is a long way from the Ehrenburg thaw. This is a return home, to family values, to private life, from which you can now see, through the window, what it means to indulge in a fatal dream.

•

Called back from Stockholm to work as Molotov's aide in 1944, father became a witness of, and vehicle for, the USSR's war-time policies. A huge number of letters from Stalin to Roosevelt and Churchill were drafted in his presence.

"Stalin conducted the war in a way that was calculated to promote revolutionary ideas in Europe. In a conversation with Maurice Thorez, with me interpreting, he said that if it weren't for the Second Front we would have gone even farther, and the French communists would have overthrown the *status quo* in their country."

Even before Churchill's speech in Fulton, Stalin, according to my father, "was gunning for a third world war. His plans were global in nature. Unlike Hitler, Stalin went so far as to contemplate taking on — and defeating — the United States. He wanted *everything*. He was firmly set on worldwide revolution, on establishing supremacy all over the world."

"I also allowed for the possibility of worldwide revolution in the long-term," father added.

"So *we* unleashed the 'Cold War'? I asked, realizing as I did so that I was mimicking his use of *we*, rather than referring to the Soviet authorities in the third person plural, as I usually did, being a representative of the liberal-intelligentsia.

Father nodded slowly.

"Did you like Stalin?"

Father gave different answers to this question as the years went by. At first he answered in the affirmative, but thereafter he found it increasingly difficult to give me an answer. But he never gave a negative answer. He saw in Stalin a "magnetic" personality of global significance.

"The first time I saw him I was taken aback. His swarthy, earthen, stale face was all pockmarked. His left arm hung limply by his side. He used to lift it up with his other hand and put it in his pocket. But even when I was sitting with my back to the door I could sense when Stalin had come into my office. Stalin would fill a space, displacing everything else in the room.

I reminded him of what Khrushchev had said about Stalin having waged war on the entire globe. It was this reference to the globe, incidentally, that undermined my mother's faith in Khrushchev's secret speech — she found the words unduly vindictive. Father burst out laughing. He had been present during a conversation between Stalin and three Western ambassadors when the Berlin crisis was at its worst, in early August 1948. As the newspaper headlines like to put it, the world was on the brink of war at the time.

Stalin remained calm and carried on smoking his favorite thin cigars, Herzegovina Flor, without inhaling. The cigars often went out. Stalin never held any papers in front of him, and never made notes. The conversation was about the Allied states' right to station their troops in Berlin. The American Ambassador Bedell Smith, being a general and Eisenhower's former Chief of Staff, was basing his argument on strategic, military reasons. The Soviet Union, he attempted to prove, by creating difficulties for the Western Command in Berlin, was violating the agreement between the Allies:

"The US High Command made no objection to Soviet troops being the first to occupy Berlin."

"You couldn't have reached Berlin before us anyway, you were too slow," Stalin countered quietly, staring straight ahead.

Out of pride for his country, father went so far as to rest one leg on the other for a moment, but he soon thought better of it, as he listened attentively to the soft voice. He could see Stalin reconstructing the capture of Berlin in his mind as it unfolded, one day at a time. As sections of Marshall Zhukov's First Belorussian Front and Marshall Konev's First Ukrainian Front strengthened their positions 60–80 kilometers from Berlin, General Patton's US Army was some 320–325 kilometers away from the city. After breaking through the enemy's powerful defenses at the Zeyelov Heights, the Red Army set about storming Berlin on the fifth day of operations; street battles broke out the very next day. The American Ambassador turned a deep shade of red as he listened.

"Those are the facts of the matter," Stalin concluded. "If you don't believe me, let's go and have a look at our archives, I'll show you our military field maps from the time."

"No," the American Ambassador replied, looking embarrassed. "I believe you, Mr. Generalissimo. Thank you."

The fervent Bedell Smith was defeated. Stalin had been victorious. Now he was speaking like a staunch advocate of a unified Germany.

"We'll take down our posts around Berlin. That's a mere technicality. But you must take the issue of the carving up of Germany off the agenda."

The ambassadors (father told me with a chuckle) resisted him politely, but with all the strength they could muster.

"The neutralization of Germany," I couldn't restrain myself, "would have been an absolute catastrophe for the West!"

My aggression alarmed father. I bit my tongue.

"Well, I suppose you're right," father agreed, deep in thought, as if studying a chess board. "But be that as it may, Stalin made a mistake."

"How so?"

"Stalin *promoted* de Gaulle, and supported the idea of France's greatness. He knew that de Gaulle couldn't stand the Americans. He should have aimed for a closer union with France. De Gaulle wanted the Rhineland. As De Gaulle once said to me, 'If France had got it, Adenauer would have become my sworn enemy.'

This *superstalinist* criticism of Stalin, which took the stance that the apocalyptic, mortally wounded beast of capitalism would crawl off to the British Isles, seemed all the more intriguing to me given that in the 1990s, father, unlike many other veterans of the Soviet diplomatic service, including that deceased noble with his array of medals, had made an *anti-communist* choice in relation to Russia.

"But de Gaulle thought highly of Stalin nonetheless," father added. "When Ambassador Vinogradov and I visited him in 1956, the conversation touched on the repression. He said: a small man makes small mistakes, and a great man makes big ones."

I had a hallucination about father's skewed vision. Father was unable to look at events both from within and without, the new insights he picked up-weren't edited in sync — he once openly admitted this to me, incidentally. But De Gaulle's logic, in summoning Russian diplomats under the pretext of consultations about his memoirs, in order to make sense of Khrushchev's secret speech, still seems disgusting to me even now. Either you're Nietzsche, or you're the people's servant: Europe was founded on this division of roles.

As for me, Nietzsche suited me down to the ground. The more my father doubted Stalin, the more Stalin began to interest me. I felt no desire to play around with his image, as the proponents of Sots art did, but at that particular time in European culture, when the artist had become more interesting than his works, when he had replaced them with his own being, Stalin appeared to me to be a mighty forerunner of this turn of events. He had transformed human raw materials into the ingredients for his own installation.

"Why was it that Molotov, specifically, was known as 'Mr. No' in the West?" I asked my father, putting my own personal thoughts, which I never could have discussed with him, to one side.

"It was part of a wider game," father smiled. "The distribution of roles. Molotov led talks with the Westerners to failure by playing the role of the 'bad guy'. The role of Mr. No suited his character to a tee. He was utterly devoid of a sense of humor. But then the 'good guy', Stalin, would come along, and the smiles would start to break out."

Molotov, according to my father, was dry and tiresome, although he was a learned man. However that may be, it seems he was the only member of the Politburo who, after Zhdanov had passed away, could say with any certainty that *Madame Bovary* had not been written by Balzac. He loved long walks in the countryside and ice-skating, drank soda water with lemon and adored buckwheat porridge. On one occasion he set my father a challenge:

"What do you know about the health benefits of buckwheat porridge? Find out and report back to me!"

The idea of longevity, as with many Communists, was for him a substitute for eternity. Privately, Molotov's interests extended beyond buckwheat porridge. In 1947 financial reforms were introduced in the Soviet Union. One-and-a-half years later, Molotov asked my father one evening:

"Do you have any money on you?"

"Money?" my father said in amazement, and started patting his pockets, so that he could whip out his wallet with alacrity.

The Prime Minister studied his country's financial denominations with interest.

"That's very good money," he said approvingly.

•

Based on my father's observation of Stalin over many years, the only person whom he genuinely held in any esteem was

Molotov. The rest did no more than carry out their instructions. The two men governed the Soviet Union together. Every issue in this extremely centralized state rose upward toward them, from world affairs to the cut of ladies' blouses and the lack of restrooms in Moscow — something for which Stalin chided Khrushchev at the very height of the great terror. Stalin was responsible for even the smallest needs of his people.

The role of the institute of assistants, who used to prepare their *little reports* in order to brief Stalin, consisting of 12–15 documents with annotations: 1A (the most urgent), 1 (urgent), and "others" — was hard to overstate. The 'big boss' Stalin, and the regular' boss' Molotov, valued initiative in their assistants and even encouraged them to engage in a bit of free-thinking (a trait I loved about my father; he once took the liberty of beating the great Soviet inquisitor Vyshinsky at chess several times in a row, at the Soviet dacha outside New York. The latter never forgave him for it, and used to cross him off the list of Ministry of Foreign Affairs employees desiring better housing each year. Eventually my father appealed to Molotov, who hated it when people came asking him for help in personal matters, seeing it as an abuse of office — but signed my father's request. Years later my father took pleasure in carrying Vyshinsky's coffin on his shoulders through the French airport of Le Bourget). The authorities allowed people to argue with their views up until the moment a decision was taken. It was like that even with the Americans' Marshall Plan: Molotov, spurred on by his aides, was prepared to agree to it in principle, only for Stalin to thwart him with a few sharp words.

In 1949, Molotov's wife, Polina Sergeyevna Zhemchuzhina, was arrested, accused of being a Zionist — she had suggested that the Crimea be given back to the Jews. That was pushing it a bit, wasn't it? The aides were told about the brief exchange that had taken place between the leaders.

"We can't have people not being jailed, *Vyach*," Stalin had said to Molotov, referring to him in their private conversations using a truncated form of his name, almost in the American fashion.

Stalin was fond of jailing the wives of close colleagues — Kalinina, Voroshilova, and Poskribysheva too. He would wait with keen anticipation each time to see their puppy-eyed faces the next morning, how they would squirm, which words they would use to plead for their wives. One minute Zhemchuzhina is sipping champagne in a low-cut dress at a reception at the Kremlin, smelling of perfume, reminiscing about how she was the last person to see Nadia Alliluyeva alive, smiling regally at distinguished actors, and patting the handsome Cherkasov, who played Ivan the Terrible, on the shoulder; the next, she is at the Lubyanka, naked, spreading her buttocks and showing her anus to the prison doctor at his command. When Poskrebyshev asked after his wife, according to my father, Stalin answered laughingly:

"We'll find you a better one."

Molotov put up, as did the others, with his wife's arrest, but from that moment on he would return from his chats with Stalin looking extremely irritated.

Papa, especially in the early stages, looked on the work he did at the Kremlin as a series of portraits that had miraculously come to life. Millions of likenesses of Stalin, Molotov, Kalinin, Kaganovich, Voroshilov and Beria were hung up all over the country, their features identical in photos and portraits. The depictions of Molotov looked exactly like him: in his reserved, provincial smile there was something feline, some unidentifiable sense of scorn, as if a pile of shit had just been carried past him. When this portrait lost its portrait-like properties, and came out of its frame, breaking ranks with a canon consisting of many millions of copies, it seemed as if the end of the world was nigh. Molotov turned into a furious cat (didn't Bulgakov base his character Behemoth on him?), with a pince-nez on his nose. Returning from Stalin's office one day, the cat threw a folder onto his aides' table and shouted:

"Well, what are you doing just sitting there, you blockheads?! Sort it out!"

•

When he recalled how Molotov used to scold him, my father said he had got it in the neck most of all over Ilya Ehrenburg. At the end of the war the most popular Soviet writer of the day, the eye-catching offspring of cubism and Paris, wrote, deliberately choosing not to adopt a class-based approach, an article about how the German workers and peasants with whom he had spoken about Konigsberg, which had been seized by the Red Army, always expressed support for Hitler's aggressive plans, dreaming of being able to use Russians for manual labor. Ehrenburg (when you read between the lines) was demanding, in a veiled way, global revenge, subordinating the article's Soviet style to national feeling, which had been hurt. Molotov, who, on top of all his other duties, was in charge of the foreign policy journal *Questions of the International Workers' Movement*. Ehrenburg had brought an article to its editorial offices, and Molotov demanded that it be rewritten. He ordered my father to explain to the person who had written it:

"The war is coming to an end; we need to seek out forces for good in Germany, someone who can be relied on, not blacken everyone's name."

That made sense, didn't it? My father went off to carry out an order from 'the boss'. Arriving at the writer's apartment, he felt like an emissary from on high. Ehrenburg came out into the hallway. This literary 'celebrity' seemed shorter than he ought to have been, as was always the way. Moreover, he had an exhausted, yellow face, with large bags under his eyes, as if he was always drunk.

"Come in."

The sat down in the office.

"Vyacheslav Mikhailovich strongly urges you…"

Ehrenburg understood everything on hearing this first phrase. And he grew bored, like any author who is told that something in the text needs to be corrected. Having listened to my father coolly, his face grew even more yellow.

"Everything I wrote is the truth, and I have no intention of changing any of it."

It was the first occasion father could remember on which the authority Molotov's name automatically evoked had failed to have the desired effect. My father couldn't believe his ears. He told Molotov what had happened. The latter went into a frenzy:

"You're the one who doesn't understand anything, you can't even make people see reason about obvious things!"

Father was again ordered to go and see Ehrenburg, and he did everything he could to make him change his mind.

"If you don't want to publish it, don't publish it, it's your call," Ehrenburg, who had seemed so "obedient", said to father categorically.

My father meandered over despondently to the 'boss', well aware what was in store for him. Translating these polemics from the language of bureaucracy into deconstructed thought, you can see that the traditional roles of the writer and the authorities have changed places in this case.

EHRENBURG: We must destroy the Germans, who incinerated the Jews in the gas chambers. They all supported Hitler — let's whack the lot of them. The chambers are still there — what's stopping us?

MOLOTOV: You must stop these Jewish reprisals of yours! What are you trying to goad me into doing? I have a Jewish wife!

EHRENBURG: I demand vengeance. An eye for an eye.

MOLOTOV: There's more than enough vengeance in Koenigsburg. The Red Army is buggering every German woman in sight, both young and old. Calm down, that Kopelev of yours will have something to write about this.

EHRENBURG: That's no argument! The fascists raped all our women.

MOLOTOV: Ours all gave themselves willingly, with laughs of delight, even the girls in the Komsomol. Those bitches thought the Germans had come here for good.

EHRENBURG: I wonder how many children of mixed

nationality are going to be born in Russia and Germany, after the war? Millions, probably. But that's a statistic no one will ever study.

MOLOTOV: Don't distract me with your nonsense. Rewrite the article. We don't need the ashes of Germans, we need people who are alive and can fight for Socialism. The Germans love order. They'll move from one system to another in well-ordered ranks.

EHRENBURG: They're all rushing off to the West.

MOLOTOV: You're the one rushing off to the West, to that Paris of yours.

EHRENBURG: Don't you trust me?

MOLOTOV: How can anyone trust a Jewish mug?

EHRENBURG: Are you referring to your wife?

MOLOTOV: Listen here, you bastard, what does my wife have to do with anything? We need reparations, German automobile factories! We shouldn't be spending forever and a day quarelling with the Americans. They don't support your idea about the gas chambers!

EHRENBURG: But what about the 'Cold War'?

MOLOTOV: That's a matter for another day. As for today, I've got a task for you. You're to rename Koenigsburg.

EHRENBURG: Molotovburg!

MOLOTOV: Shut it, you misanthrope!

EHRENBURG: I didn't know you were a bourgeois humanist!

Essentially, in terms of the logic of the argument, that was how the conversation went. Ehrenburg's boldness, in desiring bloody vengeance, was justified by his access of hatred, which was a position that the authorities loved. On this subject he could even resist the all-mighty prime minister. In the same way, in my father's experience thereafter, the politicians of the people's democracies in Eastern Europe often turned out to be more radical, in the degree of class hatred, than their Soviet counterparts. This was frowned upon, and if you were that way inclined you might describe it as Trotskyism, but it was more reliable than the right-wing trend. Molotov himself might, in this instance, have echoed Pushkin's words, to the effect that in Russia, the only true European is the government. What troubled papa, however, was not so much the essence of the dispute, but this show of insubordination. It indicated that writers (who didn't wear epaulettes, and weren't even members of the party) could speak and act arrogantly in relation to representatives of supreme power (my father), thereby smashing his self-esteem, which had already grown strong, over their knees. No-one could tolerate a reception like that. My father held a grudge against Ehrenburg, and against all other writers to boot, for the rest of his life. Perhaps that was why he stopped reading works of fiction from that moment on, catching the whiff of arrogance on every page of any book he looked at? That was how a chasm opened up between my father and the intelligentsia. He even 'floored' me one day (in his civil service jargon), by striking out, in his turn, at Ehrenburg's self-esteem, saying that Ehrenburg "spoke bad French". But when Ehrenburg passed away and my parents' friend Galina Fyodorovna, came running over to see us and announced breathlessly that Ehrenburg's dacha (which had chestnut trees in the yard) was being sold, my father turned this carcass down, indifferently. The Molotov-Ehrenburg dispute inspired a rebellious appraisal on my part, too, albeit an insubstantial one. Father and son therefore repeated one and the same phrase, born of father's bewilderment:

"A writer dared to contradict the second most important person in the country!"

One of us said it with marked irritation; the other with secret admiration. For me, this episode was a call to join the resistance.

•

The arrest of Molotov's wife was merely Stalin's opening salvo against Mr. 'No'.

"After the 19th Party Congress, in October 1952, there was an axe hanging over Molotov," father told me. "Molotov sat at an empty desk, looking at nothing more important than Soviet newspapers and news alerts from TASS. No other material was sent in. He was rarely called in to see Stalin. In the secretaries' office, some zealous Soviet administrators had already taken down the expensive chandeliers and the curtains."

Father became the subject of surveillance by the state security forces. One evening, an unfamiliar voice on the *vertushka* — the phone which had a direct line to the government — began chiding him in vulgar language for hiding behind the curtains when Comrade Stalin was walking along the corridor. A fantasy *à la* Hamlet. Curtains, indeed! This bit of Sots Art was ahead of its time. On another occasion, whilst he was on vacation in the South, he received a telegram telling him to come back to Moscow immediately. In my father's office, a maid — she was a KGB agent — had found a postcard with an anniversary picture of Stalin on it, painted by Picasso. It had been put inside a book, like a bookmark. Beria had deemed it to be a caricature. An investigation was launched.

Stalin's death, in March 1953, clearly seems to have saved my father from the GULAG, and me from the orphanage for the children of "enemies of the people". Beria was arrested in early summer. After his arrest, a special speaker was installed in Molotov's office, through a bit of "theater in front of the microphone" was played: my father heard it himself; they broadcast "the interrogation of that villain". He sobbed and moaned, begging them to spare his life. Molotov, who was the first person in the USSR to prise the door of the GULAG slightly ajar, by demanding, just a few hours after Stalin's death, that Beria return his arrested wife to him, at times listened attentively to these cries, and at other times he tuned out. Beria's cries gradually became a familiar sound, then disappeared altogether: he had been shot.

My father had stopped working for Molotov two years previously. Once again a mysterious flu saved him from any possible unpleasantness that might have resulted from Molotov's future fall from grace (along with the other members of the anti-party group) in 1957.

"Perhaps we had all been protected from getting sick by the constant nervous tension to which we were subjected, especially during the war. When life started to go back to normal, the illnesses came back. On hearing that I had the flu, Molotov expressed displeasure, saying "that Erofeyev gets sick all the time." I exploded with rage at that: ten years of loyal service and self-sacrifice, and that was the thanks I got! When I went back into the office, I told Molotov to his face that I no longer wished to work for him."

•

The holidays were over. The boy was clinging convulsively to the fire-escape ladder. He was afraid to climb any higher, but he didn't want to go back down — he was afraid of the stones. A third-grader was standing under the ladder and throwing stones at him. One stone hit him on the back, the next hit him on the shoulder and the third hit the intended target, the back of his head. He let out a little cry and went flying backwards.

The school's principal, like an experienced ship's captain, had led the school through the new set of problems brought about by co-education. Izya Moyseyevich, the literature teacher, was sharing his views about Ilya Ehrenburg's recently published book with Zoya Nikolayevna, who taught the elementary classes. She was young, and shy about everything. On one occasion the principal had come right up close to her and pinched her stomach through her dress. The principal had black hair, and his face was still young. Zoya Nikolayevna didn't know what to make of it. He had pinched her in a way that was not vulgar at all: if anything, he had done it playfully. She smiled at him. He clenched his fist and said: "I've got you right here, in my fist." She looked down. Then the principal said: "Zoya Nikolayevna!

I ask you, not as the principal, but as a man: don't wear those long lilac pants of yours. They're not becoming of you." Zoya Nikolayevna flared up. She felt so embarrassed she wished the earth would swallow her up. Not as the principal, but as a man. I ask you. She lay on the ottoman reading Ehrenburg, but she couldn't keep her mind on her reading. In her mind's eye she could see the principal standing in front of her: thin, and with a slanted fringe. Zoya Nikolayevna tried to make sense of her feelings. She took off her lilac pants once and for all. She found a use for them in her household chores.

The workman came in the morning. He came very early, as if he was part of someone's dream. He had a white rope in his hand. He crossed the room and flung open the balcony door, letting in the damp and the wind. On the balcony, after taking his measurements, he grabbed hold of a five-pointed star as big as a person, which was covered with lightbulbs, like eyes. He didn't get a proper grip on it at first, and cut himself, so he stopped to bandage his wound. The yard-keeper yelled something at him irritatedly from the street. He came back into the room wet through because of the foul weather, covered in sweat and weakened by the battle, and in a barely audible voice asked for something to drink.

"And what sort of films do you like?" Izya Moiseyevich said, starting to come on to her. "I love *Alexander Nevsky*, Zoya Nikolayevna answered in a sad voice, after a moment's thought. The principal had been finding fault with her quite a bit lately. Why didn't she fill in the journal the right way, why didn't she contribute to the wall-newspaper? Once, during a lesson, she opened the door that opened onto the corridor. He was standing there, eavesdropping. He looked her right in the eyes and, without saying a word, walked away. "He hates me and wants to get rid of me," Zoya Nikolayevna thought, curling up into a ball on the ottoman, and started sobbing. At that very moment, Zoya Nikolayevna's younger brother, with whom she shared a room, was heating up the stove. He was a petty hooligan, the tear away kid of the local yard. He heard her sobbing and turned away. As he passed by her, he slapped his sister's fat, meaty bottom and said, roaring with laughter:

"You're in love!"

"You fool!" Zoya Nikolayevna cried, with the pitiful scream of a wounded bird.

The workman was served tap-water. He had just enough time to take in his surroundings: an expensive television set, of a kind that was not yet on sale to the wider public; on it was a musketeer with a sword and short pants, a picture of a bouquet of mimosas in a gilded frame, a knife and a lemon. A sleepy little boy in pajamas, his head propped up on his fist,was following the worker's every movement with his black eyes from the ottoman. Above the ottoman, which had holes in it where there had once been nails, from which an old, dusty carpet used to hang, there were some thin rods with little red flags attached to them. Each time there was a public holiday, the boy, imitating the street, used to hang up decorations: stars, banners, portraits of the leaders. He used to organize a parade of captured soldiers and chess pieces on the ottoman. The horses' jaws were completely torn off.

"He's left footprints everywhere, the devil!" grandmother flew into a rage, wiping up the floor after the worker had left.

Breaking his fingers, the boy fastened the pants of his school uniform. Just before he left a huge row broke out: his grandmother ordered him to put on his new overshoes, over his shoes. Grandmother had weak nerves, of which she was very proud. She had lived through the siege of Leningrad. In a rage, grandmother pushed the boy out the door, in his overshoes, without saying goodbye. Choking back his tears, the boy kicked the iron door of the elevator, to call the elevator attendant. While the attendant was making his way up, his grandmother pushed the door open, looking joyful and young once again. The boy felt like stabbing her with a knife.

"Petrovich," grandmother said to the old lift attendant, who was wearing a rotting uniform representing some unknown army.

Have some of this cabbage soup. Mind you don't go pouring it away. Only make sure you bring the pot back. Try your best," grandmother said to the boy affectionately.

The lift attendant gave a toothless grin, and bowed. On his way down with the boy, he lifted the lid and inhaled the cabbage swill deeply, looking delighted. In his younger days, Petrovich had worked as a cook for the Yusupovs. He had gone to the "Hunter's Club" in Warsaw, and then to Paris. There were some important people living in our building, too: clean black cars used to come and pick them up. Petrovich used to draw himself up to full height and salute them. The car they used to send to pick up papa was a chocolate-colored *Victory*. The attendant's eyes had filled with tears. The boy sniffed: Petrovich stank, but it was a slightly different stink to that of the worker.

Dawn had not yet broken outside. Snow and rain were falling. You could get to school by going one stop in an overcrowded trolleybus, but the boy never did so. All along the street decorations were being taken down — for good, or so it seemed. By now the boy was utterly fed up. Even the forty kopecks he had saved didn't cheer him up that day. His cap, which had the letters *SH* on its visor, fell down over his eyes. It was too big for him, the hat, they hadn't been able to find the right size. Grandmother had sewn it up with cotton on the inside, but the cotton had fallen out. The boy trudged along with his heavy briefcase through the rain and the snow. He turned off the street under an arch destroyed by a German bomb, walked along the street for another minute, and saw the school's brick building in front of him.

The principal's window was brightly lit. The principal often spent the night in his office, as he didn't want to go back to his apartment on Marx-Engels Street. The artist Kachalov had lived in his apartment before the revolution. The principal lived in a damp room measuring thirteen square meters, a converted bathroom. The pipes were exposed. The principal was dissatisfied with himself. To think that he, a Soviet officer who had served on the front-line, was putting off a decision with each passing day. He hadn't had to think twice when it came to shooting the Germans.

The boy walked into the locker room. There was a crush. The boy hung his coat on the hook; the other boys knocked his hat off his head, and he rushed to pick it up. The boys began to chase after it, as if it was a ball. They kicked it into the corner. He bent down and got a kick up the backside. He turned round. A third-grader spat benevolently in his face. He said nothing, turned away and wiped off the spit; someone kicked the heavy briefcase and it flew from his grasp and came open, so that his textbooks, notebooks and pencil case fell out. He started picking everything up. Someone's boot had left a footprint on one of his notebooks, and some of the lined pages had been creased. Zoya Nikolayevna, his teacher, had no great love of untidy pupils. She used to show their messy notebooks to the whole class, picking them up by the corners with two fingers, as if she were picking up a dead mouse by its tail. She had managed to finish reading Ehrenburg in the end. She didn't think it was anything special. It was all about some artists or other. They kept arguing amongst themselves. It was boring. By the time he had picked up his notebooks the locker-room was empty. He stood there looking confused, wondering what to do. Where should he put his overshoes? Leave them under the hook, on the floor? Was there really any chance the other boys would spare them? The boy pictured his siege-surviving grandmother's mouth, yelling at him. The bell rang. Zoya Nikolayevna had no great love of tardy pupils. She used to put them in the corner, or send them to see the principal, whose nickname was 'Roach'. The boy's cheeks were burning. He unfastened his briefcase and tried to put them inside, but there wasn't enough room. Suddenly he had a brainwave. He stuffed one overshoe into the right-hand pocket of his pants, and the other into the left-hand pocket; the one on the left was a tighter fit: his handkerchief was in the way. He pulled out the handkerchief, put it in the breast pocket of his shirt, and there was now room for the overshoes, although the heels stuck out a little. He stretched the ends of his shirt over his pockets, tightened his belt,which was embossed with the letters SH, paused for a moment and then ran out of the locker room.

The principal was standing at the entrance onto the stairs. The principal himself. There was no way past him. The expression on his face was frightening. The principal saw the boy and walked toward him. The principal couldn't stand children. A veteran of the war, who had been awarded a medal, he had found it hard to accept his appointment at the school. He had been aiming higher. He found little boys who smelled of children's soap particularly disgusting. Suddenly something distracted the principal: Izya Moiseyevich, who was always running late, was flying towards him like a bullet. The principal blocked the path to the stairs with his body. The principal said: "You there...stop distributing that Ehrenburg of yours!"

The literature teacher took umbrage: everyone was reading him...!

"All of you! Stop that right now: all of you, I say!"The literature teacher turned pale and hissed through his teeth: "Treacherous woman!"The principal squeezed the set of keys in his fist and said: "I've got you right here, in my fist!" And he walked off, jingling the keys. The boy slipped between the two furious men. He ran up to the second floor, sprinted halfway down the frozen corridor, yanked at the door-handle and frowned. The electric light was burning brightly and dryly in the classroom. Zoya Nikolayevna was standing at the table and speaking in a loud voice, enunciating her words carefully. She finished speaking and turned to look at the boy. He was standing by the door: his head was shaved, his eyes were black and his ears were burning. His hair was tousled. His satchel was dirty. She took a closer look at him. "What's that in your pockets?" the teacher asked, looking surprised. Forty young pairs of eyes turned to stare at the boy. He said nothing. He could feel water dripping from the wet overshoes, seeping through the lining of his pocket and through his brown socks, and making his feet terribly cold. "I said: what's that in your pockets?" the teacher said, stressing every word. "Nothing..." the boy whispered. "Get over here." He walked over to her, leaning to one side shyly. Zoya Nikolaevna lifted up the corner of his shirt, stretched out her hand and pulled out one of the black overshoes, its insides utterly drenched. She held the overshoe in two fingers, lifted it up, showed it to the class and said simply:

"An overshoe."

The class gave a low rumble, and began to squeal and bark. The little children — many of whom were frail and had sickly faces — collapsed onto their desks, clutching their stomachs. They were all laughing: Adrianov, Baranov, Bekkenin, who later turned out to be a Tatar, and the mild-mannered child prodigy Berman. Dorofeyev and Zhulev laughed, hugging one another like Herzen and Ogarev; the chubby girl Vasilieva, with the protruding eyes, who was suffering from Basedow's disease, laughed with that prematurely grown-up, chesty laugh of hers; the magnificent Kira Kaplina, who would go on to be the first girl in the class to go through the menstrual cycle, let out a stream of giggles; and the little monkey Naryshkina gave a little squeal (five years later Izya would ask her: "Are you one of *those* Naryshkins? Well? Answer! There's nothing to be scared about now." But she didn't understand: what did he mean by *those* Naryshkins? She was Naryshkina from Yuzhinsky Lane). They were all laughing: Goryainova, who went off on a two-year business trip to Cuba with her husband, the restless Artsybashev — he would go on to become a fairly well-known literary figure, and join the Writers' Union; Trunina, who graduated from the school with a gold medal; Zolotareva and Doctor Guseva from the health center; and Gadova, who went gray at the age of thirty and could play the guitar. Also laughing was Sokina, with her thin little legs, who would die young after contracting an infection in her blood; the curly-haired Nyshkina had already died too, after falling down an empty lift-shaft — although the red-headed fool Trunina had had more luck, along with her husband — a member of the Central Committee, if I'm not mistaken, of the All-Union Leninist Young Communist League; Nelly Petrosyan got lucky too, and married a Hungarian — she would speak Hungarian for the rest of her life — *yegish-megish* — what an incomprehensible language! The frail Bogdanov is laughing too — two years later he was to get an almighty kick from Ilya Tretyakov: that's him at the desk at the back, laughing! — he's breaking his coccyx; the sweet-toothed Los is laughing as well, she's an informant, and Yakimenko, who would go on to throw herself out of the window whilst drunk, become disabled, and give birth to twins; Yudina was to outlive all the others: on her ninetieth birthday she would walk into the kitchen of her communal flat wearing a motley bathing suit. Her neighbors, thunderstruck, burst into a round of applause. The only one not laughing was Khokhlov, who never laughed. Also laughing were: the mathematician Sukach, who would later move to Vorkuta; the murderer Kolya Maksimov — he stabbed a dovecote owner; Verchenko the spiv, who used to beg foreigners for chewing gum outside the Peking hotel when he was just a little boy, was shaking with mirth too, along with Sasha Kherasov. Zaitsev, the bespectacled Shub and a Romanian girl from a family of anti-fascists, Stella Dickens, followed suit. The ensign Shchapov, who had been wounded in a colonial campaign, the karate expert Chemodanov and Wagner, the flat-chested Wagner, were crowing with all their might. Baklazhanova, Mukhanov and Klyshko were falling into the alleys between the desks with laughter, like pieces of fruit falling off a shelf. His face lit up with laughter, Aleksei Maresiev's son, who had been given a place in the pioneers even before his first day at school, was walking on his hands.

Even Zoya Nikolaevna was beginning to chuckle, too. The children's laughter was infectious. Zoya Nikolaevna couldn't hold back her mirth, and let out a shrill, silvery laugh. "Hahahahaha,"

Zoya Nikolaevna burst out, powerless to keep a grip on herself, "hahahahaha."

The subject of all this merriment, of this universal laughter, was standing at her desk with his dirty trouser pockets turned out. Burning tears streamed from his eyes, which were black as coals, down his long face, and suddenly, over her very un-teacher-like laughter and over the children's laughter, Zoya Nikolaevna heard the boy whispering desperately and selflessly:

"O Lord," the boy whispered, "forgive them Lord, forgive them and have mercy on them! They are innocent and kind, they are good, O Lord!"

Zoya Nikolaevna stopped laughing and, still holding the galoshes in her hand, stared at the boy. And then she noticed that over this unkempt first-year's head, above his little head, which was completely shaved, there was a thin halo, shining like a circle of ice.

"I love them, Lord!" the boy whispered. "He's a saint!" the teacher froze, and her face took on a terribly stupid expression.

"What's going on in there?!" The principal appeared at the doorway. "It's a madhouse! Stop that at once!"

A hush descended on the room. Zoya Nikolaevna stood with the children's overshoes in her hand and turned to look at the principal with an absurd expression on her face.

"You're disrupting the lessons in my school!" the principal hissed at her, with a shake of his angled fringe. "Step out into the corridor at once!"

At a loss as to what was going on, as if in a dream, Zoya Nikolaevna went out into the corridor with the galoshes. The principal closed the door to the classroom behind her — inside the room the children, left to their own devices, started howling once again.

"And to top it all off you're carrying a pair of overshoes...?" the principal said, with a face like thunder.

"One of the boys," Zoya Nikolaevna muttered, "the thing is, he...," her eyes widened, "he turned out to be a saint..."

The principal took the small pair of overshoes from Zoya Nikolaevna's outstretched hands, placed them on the broad palm of his hand and carefully examined their sodden insides.

"Zoya Nikolaevna!" he said, letting the acrid stench of his male breath hit her full in the face. "This simply won't do any longer — it simply won't. I have a thirteen square meter room at home. Right in the centre of town. Move in with me. Be my wife."

Zoya Nikolaevna let out a soft cry and fell backwards over the edge of the fire escape.

•

It was a time of great upheaval. We moved to Paris. Father was prepared to make the journey even as first secretary, but Molotov flared up again, seeing in this an unjustified lowering of his status, and ordered that father be sent as an attaché. The moment Stalin was put on display in the mausoleum, alongside Lenin, papa took me along with him. He had been specially invited: the general public was not yet being admitted. I walked along as if we were going on a jolly, blissfully unaware what we were about to see, almost dancing along; but once we had gone down the marble steps I fell down to the very bottom of all my childhood fears. Stalin and Lenin were the first dead bodies I had ever seen in my life. But whereas Lenin was nice and quiet, Stalin was quite simply awash with death. He lay there, handsome and fearsome — and he would later appear in my nightmares, alternating with the skull and crossbones from that telegraph pole near the dacha. It came as such a powerful shock to me that later, in Paris, I passed up the opportunity to visit Napoleon's tomb at Les Invalides, fearing lest he too was displayed in an open coffin.

"What *exactly* did you imagine Communism to be?"

Father said nothing.

"We believed that it was the best way to organize human life.

The fairest way. Based on principles that all people and *even* the religions would recognize."

There were no diplomatic relations at all between papa and God. He never so much as set foot inside a church — even if the church in question was a cultural monument. I can picture him now standing next to the church porches in Peredelkino, in the cold, in the rays of the cupolas, sniffing, and wearing a coat with an Astrakhan collar and an Astrakhan hat. He is talking to his friend, the happy-go-lucky Huberman (everyone was surprised when he committed suicide: he hanged himself from a door). Father was never an anti-semite, incidentally — never once in his life did he allow himself to make the sort of utterances about the Jews that Russian people, as a general rule, feel in their hearts. Mama once went into a church out of curiosity, with her friend Yelena Nikolaevna — Lyolik (who is now deceased, too — the Western abundance she saw in Paris in the 1970s drove her out of her mind, and she needed a long period of treatment afterwards) — mama was allowed to do so, but father himself never did: he saw it as enemy territory. Talking about God was considered impolite and shameful in our family. God stood for prejudice and stupidity. God was written with a small 'g' in my parents' life.

"You'll be telling me next you believe in God!" mama raged furiously against my garrulous dissidence: her grandfather had been a priest, who had had to hide deep in the countryside so as not to let his family down. In the perestroika years, when she was a little older, her godlessness was more watered-down, but she became convinced that God and I were incompatible.

"What principles do you mean?" father said, continuing our conversation about Communism. "Treating a person the way you ought to. As a human being, first and foremost. Brotherhood. Friendship. Free medical care. Free education. Each person is responsible before all the others for his behavior, for the work he does. We were raised 'with an iron fist'. If someone *went off the rails*, he knew he would have to answer for his behavior at the party assembly.

Most of the people in father's circle were extremely shy types, who would never have even contemplated behaving indecently. Take Molotov's senior advisor, Boris Fedorovich Podtserob: in his younger days he asked a girl out on a date and ended up pissing himself surreptitiously, simply because he was too shy to admit that he needed to go to the toilet. There were, of course, exceptions. My father's closest friend, the smart, fidgety Andrei Mikhailovich Alexandrov, who could recite *Faust* in German by heart, and whom the Americans (he was a key advisor to Brezhnev) nicknamed the *Russian Kissinger*, not only quoted Goethe every time every time he came to see us, without fail, but also used to pinch our maids' backsides, which drove my mother crazy. I once found the *Russian Kissinger* shut inside a cupboard in my childhood bedroom, in a passionate clinch with his own wife. They gave me a friendly wave. They were even more passionate when dragging me and my young wife into their bedroom in the prestigious building opposite the Telegraph, on the pretext of showing us a good copy of Rembrandt's *Danae*. The whole thing had the whiff of an orgy about it. In the end all they did was show us some photos of themselves in the nude, spreading them out on the antique table.

The words *modesty* and *discipline* were always of key importance to my father.

"If we fail it will be a matter of global significance for mankind," father said. "It would be a global catastrophe from a philosophical perspective." All hope was lost.

On another occasion, however, whilst we were walking along the banks of the Istra River outside Moscow, he was in a more optimistic mood — which was more like him:

"As for the (communist) ideas themselves, they aren't so bad. But we have seen in practice that in the Russian setting we simply aren't ready for them. Just as today we are not yet ready for democracy. But this experience has not failed in vain. Mankind might be able to return to this business (i.e.

communism) at some point farther down the line, with a more morally acceptable approach.

Once, during the Stalinist years, a cashier gave my grandmother the wrong change inside the GUM shopping center. She looked up in surprise:

"Aren't you scared of doing something like that? My son works at the Kremlin!"

The cashier offered to hand over all the cash in the till.

•

Stalin can be referred to like that popular Russian toy: the roly-poly Stalin weeble. Stalin: the man who created magic totalitarianism. Russians love a good riddle. Stalin set them one. Stalin was completely hermetically sealed, as impermeable as a submarine. He was our very own yellow submarine. He never actually said what it was he wanted. He had a good laugh at everyone's expense — and died without ever being known.

The endless stream of liberal books about Stalin portray him as a tyrant. But it was the West that helped the Russian revolution get to its feet, gain strength, win the Civil War, crush Russian emigration, make Stalin form a pact with Hitler and then, later, betray almost all those who fled Russia. We exist in a vacuum, fenced off from any moral criticism of the West. We find ourselves required to make sense of ourselves, and categorize ourselves in accordance with our own categories. We are in a world the like of which no-one has ever been in before. These are inhuman dimensions. This is an identity consisting of polar opposites. It is practically unthinkable for us ever to be able to return to a normal system of values. We are merely imitating common sense.

As I grew up I began to realize something: to the West, and the majority of the Russian intelligentsia, Stalin was one thing; but to many millions of Russian citizens, he was something else. These people do not believe in the *bad* Stalin. They find it impossible to believe that Stalin ever tore anyone to pieces, or tortured anyone. The people have *stashed away* the image of the *good* Stalin, Russia's savior and the father of a great nation. My father went hand in hand with my people in this regard. Don't insult Stalin!

I have no other Napoleon of the taiga, no other Communists and no *other* grandmother — nor shall I ever.

I take various figures with oval, state labels on them out of a family box. The label is a universal sign of record and control. Solipsism is the absence of a childhood trauma. I was transformed from a *bare incident* into a uniform measure of things. Here's Stalin, with Molotov standing behind him, along with Beria, Mikoyan, the other members of the Politburo and some famous foreign faces: I can see De Gaulle, Ribbentrop and Maurice Thorez smiling back at me; the dance teacher Enver Hodge is dancing for me.

In accordance with my doctrines, or in spite of them, they exist exclusively for my own pleasure. Somewhere deep within the general order of things, these people are a reflection of me, and for that reason they are *deeply* artificial. (Like that Indian near the airport in Varanasi, with a moustache broader than his speckled face and an antediluvian carbine in his slender little hands, who made a threatening gesture when I accidentally walked into the prohibited area where some sort of oily rubbish was kept, behind a bamboo fence. I looked at him and found it impossible to believe that he could ever cause me any actual harm.)

It all ended the wrong way. I guessed the truth about the solipsistic rituals. I bowed down before the solipsistic idols. I swore never to beat my father at the games he loved, particularly tennis — but to no avail. The fragility of life had been given to *us* clearly, to judge by the example of my family. The shell had been cracked. The Indian, emerging from the parentheses, fired a shot — the bastard! — into the hot air. The labels fell away. Even grandmother protested about the role I had set aside for her. After turning out to be longer-lived than the USSR,

Anastasia Nikandrovna confessed to me before she died that she had always considered Lenin to have been a 'bad egg'.

"Why didn't you tell me earlier?" I asked.

"I didn't want to ruin your life," my grandmother replied in a husky voice, resorting to theatrical intonation.

She was unaware that I had already ruined my own life, without her assistance. We hid the family catastrophe from her, as if it were an embarrassing disease. She was blissfully unaware that in 1979, hopelessly lost in the world of self-publishing, I accidentally committed a *political* patricide (all those devotees of Freud among you will probably liven up at this point).

But I have some good news for you: there is such thing as conscience. In Russia you have to live a long time if you want to live to see something. But conscience sleeps the sleep of the righteous. Hypnos is not its God and commander. It has dreams. To be continued. Come to think of it, what is Russia, if not the dreams of conscience?

3

I lost my faith in the intelligence of writers long ago. Those writers whom I deem to be intelligent are few and far between. The best Russian writers — Gogol and Platonov — seem to have suffered from idiocy. You can't really claim Tolstoy and Dostoevsky had great philosophical minds. Chekhov was an agnostic, who never allowed himself to think too much, thank goodness. Nabokov wasn't the brightest spark, either. Pushkin, with all his utterances about how poetry ought to be ever so slightly stupid, was onto something. Of the Russian writers alive today, Bitov is probably the only one who really applies his mind, like a squirrel inside a wheel. I remember being pleasantly surprised by a conversation I once had over dinner with Philip Roth, in Connecticut. Brodsky also struck me as an intelligent man, but he always had about him — particularly in the later years — too much literary generalship, which is not compatible with genuine intelligence. In short, I have something on which to base my comparison — little though it may be — and can claim to have gotten lucky: I met two remarkably intelligent men in my life: Alfred Shnittke and Aleksei Fedorovich Losev. The latter once told me one night, at his house on the Old Arbat, that in a one-dimensional space the philosopher's intelligence must be two-dimensional, and in a two-dimensional space it must be three-dimensional. Losev's intelligence was four-dimensional.

Creativity is nothing less than a reminder of creation itself. In order to become a new 'reminder', you must learn to accept being a chosen one; and to get a sense of how this process of selection comes about — the meaning of it is never clear, but it is undoubtedly proportionate to the confrontation of entropy, a four-dimensional intelligence is precisely what is required: an intelligence that is able — from the point of view of common sense — to accommodate the boundless. In literature, as strange as it may sound, the boundless consists not of cosmic phenomena, but of the details. It's for that reason that writers always failed with their autobiographies when they tried to describe how they became the writers they were. They did not have that extra dimension, they made do with insights and moments of illumination. I want to achieve what is almost impossible.

My first letter to my grandmother from Paris, sent by diplomatic courier:

Paris, September 13, 1955.

Dear grandma, hello!
There are a lot of cars in Paris, but there is no black caviar at all. I'm really miss (sic!) you. Everything's going well here so far. On Monday papa bought me a Czechoslovakian tennis racket. Today I played tennis with papa. I am already quite good. I have lessons sometimes. Our school is next to the Bois de Boulogne. There aren't many pupils in my class. My teacher's name is Kirilla Vasilievna.

What is the weather like in Moscow? In Paris it was very hot, but now the weather is pretty bad. It doesn't rain very often, though. Write me a letter, please.
Lots and lots of kisses.
Your grandson Victor.

●

The Bois de Boulogne isn't a wood at all. The Champs-Élysées aren't fields. At the end of August we went by train to Paris, changing trains in Prague. Anikin, a state attaché, met us at the Gare de l'Est, where the fog merged with the steam coming from the engines. He looked mama up and down suspiciously: she was dressed in a smart black dress with white stripes, and he was horrified by her flat-heeled sandals. We were put into a car next to some suitcases and taken across the city to the embassy.

Paris greeted us with tropical heat. Mama couldn't hide her surprise:

"Everyone's dressed for the beach, in short trousers!"

For some reason there was an upbeat mood in the car. We all got wet through. Our clothes were stuck to our bodies. A cheeky little monkey, I was in a good mood too. We drove across Place de la Concorde, as you might expect, and mama turned my head to the right:

"Look, there's the Champs-Élysées — the Elysian Fields."

Stretching across her, I stuck my head out of the window. Rising up before me was a broad street full of cars, lined with trees, which came to an end in the distance with a small arch.

"Where?"

"Right there, in front of you!"

I stared intently at the street with all my might, at the arch: I really wanted to catch sight of the fields, but I couldn't see anything, and my mother was growing increasingly puzzled. All I could see was a light-gray smoke-ring of heat, on the brink of sunny weather.

"Where? Where?"

"Stop turning your head!"

"I'm not!"

"Well, do you see them?"

"Yes!"

For me, Paris began with a lie. Mama, feeling relieved, stopped pestering me. I assumed that the fields I couldn't see were probably somewhere beyond that arch, because the street went uphill. How on earth had mama been able to spot them? Papa, too, who was holding his redundant hat in his hands, also seemed to be delighted by my 'yes', because he nodded from his position in the front seat, and asked Anikin eagerly:

"What's their view of us like?"

This had become his traditional question: from whichever country I returned, in later years, papa would always ask me, with unfeigned interest:

"What's their view of us like?"

(I always felt like giving an honest answer: fucking bad. Fucking bad in Japan and in Ukraine, fucking bad in Poland, France, Finland, Hungary, the USA. In Serbia alone, though: not so fucking bad.)

"There's no short answer to that," the advisor said with a smile.

The Champs-Élysées. In my head I pictured fields of potato crops, an endless purple space of potato flowers, of vital significance for the country in which we had just arrived: perhaps the very center of the French world, which lived off sales of potatoes, and was extremely proud thereof. I pictured hundreds of French labourers working in the fields, marching up the street with their hoes, cloths and rakes and passing through the arch to start working on the land without delay. This vision still comes back to me, to this day, whenever I walk along the Champs-Élysées, and I begin to think that perhaps there really are some potato fields out there, beyond that arch.

•

Father is mowing the lawn at our dacha in the diplomats' village of Polushkino, where every building reflects the country in which the diplomat worked. Some of the diplomats, back in Soviet days, built sturdy German houses; another group built Californian-style ones; another group built Bulgarian or Romanian ones; and a fourth group built homes made of red planks, in the Scandinavian style. My parents built something that looked a bit like an Alpine chalet. The only things missing in the village are Chinese pagodas and Russian dachas. If papa had had been sent somewhere else, rather than to Paris, my life would have turned out quite differently.

All Russians suffer from a lack of warmth. But there are two ways to counter the problems of geography: surround yourself with friends and drink vodka. What's more, every Russian has their own version of the tropics available to them: a steam-filled banya, a receptacle for red-skinned devils, sweating in the steam with a birch twig in front of a scorching oven, and angels, drinking cold beer after their session, wrapped up in white sheets.

When you fly from America across the North Pole to Moscow, the plane starts to fly at a lower altitude when you are at the edge of the Arctic Ocean. Russia is a beautiful woman dressed up in snow and furs, but the Russian refuses to acknowledge that he is a northerner — in spite of St Petersburg's white nights and the northern lights of Murmansk, Siberia and the taiga. The north is understood to mean Finland, Norway... Yakutia, at a stretch; but Russia, the spiritual center of the world, was displaced in the direction of the Arctic circle. Russia pushed northwards against its will, seeking refuge from the onslaughts by the nomads of the southern steppes in the early Middle Ages. It is awaiting the day when it will return to the warm bosom of civilization.

I experienced climate shock.

The climate in Paris suited me down to the ground. I liked the Decembers, when the roses were in bloom. I dreamed of sycamores and chestnuts for the rest of my life. Paris infects you with its climate. The climate here is carefree. The snowy desert of Russia sprouts through like a boxwood tree in the Luxembourg Gardens, which is transformed into the aroma of my adolescence, the calling card of my dissimilarity.

As you travel through Germany and Belgium in an old-fashioned long-distance rail car from the Soviet era, you always sense the tense gloominess of the sky and the instability of the weather, but the moment you cross the French border, a silent explosion rings out in the sky, the clouds disperse in all directions, the horizon expands, the sky flies upwards, the pyramid-shaped poplars grow stronger and the sun beats against the window of the compartment.

Paris does not have that same feel of a resort town, the palm-tree unequivocal nature of the south. Had I lived in Rome I would have become a hedonist; in Berlin — an eccentric; in New York — a Soviet civil servant. But Paris was the only place that could have become my second homeland.

From the sparsely inhabited island of the Moscow paradise in which I spent my early years, I was taken to the place traditionally seen as an earthly paradise, heralded, glorious and at the time, in the mid-1950s, not yet emasculated: alive and real. In the Paris of those days there were still a lot of émigré white guards, who worked as taxi drivers and spoke in an antiquated pidgin dialect; it was not entirely safe to travel by taxi if you were a Soviet. I didn't understand a great deal but got a good feel for what was going on, absorbing it by osmosis. I never danced at the *bals populaires* in that dancing city, never went to the jazz clubs, never lost my voice singing along to the latest rock-'n-roll hits from overseas, never sat in the same café as the lazy-eyed Sartre. But I was reborn, without even being aware of it. My parents began to be reborn, too.

•

I can picture them now, as if in a dream, as if I am at the theater, starting to change their clothes. Everything begins with a change of clothes. Mama's neck and arms are suddenly revealed. She grows younger before my very eyes, and her hair turns curly. Her tall haircut, which gave her a surprised, careworn look, has gone, and she is wearing her hair short. If you look at the photos of her from before we moved to Paris, mama gave off the aura of the Easternness of Russia, of Blok-esque Scythians with high cheekbones and smiling eyes; here, in Paris, this Easternness had assumed soft, Slavic features. Mama puts on trendy yellow and blue bell-shaped skirts, and tight-fitting blouses. After her gloomy mid-season coat, single-tone skirts sewn with the living remains of the National Economic Policy — by the dressmaker Polina Nikanorovna — they seem particularly multicolored and motley, like the fields outside Paris, across which I run, gathering red poppies with black kernels with mama and the new maid Klava (Marusya Pushkina was not allowed to go to Paris: when she was a child she had slept with some Germans near Volokolamsk). We are particularly fond of tearing out the poppies. We demand that papa stop the car next to the ditch: it is a remarkable gray Peugeot 403, with its yellow headlights, blinking side indicators (some of the cars in Paris back then still had arrows indicating which way they were turning, which stuck out like broken wings — a dead-end for civilization) and green diplomatic license plate with red numbers, which aroused curiosity among the French, who were still full of curiosity back then, and who made chosen ones of us even in Paris. License plates conceal divine possibilities. No matter where you leave your car — even if you park it right across the road — the traffic wardens treat you like a king. But if you really wanted to take things to extremes, you could do as you pleased with a license plate like that: crash into someone, run someone over and crush them to death — and the worst that would happen is that you'd be sent back to Moscow. As I discuss these possibilities with some Soviet boys in the stone courtyard of the embassy, I feel giddy at the thought of my father's power and impunity — something about which my father, it seems, was never even aware. Meanwhile, after crossing the ditch, we crawl along the slope of the hill looking for poppies.

Papa's wearing trendy, flowing plants. On weekends he leaves his short-sleeved shirt, with its unbuttoned collar, untucked, in the French style. He too starts to get his hair cut in a different way, at the back and to the sides, leaving more hair on the sides, like a French actor. He has already bought some large-framed dark glasses, and mama has bought some sunglasses too: they are sculpted and slightly pointy-eared, with something encrusted in them — but they aren't unduly extravagant. My parents adjust the watches on their wrists, amicably: mama's watch is really tiny, and oblong.

In France mama began to have a different scent to the one she normally had in Moscow. When she tucked me into bed, her hands had a different scent, and so did the skin on her face. There was some subtle, un-Russian feeling of alienation, which I could not quite put my finger on, in these new scents. Mama had become less heavy, less like her own mother; she stooped less, had clearly lost weight, and her gait had changed: mama had generally become more mobile and light in her movements, slipping away from me with ease. When she said goodbye to me each night, she would pat me on the arm comfortingly, without sitting down, and begin what for me was our eagerly awaited night-time chat — "come on, off to sleep," — and then she broke away easily from the sofa on which I used to sleep in the large bedroom.

It was her first long-term overseas trip. Japan didn't count. She had gone to Japan during the war as a patriot, after turning down a job offer in New York with the Main Intelligence Directorate (the GRU), as a beginner spy. In the military attaché's offices she used to cut out information from the Japanese papers that might be of use for the purposes of espionage. A stubborn girl, she learned Japanese, and this meant she was the first Soviet person to find out about the execution of Richard Sorge (she read about it in the *Government News*). At the time she didn't know who he was, but when she saw the Russian soldiers running around the embassy she realized that something pretty important had just happened.

There was a sign written in Japanese that hung opposite the embassy: 'All foreigners are spies'. Mama complained about the tactlessness of this sign. She also complained about the tactlessness of the Japanese men, who used to walk around the streets of Tokyo with their kimonos hanging open after they had been to the banya, leaving their genitalia exposed, as their wives hurried to try and catch up with them.

Later, in Moscow, she was present when they interrogated the Sorges, a Germano-Russian couple who were deported to the USSR from a Japanese prison after the war. The Russian wife had broken down inside the Japanese prison, and the couple were now awaiting their punishment. You can imagine the looks they gave my future mama, who, working at the GRU as she had done before, was recording all their testimony. But instead of being executed, the couple were quietly packed off to East Germany, a country which made heroes of them many years later. After the wedding, father immediately sent mama to work at the Ministry of Foreign Affairs, in the printing department, as it was the safest place for her.

In Paris mama didn't have to hide herself away in the embassy's bomb shelter. She was the wife of the cultural attaché. She was expected to be well-dressed, go to receptions and socialize with the likes of Aragon and Yves Montand. My parents equipped themselves with all sorts of useful paraphernalia — things that looked like toys: mama now had a red dressing-case with a multicolored braid of threads, all manner of different kinds of scissors, and a golden thimble; she dried her hair with a hair-dryer; and papa shaved with an electric razor made by Phillips, with little wheels on it. I felt envious of them — I wanted to play this game too. At big government receptions papa wore a tux and a white bow-tie. He had a whole collection of cuff-links. His tie collection was growing rapidly too. Mama is standing in front of the mirror in a red and gold lace dress that stretches down to the floor. Father is chivvying her: "We need to go."

Look this way everyone! They are having their photo taken at the presidential palace. Mama has thrown her head back a little, and papa is gazing straight ahead in worldly fashion. They are *super*-parents.

We live in the seventh arrondissement, in an expensive town-house with unkempt Russian chauffeurs running around the courtyard; a ZIS with a red flag comes up the drive;

Ambassador Vinogradov steps out onto the porch, and my parents teach me our address at the embassy, just in case I get lost: *soixante-dix-neuf, Rue de Grenelle*. A black dog belonging to Ambassador Chernomor — who turned out to be a right bastard, incidentally — runs across the embassy lawn. There are tiny golden fish in the pond. In our dining room there is a real fireplace, with a high marble mantelpiece; admittedly, it doesn't work.

I am changing too, before everyone's eyes. Starting with my underwear. Instead of Y-fronts I'm wearing white trunks which look like a swimsuit, with a complex cut at the front — I will later be made to suffer because of these trunks in Moscow — and some real shorts which stop above the knee. I am wearing a dark-blue cotton sweater of a kind that Moscow will not even discover the existence of until the 1990s, and a jacket with extra pockets sewn in. Mama and I walk out of the embassy, turn right and walk past several buildings: I too get my hair cut at a Parisian hairdresser's, where the armchairs are amazingly soft. My parents are drawn to the French style. They are young and athletically built — it suits them down to the ground. But though we are well-dressed, it is considered very bad taste to talk about this. There is a ban in effect in our family: foppery is considered disgusting. My parents are slowly but surely beginning to look like foreigners.

•

Foreigners are the enemy. Papa works in enemy territory. Paris is full to the brim with foreigners. All over the city foreign newspapers are on sale, the radio broadcasts programs about topics that are banned, the movie theaters show films that are banned, and strange foreign flags are unfurled. When the Soviet diplomats drive out of the embassy gates, it is as if they are going to war. Not too many of them believe they are going to come back with their lives. The Soviet ambassador Pavlov,

Vinogradov's predecessor, informed Moscow proudly that a whole year had gone by without him spending a single franc on receptions for the French at the embassy.

Papa arrived in France at a time when the threat posed by foreigners was somewhat reduced. They had revealed themselves to be tourists, and were descending on Moscow and Leningrad in their droves. Papa helped to organize these trips. Papa went to Paris under the Soviet slogan of reducing international tension. Anything that weakened, crushed or undermined the West, however, was to be welcomed. Of course, my papa was a genuine diplomatic terrorist. He dreamed that France would one day be led by communists, and that there would be a French Socialist Republic. I sincerely doubt he wanted to deprive the French of oranges and wine, and create lines for camembert and milk. He never thought about that. His imagination did not stretch that far. The hunger, the shootings and the purges, in Paris, would have to be organized by other people, whom he didn't like.

My papa was anti-historical. Everything he fought against ended up on the winning side. Everything he fought for collapsed, along with the name of the country from which he was sent. With one exception. Father was cultural attaché at the embassy at a time when a cultural exchange began. Soviet musicians, the Soviet circus and Galina Ulanova all came to Paris. The French howled with delight. The concert halls were packed. Russian emigrés sat in the audience, tears running down their cheeks. Emigrés are even more frightening than foreigners. On one occasion my parents and I were in the North Sea — in the Belgian coastal town of Ostend. We were sitting quietly in a café. I was drinking a cup of cocoa. Suddenly a row erupted. Some kindly people who were sitting together as a family at the same establishment demanded that the owner show us the door, simply because we were from Moscow:

"They're Soviet murderers!"

The owner didn't throw us out — we soon left of our own accord. I never finished my cup of cocoa.

"Papa, who did we murder?" I asked, once we were outside. Between the two of us there was a ditch containing millions of lives. My papa was a man who opened up cultural barriers. But papa was not overly fond of culture — he thought of it as a dreary backwater, devoid of politics. Culture, for him, meant leisure time, and a stroll around the museums. He dreams of being a political attaché, who, under the guidance of ambassador Vinogradov, could do some real damage to the West.

I hardly know that *other* father of mine: the one who thought in the language of hate, using the Leninist lexicon of class struggle; the father who uttered the words: *provocation, dirty tricks campaign, fabrications, associate, man of politics.* How exalted he was when Khrushchev, during his visit to France (in 1960), pressed the French leaders in Reims, when they were reluctant to utter the name of their sworn enemies.

"Who was it that fought alongside you in the East?"

"We can't remember."

"Shall I give you a clue? What were they called?"

"Who?"

"They were fascists!"

The French didn't know where to look. Led by a government minister, they maintained a cowardly silence. I don't know what's going on inside my father's mind. He tells me, looking very pleased with himself, about how an employee at the West German embassy tried to protest about the incitement of hatred of his country on the part of Khrushchev and his official delegation, of which my father was not even a member, but which he served honorably.

But when the deputy minister for foreign affairs, father's boss Semyonov, a former Commandant in Berlin, who used to wear a cap on his days off and sucked up to Lenin, made father read Lenin's works in the evenings to try and find the answers to current political issues, father, sitting in a yellow French armchair brought over from Paris, in his Moscow apartment on Gorky Street, surrounded by burgundy books with a picture of the leader in profile, with a pencil in his hand after dinner, looked like a badgered schoolboy.

•

This much I know: my papa is the good Stalin. Every family is a communist cell. The father is the boss: he loves and he hates. Stalin treated all Russians like children — and that's exactly what they are. I never saw my father drunk. Refined drunkenness, a predilection for whiskey, is the most common affliction affecting diplomats from all countries, including Islamic states, and also their wives; it usually ends in a retirement spoilt by alcoholism. Father loved Russian vodka, but he never drank in the Russian way, just to get drunk. He was capable of sneaking a quarter-pint of the stuff into the cupboard and drinking it, so that mama didn't notice — after suffering the trauma of having an alcoholic father as a child, she used to monitor how much alcohol was consumed in our family — but he never allowed himself to go beyond the bounds of decency. I find it impossible to picture him vomiting after gorging himself on vodka. How many times had I sat huddled around the toilet, with blurry eyes, throwing up my insides: he never did so once. I never heard my father utter a single curse word. He never even said *shit*, although the word *crap* sometimes passed his lips, on rare occasions. The story about him teaching curse-words to Scottish naval officers seems improbable to me.

It's true that papa spent his entire life pronouncing the word *chauffeur* in the French way rather than the Russian way, and saying *beauteous* rather than pretty (I copied him when I was a child, and it took me a long time to get out of the habit). But my parents shunned Russian rudeness, and didn't go to Russian taverns — it was only when they moved to France that they discovered there was such a thing as: the *restaurant*.

•

Paris consists of food. It is completely permeated with the aroma of food. All the French do is eat. They sit in the sunshine and eat. They eat whilst walking along the street. They eat lying down. French food is beginning, imperceptibly, to make its presence felt in our culture. The situation with food is more complex than the situation with clothes. Papa is one of those rare types whose attitude to food is conservative. For him, *pelmeni* are the height of desire — a cosmic Saturn — even now. *Pelmeni* orbit around my entire childhood, just like Saturn: it was a food that we ate ritually on papa's birthday, on October 9, and which was cooked by Klava. Ever since her young days, Klava had been a genuine, righteous young Russian woman, who had disappeared without trace in her own kindness: she was invisible, and existed outside all political systems; she was a selfless person who remained loyal to our family and had impressive culinary skills. Klava's *pelmeni* came out looking as if they were made of lace: they were compact, and each one was unique. She cut the dough for them using the rim of a shot-glass. Klava used to lay the circles of dough out on wooden trays, giving them a generous sprinkling of flour so that they didn't stick. Once she had boiled the *pelmeni*, and they had begun to float slowly in the large saucepan, the sacred moment of 'the tasting' arrived. Klava would bring a single *pelmen* to the table, for tasting, which she had plucked from the saucepan using a special serving spoon with tiny holes in it. Papa spread cream over the *pelmen*, blew on it to avoid burning his tongue, and swallowed it down.

"What's the verdict?" Klava said, anxiously.

"They're ready," father said, smacking his lips.

The vodka would be poured out, into the same shot-glasses that had been used to make the *pelmeni*. We had lashings of vodka with our *pelmeni*, as a special treat — but no-one ever got drunk. The combination of *pelmeni* and vodka created an invincible celebration of the Russian spirit, which was right up there on the same level as *Katyusha* rocket-launchers and ballet at the Bolshoi. When I drank vodka later in life, in Moscow, I always had *pelmeni* with it — with the family's blessing. Father and I used to wolf down at least a hundred *pelmeni* at a single sitting. *Pelmeni* were part of the Platonic idea of the endless family: it was hard to imagine Klavia's handiwork ever coming to an end. *Pelmeni* were the guarantee that no-one would ever get old in our family — let alone die. No-one ever dared refer to them in an off-hand way, using the diminutive form *pelmeshki*. Mama was not fond of *pelmeni*. Once we had had our *pelmeni*, we would sit drinking tea with lemon, recuperating. We couldn't even so much as look at any dessert — although an exception was made for lemon pie, the recipe for which mama had picked up in Paris.

Sausages purchased in Parisian shops were subjected to the same Moscow avatism as *pelmeni*, although they did not have any ritual significance — only here they were less tasty than Kremlin sausages, Mikoyan sausages and dairy sausages, though they were spicy and suspiciously reddish in color, like the French themselves.

Our rebirth commenced with wine. As they fell back, without realizing it themselves, into pre-Revolutionary times, my parents were drawn towards high society: they developed a passion for French wines, which subsequently became the family standard. At the *Nicolas* wine shops, papa stocked up on dry wine for the family, which in Moscow — again, as a concept — was seen as heresy, too sour, something that was not for consumption. The path from sweet Crimean port, madeira and sherry to Bordeaux and Burgundies was the biggest betrayal of their Soviet attitudes they ever made. Viticultural neophytes, my parents used to seduce me too on Sundays — starting with water. It was like a communion service. Soft French cheeses began to appear on our table, to go with the wine. In the first instance they were not particularly bold, and their smell was not too pungent: *Camembert, Caprice des Dieux*. Unlike the yellow cheeses in Moscow, you could eat the rind too, thereby breaking all the rules. Thereafter, cheeses with increasingly aggressive smells began to appear on our table, which frightened Russian guests and filled the fridge with an unbearably sweet smell — cheeses like *Pont l'eveque*.

In our family, the war between two powerful gastronomic systems consisted of attack, defence and counter-attack. A rare beef steak is being fried in the kitchen. Along with a glass of red wine, it puts Klava's cutlets in the shade. The meat grinder falls silent, but some dry black crackers suddenly appear on the left side. We can't resist them. The black crackers are associated, in our family, not with penal colonies, but with nostalgia for Borodinsky bread. Our whole family is nostalgic about it. Whenever there is cause for celebration, grandma sends us white, tightly sewn little bags of black crackers with a violet inscription written in indelible ink: *To V.I. Erofeyev*. Father and I walk around sucking on them; they crumble into tiny crumbs in our pockets. Yet one day, a baguette with a crunchy crust, as lively as a crank, joins battle with a sliced Moscow loaf costing 12.50, crushing it, and only those white Moscow wheatmeal loaves, those ladies' handbags sprinkled with flour, preserve their remote superiority. After a while the first salad is served — so long, *Stolichny* salad with mayonnaise! — that green salad with tomatoes and raw mushrooms, topped with olive oil and white wine vinegar, which still leaves Moscow ambivalent to this day. Marching against the French are salted gherkins, boiled potatoes, salted saffron milk caps, sauerkraut, lightly salted salmon — or aren't you a true Russian? — the *hors d'oeuvres* disrupt Napoleon's plans, and the crab salad with green gherkins and peas wins the day. It's the battle of Borodino all over again: a pork chop is trying to fight off a slice of duck breast. Wow! This chapter ought to be written on an empty stomach, so that the battle is authentic, honorable and fair. The most notable triumph of French cuisine in our household, however, is *pommes frites*. A special set of crockery is procured for it, which we christened with a family neologism: we called it a *fritnitsa* (the word later entered the Russian language as a *frityurnitsa*). We chop the potatoes up into long soapy slices, put them into the cage, then suspend the cage in some boiling oil. The whole building smells of fries. Steak, fries and Bordeaux — it's enough to challenge even the *pelmeni*. Russian fried potatoes, which always get slightly burnt in the frying pan, take a back-seat. I feel as if I am forty years ahead of my time. Mama buys a leek-peeler. A new soup finds its way into our home: poireau pomme-de-terre. With crunchy croutons and sour cream. I recently explained how to make it on the TV show *Smak*, but the rest of the country clearly didn't back me up.

Mama goes one step further. She tries everything. She tries snails from Alsace and classic French onion soup (not to be confused with leek soup); she loves oysters; she adores all types of fish, particularly lemon sole. Papa doesn't eat oysters. Like Sobakevich, he knows what their appearance reminds him of. So mama breaks away from papa in her love of French cuisine; her gastronomic liberalism knows no bounds, with the exception of frogs. She says they have an unpleasant, fishy smell, which is somewhere between chicken and fish; she finds it an "absurdity" (her favorite expression) when people claim their thighs are tender and juicy, but perhaps that is just her Russian fastidiousness coming through. It is with frogs that a line is drawn, and the Russian people's Francophilia stumbles.

I understand the fury of my undernourished fellow clansmen, who have not had sufficient affection in their lives, and who start to howl: go to hell (another phrase papa never used, incidentally), and take those damn frogs of yours with you! Their hatred of me is genuine, and very acute. In their broken lives, they have managed to find meaning without frogs or poireau pomme-de-terre, and remained true to it. They all managed to find an explanation for it, to justify it. I am glad they managed to do so. I try to stay as far away from them as I can. I have dual citizenship when it comes to culture. It has been formed from the everyday semiotics, the invisible trifles, which have got into my blood. It is this dual citizenship that entitles me to say that Russia does not belong to Europe: she is of a different nature, a nature that is often hostile to Europe.

In addition to our family, there are hundreds of other Soviets at the embassy, the trade delegation, the consulate and the other Soviet institutions. They too wander around Paris, sometimes going so far as to make a few purchases. But their main objective is to save money. They save money at every opportunity. When you look back on it, you think to yourself: why was it that my parents were born again, and absorbed Europe into their systems, whilst others — the overwhelming majority — remained completely unchanged, dressed the same way they had dressed in Moscow, and took turns to have their hair cut at home on a stool in the kitchen, smoking long Soviet cigarettes (father, who often smoked in those days, immediately switched to the French way of doing things, and smoked *tabac de troupe* — strong Gallic army tobacco)? Where had my parents picked up this predisposition for being reborn?

Many years later, various people loved to repeat two things to me over and over again: my rebellious nature stemmed from my not having received sufficient love (from mama), and my worldview stemmed from my childhood years in Paris. The first idea is nonsense: mama's hysterical concern for me, her darling, awoke my capabilities, which had lain too deep within me for too long, and pushed out my laziness. Mama's astonishing ability, which was perfected over time, to say nasty things to the people she loved (among others), to their face, often left her daughters-in-law shocked, but set me back on my feet. The second thing is the absolute truth, although it has its own particular hue. If you count the children, rather than the adults, then there were quite a lot of us at the Soviet school near the Bois de Bouloigne. But none of them were as smitten by Paris as I was. I hardly ever met those little Soviet Parisians again in later life — and as for the two or three that I did run into, I couldn't find it in me to suspect them of high treason. If my parents experienced a rebirth in Paris, then I'm afraid to say I went one step further. In Paris, I betrayed my country, in a way that was to last the rest of my life. What I betrayed was not the Moscow of my childhood, which exists only for me, but a country in which I never felt I had been accepted, in spite of all my efforts at the outset. I betrayed my country without even noticing: freely and easily.

•

To this day I still can't work out how it happened. France had got to me to a very small extent. I lived on the very edge of France, but it penetrated me fully and completely, and flooded my being. In his position as a cultural attaché, father was able to travel around the country on his own. We went to the Cannes film festival. We stayed in little French hotels along the way. For breakfast we used to have croissants with strawberry or apricot jam, and a *café au lait*. That proved sufficient.

I went to school at a Soviet elementary school in Paris. It was a very strange, informal place, with two year groups studying in each room: the first-years and third-years in one room, and in the other: the second-years and the fourth-years. On one occasion, the writer Valentin Kataev came to visit us, with a friendly look on his face, of the kind you might see in an affectionate cartoon (cartoons of writers were very popular at the time). They had clearly forced him to come and see us. The schoolchildren were kicking up a din, as quietly as they could, but I leaned on the table with my fist against my temple and began to listen to him attentively. The author of *Son of the regiment* was telling us about something that looked like a long black cat:

"Only you're too young to understand what I mean."

I can remember the cat and his words, "too young to understand" —I can't remember the rest. He was the first writer to come wandering into my life by chance, with that long black cat of his. The two female teachers spent half the lesson with the little ones and half with the older ones. They never awarded the lowest marks. Kirilla Vasilievna was not just a teacher — she was also the principal. I had a secret crush on her. In addition to her, I was also secretly in love with some girl in the year above me, whose name I forget. When that girl left the school, I fell in love with another, whose name also escapes me, and who was also in the year above me. A bus picked the schoolchildren up in the courtyard of the embassy in rue de Grenelle.

"Have you taken off your ties?" the driver asked.

We used to wear red ties, but during the journey across Paris to school they made us take them off: the embassy staff were afraid of reprisals against Soviet children. To begin with I wore an artificial tie: it was an artificial dark-red color, and had been sewn by Klava using French material. It looked more like a cowboy's bandana, and when grandma sent me a real one from Moscow it was a real cause for celebration: I never cherished my pioneer's tie so much as I did when I was in Paris. We had been brought up as pioneers, but we had involuntarily become ever so slightly rusty on the ideological front, and when we drove through Paris and along the Champs-Élysées, we gazed in admiration at the big American cars with their 'fangs'. That was the word we used to describe their bumpers: we were convinced that if there was an accident, these 'fangs' would come out of their own accord and chomp through the enemy car.

The children used to play in the courtyard of the embassy. We had minimal interaction with the French. Sometimes mama and I would go to the Tuileries gardens, but it was pretty boring there: there was nothing to do but eat ice cream, whereas in the Luxembourg Gardens I could spend hours launching the little sailing boats that were available for rent, in the pond. Mama sat down on a green chair covered in lace, which was so heavy that it had to be dragged along, gnashing at the gravel and leaving tracks, to the right spot. Back then, metal chairs had to be paid for; some elderly ladies with retentive memories went round collecting people's money in a bowl: we used to take one between two, as I didn't need to sit down: hanging over the low stone parapet, I was following my little sailing boat intently. The clock on the facade of the Luxembourg palace was always fast; time here flew by with a whistle, picking up the breeze and rustling the red, scorched leaves from the tall chestnut trees, which had been raked, and knocking over the statues of French kings, who were watching over me from afar — no sooner had we arrived than dusk began to fall, and mama closed the book she was reading, folded up her paper and shoved her magazine into her bag: it was time to go home. That moment when time seemed to stand still, when, as you throw yourself ever deeper into your favorite pastime, you forget about everything, was my way of communicating with the eternity of childhood, which consisted of endless flights of fancy.

Diplomats' children weren't allowed to attend French schools back then. Only journalists' children were able to do so. I was taught French by an elderly Armenian lady, who for some reason was allowed into the embassy's dressing room, in spite of the fact that she was an emigrée. I had private lessons with her in a bare little room (it was probably used as a meeting room) next to the corridor: she would turn up with French children's books full of striking pictures. Something extraordinary came over the children in there: they ran around so furiously, fell over so tastefully (at this point the girls' skirts would fly up, and you could see their white underwear), wept so arrestingly — large tears rolling down their cheeks — and were so unselfconscious, that by comparison the Russian children in books seemed to me to be unreal, like cardboard cut-outs. But I did not have all that many lessons with the Armenian, and, unlike my younger brother, I don't speak French fluently. Of the French I learned in my childhood, a single, cherished word remains. With this word I inadvertently insulted Khrushchev's Soviet interpreter, Dubinin, who, when he heard I was learning French, said to me:

"Go on then, say something in French."

He was subordinate to papa at the time, and treated me with an accentuated level of attention.

"*Coccinelle*," I said, shyly.

"What?"

"*Coccinelle*." My embarrassment deepened. I consisted of pathological shyness in the same way that a gherkin consists of water.

I sensed a wave of confusion running over the high, handsome brow of Russia's future ambassador to France, who, in 1991, came down so determinedly, and with such clear relief, in favor of the putsch against Gorbachev.

"Holy cow," I muttered.

•

On Sundays tents were put up at one end of the Champs-Élysées and a MARK STAMPET was set up. This was the most important MARK STAMPET of my life. In actual fact it was a stamp market, but in my over-excited state I used to get the words mixed up. Mama gave me 100 francs in pocket money each week — hardly anything really. Money was used to regulate my behavior. If I behaved badly I didn't get any money. When I saved up I was able to buy myself either toy soldiers, Dinky cars or stamps. Naturally, I wanted the lot.

I was only a dilettante when it came to stamps — the things I can say about it bear no real relation to philately. My parents and I used to go and buy stamps for me together. The packaging varied depending on the price: there were either large, transparent envelopes, which usually contained pale stamps depicting Marianne holding a flag, and other French stamps, with a few German, Belgian, Dutch and Spanish stamps — showing Franco's fat, thick-set profile — mixed in, and from time to time some pre-revolutionary Russian stamps with the two-headed eagle — or small envelopes, which contained whole series. Expensive stamps could only be bought on an individual basis, and were too expensive for me. If you wanted to you could buy up a whole load of cheap ones in one go, which was what my parents cautiously advised me to do, then spend the whole day sticking them into an album, with the hereditary patience that had been passed down to me from my grandpa — a bookkeeper at the October Railway — and my mother's mother Serafima Mikhailovna — an accountant from Novgorod. Alternatively you could buy some stamps showing the British colonies, and choke with happiness. I adored stamps from the British colonies, depicting the king or the new Queen Elizabeth II, wearing her crown, in a circle. Some island named St Helena sent me into raptures, and the power of speech deserted me — not that I spoke very well in the first place. But what I loved above all were stamps from the Portuguese colonies, depicting the fish, butterflies and fauna of Angola and Mozambique. To this day, I think of these countries as brightly colored stamps, which overcame the socialist misfortunes that later beset them. I loved the diversity of the stamps that came from tiny, dwarf-like states: San Marino, a place I later visited for the sole reason that I had once collected its stamps; Monaco, Liechtenstein and Andorra. I always fell for the simplest of tweaks in design: I loved the triangular stamps made in Mongolia, and stamps with no teeth along the edges — they seemed to me to come almost from the age of the dinosaurs.

My parents bought me folders and stamp catalogs. In a two-volume, detailed catalog, inscribed with a small typeface, I sought out the stamps I had bought and registered them, drawing a horizontal line in blue pencil under the description of the stamp: bought. The notion of buying all the stamps in the world seemed to me to be achievable. Essentially, I was buying up the world, and I was not much bothered about whether the stamp had been franked or not. I put the best stamps in the album using little transparent stickers (the stamps occasionally came unstuck); the ones in the folders had a tougher time of it — they were kept tidily but in groups, like passengers in economy class.

My collecting led me to a rational objective, which made my parents happy. The world had become a place that was familiar to me — it had come through the stamps and remained in me forever. My sense of oneness with the world transformed me from a little cosmopolitan, who was able to appraise his country objectively, into a young rationalist capable of working out his political views. The Soviet stamps which grandma sent from Moscow evoked mixed feelings in me. I wanted to like them, and was initially inclined to do so, in the same way that Americans treat their guests: they don't look for their flaws, or try to seek them out — they put them on a pedestal, and it is only later that the slow descent begins. The Soviet stamps featured the world of letters and financial symbols that I could understand: the sight of rubles and kopecks made me happy. I was even happier about the fact that I was able to recognize the people, places and events depicted on them: Pushkin, Tchaikovsky, Chkalov, Red Square, the storming of the Winter Palace — that was all wonderful. But ultimately they conveyed seriousness, maturity, constraint, a feeling of repetition, a sense of fatigue. They were pedagogical stamps, which had to be reckoned with. The little ones were too faceless. The ones that celebrated anniversaries, and featured portraits of public figures, were boring reproductions of paintings. They were not a patch on the butterflies from the Portuguese colonies, which were far more interesting than the gloomy Portuguese stamps themselves.

The 'mark stampet' at the end of the Champs-Élysées drew me in like a magnet. The stories I dreamt up to try and entice my parents to take me there! The boy in the blue French beret had ceased to exist. He had turned into a passion, pure and simple. I loved the French fairground rides, loved practicing at the shooting gallery; I was such a good shot that the owners of the shooting gallery had it in for me because of the number of prizes I managed to win. But I wouldn't say I loved the mark stampet, or adored it; it was more than that — I idolized it. It was my childhood religion. I used to gaze at the counters and stands with a pale, withdrawn look. Stamps were my sex, my creativity, my all. From that time forward, my life turned into a series of magnets. When I found myself living in Paris again as a student, I used to go to the Russian bookshops with the same manic zeal. The store that was most out of bounds, YMCA-press, which sold astounding anti-Soviet literature, and across from which the KGB, as I was informed in an effort to intimidate me, had rented an apartment so that they could spy on the customers, cropped up in my dreams for years: I was walking towards it, getting closer and closer. The mark stampet brought my innate manic zeal to the surface.

•

As he extracted from the world of culture only the political roots, father set about the struggle against the West so actively in Paris that the French intelligence agencies gave him the title of 'spy'. The French ambassador, Froman-Meris, who was my father's partner at the Quai d'Orsay at the time, gave me an unfriendly assessment of him many years later, as a tough, obstinate diplomat.

Paris was at the time aglow with world-famous stars: father skilfully befriended all the right people. He has on his conscience Yves Montand's tour of Moscow following the events in Hungary in 1956, which caused indignation among many French people. Father knew Picasso fairly well, and used to go and see him on the Côte d'Azur, but he took far greater pride in the fact that he managed to rescue a granite bust of Lenin, made by a French sculptor whose identity was unknown; the leader of the revolution subsequently spent many years gathering dust in the 'red room' at the embassy. In father's eyes, the biggest enemies were the Americans. Once, on a pleasure cruise along the Seine, with music playing in the background, we were standing on deck next to some uncouth guys in colorful shirts, holding glasses of beer and speaking loudly in English.

"Careful! They're American soldiers in *civvies*," my father warned me sternly.

I was nine at the time — and I looked at these enemies on leave with a holy terror.

At the same time, father was too much in love with life not to appreciate the charm of the fog and sunshine of Paris. He possessed an inherent delicacy, which did not sit well with his ideology. There was no totalitarian regime in my family. And, essentially, that was what led to my father's ruin.

•

I was a god of war. I played at toy soldiers with such inspiration that it was probably the first manifestation of my muse, which couldn't find a more worthy application in my childhood, in which I was never close to the kind of family set-up in which children demonstrate that they are gifted from an early age, and have all eyes on them, so that the child can one day be declared a young genius. My military muse appeared to me on the dining room floor, under the round dinner table in our apartment in Paris. I had two armies ranged against one another: their fate was determined by how accurate I was with a rubber band which flew from my thumb or from a pencil. I performed the neutral role of chance. Victory by one side or the other was never predetermined.

The Russian toy soldiers of that time, which I had bought in Moscow, had their legs together and their arms by their sides. They were all roughly hewn, in a bureaucratic way, and positioned on identical round stands. The only soldier that looked different from the others was the standard-bearer, with his red standard, but before long the green paint had peeled off on his uniform, too, revealing a gray, metallic nudity.

In France you could buy various types of soldiers. There was no such thing as political correctness back then, and you could play at cowboys and Indians. They were made using the same type of plastic, but it was clear whose side you were supposed to be on. The Indians had slightly hooked noses, bows and tomahawks. Their terrifying, painted faces were twisted with rage. You were left in no doubt that they were the enemy. The cowboys, on the other hand, with their red shirts and lassos, and pistols or rifles in their outstretched hands, were heroic guys with impudent smiles on their faces. Some of them even rode horses, valiantly. The cowboys and Indians were never discussed by my parents, but they were just what I needed: victory in the war was aesthetically predetermined.

I was utterly ambivalent about the soldiers from the Napoleonic wars, which were expertly crafted. I was not yet mature enough to have an interest in history, and didn't feel like playing around with the past. I wanted tanks, not cannons and cannonballs. I liked the modern French soldiers. They were mobile and plastic, and their skin seemed almost alive, but somehow the plastic was too light, and knocking them over with a rubber band was a piece of cake. I can picture the metallic French commander vividly (I used to call him the captain), in his green-and-brown uniform and helmet, with the French tricolor on one side. He is marching into battle, holding a pistol in his right hand. He has bushy black eyebrows — perhaps *too* big — which bother me a little. In every other respect he is an icon of war. Charging into battle behind him are some more simply-dressed soldiers, but they are armed with machine guns, grenade-launchers and all kinds of vehicles, including jeeps. The Soviet idols kill them in vast numbers — but when they die it is of no consequence. The French army, led by the captain, demonstrates a capacity to be flexible.

I used to fire the rubber band by turns first at one group, then at the other — and they would charge, taking cover behind the legs of the chairs. Soldiers who fell over were considered dead, whilst any that fell 'halfway over' were considered wounded: they might have fallen against a tank, or against one of their comrades in arms. Wounded soldiers had to sit out three turns before entering the fray once again. I spent whole days on end playing these war games, lost to the world, as if I was rehearsing my predetermined fate, forgetting to do my homework, have dinner or sleep, and dreaming of one thing only: that my parents would leave me in peace. Sometimes the war required a huge number of soldiers, and chess pieces were called up as reservists. Split into black pieces and white pieces, they went into battle on the same terms as the soldiers, as harbingers of cosmic wars.

I shot the elastic band impartially, in the same way that I played chess against myself, but occasionally, when my favorite captain fell over on his oval stand, I would make concessions, pretending that he had merely fallen onto his arm, and was therefore wounded rather than dead. I held the Soviet troops dear because of the banner they carried, but in the depths of my soul I was rooting for the French. Had the French soldiers been not quite so well-crafted, I would not have been able to find so much common ground with them. Had France not had such a delicious aroma, and had it not been such a homely country, I would have become a Soviet.

•

As he sits down to write his autobiography, the Russian writer, with his invincible musty armpits, has one objective: to paint himself as a star hanging from a Christmas tree. Other writers are merely the additional toys that are hung up lower down the tree, and which fall from the branches but stay intact, bouncing high off the floor, impudently.

Unlike other countries with a claim on originality, Russia considers itself not just a bearer of unique values, but also a great nation which lights up the world with the rays of universal truth. Russia can also take pride in the Russian writer who, whilst claiming to be of global significance, remains in the shadows — but the moment he finds himself in the arena of fame, there comes fluttering out of him not a butterfly but a dinosaur, which declares itself tsar of all the animals.

"I recognize neither the philosophers of the West, nor the wise men of the East," says the Russian writer. "I belong to the Russian God."

The Russian God transforms the writer's autobiography into a fatalistic loop of divine order. But the loop presses down too hard on his head. Either suffer it in silence or cry out. The Russian writer is never in a serene state. He is raised above everyone else. It is not his lot to penetrate the dual world of chance and law, to hear their musical rhythm. He does not master chance. He rushes around. The chaos becomes condensed, and turns into a picture resembling a cloud, assuming the forms of a dolphin or a bear, depending on personal preference, and then being transformed once again into a shapeless fog. But if there really is anything original in the Russian world, it is not the fuel vapor, but the refraction of will and absurdity, of law and of good fortune — the secret hints at the latent flow of life.

•

Soviet clowns and ballerinas, writers and artists, musicians and actors — these were my father's clients in Paris. My father was like Cerberus. With a single coded message to Moscow referring to political unreliability, he had the power to ruin an artist's life and leave it destined for failure. He was an important, dangerous figure. People fawned over him and sought his friendship.

Papa thought they were genuinely trying to befriend him, and some of them, like Leonid Kogan, did indeed go on to become friends of his, finding in him a confidant. Papa went to Paris with Kogan to buy an exceptional violin of some sort, and his vivid description of the great care with which the violinist listened to the instrument leads me to believe that there came a time when papa would readily have acknowledged the world was governed by something other than politics.

There was clearly a reason, however, why Molotov believed that anyone who was active in the arts was tinged with decay, and that any attempt to make friends with such people could be dangerous. Cerberus must be cajoled if you are to slip into that intimate world, which the great Soviet musicians, even if they did not admit it, loved more than their own motherland, and certainly more than their state. Their passions in life were incompatible: papa's great passion in life was tennis, which he had begun to play before we came to Paris, whereas they were great lovers of music; and it goes without saying that they played with him, and used him, picking up the secrets of the authorities, from behind their barricade, as they did so.

When Rostropovich and I were preparing to put on Schnittke's opera *Life with an idiot* in Amsterdam, in 1992, he spoke to me in complimentary terms about my father, expressing delight in him as a man who broke the mold of the Soviet bastard. It was gratifying to hear this, and I called my father in Moscow, sending him Rostropovich's regards; he was proud to receive them. To him, this greeting from Rostropovich was a sign that his life had been a success. Unlike my mama, he never had much of an ear for music: I never saw him putting on a classical music record of his own accord, for his own pleasure: at best he thought of music as a backing track to life, but Rostropovich's friendship was a boost to his vanity.

I invited my parents to the premiere of the opera. I know what they thought of this opera in their heart of hearts; but when the Queen of Holland got to her feet to begin a standing ovation after the final curtain, I knew what their reaction would be. At the banquet papa bumped into Rostropovich, and they exchanged ardent kisses a short distance from me, almost on the lips, clapping one another on the shoulder and entering into some gleeful repartee. Rostropovich flew on to the next person, then went all round the room, kissing everyone, before bumping into me:

"Hello there, where's your father? I should like to see him!"

"You just kissed him!"

"When?"

"Just now!"

Rostropovich frowned, trying to remember, but he couldn't, and a moment later he was nowhere to be seen. The next morning papa told me how warmly Rostropovich had greeted him.

Papa protected the Soviet artists from a descent into sin, and seduced the French ones. My parents were intoxicated by their friendship with Montand and Signoret. Photographs of them together at the actors' villa on a warm, sunny day are among the most treasured items in my parents' memory bank. Their friendship with Montand ended in very peculiar fashion. When he successfully talked him into going to Moscow following the events that took place in Hungary, father saw this as a personal victory.

Various interpretations can be put on what happened next. Moscow went into raptures when Montand arrived. For the weary Muscovites, who did not understand a whole lot about the Hungarian Revolution, his arrival was a sign not of Soviet ideological cunning but of the post-Stalinist thaw. Looking at it objectively, Montand's presence in Moscow worked in favour of the liberalization of Russia. Khrushchev attended the concert that he gave with his entourage, and it was transformed into a political demonstration. Montand returned to France feeling as though he had been tricked. For many years my parents told me, with annoyance, that he had had problems with his performances for the radio, and producing records, and that he had been boycotted — that was how they punished him — and that Montand, who could almost be described as a communist in his politics, had been forced, like Shalamov in the Literary gazette, to defend himself for his Kolyma tales in the right-wing *Le Figaro*. On his return, his friendship with my parents cooled dramatically.

After the Soviet intervention in Czechoslovakia, Simone Signoret wrote a book with my father's name in the title: *Farewell, Volodya*. It may be that he was a symbol of her split from the communists. Montand became an anti-Soviet and starred in *The Confession*. He brought the film to Moscow during the Gorbachev era. Father attended the première, so that he could catch up with his old friend. He caught Montand's eye after the concert. Unlike Rostropovich, Montand recognized him — and one can probably imagine why. Both men had grown old but still held themselves well, though they both had vapid eyes that spoke of old age. Russia had changed by that time, too. Montand waved his hand from a distance and, surrounded by a throng of people, said loudly: *A bientôt! A bientôt!* *but didn't go over to him, invite him to the banquet, embrace him or kiss him. Papa went home feeling upset. The subject of Montand's friendship was carefully removed from the list of acceptable topics of conversation in our family.

●

Whenever I'm in Paris I step into Notre Dame, light two candles 'for good health' and, like an overweight merchant woman, ask God to grant my parents a long life and good health. They turned their backs on You due to historical circumstances, but they are old now, and they need understanding, affection and God's kindness. I walk along the embankment past the booksellers' stalls, where you can buy magazines from the fifties: their covers, so scandalous when they first appeared, now seem like something from a quiet backwater — and suddenly it all comes back to me again. Our family was decayed by the Impressionists (mama had taken a liking to them back in the late 1930s, in Moscow). There was a reason the Soviet art historian Kemenov struggled against them until his dying day. Perhaps justifiably, he felt that they were undermining the concept of objective truth, destroying the fabric of meaning and exaggerating the effect of chance. Kemenov was working in Paris in those days,

---

* See you soon (*fr.*).

for UNESCO; he loved Benoit, and used to play a city-naming game with my parents when they went on walks:

"Kaluga!"

"Alma-Ata!"

"Krasnoyarsk!"

"Enemaville!" Kemenov said.

We all burst out laughing, me included, but my parents stopped inviting him round after that: he was a sly old devil, and might discover mama's secret love of Monet. Long before I discovered the early works of Mayakovsky, my first (and last) idol, a picture of whom hung above the door in my room and who was a legitimate idol on the face of it, but a deeply disruptive one on the inside, the Impressionists, and then Van Gogh, Gauguin, Modigliani *et al* — had all tempted me. If it weren't for them I would probably have been ended up at the Institute of International Relations, and dreamed of becoming a Foreign Minister — I might even, perhaps, have become one. But those artists knocked me off the straight and narrow, cleaned out my mind and set me on a road leading straight to the abyss. Then, on top of that, along came the Cubists, the Abstractionists and the Surrealists. My mother introduced me to the Impressionists when I was very young. You didn't need to read what they had to say, and master it: you fell for them at first sight. They fell neatly into the rhyme scheme of my poppies outside Paris, my Seine, my Marne, and my chestnut trees and sycamores.

•

The more time I spend on this book, the murkier my understanding of the contradictions of my parents becomes — both the secret ones and the ones that were self-evident. I know what they are: they are the UFO in my life. Analyzing your parents is a form of intellectual incest. No matter which demons preyed (as my mama likes to put it) on my soul, I always found dozens of reasons not to delve into my parents' secrets. I don't know my parents very well, and that doesn't bother me in the slightest. How am I to know why they submitted to European taste so quickly, and why the stamp of Europe chose to make its mark specifically on them?

In addition to food and clothes, Europe slowly but surely began to win them over with its lifestyle choices. Papa began playing tennis, and forgot about chess altogether. He bought rackuets made by Dunlop and Slazenger and stocked up on fluffy branded tennis balls; he bought white shorts and a white polo shirt with a green crocodile on the chest. Equally significant was his purchase of an eight-millimetre video camera. To begin with it was the tourist version, in keeping with the thaw, but later, by all accounts, a moment of enlightenment was supposed to arrive. The camera involuntarily demanded that you make a decision: what should you film, and why?

Amateur home movies are like a war on death. My parents' place is full up to this day with little reels of narrow film. I haven't looked at them for ages (our old projector is broken), but for many years we had a set routine: after having lunch with our visitors, father would take the collapsible silver screen into the dining room and load the reels into the machine, and the chirruping of the ritual screening of short amateur movies would begin, featuring the chateaux of the Loire, Fontainebleau and other French architectural wonders with green lawns. Papa never made any videos in Russia. I can see myself now, angular and pale-faced, in my French beret, with an angular smile — an ever-present character in these movies. By comparison with the sturdy examples set by my parents' friends, I was always somehow *different* — an object that was slipping out of reach, like my handwriting, which had dozens of hues but had long since been abandoned because of the advent of the computer. Father bought a little editor's table with a screen on it, and spent hours at it in the evening, cutting and pasting. At first the films were black-and-white, with mid-range and long-distance shots. There were hardly any close-ups — father didn't want to invade people's personal space. I never saw him shouting, stamping his feet or losing his cool. One of his undoubted strengths was his self-control, which I inherited in far less fundamental form. I wouldn't say he was a particularly good cameraman or film director. Father entertained the idea of self-knowledge, but perhaps never accepted it in full. He was clearly interested not in art but in the objects themselves, the collection of what he had seen, an unacknowledged account of a *life lived*, and only in its weakest form — the fact that he was the chosen one. He never filmed anything daring, and on one occasion, after being given a thin strip of film by the short-sighted Galina Fyodorovna, who clearly amused him, from her trip to Mali, he ruthlessly cut out, on the editing table, an African shaking his penis in front of the camera — to the great regret of those who had gathered at the house to watch the film.

Our home cinema cut my family off from the world of the embassy: we lived within ourselves and for ourselves.

We often played music as we watched the home videos, and Europe won out here, too. Unlike the low-ranked embassy employees, who listened to Leshchenko on the quiet — his music was by then only semi-prohibited, rather than prohibited — my parents, who didn't like bravado, preferred to listen to French songs instead. They adored Edith Piaf. They listened to Brassens, too. Then came Aznavour and many others. My parents became great friends with Yves Montand and Simone Signoret (another of the powerful initiation tests of France was meeting people like that, but I hardly ever saw him: I wasn't introduced to such figures). My parents never got into jazz. We were never lucky enough to have Frank Sinatra sing for us at home, but French chansons were our common pastime. To this day I sometimes find myself singing a little refrain:

Marjolenne, tu es si jolie… —

at first I can't recall the words, then I remember them again, almost to the very last line.

•

Life at the embassy was countrified — it was the patriarchal life of the landowning gentry. Chickens and roosters were pretty much the only things missing. All manner of people scurried about the courtyard, from maids and code-breakers to low-level KGB officers and chauffeurs, and the supply manager would come in looking run off his feet. Overseeing all of this, with his hands in his trouser pockets, shifting his weight from one leg to the other, in the Soviet style, was the baron, Sergei Alexandrovich Vinogradov: a diplomat more by luck than design, he had been pushed out of the construction trade and ended up in diplomacy. His face, with its bushy, fair eyebrows shone with success and glory. In the conversations my father had with his friends at home — my parents were friends with two couples in Paris: a big jovial chap who was the correspondent for *Pravda* in Paris (a fact of which I was aware), and a middling KGB officer (a fact of which I was unaware), the handsome Lodik – the word *ambassador* was sacred. In my childhood consciousness, as I sat at the table, a certain Enes was able to compete with him: both names were uttered in hushed tones. But Enes, it seemed to me, was less important than the Ambassador, though he too was a person of considerable esteem. I did not feel like penetrating the grown-ups' secrets: I had my own to worry about, and only years later did I work out that Enes — N.S. — stood for N.S. Khrushchev. Yevgenia Alexandrovna carried herself even more regally than her husband, and spoke in a breathless voice, throwing her head back. Blessed with the appearance of a tsaritsa, she had been a Latvian electrician in her youth. Whenever the ambassador and his wife began to get bored late in the evening, they would invite my parents round to watch French TV. The ambassador ate nuts and drank beer, and often spoke directly to the newscaster.

"You're telling a pack of lies, mate!" He pointed his finger threateningly, and knitted his brows. "We've got you sussed, you American stooge!"

"He can't hear you, you know!" Yevgenia Alexandrovna admonished him.

He turned to look at her unhurriedly and maintained an eloquent silence. Like many of the wives of people in positions of great responsibility, she derived pleasure from the fact that she alone was capable of controlling her husband. Taking a ride in their swanky Citroën DS was more than I could bear.

When Sergei Alexandrovich was behind the wheel, she would shout at him:

"What are you doing, chasing that French idiot like that!"

Sergei Alexandrovich once again maintained an eloquent silence. My parents weren't sure who would have the upper hand in the end, and nodded their heads indeterminately — but their remarks weren't taken into account in any case.

Mama experienced suffered a considerable amount of pain as she was reborn as a European woman. She suffered bouts of melancholy due to being in a constant state of over-excitement, and would start getting annoyed and weeping for no apparent reason, lying down on the bed and closing her eyes as if she was dead. The telephone rang. In those days the telephones rang with a sharp, urgent sound. Black and heavy (yet brittle, too: it wouldn't have survived being dropped on the floor), father's telephone stood in pride of place in the dining room, on the shelf above the fireplace, with a taut little dial and a large, gleaming bell, and was reflected in the antique mirror above the fireplace, like the spare wheel placed on the trunk of many of the cars from that era.

The telephone was father's boss, and he rushed over to it in order to report for duty: "Erofeyev!" Mama crawled out of bed.

"Well, are you coming?" I heard Yevgenia Alexandrovna's voice saying.

"We've already gone to bed."

"That doesn't matter — you can get up again!"

If the telephone had rung in a more amicable, ingratiating way, she might perhaps have obeyed, but at that moment a form of dual violence kicked in. In her depressed state, she felt it was beneath her to give in to him. This night-time refusal was not without its consequences in father's fate. It was probably the first barrier that was erected between him being 'one of ours' and 'not one of ours'. Those who are truly 'one of us' never say no, even on their death bed.

When Stalin, Voroshilov and Molotov called on Gorky as he lay dying — possibly after being poisoned on the leader's orders — the writer got such an adrenaline rush that he stayed alive for another week. The dual organism of my parents ceased to maintain the required levels of adrenalin: they forgot, in their haste, about the career ladder, like an actor's nervous trembling before a performance, the fear felt by civil servants, which — as mama observed on several occasions — had caused the wife of the Soviet resident spy in Paris to have quivering lips and bowed legs when she curtsied for the former Latvian Yevgenia Alexandrovna: my parents were kept away not only from televised events but also from intimate receptions, where the great and the good of the ambassadorial world mingled — they began to lag behind in the race for power.

But my parents, somewhere deep down inside, had cracked as a family unit. Mama, who, thanks to having lived with my father, had an awareness of the scale of both people and events, with that uniquely female ingratitude which often causes successful men to suffer, as if it is a metaphysical revenge for what they have accomplished, fostered a treacherous scorn for my father in her heart of hearts, because he was a civil servant.

"What am I to do with him? He's a *civil servant*," she later said to me on numerous occasions, fully aware of the insulting estrangement from real men that this Chekhovian term implied.

She was not satisfied with what father's intellect had to offer: through the misty smoke she dreamed, if not of a poet, then at the very least of a humanitarian academic, a learned reader of novels.

The subcutaneous individualism of the Impressionists, who influenced mama — their ranks were not swelled by Proust, whom she never quite mastered — was sufficient to prompt her to form her own impression of her husband: in the conservative Russian tradition this would have seemed disobedient at the very least, not to say downright illegal.

Papa, with an individualism of his own, which had been infused in him on the pastures of his career, clearly needed more adoration from his spouse, needed her to be more tactile.

His fate had economized on affection. My parents were already beginning to find that I was not enough. They urgently needed a second child. But the sad truth is that even if they had had ten children it wouldn't have been enough to bridge the internal rift between them. In the depths of her consciousness mama was convinced that the forecast was always going to be gloomy, that the sun would never emerge from behind the clouds. Dissatisfaction with the way the world behaved — with the exception of the Impressionists — had accumulated within mama, the subconscious theomachism of the atheist who is convinced there is no God. But as regards individualism, I had much in common with both of them.

On November 7th, the anniversary of the Revolution, Yevgenia Alexandrovna gathered all the children in the embassy together in the dark, ceremonial hall two hours before the gala reception. The tables were creaking under the weight of all the treats on offer. An assortment of wines and juices had been put out. We listened to the grown-ups congratulating us on this special day, and we were asked how our studies were going.

"OK..." the children from the embassy replied in woolly voices.

A fat-faced maid in a white apron stood by the window, a stupid smile on her face: one of these children unexpectedly showered with affection, was her very own Dima. Although no-one had got any bad marks, the children weren't given any treats at all. Feeling incredibly shy, I asked if I could have something to drink. Yevgenia Alexandrovna repeated my question:

"You want something to drink?"

I nodded, turning red at the thought of my request, but at the same time I felt subconsciously impudent, and very unlike the clean-shaven children of the chauffeurs and cipher clerks; I had an oversized head and was internally insatiable, and was hinting at a sandwich, at least. Turning her head to the side and pulling a white handkerchief from her sleeve, she addressed the maid, who had a frugal look on her face all of a sudden.

"Bring him some water."

They brought me a glass of tap-water. Soon afterwards, the maid was sent away to Moscow: she screeched at Yevgenia Alexandrovna like an animal, then flew into the ambassador's room and started yelling, because the embassy's doctor had not come to see her son Dima, who was suffering from a serious illness.

"Our children lack a natural sense of subordination," Yevgenia Alexandrovna complained to my mama, with a sigh.

•

My parents flogged me that very evening. The revolutionary celebrations at the embassy were characterized by church-like splendour. The huge gates of the embassy opened like the gates of an Orthodox altar, and a series of incredible cars drove one after the other into the world of the Soviet dream. It was considered fashionable to go to the Soviet embassy. Cars bearing flags, and cars with no flags, stopped in front of the semi-circular, ceremonial entrance, which combined rococo with GOELRO — the State Commission for the Electrification of Russia. Chauffeurs came scurrying out of the cars and opened the back doors, giving a half-bow: French people and other foreigners climbed out of them, looking sleek, like clever sea animals. I couldn't bear to miss this spectacle. The other children at the embassy and I were forbidden from leaving our apartments. But no-one was supervising us just then. Everyone was preoccupied with the work they were doing as part of the celebrations.

I ran down the side staircase of the luxurious town-house like a shadow, or rather, flew down the twisted bannister, opened the side-door into the courtyard and, hiding behind some big, polished cars, started watching the festivities, greedily. Essentially, this was a feast for my childhood voyeurism. My short games of chase and hide-and-seek, and my reckless desire to shoot diamond-studded old woman with a toy gun ended up causing considerable alarm among the embassy guards. They didn't grab me by the ear, but they followed my every move and reported back on me. It may be that Yevgenia Alexandrovna said something to my parents.

When I arrived back at our apartment that evening after a successful reception, covered in perfume and electrified by having come into contact with the great and the good (after receptions they usually lay in bed talking everything over, sharing their impressions and having a good laugh), my parents burst into the house noisily (they usually came in on their tip-toes, so as not to wake me).

I was already tucked up on the sofa-bed.

"Vitya!"

Silence.

"Vitya, are you asleep?"

There was something unpleasant in their tone, but, as someone who loved night-time conversations, I made the misjudgment of responding.

"I can't get off to sleep," I said, smiling insincerely — I had climbed quickly into bed on hearing their voices on the stairs.

They dragged me out of bed, stood me in front of them in my shorts and t-shirt, and flew into a rage. They shouted at me and burned with rage. I had never seen my parents enraged before — not both of them at the same time. Usually I only had to deal with one of them yelling at me at a time. But now they had turned into a pair of wild dogs in a dinner jacket and ball gown.

"Where's the belt?!" mama shouted, shoving me into their bedroom.

Papa tried to take off his belt, but the belt that was used for floggings wasn't part of his get-up for special occasions, and he stuck his head into the cupboard, looking for it among his ties. I watched him, hardly believing my eyes.

"Lie down!" my mother ordered.

"Where?" I said in surprise. "I won't lie down!"

"Why did you go into the courtyard? What did we tell you?!" my father said, pronouncing the verdict.

"So what if I did?" I said, still refusing to believe what I was seeing.

"What did I say: don't you dare!"

They grabbed hold of me, but I evaded them, in my half-naked state, and hid behind the curtain. Father caught hold of me, and I broke away, rushed back into the dining room and sprinted around the table, upturning the chairs in my haste; they came running after me. They were no longer my parents, with whom I could always reach an agreement. They had slipped out of character and departed from the track to which I was accustomed: they were now executing a government commission, they were hired executioners. Eventually they caught me. Mama took a painful grip on the arm, near the elbow, and dragged me back into the bedroom. I grabbed hold of the door post and they pulled me into the bedroom. My ears, hands and face were burning. They laid me out on my stomach on their double bed, and mama started to tear my shorts off violently, pulling them by the waistband. This was such a blatant violation of all the principles on which our family life was founded that I fell silent with horror. They feasted on my tiny body. I don't know whether or not they had been flogged when they were children, but it seemed as though they knew the fundamental principles of flogging thanks to some sort of historical memory, although in practice it turned out to be awkward, inept and clumsy: I broke away and crawled off the bed, only for them to catch me again, squeeze me, and press down on me. I started suffocating. The belt slashed my naked back.

"Hit him lower down," my mother's voice rang out.

The belt moved down to my naked butt — I started howling, and the tears came. My screams filled the whole apartment. I broke away and resisted with every fiber of my being: I had done nothing wrong. Whether they began to worry that they might wake the ambassador, or whether it was just that the punishment was over quickly, like when teenagers have sex for the first time, I was soon left in peace. I was no longer screaming, but howling into the bedclothes. They smelled like Omo detergent, the box for which used to contain multicolored glass balls — the dream of our whole Soviet school.

"Go to bed!"

I lay on my sofa-bed with its messy sheets, my butt all swollen, and no-one came to say sorry. They got into bed in treacherous silence and turned off the light in the bedroom — I was shaking after what they had done to me. I was overcome with anger, and cursed their public holiday festivities.

My parents had spoilt one of my most important pleasures. My disappointment in them was short-lived but deeply felt. This was the only flogging I received in my life. But it split my childhood world in two, opening up the account for my complaints about my parents. I began to live two parallel lives with them, the way a husband and wife usually live: when we were at peace there was one story to our relations, and when we were at war I can recall another list of events, which grew bigger with each new scandal. On the night of the flogging, I remembered something that was to happen many years later. I remembered how my papa, losing his self-control, ran into our kitchen in Moscow and demanded that Klava and mama immediately stop chopping up meat on the chopping board, which lay on the floor: that man Vinogradov had been living on the floor below us for some time, and papa had a cowardly fear of him. I recalled how, in that same Moscow apartment, left without a maid, mama did the vacuum-cleaning in my room in a foul mood, and — I can picture it now — the wire of the vacuum-cleaner became detached, and the vacuum cleaner kept howling of its own accord, and all of mama's actions were absurd, just like in a Charlie Chaplin movie. I start laughing, and she suddenly boils over and, not getting the joke, hits me across the face with all her might. Yevgenia Alexandrovna, who was over-excited by the reception too, shouted at the waiter in a terrifying voice:

"How dare you offer Duclos cigars after dinner? Are you out of your mind? He's a communist!"

The former electrician was an artist, too. She used to paint in the garden and at the ambassador's dacha outside Paris. Father praised her landscapes and still lifes cautiously.

"That cloud you painted — it's so life-like."

Yevgenia Alexandrovna turned around at the compliment, looking flattered and condescending. Many years later I happened to be at Yevgenia Alexandrovna's new apartment in Aleksei Tolstoy Street, an exclusive Soviet street, with Veslava. Yevgenia Alexandrovna took us to look at some paintings, breathlessly.

"Those ones are mine," she said, pointing at some oil paintings, "So are those; those are by Picasso, those are by Chagall and those are by Léger — the rest are mine."

The French loved them, supposedly. The Vinogradovs died — their apartment was burgled, I seem to remember. Then again, perhaps it wasn't. Everything has got mixed up and lost all importance.

•

"Have you heard the news? You've got a brother!"

I was running around a big meadow with some important aim, concentrated like a spring, when Kirilla Vasilievna grabbed me by the arm. I was taken aback by what she said. Not only was I unaware my brother had been born: I didn't even know mama was expecting. She had kept it so well hidden that I didn't suspect a thing. In my family, physiology was not so much forbidden as non-existent. There was no such thing as a naked mama. There was no such thing as a naked papa. They were always wearing something. It was impossible to imagine them with no clothes on. At the swimming pool papa got changed in a separate cubicle, like a true Frenchman. On one occasion, mama, when there was no hot water, called me into the bathroom to help her wash her hair, by pouring the hot water from the pan (back then, objects were used to perform functions that they were not designed for): I went into the bathroom in a panic, as if I was going down into the mausoleum again, afraid I might see her naked, but she was dressed in her underwear and had a bath-towel wrapped around her shoulders — that was as close to nudity as mama got. As for all the excretions, waste and dirtiness produced by the organism — none of that existed either, or else it existed in such small proportions (hair pulled from a comb and thrown into the toilet, for example) as to be insignificant. Blood was the only liquid produced by the organism that it was acceptable to take a closer look at in our family. My parents never had those life-saving conversations with me about the birds and the bees.

The Soviet colony was living it up in Mantes. We made the journey in buses and cars. In Mantes, May-meetings were held on the grass. In the summer, the children were sent to camps. It was here that I first started reading. Prior to that I couldn't bear it: I read haltingly, agonizing over where to put the letters in the syllables. Mama was horrified. But I got really carried away. During quiet time I read Jules Verne. Volume after volume. His collected works, in a dark blue binding. My intoxicating reading was an illicit activity. Literature was forbidden during quiet time. Supervisors wearing wolf masks used to come in. I hid Jules Verne under my pillow.

Kirilla Vasilievna looked at me with a curious expression. I said:

"I know."

I don't know why I said that. Perhaps because I was in love with her. Kirilla Vasilievna looked at me in surprise. Then mama, who had heard from Kirilla Vasilievna that I knew, looked at me with even greater surprise. But mama didn't ask how I knew. In my embarrassment, I ran into the overgrown cherry orchard.

•

A real Frenchman used to hang around there — a big guy with an absurd expression. I don't mean to offend the French, but in my opinion this boy was a half-wit. The two of us were able to communicate because we knew roughly the same number of French words.

"*Coccinelle?*"

"*Coccinelle!*"

But they weren't 'coccinelles' — they were a cross between ants and ladybugs — little 'firemen' with flat, spotted lids, which crawled all over the forest. The idiot and I collected these little firemen in empty matchboxes. He wanted to show me something. He was forever hitching up his pants. We lit a fire. I was scared to think that they were burning in their boxes, but I sat there with an imperturbable expression on my face.

Stories about the cherry orchard were rife at the camp. You weren't allowed to run there. It was said there were snakes. The idiot was clumsy, with hands like a gorilla's — I liked him. We became friends. We tore off the red and yellow cherries together, sitting in the trees. But occasionally he used to howl. He would come to a standstill in the middle of the orchard and start howling. On one occasion he made a fist with his left hand, and shoved the index finger of his right hand into the hole. I knew what he meant. A lot of people came here for that. He could show me where they did it. I pretended I wasn't much interested. I was proud to be friends with a Frenchman.

He decided, out of the goodness of his heart, to teach me to smoke. He pulled a crumpled blue pack of filterless cigarettes out of his pocket. For the first time, I held a cigarette in my lips, with my left hand in the pocket of my shorts, but I couldn't bring myself to start smoking. Crumbs of tobacco got into my mouth and pinched my tongue; my lips stuck to the tobacco paper and I couldn't tear them free. I was afraid lest smoking just one cigarette might have fatal consequences for my health. My imagination conjured up fearful images. My suspicions receded when I caught sight of a bottle of beer.

"Want some?"

"Yeah!"

We drank the beer straight from the bottle. I got scared again: what if idiocy was passed on through saliva? I pictured myself going back to camp as a clumsy idiot — with a cigarette in my mouth — and scaring Kirilla Vasilievna — she would start shouting — I would respond with an inhuman howl — the children would run away — Vitya Erofeyev has become a devil — I would crawl over to Kirilla Vasilievna, to kiss her on the lips — but what if he's the devil? — there was a reason his trousers kept falling down — there was a reason we weren't allowed to run in the cherry orchard — there was a reason we set fire to innocent children in matchboxes — *coccinelle* — our parents would arrive after getting a phone call, and I wouldn't even recognize them — Vitya! Vityusha! — you didn't love me enough — and for some reason brought my brother into the world — you spoiled him — bought a stroller for him — yes, I'm a devil — you've forgotten about me — I'll forget Russian, I'll stand here chattering away in French — do you believe in God? I burst out with:

"I want him to believe in me too."

"But why should he believe in you, of all people?"

"What makes you say that?"

"Take a look at yourself."

"Well?"

"Wasn't it you that set fire to the firemen, in the forest?"

"Yes."

"Well then, there you have it."

"God's not an army colonel," I objected. "He loves diversity."

It seemed as if the sky was falling in on me, and the cherry orchard was floating. I began to blink my eyes, and the idiot laughed. Through this idiot, France corrupted me. He didn't have a name at all; and as far as he was concerned, neither did I. This meant we could do what other people, who had names, weren't allowed to do. We climbed up to the very top of a striped cherry tree with sweet resin in it, to spy on couples. We sat there like two oversized birds: he sat with his pants halfway down his legs, with saliva on his lips, and I sat in my shorts, my knees bleeding. No-one came. Another time, we spotted a couple walking through the orchard, and we hid. My heart started pounding. They sat down in the long grass — and disappeared from view forever.

•

Capitalism penetrated the dining room. Money was depicted in the room, in colored pencils. The yellow pictures were the most expensive: 10,000 francs. For that sum you could buy enough bananas to cover the table, or some cherry Danone, the precursor to modern-day yoghurt. The greedy bought cutlets. The teachers used to turn the children's pockets out. I was exposed. It turned out it was me that had come up with the idea of drawing money, on squared paper with big, French squares. The teachers came to the conclusion: Vitya Erofeyev has been making counterfeit money.

Drawing money was the first ideological scandal of my life. Had I been the son of the ambassador's chauffeur, they would have dealt with me good and proper. But I had a charter of immunity: they thought better of making trouble for the son of an attaché. They complained to my mama, cautiously. She scolded me; I could not see where the harm was in what I had done. It was a game that we had taken on loan from foreign life —

I doubt I would ever have drawn money in Russia. I realized that the 100 franc coin my parents gave me every Sunday amounted to a transaction. Officially, the coin was given to me for doing well in my studies and for good behavior, but there was another objective at play: 100 francs was a lightning-conductor. Having money of my own put a limit on my consumer requirements, which would otherwise have been boundless. My drawings of high-value currency were a vector of my dreams. Furthermore, Kirilla Vasilievna suppressed the scandal for reasons of her own.

Saturday was bath day. Everyone was in a state of excitement from the early morning. The children were given their baths after lunch, when we normally had quiet time, and were scrubbed right up until dinner-time. There were several baths in the bathroom, like at a bathhouse. The children were bathed separately — first the girls, then the boys. It was Kirilla Vasilievna's turn to bathe me.

Evening was coming on. Kirilla Vasilievna was sweating after having scrubbed so many children, and looked worn out. Her hands were all red, and water was dripping from the ends of her hair. She wiped her face with her hand, the way Russian do. Papa had a lot of time for Kirilla Vasilievna. He shot movies of her: here she is sitting in profile on the grass in Mante, looking straight ahead with an interested expression. Suddenly she starts applauding furiously, so furiously that her hands turn blue. Then she stops and tears at the grass. She sits there chewing it. Papa never played this reel to anyone — he considered it his own personal success. This one wasn't black-and-white — it was in color, and looked like a dream. One day, out of the blue, papa came home looking upset. His video camera had been stolen from his car. It was a square video camera made in Czechoslovakia, which you had to wind up mechanically, like a watch. I was never allowed to touch it. My parents came to the conclusion that the camera had been stolen by the French secret service, but they told me it had been taken by burglars. Was my father a spy?

•

You skim over the text, drawing it in your mind's eye as if on a piece of plywood, and suddenly you slip through, as you catch sight of your own eyes deep down inside it.

"Your skin's soft, like a girl's."

Those were Kirilla Vasilievna's words, as she scrubbed me in the bath. I was overcome with embarrassment. On September 1st we bought a bouquet of flowers again, and went to school again. School was like a plaything for me — I found my studies easy and enjoyable. During breaks we used to run outside into the yard. The paths were strewn with gravel. We threw little stones at one another. A boy named Orlov, who had a straight black fringe, knocked out one of my molars, thereby ensuring his place in the history of literature. I went up to him with a resolute look on my face, but refrained from hitting him: we weren't in the habit of having fights at that school.

In May we went to the Cannes film festival, taking a protracted route through Bordeaux, Biarritz, Lourdes (where the crutches of the cured hung down from the sky) and Toulouse: my parents stayed at the Carlton, which had a sea view; I had a separate room, on the top floor. I felt like a pigeon living up there. At the Cannes festival I found out what complete loneliness was all about. My parents used to go out in the evenings, smelling of perfume. Mama — wearing a black dress with a big, turned-down white collar — seemed alien to me. Long ago, in my early childhood, I had dreamt up how my parents ought to be, from the first detail to the last, and ordered them not to change, and they had obeyed my commands: they lived up to the template, but whenever they weren't quite themselves for any reason, as was the case in Cannes, it felt strange.

"Whatever's the matter, honey — you'll be safe and sound in a hotel, no-one's going to come and kidnap you." Mama tried to talk me round in a voice that was tender but put-on. She was hurrying to rid herself of me, and I felt embarrassed for her. After all, I was sick. I had bandages on my hands. During the journey to Cannes I had spotted a cactus for the first time ever, on the Côte d'Azur. Objects were forever overtaking my consciousness with their names. The cactus was the continuation of my flight from the North. Having begun this flight in Paris, I could no longer stop. Forgetting that I had got out of the car to go and pee, I rushed towards the cactus and grabbed hold of it, so that I could pull it out by the roots as a trophy from the south. The cactus was swift to take retribution on me.

After kissing me goodnight, mama rushed off to the star-filled reception. I lay there and thought about the fact that my parents were going to get divorced. They used to swear at each other all the time when they drove to the south. Mama accused papa of coming the wrong way, but they were in no mood to argue after seeing the crutches in Lourdes — the cripples had left us all feeling alarmed, but then they set to it once again. It was late when I finally got to sleep — sensing that I was already in a broken, divorced family — when the hotel staircase was filled with the noise of happy people and the elevator doors were slamming. The only time of day when I had fun in Cannes was in the morning. Over breakfast people came up to us speaking in Russian. They asked why I had bandages on my hands, and gave velvety laughs when they heard my response. The beautiful women were like horses. Their nostrils trembled. Once they had moved away from our table, mama criticized them:

"Look at that: the shoulder-strap of her dress is secured with a pin!"

Papa chewed his croissant in silence.

"You ought to say something! They'd have been better off wearing what they wore for the journey from Moscow. It's unusual, to say the least. They've stocked up on cheap sweaters at Tati! The African women — did you see them? — even they were better-dressed! What a disgrace!"

Papa finished his tea in silence. He almost never criticized women — certainly not the ones that looked like horses. *The Cranes are Flying* won the top prize that year, I seem to recall.

Mama had begun to get a feel for the French template. The maid at the embassy said to her, in my presence:

"The French are very dirty people. When they do the vacuuming in their bedrooms, they put their shoes on the bed."

"What nonsense!" mama exclaimed.

I noticed the *way* the maid looked at her. To all intents and purposes, it was as if the maid had said that Jews were greedy, and mama had promptly refuted the statement.

•

What am I to make of this maid? In what way is she better than the Russian authorities? What historical *fear* had led her to conclude that the French were "very dirty people"?

Russian power is transparent. It was created in order to carry out acts that would cause revulsion in the West. The persecution of Pasternak, Khruschev's shoe at the United Nations, Soviet troops entering Czechoslovakia — all these things have the common traits of intimidation. The art of such acts is the boorish mockery of the humane values on which civilization is founded. When we were children, our parents said to us: it doesn't matter how you fart if you're sitting in a puddle. I am awe-struck by the Russian state's ability to ruin its own reputation.

But I can understand the growing frustration of those in power, and to some extent I sympathize with it. There is no basic order in this country, no rule of law. Russian law has always been so inhuman that circumventing it is not so much a crime as an act of valour. Those in power in Russia do not want a return to Communism, but rely instead on a basic model of Russian statehood, which recognizes a single power structure. The eternal fear that if it is ruled in any other way, a country as vast and long as this will break down and crumble like a baguette, is the nightmare of Russia's rulers. Russia slides towards authoritarianism of its own accord, regardless of the ideological system imposed on it. Money — particularly when there are large quantities of it, in private hands — has never been seen as a force for good in Russia. In that set-up, the leader is chosen by the security services — the *oprichnina* (under Ivan the Terrible) or the secret police — in order to struggle against gravity.

Power, fearful of its own reflection, arms itself with the fear that its subjects all have of it, as the only firm cement that can bind the whole thing together. Fear, though, freezes up not only Russia's wild diversity, but also its productivity. Russia longs to move forward in a civilized space, but it clips its own wings, whilst thinking that it is only clipping its clipping its predatory claws. It is a cycle that is so simple as to lead one to despair.

A way out of this situation would be a new wave of shame at this indecent conduct, repentance, and a promise to live truthfully henceforward. But will this new wave come in time? The speed at which western technology has developed leaves Russia unable to hide away in some backwater. She doesn't have a choice. She has been sentenced either to be part of the civilized world, or not to exist at all. Russia's liberal resource is too small — again, it is undeveloped and untested, from a historical perspective. The maid brandishes her mop. This is the electorate. The upper echelons of power in Russia have sensed, once again, the weakness of the western-style liberal resource, after the chaos of the 1990s. Present-day Russia is like a cow tied to a rope: the liberals are pushing her towards the western market, but she is refusing to budge, in the belief that over there she'll lose her honor, or perhaps even be eaten alive.

•

I was probably born to write Hollywood scripts and soap operas. Be that as it may, my boyhood period of creativity — a home of creation! — creativity? — degeneracy! — my boyhood period of talent — damn it! none of that sounds right! — the language of literary theory has become obsolete — but one thing's for sure, whatever it was, *it* was closely related to these genres. I would go so far as to say that the genres I used as a boy, the first babblings of my imagination, were the best guarantor of success in life: what more could the public want? Generally speaking, I would begin with insurgents, witches, spies and heaps of dead bodies.

On the way back from Cannes to Paris I noticed a strange divergence behind me. Glancing out of the car window at the sycamores which could be glimpsed here and there along the national road (there were no superhighways back then) — the sycamores interlocked with their foliage above it, transforming it into a high-walled green tunnel — and examining the notices at the Total and Shell petrol stations (we filled up the tank using diplomatic coupons), and the streets in the provincial towns, I suddenly found myself in a different world. The people in this new world looked real, but their reasons for doing things were different. Hooking my consciousness onto some car with a spare tire on the luggage rack, a chance word from my father, or the rustling of the map with a little man made of tires on it, in mama's hands, I turned into a hyper-sensitive device, through which there ran the currents of all sorts of vague stories.

The stories were interwoven with one another, and engendered new stories about plots, getting stuck because they couldn't find a way to be continued; they drove down dead-ends, turned round and kept going as if nothing were the matter.

In my stories there would always be a gun in papa's pocket, more real than in a work of realism, and I used to tell a classmate of mine, Orlov, who once knocked one of my teeth out, that my papa carried a weapon. To my surprise, on opening a drawer in his desk one day when he was at work, I discovered that a weapon had materialized inside it: it was a small, heavy pistol — a pump-action one, admittedly. In these stories we were always being hunted by policemen dressed as peasants and cyclists. Snipers would fire at us from the tops of the platens. We were driving around with a secret mission: to free Kirilla Vasilievna, who was dressed in a torn dress covered in mud, from captivity. On another occasion we were carrying sacks of money around. We may just have been closer to the truth than we imagined: Vinogradov and my father used to supply the French communists with laundered money, in secret. Moreover, people who were connected to the embassy weren't allowed to move around the country freely — they had to have permission from the French Ministry of Foreign Affairs, and the exact route and dates of travel had to be specified (there was a similar restriction banning foreigners from travelling around the USSR); I didn't know back then that for us, you had to jump through all kinds of hoops before you could go to France.

We stopped for an early lunch, turning off into a country lane. I looked around vigilantly. Where could I find a safe place? It wouldn't be easy: there was private land all around us — occasionally we were chased away, and my parents' Soviet souls boiled over with indignation. I peopled the forests and fields with bandits, my classmates, little girls from French children's books, my parents' friends and stall-keepers from the market. Orlov invariably played the role of the traitor. We made our way to the Alps, taking the country roads. When we looked at the alpine road on the map, it made our stomachs turn.

PAPA: The crossing's coming up.

MAMA: What air! Shut the window. There's a draft.

I felt sick each time we turned a corner. Our objective was the border. Making the shape of a gun with my fingers, I would quietly shoot at the oncoming cars and then, glancing back, see them flying into the ditch by the side of the road and blowing up. Sometimes I would manage to shoot down a passenger jet. Anyone in a uniform was certainly not on the side of French law. As I shot my gun, I let out a noise that sounded like 'poof'!', and from time to time mama would turn and look at me, looking bewildered.

MAMA: Who are you shooting?

Mama was not part of this other world, and in this instance she was only getting in the way.

"I'm not shooting anyone," I always answered.

She didn't believe me. She asked me to stop shooting my gun. It was even worse when she started playing jokes on me. It was unbearable, and it spoilt my stories no end. I wouldn't go so far as to call them thrillers. They contained material that was worthy of a thriller, but the plot itself went on forever. I would be my father's bodyguard, putting my body on the line for him with the selfless loyalty of Alexander Matrosov. Some nameless French simpleton would be transformed into a handsome beau, like Valentino, but I never knew what to do with him next, and bitterly made him fall victim to a stray bullet. We used to have dinner at little hotels. Sometimes there would be French people around drinking red wine and singing songs to mark a special occasion — a wedding, or a party. A lot of them were under the influence, and were as simple as the trunk of a pine tree. Most of them were spies, who were tailing us. I used to annihilate weddings too, putting my fingers together. The thin hotel landlady was a witch, and was trying to poison me at dinner. I said no to a glass of water, and played roulette with my food: this bit is poisoned, but that bit isn't. By the end of the meal I was almost going cross-eyed. The hotel room was infused with the dragging aroma of miserly French comfort. The floorboards creaked. A brown crucifix hung above the bed. I wasn't afraid of anything, but the crucifix frightened me. Instead of pillows there were rollers, which were enough to give any normal person neck ache — my parents asked the witch to give us some pillows. I came up with untold numbers of stories on the road. They came back to me before I went to sleep, in an altered state. Some sixth sense told me once again that my parents were close to getting a divorce. I pictured myself as a miserable orphan, committed heinous crimes out of maliciousness, and prison wept for me. In the morning the sun shone through the closed shutters. From somewhere nearby I could smell the inviting aroma of good coffee. We had to keep going with our dangerous mission. And then suddenly my brother was born. Taken aback by the fact that I knew about his birth, Kirilla Vasilievna began to keep an eye on me. She was right to do so: I had solved the mystery of both my mother's immaculate conception and my brother's immaculate birth.

•

Kirilla Vasilievna put some soap on an orange sponge. You couldn't get sponges like that in Moscow. The sponge was big and porous, with holes in it, like cheese.

"Turn and face forwards," Kirilla Vasilievna said, and turned me round herself, holding me by the hand.

I always shuddered when I heard this command, and would try to be the last one to be scrubbed, postponing my moment of shame. She turned me around, bent over me and started scrubbing my knees. From above, I could see her pale breasts with their nipples swung to and fro under her red-and-green robe.

"Look how many scars you've got!" she said, with a laugh. "You hero!"

The door opened and a governess in a white robe walked into the bathroom, which was filled with clouds of steam:

"Kirilla Vasilievna, don't be late for dinner!"

"This one's my last."

"Let me help you."

"It's fine, he's a big boy, he can scrub himself! Can you do it by yourself?"

I nodded. She put the soapy orange sponge in my hand.

"What about you, though?" the governess asked.

"I'll do myself in a moment," Kirilla Vasilievna laughed, wiping her brow. "Phew, I'm tired!"

The governess walked up to a bath next to the same tiled wall where mine was, and turned on the hot and cold water. The water came pouring sharply into the bath.

"It's hot today. I'm all sweaty!"

"You're telling me!" Kirilla Vasilievna scratched her armpits.

The governess unbuttoned her white robe. After taking it off, she put it down on a stool, pinching its surface before she did so: was it still dry? She was now wearing nothing but pink panties up to her belly-button and a white bra. Lifting her thin legs high in the air, she took off her pink panties and stayed in her bra for a short while, testing the water in the bath with her hand. Turning to face us, she took off her bra and, grabbing her little breasts in her hands and as if kneading them, crawled into the bath.

The example she set inspired Kirilla Vasilievna. She too turned on the tap in the bath opposite mine, next to the other wall, and walked up to the door: the latch clicked. Now she too unbuttoned her robe, and threw it on top of a different stool that was fairly wet and soapy. She had nothing on under her robe. Kirilla Vasilievna had a small but perfectly formed butt. I looked at my teacher shyly. It was fair to say I was in love with her. Whenever she explained adverbs to us in the classroom, breaking the long French chalk in her fingers and standing side-on to the brown desk, she looked like a vixen. Kirilla Vasilievna shook her leg as she crawled into the bath, and for a split-second, as if in a flash of lightning, I caught sight of her tiny brown asshole, some pink lips, spread apart, and the black hairs of her female essence. I stood in my bath holding the orange sponge in my hand, neither dead nor alive. No nameless French idiot could ever have provided me with more sound information. Finding herself up to her knees in water, she bent over towards the washcloth and soap, revealing the details of her large breasts, which moved and swayed.

"Kirilla Vasilievna!" the governess shouted, from her bathtub. "Do you want me to scrub your back?"

Kirilla Vasilievna straightened her back and turned towards me, revealing strands of black hair beneath her stomach.

"I'll do it myself!" she giggled. "I'll ask this young cavalier to do it. He's already finished washing."

That wasn't quite true. I hadn't quite finished washing.

"Will you scrub my back for me?" she said, giggling once again.

•

Why do writers write autobiographies? If you ask me, it's a serious affliction. It's like carving your initials into a bench. The writer's task consists in not writing an autobiography, in evading this task, in feeding it to the fishes. Gorky filled his autobiographical trilogy with kilometers of dialogue, each one as plausibly realistic as it is false. The leaden abominations of Russian life are sold for a hundred pounds of bitterness. There is nothing revolutionary about this grief: it is like Sologub's conundrum. Zero equals zero. Nabokov, on the other hand, maintains that he lived in paradise. For him, this paradise consisted of the vainglorious details of the sated life of an egotistical young lord, whom the revolution later took great pleasure in punishing. Nabokov struggles to try and find the rhythmical cycles in his life, and strikes matches in order to celebrate its meaning, but, being an agnostic, he falls into the trap that he himself has set, and goes off on a tangent. His flight from chance is like a slalom. He comes across as disgustingly pleased with himself in his memoirs. It is the very vulgarity on which he had declared war. Gorky and Nabokov represent the two poles of Russian literature: they turned their autobiographies into an identical product — verbal diarrhea.

The life of the writer flies in the face of the meaning of life. It is not sustained by a million details, like other people's lives. Unlike the writer's words, it is smaller than the writer. It has a reductive effect on him. His metamorphoses are of interest only as an example of pure suffering. It is an unreliable account, and treachery is its abode. Dostoyevsky dedicated the epitaph on his mother's grave to the torn-off 'member' of the useless hero:

Rest in peace, dear remains,
Until the joyful morn.

That is our only salvation. Whatever a writer does, he merely wastes his time. Unworthy of himself, he consists of nothing but wasted time. He befriends revolutionaries then becomes a hermit; he flies into a rage, then grows calm; he is eternally indebted to his parents, whom he doesn't understand; he pours tenderness over his head, like fir trees: all this is childish babble. When painting his portrait of the artist as a young man, Joyce got so carried away by the subject of sanctity and lust that he forgot about the most important thing of all: the fact that the writer is neither lusty nor saintly. He is a sheet of paper. Otherwise he amounts to nothing more than perpetual masturbation.

Hastily changing into the clothes of his double, Bunin torments the reader with an endless description of nature, which he links to his childhood: millions of sunsets, roads covered by blizzards, the moon above the fields. But his greatest talent is for incredibly vivid descriptions of dead bodies in coffins. His neighbor, his father, a great prince, a child — all of them deceased. All the signs of their decay: the color of their lips, the veins on their temples, their eyelids, their hands — all these things are described by a master of observation. But this engaging necrophilia — to which I can relate closely, due to my sense of the horror of death — ultimately resulted in an autobiographical failure: out of a charming, lyrical boy-hero there grows a neurotic, jealous young man, demanding with an authoritative voice to be loved, and writing poems about that same nature. He preaches aestheticism and is genuinely indifferent to the suffering of his people. The writer deceived himself.

Ambassador Vinogradov tasked papa with visiting Bunin's widow, in order to buy the writer's archived documents from her. Papa fearlessly set off to see her at her apartment. She greeted him with suspicion. She looked down at him through the rails of the banister:

"You Soviets never go anywhere on your own."

She thought papa had brought with him a Soviet tail. When the widow at last let papa into her luxurious apartment, after being brought to ruin by poverty, she gave him a bit of a scare:

"An anti-Soviet committee meets here once a week, on Thursdays!"

Papa kept his composure:

"That is no business of mine, madam."

The poor widow sold the manuscripts to him. Papa took pains to make sure she was provided with a life-long Soviet pension, paid in local currency. As regards his politics, papa considered Bunin to have been 'muddle-headed': this was a mild, all-forgiving description that was convenient whenever the conversation turned to members of the intelligentsia who were "not on our side". Chagal, Annenkov, Serge Lifar, Larionov and Goncharova — all the emigrés in the creative sphere gradually became 'muddle-headed'. In the end the matter reached Berdyaev — and he too became 'muddle-headed'.

One sunny day in Deauville, where, at the age of nine, I had seen the sea and sea shells for the first time, we strolled along the coast (I was a student by this time), accompanied by the rustling of the flags on the beach and the clapping of the fabric on the deckchairs, in the wind — our stroll was like a scene from a French movie — a chubby man named Volodin, full of vitality, a pretend attaché from the embassy (he was one of the resident spies) with a charming wife who played piano at the Bolshoi Theater (mama used to dream of having her over for dinner in Moscow, but the pianist wouldn't agree to it — there was a certain hierarchy at play there), discussed Berdyaev's archive. He said that Moscow had expressed an interest in the collection of this 'muddle-headed man'. Father, who had never read a single line of Berdyaev's work, nodded his head. Suddenly Volodin stopped:

"If they were to attack us now, how I'd love to give them a good seeing to!"

In his eyes one could detect pure, undisguised hatred. I looked about me, sizing up our potential enemies. It was a windy, sunny day. There were children running around. The spark of hatred slowly ebbed away. We went off to have lunch. That sort of thing didn't happen with papa. His hatred was never expressed physically. It was expressed only in the determined look on his face. The word 'muddle-headed' was a fake word, coined by the KGB, but it had a distinct meaning. Writers are indeed 'muddle-headed'. There's no better way of putting it.

All writers find themselves agreeable: they are all inquisitive, observant, false and lustful, and have eyes that look inward. In portraits, writers always look as if they are deep in thought. The chances are I am not a writer: I come across in photographs as someone who has been appended to life by accident. Thirty percent of any writer's make-up consists in a deep-seated feeling of complacency. Twenty percent consists in an awareness of death. The remaining fifty percent consists in faith in the fact that they are unique. Writers don't believe in their birthdays — they arrived in the world from outer space, and are destined to become part of outer space forever. Writers search for secret marks on their bodies. Take me, for example — I have a birthmark under my left nipple. I've checked a lot of people — and no-one else has anything like that. It probably stems from my past life. In that life I was a demi-god. If you take away a writer's feeling of uniqueness, he's done for. This sense of uniqueness is particularly aggravating. Tolstoy, mixing up the traces of his life, constructed a moral vessel out of his autobiograhy, which ended in Tolstoyism. Dobychin chose a diametrically opposed path: he combined the important with the insignificant, as a result of which his narration attained the meritless status of a moral letter. Mayakovsky makes mischief, Pasternak philosophizes. Proust told us he consisted entirely of pure chance, from head to toe. Writers interrupt one another to share the details of their lives with us, convinced that someone will find what they have to say of interest. Somehow I never quite got *The Childhood of Bagrov's*

Grandson. Perhaps this was an exception? The autobiography is by its very nature a dead-end genre. All it took was for me to read a few dozen autobiographies in order to reach the conclusion that I would never write an autobiography.

•

I noticed that the nanny had suddenly gone quiet in her cast iron bathtub with its little legs. I have just remembered — as if I was transported back to my childhood momentarily — that she was the young wife of a trade delegation employee; she looked very French, and was more stylishly dressed than my mother; she had decided to earn a bit of extra money during the summer. We used to go to the trade delegation to watch Soviet films: we were particularly fond of *Carnival Night* and a Khrushchev-era propaganda film in which weeds went on the attack against corn. The weeds sang American boogie-woogie tunes and swept up everything in their path. Wearing a bell-shaped skirt, the employee's wife used to hang around near the men at the entrance to the auditorium: she always looked excited. My mother used to judge her because of that. The way mama saw it, if your husband worked in Export trade, you ought not to work as a nanny: it was not good to sell yourself for money like that.

"OK," I agreed, like an obedient pupil. Kirilla Vasilievna was resting her back on the edge of the bathtub.

I already knew that this experience was going to live with me for years. I realized, exactly as if I had been an adult, by leaping from one thought to the next, that she had only dared to suggest that a schoolboy scrub her back because the wife of a trade delegation employee was present: if the two of us had been alone, nothing would ever have happened.

I walked over to her bathtub, took the sponge from her hand — it already looked utterly Russian and was all soapy, and, for the first time ever (life consists of the pulsations of those words — 'for the first time'), started to scrub someone else's back. Red spots started to appear on her back.

"You're good at it!" she said, as if giving me a grade for solving a math question. "Do you remember," she went on, "when I asked the class when you were welcomed as pioneers, where the name came from — pioneer — and you put up your hand?"

"I remember," I spluttered.

"'Pioneer', you said, when I picked you, 'comes from the word PEONY! Pioneers are as red, with their ties, as peonies!"

Kirilla Vasilievna burst out laughing. There was no reaction whatsoever from the nanny, however, in her bathtub, and I blushed again, just as I had done back then in the classroom — I had gone all red like a PEONY.

"What a peony you are!" Kirilla Vasilievna said, unable to remain calm. She stood up in the bathtub, stretched her hand out towards the wall like the captured Algerian in the photo in *Paris-Match*, and bent down, spreading her legs slightly:

"Go on then, keep scrubbing! Since you've started, you'd better finish the job." I put soap on the sponge again.

"You little fool!" she said, turning round. "You're supposed to use your hands for that bit." I put soap on my hands and started wiping her bum. She stood there, moving her buttocks rhythmically. Leaning her head against the wall, she put her hands behind her back and spread her buttocks:

"Wash me there too. But do it gently."

Once again her small brown anus opened up before my eyes. I washed the reddish groove of her bum, touching her anus with my fingers. By that point I was no longer there. This was all being done by someone else. My heart nearly burst out of my chest. Her anus was springy, powerful, capricious — like Kirilla Vasilievna herself. Suddenly it tightened up, as if inflated with rage — and expanded, turning pinkish-red: with a hiss, a jet of gas came out.

"Sorry," she said. "I can't hold it in any longer."

I thought she had got tired of being scrubbed, moved slightly away from Kirilla Vasilievna, and suddenly saw that she had spread her legs slightly farther apart and was pissing into the bathtub, with a powerful jet of urine. Once she had finished pissing she said to me in a half-whisper, in a voice that I didn't recognize:

"Wash me down there."

I didn't know what she meant.

"What do you mean?" I asked her to repeat the question.

She turned to face me and put my soapy palm on her curly-haired pubis.

"Here," she said.

I started to rub the hair. She pushed my hand slowly downwards, where there was no hair and it was all slippery. I felt a little protuberance.

"Touch it," she said. "Touch my clitoris." I started touching it, pinching the mound between two fingers.

"You see, I've got a big one," she moaned, "like a little penis."

I carried on touching the tender mound, the very existence of which I had not even suspected just moment ago.

"Do you like it?" Kirilla Vasilievna wheezed. "Now go lower down. Put your finger in my pee-hole."

My finger sank into her moist pussy. I put another finger in. Kirilla Vasilievna stomped her legs like a horse.

"Your fist," she said, "put your whole fist in!"

I shoved my fist in and started moving it from side to side. Kirilla Vasilievna coiled up in the bathtub.

"Say: I love your pussy," Kirilla Vasilievna asked, already in complete delirium. "Say: I love your pussy."

"I love your pussy," I said hesitantly, continuing to move my fist around.

Suddenly she opened her eyes, which had been closed for some time, looked at me with a lost expression in her eyes took hold of my balls gently. She moved her hand and grabbed my twinkie, moving the skin to one side with her fingers.

"It's up!" she said greedily, holding me tightly in her hand. "It's up, my little boy, it's up!"

Kirilla Vasilievna was twitching even more fiercely, her mouth had fallen open, and she looked as though she was in great pain, as if she had just had a tooth pulled out. She came with all her might onto my fist, which had got lost inside her, and began to twitch as if she had been hung. At last, heaving a sigh with her whole body, she slowly began settling in the bathtub, delicately, extricating herself from my fist in a ladylike way. She put her head in the water and sat there looking all pasty, like an underdone fried egg. After a short while she said softly, without looking up:

"Did you come, too?"

"Yes," the nanny answered, as if in a dream. "I've spilt all the bathwater."

"Did you see him?" Kirilla Vasilievna asked.

"I came while looking at him," the nanny said. "He hasn't even got any hair yet, but what an erection!"

Kirillia Vasilievna, looking tired, touched me on the twinkie again.

"Well done, peony!" she praised me. "And now it's time for dinner!"

The women, like two waterfalls, stood up and go out of their bathtubs. Kirilla Vasilievna kissed the nanny on the lips; the two women flattened each other's breasts in an embrace, and she said with a laugh:

"And there you were saying: there aren't any men!"

Once we had rubbed ourselves with towels and got dressed, Kirilla Vasilievna, her hair sticking out to the sides, asked me sternly:

"You promise you won't draw any more counterfeit money?"

"I won't."

"You won't need any counterfeit money in life."

I don't know how she came to be so sure of herself. Her prediction turned out to be only partially true. After this incident I began to get a sweet aching sensation in my groin from time to time. I didn't get scrubbed by Kirilla Vasilievna in the bath again after that. I saw the nanny again many years later, in Moscow. I was walking along with mama and she was coming towards us. She told us her husband had died in a car crash on the Mozhaika. She looked at me as if I had never seen her shaved pubis, when she took off her white bra.

•

We never had pets at home. Everyone else used to have pets, but we didn't. My parents didn't like cats or dogs. My parents would wrinkle their brows discreetly whenever they came into contact with pets, although a sense of diplomatic courtesy made them feel obliged to ask their friends' cats and dogs:

"What's your name, then?"

They got on well with Chernomor, however. They used to put my brother in the embassy garden in his stroller, illegally, in spite of the fact that Vinogradov had imposed a ban on being there, which extended to cover absolutely everyone. Yevgenia Alexandrovna said:

"Chernomor's getting agitated. He doesn't like children."

But the stroller stayed where it was. I find it hard to imagine my parents stroking a pet. We didn't know the names of any breeds of dog at home other than German shepherds, nor did we have any wish to. In Paris I dreamt that my parents had bought me a monkey; they never bought one. They didn't even buy me so much as one of the fish that were sold near the Samoritena, on the banks of the Seine. There were no rats, rabbits, squirrels on wheels, guinea pigs or songbirds, either. We never heard the awful voices of parrots in our household, either. My parents never rode horses or reared chickens. Not a single turtle was ever seen crawling around in our house. In the end, my only household pet was a vagina. A vagina was my comrade-in-arms. A vagina was my artistic performer. A vagina was the shot that was fired through my freedom. Vaginas get in the way of writing. The vagina is my life-long friend.

•

When I spotted the French simpleton in the cherry orchard again, I wanted to tell him about Kirilla Vasilievna and the bathtub, but my French vocabulary didn't stretch that far.

"*Tu habites où?*" I asked.

"*Ici,*"[*] he smiled hesitantly, staring straight ahead.

We sat on the wall of the garden, which was overgrown with violet Bougainvillea and some nameless red flowers that looked like pipes, which were always swarming with ants. Behind us we could hear the swaying of the beech trees in Mantes park. He handed me a cigarette. By this stage I had nothing to lose. I took a drag on the cigarette, barely inhaling, and spitting out crumbs of tobacco. Suddenly we spotted a French couple walking through the garden. They looked shy, and were stealing along, glancing over their shoulders occasionally. But it was clear they really wanted to do it. They sat down under a cherry tree and started kissing. I watched them ironically, with a crooked smile; we were too far away to make much out, and after what had happened with Kirilla Vasilievna, this was small fry.

"The sky is full of stars, at night," the boy suddenly blurted out.

"Yes," I agreed.

"Do you like stars?"

"Yes."

"So do I. Come out here when it gets dark. I'll show you." He stretched out his hand broadly and hospitably, to take in the whole of the French sky.

"OK!" I said happily.

They lay down, there was a flash of white between her legs, and after that you could hardly see anything because of him. Just her flinching legs. But when I looked over at my French friend to point out that we could have done with a pair of binoculars, which I had always associated with spying, and a detailed

---

[*] "Where do you live?" "Here" (*fr.*).

examination of someone else's life in the building opposite, rather than with a première at the theater, where I never asked the cloakroom attendant for binoculars even if I had a seat near the back, I was amazed by what I saw. He had unbuttoned his trousers. His belly was bare. There were yellow hairs on his belly. There was an infinite number of freckles and birthmarks. And a penis of enormous proportions. Staring at what amounted to hardly anything, my friend was tugging at it rapidly; and it was shaking its pink tip from side to side, tautly. Catching my gaze, the idiot, with a low moo, suggested that I do the same thing. But I remained loyal to my principal, Kirilla Vasilievna.

Now, as I look back on this story, I can't work out which bits have been invented — the result of me turning it over multiple times in my mind — and which bits are historical truth. This story has been in my mind since the mid-fifties — as immutable as a cliff-face. I remember the exact outlines of the yellow counterfeit money, but I find it hard to answer even the simplest of questions: was Kirilla Vasilievna an erotomaniac? Or had the fancy merely taken her on that one occasion, as is sometimes the way? But if that was the case, why did she ask the pseudo-nanny that question about men? Perhaps the question came much later? But how had she dared to do it? And was she the only one?

A huge row broke out at the embassy. One of the staffers had taken his lover with him to Paris and pretended she was his wife, handing photos of her to the HR department. Yevgenia Alexandrovna, who normally didn't bother to get to know even wives from second marriages, unexpectedly made friends with the lover, who was brazenly going by the name of a completely different woman (the thought of whom was surely not very agreeable to her) in public. This bit of extramarital smuggling was only discovered when the wife, alarmed by the fact that her husband hadn't written to her from France for some time, started making calls to the ministry. By Soviet standards, it was a plot to rival *Romeo and Juliet*. All I remember of Kirilla Vasilievna are some miserly snapshots from an amateur chronicle. I can picture her applauding us: five of us — five boys — are building a pyramid in a meadow — and having a great deal of difficulty doing so. There is a diamond-shaped paper 'D' for Dinamo on my blue sweater, and I am well-groomed again. She watches us, claps her hands, tears at the grass and puts it in the corner of her mouth.

•

The first time I saw Picasso was on the Cote d'Azur, on the terrace outside a cafe. Papa had come to town with the great actor Ch., who had worked with Eisenstein. Mama got talking to his wife. During our trip to the Soviet government health spa in Sochi that year, when I learned to swim, Ch's wife said to me, as we wandered around a sub-tropical park:

"You can't imagine how sad it is to grow old with a stupid person!"

I remembered those words for the rest of my life. I had occasion to meet many actors later in life: the ones that weren't stupid were bad actors. Picasso appeared: he was short and wearing a vest, and had bulging eyes. He had a bullish look in his eyes. He greeted papa and the actor, and we headed off somewhere. The actor was supposed to recite something by Mayakovsky. The poet Aragon joined up with us along the way. He was friends with papa, and whenever he had had an argument with Else Triole he used to come to the embassy and complain to papa about his wife, the cook, and women in general. I knew he was a communist. Aragon the communist liked looking at himself in the mirror. If he had had a mirror in his room, he wouldn't have been able to tear himself away from it. Then a stocky man came up to us — it was Maurice Thorez. We went into a building of some sort. The actor Ch. was playing the roles of Mayakovsky and a woman, in Russian. It was apparent that they were not going to live together, and I desperately wanted my parents not to get divorced. After the play, the men sat down for a glass of wine. Picasso took my hand and said:

"You've got the fingers of a musician."

Rostropovich later said the exact same thing to me, as he grabbed my hand when I opened the door of our Moscow apartment for him: he had brought me a letter from my parents — but I don't have an ear for music, and my fingers could do nothing to change that.

"What do you want to be when you're older?" Picasso screwed up his eyes powerfully and unsmilingly.

"Nobody," I replied, turning my head to one side under the gaze of the pop-eyed artist. I noticed that papa had begun to worry and was trying to come to my aid, but Picasso suddenly burst out laughing:

"Good answer."

Everyone else stared at me with affection. I picked up a napkin and a pencil, put my hand on the napkin and, while they were talking, traced my palm and outspread fingers with the pencil. I gave my drawing to Picasso. He said that I was a quick learner — and tapped his fingers against his temple. Picasso picked up the drawing and started painting my fingers with red wine, after dipping his finger in his glass. Everyone was pretending that they weren't paying any attention to him, but once the outspread fingers had been filled in, Aragon, papa, the Soviet actor Ch. and France's most prominent communist were in a state of holy delight and kept repeating, one after the other, that I would remember this moment for the rest of my life. But Picasso looked at me and said that my eyes were as sad as Cocteau's. I didn't know who Cocteau was, and only found out later. As for what became of the drawing of my hand, I don't know — but I remember that Picasso signed it with the very same pencil and gave it to me. It's within the bounds of possibility that my hand is currently hanging in a private collection in Switzerland, and has been valued at a million dollars.

Then papa went to visit Picasso in the south again, without

me this time — he brought back a whole series of photos of Picasso taken by papa, just as I had seen him but wearing different outfits. In one of them he was wearing a clown's nose. Papa said that Picasso had expressed interest in my artistic successes. For me, he was a timeless artist, who remained unaffected by age and never fell out of fashion. When he painted my fingers with wine, it wasn't just a monochrome painting: one finger was a particularly deep red, and another was completely pale. Everyone agreed: the outspread, wine-colored fingers of this boy were a chef-d'oeuvre. There was something inexpressibly alarming about this drawing, though. It was as though it had been painted not just with wine but perhaps with blood, as well.

•

Our embassy came under attack: it had eggs thrown at it. It happened in the fall. The white walls of the embassy were showered with red paint. It was said that some hooligans had arrived in cars early in the morning and started throwing eggs containing red paint at the embassy, and that the police hadn't lifted a finger to protect us.

"If you ask me, it's an act of provocation," I said.

"There's no doubt about it." As a precaution, mama started carrying my little brother around the apartment in her arms.

"Or is world war three breaking out?" Mama pressed my brother against her chest.

"What are you talking about!"

A sense of panic fell on the embassy, and it became as busy as a beehive. Everyone was rushing around madly, papa included. My brother was born the year the earthquakes began. That summer, in Mantes, while I was in the toilet, I noticed a newspaper cutting containing something about Stalin's cult of personality. Stalin did not mean all that much to me. I myself was Stalin. It was probably the sensation that I was at the center of the world, rather than the soap operas with their thrilling plots, that transformed me into a vulnerable, lonely, suffering creature. I suddenly sensed I was being restricted, and shifted to one side: the world had become far more dressed up; my parents whispered and gossiped, and didn't let me in on their grown-up conversations. There was a plot against me.

On seeing the walls of the embassy all red — the first ever abstractionism in my life — I felt a terrible anxiety. I had heard that you could play with things other than railways and soldiers, and that stamps were not the absolute limit of desire. In this world there are far more important things you can do. As it turned out, you could wreak havoc by throwing eggs, after first filling them up with red paint. Some cardboard boxes appeared in the corridors of the embassy: word was going around that the embassy was being shut down, and that everyone was leaving for Moscow. We were banned from going to school. It was a public holiday. Everything was cancelled. I found out that there existed in the world a group of people known as Hungarians. I came to the conclusion that Hungarians and hooligans were one and the same thing. They were rioting. In Paris-Match I saw pictures of tanks moving into the city. They had things thrown at them, too: rocks this time, though, rather than eggs.

The Hungarian Revolution marked a critical juncture in my life. It woke me up to adult life. At long last I felt a desire to find out more about it. I started asking my parents about grown-up things. The world had suddenly grown bigger. My parents evaded my questions. That only prompted me to think up new ones. Mama said ponderously:

"We may be required to leave for Moscow."

There was no joy in her hazel eyes. I too began packing my things. I gathered up my toys, my textbooks and my stamp folders. I could see some workmen washing the paint off the walls. The embassy stood there looking lost. Something had taken place in the world. My childhood world, which had been complete and indivisible, was no more. In that childhood world there had been a clean embassy, into which there was strictly no admittance to anyone other than those who were 'with us': it had a duty officer sitting in the corridor; he must have been important, for he too carried a gun (a fact of which I was aware). In that world, Chernomor the dog did laps of the garden. Ambassador Vinogradov would come out onto the porch and either get into a Citroën or drive off in a ZIS. I knew the address: my parents had taught me it, just in case I got lost: I live at *soixante-dix-neuf, rue de Grenelle*. That was my first ever password in life. Suddenly all that had been destroyed. Words had lost their former meaning. The red flag had been torn from the gates of the embassy. I couldn't quite get my head around that. Tear down a flag? Who had dared do such a thing? A secret apartment had been opened. The world had been tilted to one side. Who was to blame? Those hooligans who had thrown eggs. They had bred new hooligans. The New hooligans came along every day with their slogans and banners, waving them at us and shouting into loudhailers. They tried to storm the embassy. Police had now surrounded the building. The situation become very interesting indeed. It was impossible to make any headway down the narrow rue de Grenelle. I wished I was a hooligan more than anything else in the world. Wished I had been the one who had dared to act. The one who had caused all this uproar. The one who had caused the road to be blocked by police buses and armoured vehicles with aerials stretching as high as the second floor. The policemen put helmets on. The embassy staff collected boxes and put them in front of the doors of the apartments, in case they had to leave. They were boring and moribund — they weren't hooligans. Soviet tanks were driving around the streets of Budapest. I decided I was going to be a Hungarian, as terrifying as an Indian. I wanted to be one of the ones throwing eggs. That feeling has stayed with me forever.

•

It was about three o'clock in the afternoon. My papa, as usual, was having lunch in one of Paris's restaurants. On this occasion he was drinking beer and talking to someone for whom he had a great fondness. The conversation was conducted in French, although neither man was a native speaker, because my papa never got round to learning English. The man he was talking to was a man named Libik: he was an attaché from an embassy, just like papa — it was fair to say he was papa's double, only wealthier and from foreign climes. They were nearing the end of their meal.

"Listen," my father couldn't help saying, "why did you decline my invitation to join me at this restaurant?"

"I'm not telling," Libik sniggered.

"Please tell me!"

"I came here once before. Two waiters served me. One was an elderly fellow, and the other was clearly a trainee. This young trainee was so nervous that his hands were shaking, and he spilt hot oil from a pitcher on me!"

The men chuckled amicably. The French people sitting nearby glanced over at them. Dessert was served. Papa had ordered peach-melba ice cream, while Libik had opted for apple pie. Over dessert they discussed all the most sensitive things.

"You really gave us a headache with that Hungary of yours," Libik smiled wearily.

Papa noticed his use of the word 'yours' and sat in silence awaiting the continuation. Outside a persistent rain was falling. The pigeons sat under the canopies. The black gratings of the Parisian balconies looked like obituaries. Libik appeared in father's life at a time when cataclysmic events were taking place in the world. Libik used to invite father to classy restaurants, while father took him to more modest ones.

"What exactly is going on over there?" Libik asked.

"It's a fascist riot," papa said, breaking his peach into little bits with his teaspoon. He lost his grip on the teaspoon and it clattered against the glass table jarringly.

"A riot?" Libik asked in an ironic, yet at the same time slightly menacing tone. The entire military might of the United States had gathered behind him. But neither his irony nor his military might frightened papa.

"I'd say so, yes," father said — "a riot".

"I love the rain in Paris," Libik remarked. "How incredibly peaceful it is! It makes you want to have an afternoon nap! Do you take naps after lunch?"

"On weekends, yes, I do," papa said, spilling the beans on a domestic secret.

"How long for?"

"An hour and a half."

"So what are you going to do about this mutiny?" Libik yawned, covering his mouth politely.

"The Hungarian people..."

"I understand all that. But what about you?"

"We're providing them with brotherly assistance."

"Vladimir," Libik said, "you've got one week. If you bring the operation to an end within a week, we won't intervene. Glass of cognac?"

"It's on me this time," father said. "Two cognacs," he said to a waiter dressed in a long white apron. "And the bill, please."

"I wish we didn't meet up quite so often." Libik clinked glasses with him. "But I fear it will stay that way."

"I should go." Father drained his cognac in one go. The two men stood up and shook hands.

"That's a magnificent tweed suit you're wearing," father said.

"It's from Scotland," Libik nodded. "From Edinburgh."

"I spent time there during the war."

"I know," Libik smiled. "I'm going to stay awhile. I'll smoke my pipe."

Father walked out of the restaurant calmly, picking up his light-gray, double-breasted coat at the door. He climbed into a Peugeot 304, drove off the pavement and roared along the Boulevard Raspail towards the embassy, making the dead leaves from the chestnut trees, which had fallen on the front windscreen, scatter like street-sweepers — they gave off the sickly-sweet smell of death.

"*Les feuilles mortes*,"[*] father muttered. He pictured the tall, portly Libik bending down to dial his embassy at that very moment, in the cramped telephone booth next to the restaurant toilet, surrounded by old advertising posters.

"Well?" Ambassador Vinogradov asked, raising his thick brows tortuously. He had been waiting for father in the hall, like a little boy.

"We've got a week," father said in a quick, soft voice.

"Send a telegram," Ambassador Vinogradov sniggered. "Right to the man at the top. You're a writer, after all."

"I've had enough of cultural stuff," father remarked in passing.

"Understood."

The ambassador thought of people as either writers or non-writers. He himself was in the latter category.

"We'll sign it together, if you've no objections," he added, stuttering slightly in front of my father.

•

"Just think," I said to mama at her gleeful words, "it's orbiting the Earth!" Beep-beep-beep! There's no space up there!

"You don't read the newspapers. The whole world is amazed!"

"If he'd gone to the Moon, now that would have been something!"

"Where did you pick up this contradictory spirit?" mama said, unpleasantly alarmed.

She was right. I hadn't appreciated the significance of the first ever satellite. A spirit of contradiction had got into me. I didn't know where I had got it from. But a spirit was definitely what it was. I was shy, yet I had a contradictory spirit. And it had grown oversized. To begin with it had been tempestuous. It wasn't that I was trying to make fun of anything in particular. I simply liked having my own independent take on things. The

---

[*] Fallen leaves (*fr.*) — an Yves Montand hit.

contradictory spirit that had got into me hit out at various things, from satellites to shoes, and didn't leave mama unaffected either.

I saw a model of the satellite at the world exhibition in Brussels, and was disappointed once again: it's so small! Moreover, a girl from my school was there at the same time. I was in love with her, and my attention was focused more on her than on the satellite. We stood side by side outside the entrance to the Soviet pavilion, a short distance from the Atomium, which was gleaming like the dog's bollocks. She was a year older than me. Our parents were having a chat, and she was japing around and making silly shapes, so that I felt ashamed of her, in spite of the fact that I was in love with her. We didn't say a word to one another. But in my parallel world I included her in all my detective stories. She would be wounded by the baddies — and I would tend to her wounds. The adventures I had when we were on the road were a lot of fun — they always involved me being covered in glory. By contrast, the adventures I had at night, before I went to sleep, were agonizing. I would always lose out, in every possible way: my parents would get divorced, the girl I loved would die, everyone would die. There were fears living inside me.

On the way home, we stopped off in Reims to have a look at a smiling angel. My parents went into the catholic cathedrals in France as if they were museums — to marvel at their gothic interiors, green guidebooks in their hands. They liked the stained glass windows, which I liked as well: Saint Chapel, Notre Dame, Chartres — all was as it should have been. But even this *museum-style* induction into Catholicism knocked me off the path of Orthodoxy for good. I must become a knight of the holy Virgin. For me, beyond the worship of women, there was no such thing as religion. In my fitful imagination I probably had a great need for faith. I was forced to cope with the horrors of death on my own, without any outside help. Nobody ever told me that God existed. But if I had believed, I would probably never have become a writer.

Writing turned out to be a substitute for faith in my life — initially, at least. I had lived through the godforsakenness of the 20th century, which was born of formal religion, weeping on other people's account.

Mama, just like me, was always afraid of dead bodies, afraid of going near them or touching them. To her, her grandfather was no more than a cold dead hand that she had been obliged to kiss. My mother's fear of dead bodies, which I inherited, was reinforced by my father's valetudinarianism, which was passed down to me in full measure. Mama teased him constantly about this. Incidentally, that's the wrong word: teased. This word was never used in my family. The moment I use it, my family becomes hidden from view: it is something that doesn't apply to them. There is a whole plethora of words that were never used in our family life. Mama didn't tease him — papa's valetudinarianism clearly irritated her, but she resisted it with all her might, and that was obvious too. It was in papa's moments of valetudinarianism that I felt my heart beat faster, and realized papa was not her ideal husband. For me, my parents' lyrical relations are enveloped in a layer of gloom.

●

Whereas during the Moscow years my family had been a silver ball that contained the whole world, that ball was broken to pieces in Paris. Mama began to float off, like a mermaid, towards liberal values: man as the measure of all things. She believed in the processes of de-Stalinization, which in actual fact never became processes. Russia had had her eyes gauged out: she could do nothing but spin around on the spot or feel her way, blindly: either forwards or backwards. Mama submitted not to women's wisdom, but to the views of the close but impartial observer, something that the moral court of women in Russia had always done, from Nadezhda Mandelshtam to our times.

The principles of women's moral court were unsteady. They were the women of the century of unbelief. But the more unsteady their principles were, the stricter they themselves became. Mama had gone down the route of underground liberalism. She was irritated by her husband's Stalinism. My father, an important figure at state level, saw how effective Stalinism had been during the war and in the years that followed, and was unable to discount this.

I gradually began to get annoyed. In cultural matters I was increasingly inclined to agree with mama. But in terms of their core outlook on life, I felt more sympathy for my father: life was about energy, willpower, experience, war and games. Books remained firmly on my mother's side. The birth of my brother relieved a lot of the tension. My brother immediately became mama's favorite: it was impossible to compete with him. This distanced me from mama, whilst papa never showed any preference for either of his sons. He definitely preferred us to his work. A protégé of Molotov, father never lost sight of the most important thing of all: the things he had been taught about worldwide revolution. He later told me that whenever he spoke to bourgeois figures he used to think: he was in the right. So the real truth about my father's liberal thawing is of limited significance. He never made the shift towards a position of aggressive Stalinism, however, like Podtserob, who is prominently positioned in the photos of the Soviet delegation led by Stalin in Potsdam. Podtserob was openly critical of Khrushchev in father's presence and had a portrait of Stalin above the cupboard in his study, and a shrine containing Stalinist books, photos and notes inside the cupboard. A circle of admirers of Stalin, made up of men who had formerly had close ties to the Kremlin, used to meet in his study. They were the true knights of the Gulag. Khrushchev, whom the West saw as a staunch Communist who had only distanced himself from Stalin for tactical reasons, and who wanted to stick two fingers up at the West at every opportunity and snuggle up to America during the Caribbean crisis, was, in the eyes of the true believers, not just a political namby-pamby, but also a traitor. On the day Khrushchev was ousted, Podtserob knocked on the door of our Moscow apartment early in the morning holding a copy of *Pravda*. He was in raptures. Podtserov was died-in-the-wool; papa wasn't. Papa didn't have sufficient philosophy to cling to — he had been cast adrift. The spirit of Stalin did not live on in our home. Father did not cross the threshold of the dissidence of the anti-party group, but when he talked about his work at the Kremlin you could tell by the gleam in his eye where he felt he had spent the most important years of his life.

•

I loved to lie when I was a child. I would like even when it wasn't in my interest to do so. I would color the world with my lies, making my audience shudder with my fictions. The people I most enjoyed lying to were, by turns, Marusya Pushkina, grandma and Klava — they were the easiest to deceive. Later, I moved on to my classmates. I told them that at the universal exhibition in Brussels I had been invited to circumnavigate the earth in a satellite; that I had learned to drive and had driven three hundred kilometers on my own; that I had fired a real gun; that I had seen a 100kg diamond in Paris. I told grandma, who had never been abroad, all sorts of improbable stories — not just the one about the diamond — related to our time in Paris; I told her that I had climbed up the side of the Eiffel Tower — up the iron girders — and she believed me, which filled me with glee; but when I told her that roast chestnuts were a popular snack in Paris, she didn't believe me. I took delight in lying to the Armenian émigrée, who had taught me a little French, about Moscow. I told her that in Moscow there were blue and yellow trolleybuses that were driven by auto-pilots, and knew where to stop without being told; I told her that I had started drinking vodka at the age of three, like all ordinary children in Russia, and that I had touched the stars on top of the Kremlin with my hands.

"What are they like?" the Armenian said with a gasp. "Are they made of precious rubies?"

"I don't know," I replied. "But they're sharp — I cut my nails on them."

"Is it true what they say — that schoolchildren in Russia wear blazers?" the Armenian asked.

"Yes," I answered. "Each one carries a little dagger on the side. Everyone owns a blazer in our country: the workers, the peasants...my father, too."

I felt as though I was about to burst because of this mixture of lies and vital truth, and we lost track of time. Eventually the Armenian came to her senses, and looked at her slender watch with her sad, Armenian eyes, which had big black bags under them:

"*Et bien. Nous allons, vous allez, ils?..**

But it was too late: it was already the end of the lesson. Mama dashed into the room with light steps, wearing a wide-hemmed dress. Due to my lying, the only new word I had managed to learn was '*coccinelle*'.

"She's delighted with you," mama said to me.

It was hardly surprising: the Armenian now had plenty to tell the émigré community.

God alone knew what lies I had told, and might have to answer for. I had got carried away. I told grandma that I had drunk a whole ink-well of ink for a bet without getting food-poisoning; that I had got into a fight with Orlov and broken his arm, and that he only had one arm now; that I had a diplomatic passport, and the policemen in Paris paid their obeisance to me; that I had a gold watch that I had found in the street; that papa was in fact more important than Ambassador Vinogradov. I told grandma: that I hadn't slept for ages because of the homework they gave me at the school in Paris; that I had supported five girls on my shoulders during a physical culture lesson, like an acrobat at the circus. She sighed and gasped, growing anxious

---

* Right then. We go, you go, they...? (*fr.*)

and terribly concerned. Sometimes she couldn't help but intervene: she would speak up on my behalf to my parents. The latter would be horrified, and would start chasing after my lies. Mama and papa were no fun to talk to. I tried my best never to lie to papa; and when I lied to mama she quickly discovered the truth, got angry and started calling me Baron von Munchhausen. At such times she would grab me by the ear and say:

"By the ear and into the light."

It was horrible. I can't remember when I first learned to tell lies. I think I was just born that way. I loved it when the world reverberated because of my imagination. Lying shook up my view of the world. I saw the world bending under the impact of my lies, and stopped believing in its solidity. It seemed to me that the world would be a boring place without my stories — flat and utterly absurd. I was the protagonist of all my lies. My attitude to words was born of my lies. The whole of humanity sounded different to me. For example, in Krylov's fable about the Grasshopper and the Ant, I heard (while I was still in the toddler's group on Tverskoy Boulevard):

With an evil sadness at the cockerel's place
She goes to the Ant.

And then: *"Don't leave me, madearie..." 'Madearie'* seemed to me to be the most tender word in the world. I liked the cockerel more than the Ant and the Grasshopper. To this day I prefer *cockerel* and *madearie* to the original words. At school I was very fond of the name of Griboedov's play, *Woe from weather!* When I found out what the real title was, I was upset by how banal it sounded.

•

The things I hate more than anything else in the world are women's underwear and spies. I have a lot of issues with lacey women's underwear. At that time, when my grandma, in an effort to keep me warm, sent me off to start the first grade in a home-made white bra under my school uniform, with huge buttons and elastic bands holding up my brown socks, and I stood there in the morning, in the mid-season gloom, before the mirror, looking like a young Moscow transvestite with my willy on show between my female accessories, my natural masculinity revolted. I walked around in the bra like a pig on its way to the slaughter-house.

To this day I can't bear the sight of a woman wearing tights. I refuse to recognize women with *Wild orchid* fantasies. I'm disgusted by the thought of the can-can being performed in pantaloons, too. I hate the very concept of women's bras, which grab women's breasts and are fastened on their backs with vile hooks. I refuse to recognize either American sports bras, which have declared war on nipples both in Hollywood movies and in real life, or the frilly underwear of the Old World. When a woman turns out to be wearing underwear, I turn away in disappointment. It's not what I go in for. We've my grandma to thank — sexual desire is not something to be messed with. I like women who don't wear a bra at all, and let their breasts hang free.

I hate spies in exactly the same way. When a sweet-natured admirer of mine in Moscow once told me that she could only see me in one of two manifestations: either a writer or a great spy, I said to her: "Darling, don't put me in a white bra with elastic straps." I don't even like James Bond, the ironic manifestation of them. His enemies are the same as mine, but I nonetheless find his English sense of humor vomit-inducing. Spies are born to lie and rape. I don't like men who go about their business by speculating about brute force. They make my stomach turn. Fundamentally I have nothing against the idea of *retribution*. Going back to Ehrenburg, I must admit that the image of Jews sending Germans to the gas chambers at the end of the war in an equal proportion of 6,000,000: 6,000,000, and letting out the smoke through the pipes of a Jewish crematorium to the sound of triumphant Jewish melodies, intrigues me. Now that's

Jewish humor for you. The idea of the Red Army raping every German woman it came across is also something that I can understand, something that even appeals to me to some extent. But James Bond is not my kind of hero. And what did I end up with, once I had put everything in its right place?

•

Allow me to introduce you: Vladimir Ivanovich Erofeyev was an extremely significant figure in Soviet espionage in France. This is perhaps precisely how the objective historian of Franco-Soviet relations in the mid-twentieth century will record my father for political posterity. Poor papa! In France he got caught between two espionage agencies. What pigs those French are! In October 1996 the magazine *L'Express* — which papa had read every week for years — accused him of being a spy.

The effect this had on my father! He was at the Central Clinical Hospital at the time, but after asking permission from the head doctor he rushed home, where he gave an interview to French television. I could see from his instinctive, naive reaction that he was troubled to the very depths of his soul. An act of provocation had been organized against him. I can see him now sitting in the dining room, in the yellow armchair in front of the video camera, wearing a dark suit and expensive tie, ready to offer resistance, but mama doesn't let anyone into the apartment in their shoes — they have rugs and carpets in the house, the place has an Asian feel in this regard, and the maid only comes once a week, so papa is wearing house slippers on his feet — good-quality black ones, which are probably French, too, but are slippers nevertheless — which are coming off at the heels, and are not in keeping at all with his thunderous expression, and I see some bastard cameraman complaining about the slippers, in order to make my father a laughing stock in front of the whole of France, and I sit there in the corner of the room in silence — I feel like getting up and punching this cameraman in the face for bringing shame on my papa, but I sit there in silence and feel sorry for him.

I sit there and it occurs to me that papa, essentially, is just like some sort of Nazi diplomat, revealed to have been a spy after the war, what difference did it make that he wasn't a Nazi, and wasn't a Communist — he was my papa, my ageing papa, the papa whom I killed in 1979 and who had forgiven me for that; and I remember how once, in Mannheim, I had been taken into some back-rooms in my friends' apartment and been shown a portrait of their grandfather in full Nazi attire, with a swastika on his forehead; there was a big bouquet of fresh flowers underneath him, which was changed every day, like the changing of the guard, and I was told that he had been involved in the conspiracy against Hitler — I was told this in a kind whisper — and that he had been hung from a hook, but for me the uniform was more important than the conspiracy — in that it had belatedly rescued his officer-general's skin — if only that had happened earlier — prior to Stalingrad — because I don't give a damn about the Germans' complaints regarding the British and American bombs dropped on German cities, don't give a damn about the ruins of Dresden — I like these fire storms of revenge — and I was unable to overcome any of this and feel sympathy for someone else's grandfather, who had been hung from a hook. When the TV interview came to an end, I told my father about the slippers and he turned pale, but assured me that he wasn't a spy. And then I told him what I had been thinking during the interview: I thought that the only way I could get at the truth was by being tough with him. The next time I was in Paris I went to see my friends at *Le Monde*. But before I went I said to my father:

"You promise you weren't a spy?"

Father denied it.

"But you probably gave money to the French communists, illegally, right?" I asked, on the off-chance.

"Yes. Vinogradov used to take me with him when he handed over the money."

Le Monde printed my father's refutation. Father was very pleased. I said to him:

"What do you think, is there any difference between a Nazi diplomat and a Nazi spy?"

Father pondered my question.

"Is there any way a Nazi diplomat could have been a worthy person, a faithful servant to Hitler?"

"I doubt it," father said.

"Take occupied Paris, for example. Can you see any difference between a diplomat like Ribbentrop and a Nazi spy?"

"What do you mean?"

"To the French, you were a Nazi diplomat. Only you were working for Stalin rather than Hitler."

"That's not the same thing."

"That's what you think. But to the French it amounted to the same thing!"

He stood there looking pale, with trembling lips. They made him go back to hospital. But he was glad that *Le Monde* had printed his refutation.

•

The spy scandal in which my father had been embroiled escalated. The French suddenly gained an insight into the matter. They got into the archives of the Ministry of Foreign Affairs of the Russian Federation and read, amongst other things, the encoded telegrams sent by my father and stamped 'confidential'.

Who could have dreamt — and could my father ever have imagined, even in his worst nightmares — that those telegrams from the 1950s would one day fall into the hands of the enemy? An enemy from the past, of course — but an existing one nevertheless. It was at that moment that the good Stalin made his presence felt: my father, like a prehistoric dinosaur, spoke up for the honour of his non-existent motherland. In a series of encoded telegrams he provided information about how many French troops were in Algiers, about their political purges and about incidents of torture — and he also revealed the addresses of the US secret services in Paris. How did he know all this?

The French historian Thierry Wolton had prepared a sentence for my papa (with which it was hard not to agree, from a political standpoint): "Every diplomat who met a political figure or journalist was required to present a report about their meeting to the resident KGB agent. This meant that any Soviet diplomat who worked in the West ended up becoming a secret service agent. And Vladimir Ivanovich Erofeyev, it seems, was no exception: he remained in constant communication with Charles Hernu while he was an attaché at the USSR's embassy in Paris, from August 19, 1955 to June 24, 1959."

Please accept my thanks, historians. I now know what day it was when I failed to see the Champs-Élysées.

In France, Erofeyev was seen as someone with great knowledge of political and cultural life in the country, and during the normal course of his activity he had occasion to meet artists such as Yves Montand and Claude Autant-Lara, as well as politicians (Leo Amon, Jean de Lipkovsky *et al*). He had breakfast with Charles Hernu on April 24, 1957, for example, at the restaurant *La Rotisserie Perigourdine*.

I can vividly picture my father having breakfast (or looking at it from a Russian perspective: having lunch) in a Parisian restaurant with a person whose hatred of capitalism was as strong as my hatred of communism. When I met some French diplomats at their embassy in Moscow, whilst a graduate student at the Institute of World Literature, I had such an overwhelming desire to say something anti-Soviet to them, and to give away every secret imaginable, that they made up their minds I was a spy and an *agent provocateur*. My naïvety, which had been passed down to me from my father, prompted me to go to even greater lengths. I tried to persuade the American ambassador that his Russian chauffeur must be working for the KGB.

I was promptly called in to the KGB's offices at Kuznetsky Most because of having ventured into foreign embassies: they began trying to scare me with vague threats, but by the end of the conversation they were asking me to collaborate with them. I told them that I ought to let my father know about this, and ask his advice. As strange as it seems, this threw them into confusion. They harassed me on a further three occasions: one of them, a young, restless chap named Boris Ivanovich, stuck out.

"We've rounded up all the young writers," he boasted. I ignored this, along with everything else that didn't concern me directly. The two of us were sitting at a table in the brightly-colored cafe at the Central Home of Writers.

"Listen, could you do me a little favor?"

"Go on?"

"My sister's got mixed up with some guy in India. Could you somehow get her called back here, via your father?"

"What's wrong, is she a virgin or something?" I said rudely.

He flared up like a little werewolf. To tell the truth, I too felt somewhat taken aback by my own sharpness of tongue. But an ambassador's son was out of his league in this matter. Besides, my wife was a foreigner — a Pole, admittedly, but still not one of ours. It must be said that there was a difference between me and Hernu, though. He had been tapped up by the Bulgarian intelligence agency, and had received money in exchange for information — but when he lost the trust of the Bulgarians, the Russians picked him up; in the intervening period he met Vladimir Ivanovich four times. Papa said he was unaware that Hernu had been tapped up by the Bulgarians. Strangely, though, Hernu ended up becoming France's Defence Minister.

The French, as flighty as ever, suddenly caught on and discovered, in a historic moment, what had long been clear to the naked eye: France, pushing Washington ever further away, and over-saturated with Communists of its own, was easy prey for

Moscow, which sent all manner of "agents of influence" to Paris, and my father may well have had a diplomatically small slice of this French pie for himself. When the French caught on, their first move was to expose my father. Father sent a refutation to *L'Express*, via me. The journalists there were probably surprised that he was still alive, and sent no response. They decided not to print his refutation, which was impolite at best.

Father pressured me to try and influence the French press using the connections I had amongst French journalists. He even went so far as to complain to Bella Akhmadulina on one occasion, such was his anxiety.

"What am I to make of it," she said unsympathetically, performing the role of the eternal conscience, "take me, for example: I had a friendly chat with a diplomat I know, and he denounced me to his superiors. I find that dishonest — I would even call it dishonorable.

"In diplomatic practice," my father explained to her, drawing back the veil a little on his secretive profession, "there are set ways of working; keeping records of business conversations is something diplomats do all over the world."

He added that recording conversations was an important source of information about what was going on in the country where the diplomat lived...

Style maketh the villain.

In short, it enables him to draw up specific measures with regard to how best to develop and deepen connections and interaction with the country in question. Records of conversations such as this are sent to HQ, to an approved list of people, including the minister, his deputies, and the heads of the relevant territorial divisions.

When my father revealed the secret to the musicians, they paid attention: to them, the minister, at the end of the day, was an important man — but there was no "interaction" with the poetess: the conversation began to drown in their mutual alienation. What's more, the Russian journalists, for their part, who — in father's opinion — ought to have adopted a patriotic stance, began to express support for *L'Express*. For some reason my father began to refer to them as Soviets, call them to order, and complain to my former neighbor in the diplomatic house (my father had got me a position on the staff there), who at that time was the head of the printing department, and asked him about holding a press-conference, but he brushed father off like an irritating fly.

My father escalated the matter, taking it to Minister Primakov, but Primakov didn't have time for this pensioner. The Deputy Minister agreed to see him, though (this gave father no small measure of satisfaction, as you might expect of a civil servant), and father started cursing the French, in order to emphasize at every opportunity the fact that he was no spy. And then that good-for-nothing French historian came along and wrote that father had been a spy when he was in Sweden, too. As it happens, this wasn't news to me at all. During the Soviet era I had read a book by an American author (his name was Smith, if I'm not mistaken) about the KGB (my parents had it on their bookshelf), and I had spotted my father's name in it, in connection with his activities in Sweden.

The Frenchman and the American both maintained that father had provided valuable services to the GRU when they were in Stockholm. As for father, he was proud of this.

FATHER: On Kollontai's orders I stayed in constant touch with the Danish and Norwegian patriots who were fighting Hitler, and who often came to Sweden. They told me about the Nazis' military exercises, and I passed on what they said to Kollontai. She would then pass this information to Moscow, and to the Allies. By way of example, she passed on to the British Ambassador some information that I had picked up from Danish patriots regarding the locations of Hitler's Fau-1 and Fau-2 rocket launcher sites, from which he planned to launch rockets aimed at England, predominantly at London. The RAF immediately dealt a crushing blow to these bases.

"Only false patriots," my father said to me, who did God knows what during the war — men like Thierry Walton, are capable of reproaching us, Soviet diplomats sent by the Ministry of Foreign Affairs of the USSR to take up diplomatic roles..."

I stopped listening at that point. I thought about the meaning of the word "patriot", and about the fact that for Soviet diplomats, the war did not end in 1945. That being against the Germans was good, but being against the Americans was bad — was that it? I was torn between my family and history. I was not tempted by the role of a latter-day Pavlik Morozov, betraying my father not just to Akhmadulina but also to Thierry Wolton, whom I didn't know. I tried to imagine who this Thierry might be like (I had seen a fair few professors like him; they would call me and try to befriend me): a dull-as-ditchwater university academic with cheap Parisian snobbery, an ugly old wife, a filthy Renault and a modest, pedant's apartment — or a clever, sympathetic misanthrope, like a friend of mine from Nanterre, who, during the Soviet era, while working at the French embassy — it was there that we met — used to bring suitcases of money for Soviet dissidents, illegally.

But papa not supposed to talk to the French Communists? So Pavlik Morozov was nothing but a moral fiction? But how on earth had papa found out the addresses of the American agents in Paris?

•

On June 24, 1959, papa left France, against his will. France forced him to learn to love the French way of eating and drinking, then spat him out. Surely the French didn't declare my father a *persona non grata*?

My parents packed their things hastily. To make things worse, Ambassador Vinogradov made life difficult for them. At the last minute he housed a party bigwig from Moscow in their apartment, and they were forced to move upstairs, almost into the attic. And yet just a short time earlier, no more than a month ago, in May, Ambassador Vinogradov had put in an official request to Moscow asking for father to be made the number two man in the Soviet embassy: an attache-envoy. This later opened the way for father to make his next move in this game of chess: to travel to Switzerland or Belgium as an ambassador. And then suddenly he moved to Moscow.

The resident KGB agent in Paris was not fond of papa. The longer things went on, the more he realized that in terms of his spirit, there was something not quite right about papa. He didn't know how to explain this, either to Moscow or to himself. At first glance everything seemed absolutely fine with papa.

At heart, the resident spy despised all diplomats: their knowledge was superficial and unreliable, and most of them had come to Paris merely to show off and buy some new glad-rags. Ambassador Vinogradov seemed to him to be a "braggart". The resident spy scorned his near neighbours among the Soviet counter-espionage agents as well, who were secretly spying on him. The resident spy loved the underground illegals, who, at his orders, took their lives in their hands by putting microphones in the officers and apartments of the French ministers, and got rid of undesirables and traitors. It was business. "There's a reason why the Committee members refer to us as "carving knives", the agent smiled to himself. But he knew that something disagreeable was happening to him, and that he had fallen off the straight and narrow: he was slowly but surely becoming a drunkard, and would soon be an inveterate one. He found it hard to shave in the mornings. He had twice beaten up his wife, who gave free English lessons to diplomats' wives and brought tasty meat pies into her lessons. He had once broken down the door of his apartment, after his wife locked it to stop him going out drinking. The referent knew that the nearest neighbors were aware of this.

The referent did not scorn my father. He thought of him as an active and well-qualified worker — his denunciations to

Moscow were useful, intelligent, one might even say brilliant, that was all true, but the resident followed his gut instinct. It wasn't about the way papa dressed, his gait, or his speech — but in his way of dressing, his gait and his speech the agent saw something that was a threat to his very essence. Papa never stood still: he developed and grew, like a tree, but some strange fruit appeared on that tree. The resident KGB agent began to see, in papa, a silent danger to himself as a living being. If Vinogradov had never proposed that Moscow make papa an envoy and adviser, all this could have been avoided. But the resident spy was supposed to give his opinion on this course of action, and rubber-stamp every step papa took; he now had a reason to do so, and he began to think deeply about him.

We are all of us disliked by a whole assortment of people — their gut instinct is to be irritated by every movement we make — but the key thing is not to give them a reason to form a particular opinion about us, not to become dependent on them, not to give them an opportunity to strike us with a sharp Japanese sword.

Papa was replaced. He had wanted a promotion — his scent was supposed to spread throughout the whole embassy. It was all decided at the level of scents. In this silent struggle between a nameless resident spy (papa never told me his name, out of a patriotic fear that if he pulled on that little cord the whole chain might unravel, right up to the present day and Russia's spies in Europe; mama told me that he apparently had a false name, and added that he was "no idiot") and papa had already become a paradigm for my relations with people in the future. Papa laid the groundwork for alienation thanks to his charming aura of success, which came naturally to him — the people known as KGB residents do not like that at all. The latter had a high-quality French car (the French counter-intelligence officers could easily tell who the Russian spies were based on what car they drove: the diplomats' cars were not as good, but the residents didn't even hide away: they were able to hide in the open), a talkative wife with a pathological fear of Yevgenia Alexandrovna, money, and useful ties in Moscow, but he didn't have what my father had: the ability to flutter through life like a butterfly. Papa set a riddle for my very existence.

What happened next had been predetermined. According to the resident spy's information, all manner of suspicious individuals had suddenly appeared around father — such as Bonner, who owned a tobacco store — enter Flaubert: this one was a character right out of one of his books — and his wife, who ran a fashionable shop on the right bank of the Seine; these were people of means, people who were of use; according to father, to the USSR, insofar as they used to take the steam ship to Odessa (the Soviet customs agents pierced oranges with needles on the border, whether in search of seditious material or to stop the French selling them on the coast) and told everyone that they had liked it there. The Bonner family was another family that was interested in culture (mama first got them interested in it): they used to accompany my parents on theatre trips, and discuss what they had seen; they invited my parents round to their place.

Meeting my father in the middle of the embassy's stone courtyard, the resident, acknowledging how efficient my father had been, said openly:

"I have told Moscow about your suspicious contacts."

Father explained to me that at that time there was an unspoken but very distinct ban on maintaining relations of an informal nature with foreign civilians. And he and mama were engaged in *treacherous* relations with the Bonners.

But worse than that, in my opinion, was this: papa and mama were significant *French* agents of influence, in that they used to take all sorts of fine things to Moscow, like furniture, German silver, tablecloths, and albums of works by the Impressionists, and these items used to bother visitors. Moreover, papa brought his branded tennis balls to Moscow. They were far better than the balls I used to buy at Dinamo, when they were in stock.

Everything seemed complicated and confused. My parents

had some close friends, Lodic and Galochka (Galina Fedorovna), and they had a daughter called Irochka, who was a friend of mine. Once the grown-ups had gone out to the cinema, I put Irochka in the bath and turned on the shower. She got wet through, because she was dressed. At a loss what to do, I propped her up against a tall radiator, by the window, and she stood there, drying out slowly, until her parents arrived. At first they were unable to work out what had happened, and took fright — in their alarm they suspected me of sadism and eroticism (all of which had perhaps played a role, under the surface), but later, after they had boiled over, they burst out laughing, such was their relief.

On one occasion papa decided to seek advice from Uncle Lodik, who worked in the same group as the resident, under the banner of UNESCO. There was something about Bonner's behaviour that put papa on alert. Uncle Lodik was a "distant neighbor" and a very handsome man. Papa began to confide in him. But his wife Galina Fedorovna, on the other hand, also had ties to the KGB in my parents' view, because after mama told her that they were going to the theatre with the tobacconist, Lodik and Galochka suddenly appeared near the buffet during the intermission — what a charming couple they were — and started getting to know the Bonners. Papa told Lodik that Bonner wasn't a counter-intelligence agent, but the latter once told papa in confidence that France had developed a means of transporting oil in dry form.

"In granules," Bonner explained over a lemon pie (mama had adopted him) in his apartment.

Papa had long experience of being on a high state of alert. He sensed something was not quite right about this oil in dry form, the formula for which Bonner had not really suggested, but there was a hitch, and papa was on his guard internally.

"I'm no expert in these matters," papa said quietly, warding off the danger, "but you could mention it to the Trade Mission, by all means."

"It's an interesting film," Lodik answered.

"What was it he said: in the form of granules?" Lodik asked once again, after pausing for thought.

He promised to take care of everything. An hour later Uncle Lodik was with the KGB resident, wanting to toady up to him. It may also be that he wanted to get revenge on me over his daughter, whom I had washed in the bathtub with vague erotic ideas going through my mind. He was a gentle man, nothing like an intelligence agent in temperament, and they wanted to send him home — all the more so given that his wife Galina Fedorovna accidentally spilt boiling water from the kettle onto his pants, and for the first time in his life he swore at her, but then he saved the embassy from having to recruit an attaché.

The resident, who was known to everyone because he made no effort to conceal his identity; who, whenever they went to Mantes, would sit on the lawn boozing on vodka and eating kebabs; and who felt no love at all for Paris, for the bridges over the Seine, the sycamores and the rotting chestnut trees, surrounded as he was by others just like him, near neighbors and more distant ones, such that he only seemed conspiratorial to a mild degree — not just to the journalist from Humanity who just happened to be at the party ("They stick out like a sore thumb," he whispered to papa), but even to us, the children — decided to send papa home, quickly and without any fuss. Some sixth sense told him that papa had misunderstood the primary objective of his work: he didn't want to get his hands dirty. Essentially, he and the resident were part of the same circus troupe: the only difference was that papa operated using white gloves, whilst the resident operated using a whip. They were both striving towards the same outcome: for everything to fall apart, and for France to have to start again from scratch. One day the Ambassador received a telegram.

"Volodya, I can't make head nor tail of it, but you're being called home. Look."

The ambassador showed him the telegram amicably. He

might have spared him having to see it. The two men looked into one another's eyes. They didn't waste their words.

"I'll find out what's going on," Vinogradov said, knitting his brows.

Ambassador Vinogradov would have stepped in on papa's behalf, but, just as in the incident with Kollontai, the ambassador proved to be powerless. The KGB crushed papa. Shaken, disillusioned by a false friendship, full of adoration for Paris, insulted, and frustrated, my parents left for Moscow.

But the Ministry of Foreign Affairs — my parents' religion — did not let them die. When papa, on his arrival in Moscow, appeared before Gromyko, the Foreign Minister was entirely justified in saying to him, in a weighty manner and with a pious expression on his face:

"We trust you. You're going to work at the Ministry of Foreign Affairs, just like you used to."

Everything was fine. Only Paris was no more.

•

Memory is like a corpse. Where have all those events disappeared to — the ones I wrote to my parents about once a fortnight, to various foreign destinations, painstakingly avoiding writing about myself? Where have those hundreds of letters got to — the ones I had to hand in at the Belarus Station, hurrying to get to the Moscow to Paris car, or take to other people's apartments, or to Smolensk Square, and toil in the gothic vestibule of the Ministry of Foreign Affairs? The specters of Oswald Spengler and Danilevsky haunt the pages of my book. I am jumping away from this topic. The direction of one's life is determined by the direction of one's mind. It is fraught with solitude, which can deceive you with its stream of entertaining diversions. Wisdom is a blind alley too, if we constantly maintain that there is a difference between faith and knowledge. Wisdom causes a drawing in of the mouth. Education can get in the way of enlightenment, but intellectual restraint only serves to encourage wild behavior. I come across a bill from the Berlin restaurant *Sale e Tabacchi*, for €49.50. You must feed a woman up first — then you have sex with her. Four glasses of mediocre Italian wine. Would you like your water carbonated or uncarbonated, sir? A bottle of Evian. A pheasant with a pear. I don't know how to live on my own. I can't get by without those reflections — the ones that my crushes for women always turned into. I used to turn women on like lamps, always trying to change the lighting, with which I had grown tired. What were their names? I can't remember half of them. Luck is the extreme form of the challenges life throws up. Jealousy, spite and vanity fell off me like leaves off a cabbage. With my impeccable manners, I am turning into an exemplary cabbage stump. I am burying myself in star-studded sand.

•

I keep procrastinating: I ought to have packed away my little books already, and my textbooks and toys, and gone home to Moscow — and yet I'm still here. My parents are going to spend another whole year without me in Paris, until they get called back, but I have to leave: there is no Russian middle school here on the banks of the Seine.

I have learnt the route home off by heart, just as I learnt the poem 'I love the storm in early May'. Little has changed since the days of de Custine. Back then, when I was a schoolboy, and much later, when my father returned to Paris to deputize for the Director General of UNESCO (the Ministry of Culture mocked the decision, and didn't want to let my father go), and I started spending time in Paris once again: I began to gain an understanding of the route back to Moscow with growing clarity, just like the noblewoman Morozova's exile to Siberia.

The fuss of packing kept me from sad thoughts, but the moment my suitcase was carried outside and put into the trunk as if in a funeral ceremony, I began to struggle manfully against my own pitiful appearance.

"What's got into you?" my parents asked, as if in earnest.

"I don't want to go," I smiled with all the strength I could muster.

We drove slowly along the Boulevard de Sebastopol, held up by the traffic lights, towards the Gare du Nord; Parisians walked along the pavement with a springy gait, carrying their baguettes, and I wished that the railway workers would suddenly go on strike or that we would get stuck in a traffic jam and miss the train.

A Soviet car, as heavy as an armored vehicle and manufactured in East Germany, stood at the station. There was no sign of the conductor. He had gone to the station kiosk at one end of the platform. He was flicking through the pages of an erotic magazine full of titties, lasciviously yet with an indifferent expression on his face. He came back, short of breath. He was a man of many faces. He looked like a guard keeping watch at a warehouse; a yard-keeper who had come out to sweep the street; a Chekist; a comedian; a mountain eagle; a soldier and a commander. To me he was already all Russia, cornered in the dress uniform of a railway worker. As he inspected my ticket, he demonstrated a Byzantine slowness of thought. We didn't have far to go. Europe was far from being like the Trans-Siberian. Saying farewell can be a crafty business. After opening the upper quarter of the window, which you would never dare stick your head out of, you wave towards your parents absent-mindedly, and in response they wave at you with great care, right up until you disappear for good.

We had not yet left the web of tracks outside the station when the guard fastened all the doors. He had turned from the joker into the prison warden, who brings out the tea in glass-holders. Usually it is the last car of the train. You can go out into the corridor and be transformed into a rear-view mirror. Now we are passing through France, Belgium, West Germany — this is the section of the journey when the guard collects our passports — out of concern for the passengers, on the face of it; the Western border guards put stamps in it, they don't bother you, but, most importantly of all, they make sure no-one has fled the train.

The train hurtles madly across Europe; the immutable station of Huy, in Belgium, flashes past; West Germany grows before you in leaps and bounds. The train moves into the dense strata of the atmosphere: the border with East Germany. But there's still something left to indulge in: the West Berlin station of Zoo, where the guard always gets nervous, and watches you buying beer, nuts and chocolate with what little money you have left. The train knocks harshly on the bridge, the wall and Friedrichstrasse come into view: you've arrived.

A sudden change comes over the conductor — he becomes more down-to-earth, and changes completely: he is transformed from a benevolent supervisor into an old man overgrown with stubble. We are all equal, but he's the top dog here. Grumbling, he hands out our passports — you're on your own from here. The East German border guards unscrew the ceilings, poke around in the toilet and all the cracks with little torches; the Poles are indifferent in their caps with eagles on — what do they care — and Warsaw sails past through the window, with the Soviet house of culture — beyond that is a crossing in the woods, a stream — and then you stop. Before we reach the border, the guard changes clothes — he looks like someone's bride now. The bridegrooms will be along any minute now. It's raining bridegrooms. At their officer's abrupt command, they hurtle towards the train. The border guards walk into the railway cars with a clatter, along with German shepherds on leads. The passengers freeze. The German shepherds poke their noses around in the compartment (everyone out!) and jump onto the beds. The train stands there for hours — it has its wheels changed, as though there are some public systems at work. Some women roll up, and offer you fresh fruit and veg. A group of passionless male customs officers and perverse female customs officers, with sadistic disc-shaped accessories instead of eyes, come in, as if by way of punishment; they take away the women's magazines, rummage around in your suitcases, check your pockets, and take one or two people off the train.

Then the motherland begins. The train starts moving, and all the passengers — after being frisked — gaze out of the window with trembling cheeks. In Brest, lads in tracksuits, on a field trip, are running along the platform looking for beer. The motherland smells of Zhigulevsky beer. The motherland unfurls itself out of the nothingness. The Belarussian fields. The Russian forests. The teaspoon tinkles in the railway glass, in its glass-holder. Suddenly, you remember that there are such things as wooden huts — *izby* — in the world. The railroad worker in the padded jacket stands by the barrier holding his yellow flag aloft, forever.

Nobody bothered us in Brest — my parents had diplomatic passports. We were left in peace, and shown respect. People saluted us. On that day, when I left Paris for Moscow with my parents in the summer of 1958, my childhood came to an end.

4

She put her old blue panties on the floor in the hall, in front of the door — like a flag that is hung up when power changes hands, rather than a rag on which to wipe dirty shoes. She had covered the chandelier with old sheets; she had even thrown a sheet over the painting in the dining room; she covered the sofas and armchairs with rags — to protect the furniture. When my parents, making the most of their leave, left for Paris, grandma turned the apartment into a dressing room. She dressed me up in clothes that she had sewn herself. My paradise came to an end, along with my childhood. I had been given up to grandma. I had been thrown into her care, like a cuckoo's egg. At first I didn't understand exactly what was going on, but I soon figured out that this was a children's penal colony, a prison for young criminals. I wasn't allowed to sit on the sofa, and I wasn't keen to sit on rags. I wasn't allowed to be someone that I couldn't be in reality. Grandma's nerves were completely shot. She used to yell at me. She shuddered loudly whenever the piano was opened. Not a single aspect of my behavior was to her liking, because the world was not to her liking. She lived in this world on loan, saving things up the same way souls are preserved. She waged war against moths. There was no logic in this at all. My parents later threw out the sofas and armchairs without a moment's hesitation — and she picked them up and took them back to her place.

It took just a few days for my relations with grandma to be ruined. In the past she had been my favorite grandma; now she was my torturer.

I wasn't allowed to bring other kids home with me — they might turn out to be thieves or snitches. Grandma stuffed me into a glass preserve jar, like a tomato. I spent a whole year floating in that jar. I plunged into a desperate loneliness, one that clearly came to my rescue — I plunged into myself. Grandma had completed four years of schooling, just like me. She had not been able to make head nor tail of anything she heard in her lessons. She kept an eye on my grades.

My parents had sent me back to School No. 122, where I had already spent a year — the first year — in Palashavsky Side-street, near Pushkin Square. The dissident Bukovsky was a fellow-pupil, but he was older than me and I didn't know him back then. When I met Bukovsky in Cambridge, and stayed up all night with him drinking red wine, we reminisced about the teachers, including the deputy head, a geography teacher nicknamed Roach. I could have been sent to a school for children from privileged families, like the Podtserobs. I don't know how that would have turned out. Aleksei, who had raised his glass of tomato juice to Stalin on my birthday, went on to become a diplomat, and the other son became a drug addict. I grew close to Kiryusha, who later became a drug addict. I found him interesting, and close to me from a social standpoint. Children from the side-street basements and communal flats on Gorky Street studied at my school. Half the class had to put firewood in the stove each evening. My classmates seemed to me to be ragamuffins, little clochards.

The difference between Paris and Moscow was so striking, so deafening, that Moscow came across as a sort of imaginary city — a city that didn't really exist at all. I set off to do some reconnaissance on the non-existent. Kiryusha and I walked around the city in the evening. He showed me all the dangerous places. As I saw it, every place was dangerous. Some garbage was ablaze in the rubbish dumps in Krasnaya Presnaya. Taking the side-street on the journey home from school was a risky business. Hooligans would come up to you:

"Got any money?"

If you said "no", they asked you to jump up in the air. If they heard change jingling in your pockets, they would beat you up

for lying and take your money off you. If there was no jingling —
they would beat you up anyway. I soon realized that there are
some experiences that cannot be conveyed in words. No-one
understood what I meant when I referred to Paris. During the
transition towards the warmer season, crowds of kids would
rush around after a football in the schoolyard. On the site of
the school there had once been a cemetery; executioners had
once lived in the side-street. Anyone who could afford better
clothes was scorned; envious of a passer-by in a hat, they would
shout out:

"Look, there's that hat going past!"

My stamp collection languished. I was scared of the young
traffickers, who sold the British colonies on the black market,
at the gateway onto Kuznetsky Bridge, near the philately store.
The bakery sold tasty *kalach*, though. Life had turned into a
comparison. In winter there was an ice-rink at Patriarch's
Ponds — that was something you didn't see in Paris. If you
steered clear of the hooligans, you could have a nice little skate
there. But there were hooligans on the ice, too. They had grown
adept at fighting on skates and insulting young girls. In actual
fact I got away quite lightly. I was brave. But I didn't like fighting.
There were two scary older boys who used to patrol the school
corridors. One day they punched me in the face — for no reason
at all. It hurt. I had a crush on Kirilla Vasilievna — I couldn't
get the image of her light, naked body in the bathtub out of my
mind. There was a bit of eroticism at school, too. We used to look
at the girls when they were getting changed for gym class. But
they wore strange pinkish-auger and raspberry panties which
reeked of poverty, and were lice-bitten and sickly pale. The only
thing I was good for at school was as a supplier of chewing gum.
My parents never bought chewing gum in Paris, but everyone at
School 122 dreamed of getting their hands on some American
chewing gum. One day Kolya Maksimov was round at my place.
He noticed what looked like little pillows in the kitchen, and
started to eat them. As it turned out, this wasn't chewing gum

at all, but French glue. I can still picture him now, his mouth all glued together.

If I had been a little more cunning, I would probably have bought off the hooligans, but I didn't have a cunning bone in my body. I became not so much a cynic as a John the Baptist, making promises to all and sundry that Moscow would one day be lit up with fire and gleam with advertisements; that the time of *perestroika* and a new life would come. People looked at me as if I was a degenerate. Moralism became incredibly popular, becoming more obdurate with each passing year. I preached a different, higher quality of life, in which there would be no hooligan-like aggression, no poverty or lice. Mama has maintained this preachy nature right up to this day. Diplomatic etiquette became her god. Yet she never taught me how to use a knife and fork the right way. I would lean over my soup with my face almost touching the bowl, and gulp hot tea with a slurp. Tell the doctor I don't need him. My school days were a sluggish torture. Never in my life has time passed as slowly as it did during my lessons at school. The square clock that hung above the door at school was stuck on to a dial. 45 minutes seemed an eternity. I sometimes find myself dreaming about that ropey time.

·

Mama, after her final year in Paris, saw me at the Belarus Station. Instead of kissing me, she put her head in her hands. When we got home she dressed me up in Parisian finery. Life with my parents became easier. I began to find my feet at school. My favorite pastime was to go to GUM and buy some ice cream. In Soviet days the ice cream there was incredibly tasty. It was sold in a little glass costing 20 kopecks (after the monetary reform in 1961). They served it in aluminum trays: strawberry, blackcurrant, crême-brulée or plain old vanilla. Nina Sergeevna, the wife of *Pravda*'s correspondent in Paris, used to say:

"If we did everything to the same standard as we make ice cream, we would have built Communism by now."

For some reason this never quite happened. As well as ice cream there was also the summer. We used to drive out to our dacha. There were tall birches in Chkalovsky. It was an area occupied by staff from the Ministry of Foreign Affairs. They used to play tennis there. There were even some former 'British' spies with thin, freckled faces and legs — they had sold the secrets of the atom bomb to our country and were now playing tennis without a care in the world. It was raining cats and dogs. It was not so much a shower as a downpour. Everyone crowded into the big hallway in front of the dining room. I stood right in front of the door, smelling the scent of the rain. I always loved being on the edge — between the warmth and the icy cold, between truth and lies. The threshold was the motherland to which I was so accustomed. Two short figures were standing in the darkest recesses of the hall, right back in the corner away from everyone else: I sensed that no-one wanted to pay any attention to them. One of them was Molotov, the eternal water-carrier, the man who organized the Soviet collective farms, the man of the universe. Alongside him was Zhemchuzhina, who was the last person to see Stalin's wife alive. The rain came to an end. Everyone rushed outside into the wet surroundings. My parents, embarrassed by how cruel mankind could be, went over to their one-time hosts. The latter couple had once invited them to their dacha in Sochi. When the rain stopped, my parents invited them to join them on a walk. Heavy drops of rain were falling from the birch trees. My parents talked about life in Paris. Molotov said absent-mindedly:

"Is that so?"

Zhemchuzhina sang the praises of Khrushchev, who had kicked Molotov into the long grass. After his descent, Molotov became our neighbor: he lived in the dacha next to ours.

After she came out of prison, Polina Semenova remained loyal to Stalin till her dying day. Mama could not get her head around this. She had once spent three days in the same ward of the Central Clinical Hospital as Polina Semenova, and was struck by this Russian passionary. In the mornings, Zhemchuzhina would listen to summaries of the latest news through her earphones, and would read all the main newspapers, a pencil in her hand. That was apparently her way of casting a spell on death. The sick women got onto the subject of Fyodor Raskolnikov, who had been the Soviet ambassador to Bulgaria during the purges. Raskolnikov was known for being the grandson of a man who came straight out of a well-known novel. This sometimes happens in Russia, and it is confirmed by Daniil Andreev. After receiving a list of books by "enemies of the people" which had to be confiscated from the embassy's library, and seeing that his book was included on the list, Raskolnikov decided to defect. The protagonist's personification process was interrupted when the KGB threw his grandson out of a Paris window some time later. Zhemchuzhina said:

"Better to die in one's Socialist motherland than live in a capitalist country."

The women engaged in some hostile bickering, unable to find any common ground. Zhemchuzhina, who was dying of cancer of the liver, referred to Stalin affectionately as "Josef". Molotov called in on her every day. Zhemchuzhina was right. Stalin is the only guarantor of Communism in Russia.

No matter how much dirt is thrown over him, he lives on. He lives on, though his immediate surroundings destroyed him. He lives on, in spite of the 20th party congress. He has risen up from hell, despite the fact that the mystic writer Daniil Andreyev condemned him to the very bottom of the underworld in his work *The Rose of the World*. He lives on, in spite of *perestroika*. He has emerged out of the depths, like a drowned man. He has emerged and is risen again. Stalin has the copyright on magic totalitarianism. In the end, Stalingrad will once again be named after him. Stalin needs no rehabilitation, because he has already been rehabilitated. The Russian soul, by its very nature, is Stalinist. The further back in time Stalin's victims go, the stronger and the more enlightened Stalin becomes. His victims are a little cloud of time. Russians have a sweet taste in their mouth when they watch films about Stalin, when they hear jokes about Stalin.

Stalin is walking down the stairs in the Kremlin — an Uzbek in an oriental robe rushes towards him with a bunch of flowers. Stalin has even managed to please an Uzbek. Stalin's resurrection is going to be permanent, just as Trotsky's revolution was to be permanent. Every boss in Russia uses Stalinist methods — even the bosses of railroad stations radiate Stalinist ideas. European liberalism in Russia lacks the energy not only to evolve, but also to reproduce other forms of government. Every ruler of Russia involuntarily aligns himself along Stalinist lines.

"Why would I want to drown Vitya?" mama said, pondering Dostoyevsky's words over.

We slowly moved away (like Bryulov in *The Last Day of Pompeii*), stooping, from a polite world in which the lovers in films at the cinema used the formal form of "you", in spite of Stalinism and everything it involved. The destruction of the polite Russia — about which de Custine had written with such admiration — outlived Stalin. I ended up with the remnants of it.

•

"Boy, if you've got a grandma — if she's still alive — do something that will hurt her. Break her arm, bite off her withered nipple." That was what Uncle Slava advised me to do. Just like that. No other way. Do it exactly like that. Bite it off and spit it out. Gross!

That summer, grandma passed away. In her heart she sensed me screaming at her: the devil's woman. Begging forgiveness, she fell to the floor and sobbed. She didn't forgive me: father was called, with tragic laurels. Grandma demanded vengeance. Near our place was a village for future cosmonauts. Gagarin, as yet unknown to the world, used to look up at the stars at night, and the dollar signs flashing in his eyes were so big that they were enough to make a grown man get down on all fours wipe his ass. That place was marvelous, simply marvelous. The birches were tall and the grass was tall. Walking down to the large pond, up to your knees in grass, was really pleasant. I remember waiting to be hit, my face darkening in fear, here it comes, here it comes, my cheeks went numb and there was a ringing in my ears — but father didn't strike me.

I don't know how Uncle Slava cooked his food in the dacha next door, but we cooked ours using a kerosene burner. Granny didn't believe in electric stoves, because the power had a tendency to go out. Oil stoves were slowly becoming a thing of the past, but the kerosene burner wasn't — oh no — it towered above life and utensils, like a high-priest's headdress, and it had a fun little peep-hole in it, like the stove in which they cremated the dead in those days. The butter went in, and the chunks of smoked sausage — rationed sausage, *Doctor's* sausage — jumped around and gleamed, and began to look like ears. Granny sang out into the garden, in a soulful voice:

"Come e-e-e-e-e-eat!"

I was in the garden: thin and big-headed, an egg-head who had not been awoken. I was not yet myself, though. I was some sort of pre-me. This me-but-not-me was about thirteen years old, and was utterly worn out with loneliness. There was music playing somewhere in the park. I got the panicky feeling that life was passing by, and would pass by me without me noticing. I would sit down on a pile of sand as if it was a pile of manure, submissively, but I enjoyed playing on the railroad. It was the national railroad, ugly and solid, and I did not throw the frame of the railroad tank car into the trash chute until I after I got married. Or I would read until I made myself sick. My loneliness transformed me inexorably into an educated young man. My complete lack of acquaintances prompted me to make friends with Uncle Slava.

I didn't call him Uncle Slava straight away. Our dachas were official ones, for middling civil servants; no provision was made to have fences between them. We washed in the kitchen, among the pans and the nocturnal butterflies, or on the porch. Or on the veranda. I always hated having to wash my feet in the basin before I went to bed. Granny poured some boiling water out of the teapot. "Is it hot enough?" Three knees. "What are you doing talking to him? You'll do your father some damage too, if you're not careful. Don't spray water on the floor."

You touch the water with your thumb. "Ooh, make it hotter!" She would pour the water in, her bra straps making my eyes ache; the smoke would come, and suddenly it would scald me. What then? I began to worry that she would smother me in my sleep, because I was young — out of jealousy, that is. "D'you hear? He's a bad influence on you. Look, no-one gives him the time of day." And then you wake up in the morning: the sun's shining, it's warm: she didn't smother you after all. You run outside in bare feet to get washed.

So right from the outset our friendship was not legit. Granny began to scare me with stories about men from an early age. "He'll tempt you into the forest with a sweet, then undress you — and you've had it!" Frightened, I pictured a scary man stuffing children's summer clothes and sandals into a bag and walking off, rustling through the fallen leaves, leaving me naked in the forest at the mercy of fortune, with nothing but an empty sweet-wrapper. I swore to her that I would never believe anyone, and she stroked my head with her furry hand; at times it seems to me as though I have kept that oath.

As well as grandma, who was like a soulmate to me, I also made enemies with the cat that hung around the rubbish bins — the rubbish bins that I shared with Uncle Slava were communal — a huge, foul-smelling pit. I first began — first dared — to call him Uncle Slava in August, when the meteor shower began, and, sitting side-by-side on the bench, the back of which was bent in the boulevard style, distracted from our primary task, we made wishes, keeping them secret from one another — there's another one, I would say, and there's another! — I wished someone would give me a hug, and press me close to them — yes, there are lots of them falling down, Uncle Slava suddenly agreed, in a pained voice. He hardly ever left his dacha, living his life in peace, and each time he went to Moscow I felt deeply hurt.

A black ZIM that had seen better days pulled up at the dacha; the trunk, as small as a dressing case, opened up; the chauffeur wandered around sluggishly; and some ghostly maids appeared: he came out dressed in an impeccable dark suit, dark tie and dark hat. Precise in his every movement, prim and looking ever so slightly lost, he plunged, stooping, into the ZIM, sat down unhurriedly on the back-seat, which had been covered slightly — so that he didn't get it dirty — with a plush dark-red case, as if to taunt him. I remember the smell of gray smoke that came out of the exhaust pipe of that ZIM. It was the smell of our separation. As he drove past a thin teenager with a large, timid mouth, he raised and then put down his arm, which was bent at the elbow. For a split-second, an indistinct, swollen, painful smile seemed to hover on his face. I too threw up my hand to bid him farewell, and stood on the pavement for a long time, feeling the Earth spinning the wheels of his car as it turned on its axis.

One day some glazier dropped a huge sheet of glass on the pavement, and the fragments lay there glimmering in the sunlight like hundreds of copies of Uncle Slava's pince-nez, and my granny, whose husband — my deceased grandfather, in other words, who had been a railway accountant — had also worn a pince-nez all his life, said sympathetically that a pince-nez made a man look quite handsome. And she wiped away a tear, in true widow fashion. Whenever she was in a bad mood, she used to say it was me that had killed grandpa, because I used to torture him with my caprices and forced him to carry me, which had led to him having a heart attack and dying disastrously early, before he had a chance to receive — grandmother's eyes went all dreamy — the Order of Lenin which had already been promised him; or that I was ungrateful, for how dare I not be able to remember grandpa, who had done so many good things for me, and who had taken me to the dacha at Razdory, made whistles and crawled on his knees playing at cars, and one day I suddenly caught sight of him: in over-sized pajamas and an utterly absurd cap, and, alas, no Order of Lenin on his chest, rocking a yellow-and-brown trolleybus...

"How great it is to be a traffic warden," grandpa said breathlessly, with a little wink. "You shake your stick one way, then the other."

"Come e-e-e-e-e-eat!" granny started yelling.

Time was when they would have had that glazier pick up those fragments of glass and eat them. After lunch grandma lay down in the garden on the folding bed, in her blue cotton sundress, wrapping a blanket over her legs, and I sat on a pile of sand and pushed the railroad tank down the rails — suddenly granny rushed off — the milk had boiled over and dripped into the kerosene burner, giving off an awful smell — she tore off the blanket, and I saw that under her sundress she was wearing: nothing at all, besides black hair, and a pink incision which flashed before my eyes for a split second — with the cistern in her hands.

The fragments of glass were now crunching under the defenseless tires of the ZIM. At the dacha, Uncle Slava walked around looking cheery, wearing a bright-colored hat and no tie. He loved circular walks, and never strayed too far from the dacha. And he would always carry his walking stick with him. It was a simple stick with a simple handle. It was rigid and agreeable, like a little safe. The other holidaymakers, on catching sight of Uncle Slava from a distance, used to turn and walk the other way — and the ones who crossed his path walked on by without looking up at him. Smoked sausage with macaroni. My favorite dinner. But if you eat too much sausage you get indigestion. I was tortured by indigestion and loneliness. Dinner would end with a big row and a glass of weak tea. Grandma didn't let me listen to the transistor radio. She thought that the radio would get spoilt if people listened to it too much. Back then, transistor radios were a gob-smacking novelty, something completely unheard of among the locals. Granny wrapped the radio up in a rag and hid it in the cupboard. It was kept in a tempting box, a bright-red one with a white plastic handle, which had been made in Norway, of all places. When I took the box over to the big pond, without telling granny, the locals were overcome with something akin to insanity. They swarmed all over me, curious and suspicious, and it was plain to see from their faces what they were thinking: a radio can't play without a wire like that, on its own. Standing there with my radio, by the lake, I felt like some incomprehensible young god. "Papa said I could," I said. "What did he say you could do, exactly?" granny said. "You ruin everything, and you'll ruin this to boot." She used to wrap up anything she could lay her hands on: the headlight from my bicycle was kept in a rag too. "Papa said I could!" "I won't let you!" "Yes you will!" She would reduce me to tears, and then hide and take the radio away, with the hapless expression of a bulldog that feels hurt. And I would run into the garden: it was wet with dew, and I was wet with tears. When I had shed a few tears the world seemed an even more wonderful place.

Uncle Slava and I used to meet at about nine o'clock each evening on a bench between our dachas, under a tall birch tree. Granny never came near us and couldn't hear what we were listening to. All she did was frown: "What does he want from you?" — but she respected him.

I would always be the first to show up, and would worry that he might not come. Uncle Slava would turn up thirty seconds later. At a distance of thirty-one meters I managed to get a signal out of the chaotic noise coming from the radio. First of all, as is usually the way, there was a brief summary of the news, then the full-length version was broadcast. Uncle Slava put his palms over the handle of his stick and rested his chin on them — his mustache, pince-nez and hat were all in place, and didn't get in his way. We were all ears.

The voice was constantly trying to move off to one side, and we had to keep catching it over and over again. The signal had been suppressed. It stayed that way until sixty-three, if I'm not mistaken. We were allowed to listen to various unimportant news stories, but as soon as it reached us, or Berlin, the muffler was turned on, at someone's command, and it became almost impossible to listen to. You could listen to it a little bit though, and Uncle Slava would never give up, while Granny jumped up again and again from the folding bed, and stood at my headboard at night, thinking: to smother him or not to smother him? Uncle Slava would never give up when they started to muffle the radio, and never grunted, never expressed frustration or displeasure: he thought of the muffler as a natural phenomenon that was unavoidable. He remained imperturbable, and sat and waited until I found that happy medium where the sound was half-audible and half-muffled. He barely said a word but was always ready with a friendly greeting, right from the outset, and although he sat there looking peaceful and rigid, I could not shake off the worrying sense that it was mere coincidence that he was here: that he had just happened to sit down on this bench next to a boy who was fiddling with a radio; that he had merely happened to hear something that he was not supposed to hear, and that the old conspirator was innocent, but seeing as how the same thing happened every evening, he was putting on a show that this was a coincidence not for me but for the whole world — of which there was neither sight nor sound: the bench was cut off from everyone else, and was ours alone, and in these minutes we were alone in the universe, he and I, silent co-conspirators listening to something we were not supposed to be listening to, equally in the wrong, the pioneer and the pensioner: we had crossed the threshold into illegality, yet for some reason were not betraying one another. And this, as you would expect, brought us closer together, and from one evening to the next he became more and more kindly towards me; I was by now more than just a boy, I now had a name, and with imperceptible gestures he gave me to understand that he didn't hold it against me that we couldn't hear the radio, and I gradually lost the feeling of awkwardness that stemmed from the fact I was his neighbor and wasn't always able to cope with the muffler. After lunch granny lay down in the garden on the folding bed, and suddenly — the milk! The whole summer passed by in the same manner, with the recurring eruption of milk and Uncle Slava as the constant listener: he seldom listened to the comments, but would quietly get to his feet and leave after the news, and only once did we hear Uncle Slava's name mentioned in the news, when they reported — I remember it word for word — that some students at Beirut University were throwing bottles at the police, containing a cocktail named after Uncle Slava. *Voice of America* was no less a revelation for me than the black hairs under the sundress, and I stole a glance at Uncle Slava: how would he respond to his name being mentioned? Say something! He made no response at all.

He never questioned me about anything, never asked any condescending questions — and I never asked him about anything, either. But I remembered how several years ago, in Sochi, father, who had been paddling in the sea, was walking towards us — and suddenly it was announced — people ran over to the loud-speaker — that: they had been exposed. Every last one of them — and all those connected to them. I remembered how bitter my parents had felt: papa, in his swimming trunks, felt particularly bitter. Alongside me — I used to wish we could caress one another, throw paper airplanes, run around the field and kiss one another — sat the creator of a cocktail I had never heard of before, and granny was in the midst of a huge laundry operation, and, as was always the case on such days, I was left to my own devices, and I nicked from the cupboard the very thing that I was categorically forbidden to touch: my father's air-rifle, and the little pelts that it fired — and ran off towards the rubbish bins to kill the cat. There was no sign of the cat by the bins, and I sat waiting by the stinking pit for ages, feeling annoyed, until I had had enough. When I had had enough, I ran into the forest with my weapon, and as it turned out I was a pretty good shot. That day — the day of the huge laundry operation — I killed dozens of ravens, wagtails and titmice, as well as all sorts of other birds which I'd never heard of. I liked the way they fell to the ground quietly like cornets. On the way home I shot a red woodpecker: it fell right at my feet, and I didn't feel sorry for it in the slightest. Then I ran to the rubbish bins once again and, as the cry reached my ears: "Come e-e-e-e-e-e-e-at!" I caught sight of the puny gray cat, searching for food in the pit. The cat tried to slip away, but I called out to it in a treacherous voice: "Here kitty-kitty-kitty!" The cat squinted at me, suspecting some foul play — in the same way that the locals had suspected the radio without a wire must be a dirty trick. I put all the tenderness I could muster into my next "here, kitty-kitty." The cat hesitated. I carefully raised the barrel of the air-rifle and aimed it at him, a friendly smile on my face. The cat stood there, unable to decide what to do. I shot it in the forehead. The cat let out a blood-curdling hiss and charged off into the grass. Shaking with excitement, I began to reload my weapon awkwardly.

"Come e-e-e-e-e-e-e-at!"

I never saw that cat again. Uncle Slava soon left as well. Some snitch told my father that I had been running around with an air-rifle, destroying anything that moved. What bastards there are out there. I confessed that I had taken the gun without his permission and started crying, asking his forgiveness. Before I went to sleep I felt a sweet ache in my nether regions because of that pink incision. "How do you do it?" Uncle Slava asked. "Look. You take the skin...won't it get infected?" "What nonsense — infected! Like that. That's it. Go on, go on — don't be shy, buddy!" He had listened to all sorts of anti-Soviet stuff with me, I thought coldly. Communism is unavoidable. Father, in his rage, struck me on the face. Shortly before his death Uncle Slava was rehabilitated within the party.

•

There was a cinema opposite the school that was free of charge. People used to watch films there standing up — the shorter ones had to stand on tip-toes. People usually went there on their own, although they sometimes pushed each other and egged one another on. In winter, people watched films there amid the crunch of the icy crust on the snow, on which they would slip and fall over, a thin cigar clenched between their teeth. If you wore poor-quality shoes they would swell up in the snow: your socks would get wet through, your feet would freeze, and then, when you were in the warm again, they would ache, at great length and in a Russian way. The ache of thawing feet is the eternal motif of my Moscow childhood.

At this cinema, when you went in from the yard, particularly when it was getting dark, you could catch a glimpse of a whole load of naked women. The windows were polished, but they were painted not on the inside but on the outside, with white paint. The paint had been scratched off in places by various men. Some of the holes were quite big — the women used to stick wet pieces of paper over them from the other side: they had sussed what the holes were for. But they didn't stick anything over the smaller holes. Ilyusha Tretyakov told me that one day the window had been opened and the guys outside had had boiling water from the tub thrown all over them. There had been much cursing on the part of the men and squealing on the part of the women. But you could overlook that incident, Tretyakov said, because in fact the women had grown used to being looked at, and sometimes even posed for their admirers.

It was a long time before I agreed to join him at this male cinema, which he visited almost every day. I lagged behind my peers in terms of development, though I pretended I was just like them. I tripped up over a footballer's surname. The rest of the class was having a laugh about a famous player called Malofeyev. I didn't know any of the connotations this name had, and I was pressed up against the wall.

"I don't really know much about soccer," I blurted out.

I had only been to a soccer match on one occasion, at Dinamo's stadium with my papa during the May holidays, when Dinamo were playing Spartak on the first day of the season. We watched the first half, which ended with the scores level, and left, feeling disappointed by this strange, dull game.

"What's soccer got to do with anything?" my classmates said in surprise.

Suddenly they realized my mistake, and stated cackling so loudly and scornfully that their laughter tormented me by night for a long time thereafter. I was a late developer when it came to learning the slang that children pick up. I learned it only later, as if it was a foreign language. I was a late developer when it came to learning about Russian anti-Semitism, too. I thought that a "sheeny" was simply a "greedy-guts", and I was taken aback when both my trusty friends, Borya Minkov and Ilyusha Tretykov, took offence at being called "sheens". They decided to enlighten me.

"Bet you don't know what a *rubber* is, either?" Borya asked.

"I can guess," I lied.

"Where would you buy one?"

"I dunno."

"Come on, I'll show you," my friend said.

Every Russian boy has a good story to tell about a condom. Condoms are Russian childhood's answer to the balloon. We went into the pharmacy on Gorky Street, which stank — like all Soviet women on the inside — of valerian, and Borya said we had to put forty kopecks into the till. I took two twenty-kopeck pieces out of my pocket, got my check and took it up to the little window where medicines were sold without a prescription. Borya was a little further back in the queue.

"Please may I have a rubber!" I said to a young female pharmacist in a white coat and cap. She took the check from me and, giving me a sidelong look, ran off into the depths of the pharmacy. A short while later a fat old matron emerged from a side-door, also dressed in a white coat.

"Are you the one who was asking for a condom?" she said, giving me a stern look.

"No," I said, "I need a rubber."

"What for?"

"That's my business."

"Your business?" the pharmacist said in surprise. "How old are you?"

"I'm in the fifth grade."

"Come back in three years' time." She signed the check, gave it back to the cashier, and the latter thrust the forty kopecks into my hand.

Borya, to give him his due, painted me as a hero the next day: he told everyone that I had gone to the pharmacy to buy a rubber. My classmates gave me respectful looks, and the girls started giggling benevolently and catching hold of my hand as if by accident.

"Well, if you can go and buy a condom," Ilyusha Tretyakov said, "there's nothing you can't do. Let's go!"

I couldn't say no. But I put it off, and didn't go and join him until the winter, when we were in the sixth grade.

What made it so special was that it was a reality show. There the women were, playing out their lives in the bath-house, which was their stage. They washed, scrubbed one another with washcloths, chatted to one another or sat there deep in thought. They lived separate lives from me and the lanky Ilyusha Tretyakov, and yet were surprisingly tasty: one of them was strawberry, another was blackcurrant; even the vanilla-flavored old women were delicious. In the ecstasy of my voyeurism I found that women were beautiful whatever their age (from a distance, at any rate). Some of our classmates were in there: as it turned out, they already had pubic hair; and their mothers and grandmothers were there too. Some of them did indeed glance over from time to time at the windows, through which Ilyusha and I were clearly visible, and seemed to strike all sorts of poses.

I watched first with one eye, then the other, and I even got an eyelash in my eye because of the tension (it happens all the time at that age). I wiped my eyes, which were watering, and, whether as a result of the pain in my eye, or because I was over-excited, I can remember with incredible clarity the precise moment when the picture inside the bath-house began to look different. The window-pane slammed shut. What I saw was no tranquil image of some women washing, but some sort of descent into sin of the female flesh. First of all the girls, with their nubile tufts of pubic hair, moved off to one side, and the monstrous frames of some bloated women, their bellies that hung down to their knees and titties that looked like the Central Asian melons from the Central Market, and the skeletal frames of the older women. I did not stop to dwell on the fleetingness of female beauty; I suddenly sensed that death had shown its face in the bath-house. It had arrived in a pink, rubber apron, thrown onto a naked body, with a bare bum, and resembling a bath-house attendant.

This strong, adroit bath-house attendant, who looked as if she belonged in one of Moscow's gyms in the present day, started chopping up the women like so many cabbages, laughingly, but not with a scythe, like in the magical fairytale, but with a Cossack saber. Budyonnov's First Cavalry Army could not have cut people up in such a professional manner as she did. She began chopping the women and the elderly ladies in half wildly, then cut off their arms, legs and breasts. Their heads flew into the tub and under the bench, leaving red marks. Then, gleaming in the fog of the bath-house with her bloody blade, she threw herself on the girls with the quiet hint of a sickly-sweet smile on her lips, she moved onto the girls: red-haired girls, freckled girls, angelic girls, girls with fringes and without, and girls with the tender outlines of breasts. The girls rushed around higgledy-piggledy: the bath-house attendant, moving around in long leaps, like in Borodin's Polovetsk dances, didn't spare any of them. The window was hit by the howling of these dying girls. The bath-house attendant ended up by killing the little children too, both the boys and the girls, who had come to have a wash with their mothers and grandmothers, by drowning them in the blood. I had once been to a female bath house on Chkalovskaya Street, with my grandmother.

To begin with I was horrified by this spectacle: I was afraid of blood, and was even more aghast at the sight of the chopped-up bodies, but had to admit that there was art in what she had done. I turned away from the window to discuss this unexpected turn of events with Tretyakov, but I was cut off. A policeman came round the corner and pounced on Tretyakov. Tretyakov was the closest to him. The policeman grabbed him by his fur hat, which had earflaps, and tore it off his head. There was something incredibly wanton and nasty about this attack, and I found it hard to reconcile it with the idea of justice. The first incident that imbued me with a fondness for justice, incidentally, involved a bicycle. My parents had brought me a red, teenage-size bicycle with a headlight and surprisingly effective brake levers, from Paris — this was simply wonderful. I was riding it one day down the Uspensky Highway, not far from the dacha. A policeman stopped me: "You can't ride a bike here." He did a nasty thing: not only did he let all the air out of my tires, but on top of that he threw the air-vent caps into the bushes. As he was putting me through all this, a second cyclist rode past. He didn't stop the second cyclist.

"Why didn't you stop him too, if he's breaking the law as well?" I asked, my heart thumping. "It's unjust."

"If you want justice, go look for it at home, with your mother," the policeman said.

In the Soviet Union, every policeman was an emissary of the GULAG — the waves of the distorted world, its rotten breath passed through the policeman and reached me. His response, which meant nothing to him at all, suddenly seemed to me to represent the rock bottom of my country's decline. I became a moralist for a few years. I found injustice around every corner.

Tretyakov went obediently after his hat — straight to the police station. They took away Tretyakov, but they left me — dumbfounded by the chopping up of the bodies and the policeman's vicious attack — all on my own. They called his mother from the police station. I headed home and thought about what might have happened to me if the policeman had called my mother and said I had been gawping at naked women. I realized that, just as in a game of chess quality is always sacrificed, I would have sacrificed my hat for the sake of honor — and fled the scene without it.

•

I am a member of the Komsomol. I was a true Soviet only once in my life — the day I joined the Komsomol, at the age of fourteen. Everyone was joining up — and I did too. In spite of the difference between Moscow and Paris. The thing was, those who didn't join up had to go on wearing those stupid pioneers' ties, although they had already grown whiskers and had wet-dreams, whilst those who did join up were given magnificent Komosomol badges — and these badges looked much better with the uniform than a red tie.

A lot of the girls were already in the Komsomol — they were the first to join, and the boys felt too embarrassed to stay in the pioneers. I didn't even consider not joining the Komsomol. The Komsomol was probably more of a way of getting close to adult life than a decision based on ideology. That said, there was some talk of the benefits we would derive from it in the future: everyone was aware that only people who had been in the Komsomol were given places at university. When I was asked by the District Committee to name my favorite book, I said: "*The Young Guard*".

I idolized Remarque, but made up my mind that Remarque was inappropriate for a member of the Komsomol. I ran out of the District Committee with a brand new ticket, which made me feel very proud. It was my first ever official document. The seeds of non-conformism had sprouted inside me: I was overlooked. I clearly had grounds for becoming a Soviet diplomat.

•

Erika was dressed in an orange rind with a gilded fastening. But if you peeled off the rind, Erika was insanely gorgeous, even more beautiful than the two art students I had met on Chkalovskaya Street; I had spent the evenings discussing modern art with them around a fire. One of these students, Natasha Ankina, who was an ambassador's daughter, and who was next to be handed the baton in the relay of girls I fell in love with, and used to stand motionless whenever I brought her a white towel after she had been for a night-time dip in the pond, burning in the darkness, told a story back then about a man named Papanin, whom her father had known. Papanin had built himself a big dacha outside Moscow using his own hard-earned money.

"Why haven't you invited me round for the house-warming party?" Stalin said to him, over the telephone.

Papanin laid on a banquet fit for a king. Stalin was accompanied by Molotov and Voroshilov. The two Politburo members said how much they liked the dacha. Stalin said nothing. Just before they left, Stalin proposed a toast.

"Comrade Papanin," he said, "thank you. Let's drink to this new orphanage!"

"But Papanin used his hard-earned money..." I said in confusion, unsettled by the story.

"People love telling this story," some artist, whose name I forget, remarked — I used to take her a white towel, too, but unlike Natasha she was never shy in the darkness.

"Perhaps the idea is that the children were more important than Papanin?" I said, changing my opinion as I often did back then.

"Let's look at some works by Modigliani," said Natasha. She brought a sweet-smelling square tome, published by the Skira publishing house, out of the dacha.

Erika was on a higher plane than my series of crushes. Erika was a marshy, metallic color. She had tightly wrought little hooves, which made a clattering sound. Her black, sweet-smelling ribbon, which ran from one little wheel to the other; her slender fingers with letters for nails — this was real love.

Until today, it had never even occurred to me that Erika was a woman's name. It was the name of my own personal dream. Erika: that was the name of the typewriter that made turned me into a writer. Erika was the main exhibit in my own personal museum. In theory it still works even now. Products made in East Germany were heavy but portable. Why had my parents bought it? They rarely used it. It was just like the 'mark stampet' — it was mine. I grew attached to it. All the more so given that I was never allowed to use it. They were afraid I might break it. They hid Erika away from me, behind the table or under the bed. Writing was a forbidden topic all of a sudden. I typed a few words on it, made a mistake, mixing up the letters, and — something dawned on me. It wasn't about the words or the letters. It was about flights of fancy.

The first poem I ever wrote in my life, which I typed on Erika, was called *Lilies of the valley*. It was mid-May. I had seen some lilies of the valley in the forest, next to the station Razdory on the Usovskaya branch, and I wrote the poem, agonizing over which rhymes to select. I sent the poem off to Africa. My parents delicately refrained from mentioning it. *Lilies of the valley* reflected my complete lack of literary talent.

By that time I had already failed in my drive to expand my vocabulary. It had happened in the eighth grade. I had written the assignment *How I spent the summer vacation* in the tone of a formal note. I had spent the summer at the Artek summer camp. I wrote about the reinforced concrete structures in the pioneers' halls of residence, which overlooked the sea. It was like my letters to my parents: not quite right. It turned out that there was an underground Artek. It was full of the numerous children of Fidel Castro, some of whom clearly looked like the Arabs with whom I used to run to Ayu-Dag to buy beer. In the pioneer underground there was a Georgian pioneer with a huge penis, which he used to show us in the tent during quiet time, challenging us to reveal a bigger one. Comparing dick sizes: this was quite a novelty for me. There was pioneer leader at the camp who had hairs sticking out of her knickers. She liked the works of François Sagan. I wrote using dead words. Pushkin was a revelation to me. We had to write something about Eugene Onegin. I wrote something that frightened the teacher. It was absolute gibberish. My words were no longer dead: they were alive. Everything became clear. The teacher was horrified. The only thing I was missing was a printing press. When it arrived, I became a writer. Grandma Sima, when she saw that I had locked myself in the dining room with the typewriter for the night, exploded with rage:

"You're writing pornography."

What an old Cassandra she was. I wrote poems about the lilies-of-the-valley. My parents were living in Africa at the time. Grandma Sima was a permanent resident in Leningrad, but whenever she came to Moscow she read everything that was on my parents' shelves: Balzac, Dickens, Tolstoy — all the collected works. I never saw such an avid reader ever again in my life. She would soon forget everything she had read and start reading them again — as if she were doing so for the first time. She was a caricature of literature in action. In time, you forget everything. There were dark passions at work in Grandma Sima. Many years later, my third-cousin Marina claimed that Serafima Mikhailovna had lost her mind over sex: she saw reproductive organs in everything she looked at. There were probably a lot of subjects that grandma and I could have discussed — but we were never required to do so.

•

STALIN: Only a lazy liberal would not bother to draw the comparison between Stalin and Hitler. But all Hitler had behind him was a trumped up idea of nationhood. It is impossible to revive Lenin, Trotsky and Hitler. They are the trumped playing cards of history. But my fate is different from theirs. In *my* painting, not only did Ivan the Terrible kill his son, but whole peoples were moved from place to place. I worked alone not out of suspicion, but because I was lonely. I wanted to reshape the world — and that is precisely what I did.

ME: The greater my father's embarrassment about Stalin, as he fails to find any humane justification for him, the more Stalin bothers me, as an artist who made his project for the world a reality. Behind Stalin there was a great dream. This dream might equally have been made a reality in Africa, or in the USA.

STALIN: Man was made for flight just as birds were made for happiness. Man can fly. Only landowners and capitalists don't fly.

ME: Stalin created a myth about flight.

STALIN: Chkalov became half-man, half-bird.

ME: The USSR built the biggest airplane in the world. Everyone was supposed to be able to fly, and do a parachute jump (my papa once did it).

STALIN: First you should fly in an airplane — and then without one.

ME: The European and American elite believed in this dream. When I first arrived in America in the late 1980s, I was surprised how many words related to the financial markets had got into the American lexicon. Everyone was talking about credit, and transactions — they were the words in demand.

STALIN: Those words might make you rich, but they won't enable you to fly in the sky.

ME: Stalin wanted an Icarus all of his own. Stalin wanted to fly. Notwithstanding the fact that he only flew in an airplane once in his life, in Tehran — and was very scared by the experience.

STALIN: The irony was not lost on my critics in the West.

ME: I ran to Manezh Square, pushing my way past the military lorries, when Gagarin made his flight. I love that smile of his to this day. We were all infected with the dream of flight.

STALIN: But as it turns out, man is slow to grow wings.

ME: Stalin tried to destroy all of his own old guard, who had witnessed his march to power, before he died. He wanted to be preserved as an ideal coagulation of a dream — unadulterated by anything human. We see the same thing in the rejected lover, who longs for the death of all those who witnessed his disgrace. He changed his circle of friends, at any rate. Stalin used torture to try to force confessions — he wanted to find people who were genuine enemies of flight. He realized that killing people was an interesting game. He got his pleasure from sadism. He laughed when he heard a description of the shooting of Zinoviev. And the fellow who had made him laugh? He had him shot, too.

STALIN: Enough already! They were in my way, and I...felt like it. I was the loneliest person in the world.

ME: But he was a coarse, uneducated, unsubtle man. He liked the prints in the magazine *Ogonyok*. The Hermitage? He could take it or leave it.

STALIN: What makes you say that?

ME: He spent his entire life proving that people don't have wings. It may seem to some that he was hammering at an open door. But you can't say the same about the people living in Russia. When the crows fly over the rubbish tip, to while away the hours on the birch trees next door or circle in the sky, I think to myself: the Russians have arrived. They all fly by night. They have no desire to talk about credit or transactions. They still dream of flight, just as they always used to. Their dreams are overly emotional and old-fashioned. Therein lies the secret of my papa: he was a Stalinist hawk. And therein lies the secret of my country. For the sake of a dream, no number of victims is too terrifying. Millions are as nothing. The Jews can't fly — down with the Jews! The West can't fly — down with the West! But if we really have to, we'll teach even the Jews to fly. Even when

I was a little ball in a beaver hat and mittens tied together with elastic — ai! "Who's there?" "Ai!" — as we stood in the stairwell (so as not to drip sweat in front of the door to the apartment), the boys and I sang a song, pointing our fingers at the girls as if they were sub-human.

STALIN:

> Airplanes above all else, above all else,
> And girls, well — afterwards.

ME: We thought that song was quite chauvinist, we really did. We walked in pairs down Tverskaya Boulevard. My parents chose not to send me to a state kindergarten — for all their Stalinism, they nevertheless chose a private toddlers' group, the pitiful, historic scraps of the National Economic Plan. An elderly lady wearing a hat with a dark veil attached to it sat on the wooden cover of the sand-pit. She seemed to have come right out of a Chekhov play. She was Georgian, and was short of breath. She was very obviously unable to fly. Some miracle had enabled her to survive intact. Among us were some children who could fly. But our song was just one link in a long chain of flying images.

STALIN: I know.

ME: A flying waitress was one of the heroines of the sixties. The flying saucer was the obsession of the occult practices popular during *perestroika*. If not a flying one, then a moving one at least. The Russian god is a runner. Run, sail, walk, keep changing your place of work ('fly'), become a wanderer, escape from prison — anything but stand still. Having said that, we are an exceptionally inert nation. When I think about why I have racked up so many air-miles, I realize something: the dream has touched my life, too. I can fly, as well. It's possible to fight back against this dream. But Russians won't realize that. Or else they'll be born again. Russia is the aerodrome for the dream of flight. Letatlin is the connection between the avant-garde and the revolution. Everything flies. And when a Russian emigrates, he loses his aerodrome — he is the unhappiest émigré in the world. Needless to say, this country is a circus. Everyone became a pilot — only they were missing their trousers. All the pilots have killed one another. They have fallen from the sky. Their parachutes failed to open. They died on impact.

STALIN: Stalin died.

ME: I was sent here to witness all this with my own eyes, and show you on the palm of my hand: this is how things are in reality. But analysis is the enemy of all dreams. The secret is the death of the fairytale. Leave our fairytale alone! At this point Kirkegaard rises to his feet: either — or.

•

According to mama, we are all like Kai from Hans Christian Andersen's tale *The Snow Queen*. A fragment of the mirror has got in our eye: we see everything in a bad light. Including each other. Grandma Sima sat with her body in a huge heap and read novels in her spectacles, like a monument to individualism. She found moving difficult, and was not much help around the house. I got the impression she was quite cold. It wasn't that she showed no affection at all, but she was a cold frog. And a cold-blooded one. Mama had an eternal chill about her, too, like mint sugar candy. But grandma Sima really was a cold person, and gurgled with boggy passions. Papa was posted to Africa as an ambassador.

He took down a gray volume from one of the bookshelves, a hardback Soviet atlas of the world from 1940. The Soviet Union, along with the territories which had just been annexed to it, was painted in such triumphant red paint that it dazzled the eyes, whilst Poland, drawn in stripes, was referred to as the zone of Germany's State interests. Flicking through to the right page, papa showed me Africa — lilac French Africa — but couldn't find Senegal or Gambia: he was ambassador to two countries at the same time. I was now the son of an ambassador.

•

Dressed in the black ceremonial uniform of "his excellency", with its four gold general's stars on its epaulettes, father awarded certificates to the talented Senegalese poet Sengor, who was married to a beautiful Frenchwoman from Normandy; paid visits to all the local bigwigs and foreign ambassadors, like Chichikov from Gogol's *Dead Souls*; paid everyone compliments; and found favor with everyone. Now he himself was in charge of a whole diplomatic economy, from the chef to the advisers, and he put all his energy, without pausing to rest, into the struggle with what was left of colonialism for Africa's bright future. To someone from a Soviet country, Africa seemed to be a many-sided paradise. The slaves and savages of old had put on boubou clothes and were dreaming of socialism. Socialist regimes were popping up here, there and everywhere. There were, of course, the occasional failures: snow-ploughs were taken to Guinea, in the tropics, from Moscow — some wit remarked that if socialism was taken to the Sahara, it would soon develop a chronic shortage of sand, but papa set to work diligently correcting mistakes such as this. I heard only good things about him, no matter whom I spoke to: from his superiors and his subordinates, from white men and black people. When the Soviet ships dropped anchor at the port of Dakar, where there were enormous rats, the like of which not even Gogol could have dreamt up, papa, climbing aboard, listened to the reports given by the ships' captains. When the Soviet soccer team arrived, papa patted the tow-haired lads on the head encouragingly, then went to the stadium to cheer them on, unsure of the rules of this game, which he did not particularly like. Soviet film-makers arrived, and he supported them; military attachés came over and he supported them too; our neighbors from the KGB came over to talk to the resident Soviet spy, named Telega, and he and Telega found a lot of common ground. Everything went swimmingly.

If you haven't been to Africa, you haven't lived. In Africa the binding has been peeled off life, like the skin from an orange.

Africa is an extension of Russia, just as war is an extension of politics. If papa had not been tripped up by the French counter-espionage unit, he would have been appointed ambassador to Belgium, and would probably have done far more damage to the West than he did in Senegal. Busy, highly conversant and endearing, he disarmed his enemies with his utterly un-Soviet charm. He got into battle with them as if he was playing a game of chess, with unfailing benevolence, but he was unable to secure victory. He was amazed that his enemies did not give in. He believed in the color of his chess pieces.

After buying a house in the center of Dakar, he invited me round for the holidays. Papa wasn't even sure which gift he had given me. Black Africa is a blown-up photo. There's a reason why photographers adore Africa. The baobabs there are more powerful than Gaudi's cathedrals; the dancing there, to the beat of the tom-toms, is more powerful than the Karamazov brothers' conversations about the meaning of life; each stone in the savannah is more powerful than the Evangelists; and the monkeys are more humane than humankind. This was not just a new shade to life — it was a whole new dimension of it. The sunsets, the thunderstorms, medina, mosques, boubou, masks, jungles — all this was more powerful than Blok's *night, a street, a lantern, a pharmacy*. We drove across the Sahara to Mauritania, in a Land Rover, and I saw hundreds of Othellos dressed in noble rags. We drove to Ziguinchor and Gambia, where young kids sold their sisters for pennies, which the Swedish tourists really appreciated, and where the parliament was designed along the British model. I had landed in the world's resort: it had beaches, palm trees, baobabs, former slave traders, the sun directly overhead, bars and sea urchins. By then I was already ideologically opposed to my father. At dawn I went out into the ocean to catch fish. I flew out to spend the summer with my father on two occasions, in two different manifestations: as a schoolboy who still had a year left at school, and as a student who had completed his first year.

The schoolboy was a dyed-in-the-wool moralist. I was plagued by moralism, as if by measles. The world made me itch: everything about it was unjust — from my school to Khrushchev's taste in art (he hated abstract paintings). I got lost in my reading of Yevtushenko's poems as if they had been written especially for me. Professor, for some reason I don't like you, but your wife liked me, as did your son, a stubborn lad, who clearly doesn't take after his father. I can recite it from memory. That was the level I was at. I found that I was rather like that stubborn boy, and with a sharp intake of breath the bitter realization dawned on me that I too had not taken after my father. Yevtushenko forced me to feel a sense of alienation from my own father, which I tried not to admit to.

Just as in the past, I knew papa mostly through seeing him at rest — I had an ambassador at rest before my eyes. He knew how to organize his leisure time wherever he was: Dakar was a luxurious base for leisure. He and I played tennis together, with some local boys running around the court as our ball-boys. It wasn't exactly a socialist set-up, but if we had declined their services the boys would have been left without any money, so we had to make a decision: either we give them some genuine assistance, or we take the battle for socialism to the tennis club, too. We both chose to turn our backs on socialism in this instance. After the game we headed to the club's bar, where father had an open tab — he had made the reckless decision to let me use it. I used to treat the offspring of a wealthy French family, who had made millions out of peanuts, not only to alcohol but also to fried pigeon — with such generosity that after a month papa was left clutching his head, but he refrained from killing me. He was always somewhat off-hand in his attitude to money. He had no difficulty believing in the success he had made of his life, and he never envied his friends: neither Troyanovsky, nor Dubinin, nor Alexandrov, whose career trajectories had all been more brilliant than his own. Yevtushenko's poem had a prophetic significance in our family. The poet came to Dakar to attend a festival of negro art. Papa didn't take to him. They went to see Sengor together, and Sengor asked Yevtushenko who was better — Mayakovsky or Yesenin.

YEVTUSHENKO: You might as well compare a tomato with a cucumber.

Papa thought his answer impudent. He lived according to the laws of diplomatic etiquette. As for me, I was overjoyed by Yevtushenko's answer. The way he behaved, and his love for Akhmadulina, were for me an absolutely cult phenomenon. During the festival Yevtushenko fell in love with my mama, and she blossomed due to the advances of this experienced, successful ladies' man, who wrote the following lines in Dakar:

> *Put me inside a nice baobab*
> *With a few beautiful girls to grab.*

Papa exploded with rage, demonstratively ignored the poet, and made a great show of being jealous in front of mama. When mama arrived in Moscow, proud of her victory, she told me for the first time that I had a jealous papa, and that he turned pale whenever he was jealous. In this way, thanks to Yevtushenko, I caught a glimpse behind the scenes of my parents' lives.

•

I'll tell you what the poets of the sixties are. They are my latest 'market-worthy stamps'. The poets of the sixties are like the stamps from the Portuguese colonies. Akhmadulina is a lizard. Voznesensky is a butterfly. Yevtushenko is a jaguar. Okudzhava is a sea horse. They recite verses from the stage about the wonderful lives they lead inside triangular stamps from the Portuguese colonies. I get a real kick out of it. And I live with a grandmother who wraps up the chandelier in a sheet. I want to be a bohemian, too. Little is left of this particular fauna.

Kirill Vasilievich, who had a surname right out of Russian classicism — Chistov — and his wife Bella Yefimovna were the exception among my parents' circle of friends. They were philologists, and loved poetry. They lived a modest but pure life in Petrozavodsk. They gave mama some slender anthologies of new poetry. They loved Akhmatova and Tsvetaeva, whom mama and I used to read on the typewriter, on little pieces of squared paper. I travelled to Petrozavodsk, and to Kizhi — I was prepared to love holy Rus, the avant-garde, the intelligentsia, French cheese — everything but Soviet reality and my life with grandma.

At a school assembly I gave a speech, in the tongue-tied fashion of a young poet of the sixties, about the injustice at our school. For many years it seemed to me that my imagination, my heightened feelings, and my passionate love of literature and justice were things that I shared with everyone, and that there was nothing unusual about me: it was just that the others never thought about these things. They ought to be woken up! I remembered, of course, what one of my classmates had said about Eugene Onegin:

"Why does he walk around torturing himself about such stupid things! He needs a good punch in the face, to make him stop!"

Well he was a bit behind the times, I thought. I lived in a Platonic world of dreams. It seemed to me that my teachers were all intellectuals — even my gym teacher.

"But he's a teacher!" I would protest, when our gym teacher committed a slight indiscretion (he had been peeping at the girls while they got changed). An intellectual friend of my mother's snorted. But I insisted. It seemed to me that the world could be put to rights, and that there was some logic to it really. I didn't have the faintest inkling that I was the one who looked like a white crow. I was surprised when our history teacher gave me only four out of five in my final exam in history — clearly as a punishment for having deliberately chosen history so that

I could try and befuddle her with my questions. I had thought we were just engaging in polemics. As it turned out, she couldn't stand me. Both because of my questions, and because of the fact that after being appointed the class's Communist leader, I started a velvet revolution: we listened to records of French rock 'n' roll, and Johnny Halliday. I saw the way the poverty-stricken children lit up when the loud music came on — but not everyone liked it — I thought we would all join together in shared bliss, but Celia Samoilovna Palchik, who had a reputation as one of the best teachers in Moscow — a middle-aged woman with died-blonde hair — decided that it was an act of provocation. But she was afraid of me, because I was an ambassador's son. I had free reign to misbehave. I spoke at the school assembly, right in front of the female principal, in front of everyone, and gave a revolutionary speech, which was spoilt by the fact I was so tongue-tied (due to my awful shyness), and suddenly the principal stood up and announced to the whole school that I was a fascist.

A fascist! This was me we were talking about — I had been a top student, had studied English on the Ministry of Foreign Affairs' courses, knew my history, was top of the class in literature, had forced myself to be literate, and had learnt off by heart Rosenthal's textbook on the Russian language during the holidays after the eighth grade, and had written so brilliantly in the school's wall-newspaper that the teachers thought I had copied an article from the journal *America* — I was a fascist? I idolized Modigliani, Van Gogh, the young Mayakovsky. I had stolen copies of the journal *Youth* from the school library, containing Aksyonov's novel *A ticket to the stars* — out of sheer adoration. I had flown off to make the world a better place; the poets of the sixties had flown with me, in the same squadron — they had filled stadia to the rafters, and now I was being called a fascist.

In actual fact I wasn't a fascist, but a moralist, and the first protest I went through was a moral protest. In the last few years of school I thought in terms of moral categories — fairness and the justification of goodness. I became intimate with Russian literature. I loved chemistry, because I discovered alchemy in it. I set up experiments at home. I would make something light up in a phosphorescent glow in a test-tube from the 'Young Chemist' set. My parents were surprised, drew in their lips with understanding, but worried about the pink walls, with a hint of silver grape, of my bedroom walls, taken by old house-painters for hire from the Silver Age. The young chemistry teacher took a liking to me. In chemistry I sought the elixir of kindness. I furiously attempted to uncover deception. The whole world was lying — and I was uncovering the lie. Mama told lies, papa told lies, the excellent teacher Celia Samoilovna told lies, my classmates told lies, the TV newsreaders told lies, and so did the newspapers, the party and the government. Only my beloved France didn't tell lies. And Dostoyevsky — he didn't lie. I was suffocating with all this lying. I lied too, but my lying was inspired, whereas the world lied in an underhand way, maliciously, lethally. Like Belinsky, who used to go along to the Nikolaevsky station each day to watch the railway that was to link St Petersburg and Moscow being built, I believed in the progressive march of civilization: I felt delighted by each new shop-window, by the first mannequins that appeared from goodness knows where in the shop *Odezhda* in Pushkin Square, and the construction of the 'modern' *Minsk* hotel, which vaguely reminded me at that time of the existence of Le Corbusier; by the increase in the number of parking lots for privately owned cars in Moscow, of which there were never more than three at any given set of traffic lights. I dreamed of traffic jams, cafés and cocktails. I don't know why but I had a very strong belief in people: I thought of evil as no more than a deviation that could be corrected, and if I stuck to the course I was on, I would make a real mark in Russian literature, root out evil, make my mark among the poets of the sixties, becoming a younger brother to them, and that however bad things got thereafter, I would be master of my own destiny — forever. Come up to the board. Oh people — how I loved you.

•

It's about time I said something that gets to the point. I'm already getting behind due to my summary of my childhood. So here goes: before I go to university, procure my first steady vagina and finally fall in love, let's talk about secrets for a while.

The division of fantasies into day-time ones — playful and for the road — and night-time ones, related to fear, ultimately led me to a kind of creative schizophrenia, to a split between my thinking during the day, in terms of categories, and my thinking by night — in terms of crazy images. My childhood fears came to the fore because of my lack of faith on paper: it was a form of excrement that saved me, and didn't require any sympathy or support — it was a liberation.

Things were not limited to that, though — just as was the case, later, with my patricide. There was also some sort of deeper, impenetrable secret involved, related to the switching on and off of energy. Both my patricide and my liberation from phobias implied a creativity that came 'from within', a self-expression which wasn't part of the secret, and which I stirred into the mix only superficially, staying true to the secret. There is a lot of speculation related to this secret, which has turned it into a shared site of metaphysical languor. Anyone who puts any thought into the matter says that creative energy comes from somewhere inside. That is indeed quite a talent — to allow energy to pass through you. Creativity that comes 'from within' amounts to an imitation at best. Creativity that comes 'from without' doesn't come with that guarantee, doesn't improve with time, but instead evaporates. It is replaced by self-repetition.

Creativity that comes 'from without' is favorably inclined toward the generally accepted style of the times, that is to say it interacts at the level of contemporary concepts, it always operates in the biosphere of *today*. But it turns out to be outside the remit of fashionable constructions, and has a dual relationship with time, exactly in the same way as with human thought, which is why it is not easily translatable — an example is when Pushkin is translated into other languages. Translation transforms him, at best, into an elegant anthology of trivial truths.

The combination of these two variously-sized concepts has always been there, but everything got really shaken up in the 20th century, when the metaphysical roof was torn off. Creativity 'from within' possesses enormous aesthetic capabilities; I have had occasion to come face to face with its achievements on more than one occasion. The secret, however, consisted in my transformation into a *carrier*, able to reproduce other capabilities and a different world. My transformation into a carrier gave me some rare moments of genuine ecstasy, when your text no longer belongs to you, and, when you look at it, you are surprised: was it really you that wrote that? I was never drawn towards formalism, even in its forbidden form. Neither the Tartu-Moscow Semiotic School nor French structuralism ever seemed to me to be movements that would lead to the revealing of secrets. All they contained was the question: how was *The Overcoat* created?

But my feeling was that *The Overcoat* wasn't created, that its author wasn't a master, despite what Mikhail Bulgakov thought. The writer is an alarm clock ringing furiously, which goes off in order to wake up the world, and that alarm clock has been set to go off not because of a writerly concern about the state of the world — alarms like that are heard all the time — but for a different reason altogether. However, weak and deaf as he was, and preoccupied with his private life, the writer can barely hear the waves passing through him; he talks nonsense, does some *ad libbing*, and ruins the original thought, which it is his duty to recreate, as its carrier. It's for that reason that the idea of writerly arrogance seems to me to be superficial and laughable. The writer is left biting his nails because he is struggling to hear properly. His own flaws appear more clearly to him than anything else. He is a terrible carrier. He is ashamed. He wants to crawl under the table out of shame. He can't cope with the task he has been set. And he can't even share this with anyone: he has no-one to turn to. The only person I could talk to about this was Schnittke.

Everyone else is reduced to their social roles, to protest, to a flight towards glory, to creative strategies for life and aesthetic achievements, as they excrete their traumas. There are a fair few geniuses who never properly fulfilled themselves, who were vested with verbal fortune-telling, and, it seems that at first they are singing from someone else's hymn-sheet, like the early Mayakovsky. But once they learn to manipulate words, they imitate a state which is not a lifelong mandate. My own poor hearing taught me to be humble. Pride fell away of its own accord. Yet, as if not believing in my humility, I was given someone who shared my surname, who instilled arrogance in me automatically. It is said that a Buddhist monk who was once staying in St Petersburg couldn't get off to sleep one night. He couldn't get to sleep the next night either. Alarmed, his pupils, who were thirsting for his instructions, asked him why he couldn't get to sleep. "It's hard to get to sleep in your city: there are too many unrepentant souls in the trees." There are probably dead souls hanging from the trees all over the country, who have left without securing repentance. This knocks you off your stride — you involuntarily feel like reading a burial service for them. Whereas my father was sent to Paris, and thrown to culture, I was sent to a life in a country which turned out to be a metaphor for misfortune, wildness personified. I was told: this is your place of work.

But my recognition of this came much later, when mama, pregnant (unbeknownst to me) with my brother, was walking around the Louvre and the Impressionists' museum. For her, culture was a leisure pursuit which she would have liked to extend, to make it last her entire lifetime. In theory she ought to have been my lifelong ally, but it isn't like that: the consumption of culture is fatal for an artist — an artist is not supposed to swallow it, but to tear it to pieces. Mama used to dream of translating literary works — she undoubtedly had some literary ability. But, being a modest woman, she did not consider her talents to be very great. She was full of admiration for talented people. She fed off culture constantly. She would force papa to go to exhibitions, and papa would admire the works of art on show, trying to match up to his cultured wife, though I doubt he ever grasped the difference between Leonardo da Vinci and Laktionov. In this regard, too, he turns out to be much closer to me than mama: like his teacher, Molotov, he understood instinctively that culture was dangerous, that in and of itself it is a right-wing tendency, a mixture of perspectives, a weakening of the role of the state.

Even his interaction with the musicians who came to Paris, and whom he escorted around the city, weakened him with their extraneous ideas, feelings and, ultimately, the music they made. He submitted to them and let a great deal of superfluous things into his life. The most innocent of the musicians, like Kogan or Rostropovich, who were dependent on his reports to the ambassador and to Moscow, were too irregular and unpredictable. There was something "different" about them. You could never tell: were they going to overstep the mark, and buy an expensive violin or say something to one of their American counterparts (with whom they began fraternizing at once) — or would this all be for the good of Soviet culture? There are fewer dimensions in politics: bosses and subordinates, fellow adherents to the cause, co-workers, one's career, friends and enemies. So when Ambassador Vinogradov transferred father from culture to politics, father not only felt glad (though he showed restraint — I never saw my father display unrestrained glee), but sighed with relief as well. He was returning to a world that he knew well...but as I said, I am getting behind. Papa has now been in Africa for some time.

•

In August, when blackcurrant clouds hung over Africa and the air was filled with the smell of a storm, like a huge international, probably Caribbean, crisis, when the rainstorms turned into floods, papa decided to go on holiday to Moscow.

Being ambassador means that you are severely cut off from the people, and that you are always a useful person to know. Awaiting him back home was 'Pine Trees'. The holiday home for government officials, 'Pine Trees', was my *favorite holiday destination*, although I never once spent the night there. I used to go and join my parents on my days off, and plunge into a half-forgotten children's paradise. According to all the laws of my rapidly advancing, unrestrained liberalism, this ought to have been a damnable place: the people holidaying here were true enemies of the people — toadies who were high up in the government. But the moment I arrived at 'Pine Trees', my moralizing always gave way to hedonism. It was less a compromise of my conscience than the magnificent imperfection of thought of a young baron. The ideal start in life if you want to be a Russian writer is among country-bumpkins and people who have endured a tough childhood — among freaks and prostitutes. I was never forgiven back home for my disgusting background.

'Pine Trees' amounted to an annual promotion for my parents. It wasn't about the swimming pool, the doctors with their questionnaires, the absolute benevolence of the domestic servants, the boat terminal on the Moscow River, the dining room or the tennis court — it was about prestige, pure and simple. Ambassadors were entitled to stay there, rubbing shoulders with those who really were close to the men in power. They would be moved from business class to first class. There were even better places, too, like the Barvikha sanatorium — that was where Troyanovsky, Dubinin and Alexandrov went on vacation — but my parents were yet to go there (and because of me they never did). But Communism was built here, too — at 'Pine Trees', however, in the shadow of Mount Nikolina. This constructivist building, which was shaped like a ship, had already dropped anchor. In its spacious cabins, with their balconies, there was the smell of tranquility — I loved this place with a criminal love, outside any dependency on power, the party, Soviet reality or the people staying there. On the other side of the park, which was heavily guarded, was a disused church in the baroque style of the suburbs of Moscow, with grape vines made of stone — and I loved that, too. I loved everything about the place.

I borrowed papa's bike and set off along the paths that led into the distance. It was a huge park, containing mushrooms that had been untouched by anyone. Life there was on such a different level that you weren't supposed to go beyond the fence. When I was at 'The Pines' I used to forget that my papa seemed alien to me. His very foreignness seemed calculated, nuanced. His friends hated *One Day in the Life of Ivan Denisovich*; as we sat around the table for lunch at home, smoking Marlboros in the intervals between courses, they would talk about Solzhenitsyn in their lordly voices — I can hear, first of all, the voice of Oleg Alexandrovich Troyanovsky, the insistent, handsome lord of Soviet diplomacy, the ambassador in Japan and China, and the son of Lenin's fellow campaigner: his dacha in Zhukovka, with its veranda, a huge *Zenit* transistor radio, from which there come pouring the sounds of the exclusive, received English of the BBC dictors; my papa did not speak so elegantly, did not extend his syllables — as an anti-Soviet, even at a time when he was being put forward for a Lenin Prize for this story; they were furious, and frothing. But father never once condemned him when mama and I were present. He listened to what his friends had to say — but refrained from judging him. He probably never read *Ivan Denisovich*. On the home front he kept silent. And this silence was golden. On the window sill in my bedroom there was a small bust of Solzhenitsyn made of fired clay, which had been manufactured by Silas and Lamport: it was on a stand made of books and a little bit of barbed wire. It was slightly concealed from those with bad intentions by a transparent curtain, and my parents struggled with it, by turns weakly and energetically, but then hit upon a solution.

"If anyone asks, it's Beethoven," mama said.

And that was how, in our house, Solzhenitsyn was transformed into Beethoven. Mama, sitting in a blue-and-white chaise-longue on the balcony at 'The Pines', used to read thick pre-revolutionary journals such as *Niva*, and read out adverts and doctors' statements about how to ward off hemorrhoids to me and papa, with a cheery smile that created a touching horizontal fold over her upper lip; as for papa, he played tennis selflessly, and in this regard too he became my lifelong ally. When the rain fell, smelling of the pine needles that swam in the puddles, he used to say that the sun would soon come out, and then take me to play ping-pong, or billiards, or to the indoor court, with its wooden surface and very short tram-lines. Papa was beginning to show a few signs of being a playboy. He started buying expensive, eye-catching sweaters made by famous international designers.

The summer steam swirled in the air after the rain. I pedaled hard, flying around the forbidden park. A man from the time of the GULAG, an elderly guard, popping up from behind the wet bushes, grabbed my heavy bicycle by the handlebars. I very nearly fell off. He had a furious expression, as if he had made up his mind to shoot me. He was clearly thinking: here's a cyclist from the simple, outside world. But I was furious as well. It was the righteous anger of an ambassador's son. And I was in the right. I bellowed at him:

"Can't you see that?"

He was three-quarters of a lifetime older than me.

"Can't I see what?" He hadn't expected any resistance.

"The label!"

I showed him the state label attached to the spokes of the front wheel. We were two astounding bastards. He realized his chance had gone. He was transformed from a guard blinded by fury into a puzzled figure. His transformation was horrific. He went from being a puzzled old man to a frightened peasant who had wronged the baron's son. The history of Russia rose up on its hind legs. He started to bow down slightly, and apologize hurriedly — he was the one infringing on someone else's territory. Now he was the one who might be chased away.

I had never witnessed such a disgraceful spectacle in all my life. In Dakar, the diplomats under my father's command attended to my every need. The Senegalese, too, believed that since I was the ambassador's son, I would one day grow up to be the ambassador, and, when my father was unable to go to some city or other for an Islamic festival as teetotal as a children's party, where sticky orange Fanta was served, they were more than happy to make do with me, whom they saw as the dauphin, and the diplomat who had accompanied me meekly acknowledged that I was superior in rank. But these were African tricks. As for that guard, he had slipped up on his home soil. Pus came pouring out of him. He had been squashed, his uniform had been folded up. The guard had grown flat. This bearded soldier in a lousy overcoat and his brother sailor, who had come to *take* this counter-revolutionary, had come unstuck. A huge pool of stinking yellowy-green pus opened up before me. In my younger days I was a sincere believer in the Russian people, who had been worn out by history. I was drawn to the people in the same way that I was drawn to black bread. I even believed in the proletariat, enslaved by Communism, until, in the eleventh grade, I failed a school experiment at a small radio factory in Marina Roshcha. But on that path through the park the entire Russian people seemed to me to be a huge puddle of pus. It was a mystical phenomenon. This feeling was even more frightening than my childhood fears, and it demanded that I liberate myself from it. I didn't know how to go about that. My literature was still a month-old embryo, devoid of independent life. I didn't believe this embryo was capable of life.

•

I rejected reality, refusing to accept that it was real. I passed through into the world of ghosts. Grandma kept inventing new forms for the ghostly siege years: she even wrapped up my bicycle headlight in a little rag, in the almost unthinkable event of a future, post-war life. My parents wrote me optimistic letters from Africa, describing rare shells and other mysteries from the underwater realm. With a very French nonchalance that could easily be mistaken for utter indifference, they left me alone with my university exams. In an oral literature exam, when I was really put through the meat-grinder, the final straw was the question:

"In which chapter does Mayakovsky meet Blok in the narrative poem *Good!*?"

I couldn't remember the chapter numbers, but I had a good understanding of the uncomplicated meaning that Mayakovsky had put into this mythical scene, and managed to emerge from the ordeal with a 'five' that rescued me. And only when I had passed three exams out of four without recourse to any ambassadorial string-pulling, despite intense competition — in the presence of my mama, at home, who was completely walled off from my tortures — did my father suddenly appear out of the blue after taking some time off, and he and Zasursky, whom he did not know very well, came running down the narrow corridors of the philological faculty looking for the office in which I was taking my history exam, to whisper something into the teacher's ear, but I wasn't there — I had already passed the exam.

•

The mediocre consciousness of a child from the hothouse, whom two people bearing no great resemblance to one another, and who are equally superficial in their mastery of culture, have stretched in different directions, was transformed into a hungry spirit. As I passed through my first failure, my nightmares and other post-exam nonsense, I thought, using the pitiful remnants of my youthful idealism, that university was a voluntary academy. The first lecture, on the first day of the academic year, was on the history of the Communist Party of the Soviet Union. Admittedly this was followed by Radtsig, who could recite Homer in ancient Greek. He gave the rider that he was not completely sure how it was pronounced, because he had not lived at that time, but, as I glanced at this frail old man, I began to suspect him of an elderly flirtatiousness. For me, university had an efficiency rating, like a steam engine, of no more than five percent. They taught me French there, more or less, but as for everything else — it was a free reservoir of time. After my first year, the embassy in Dakar found me unrecognizable. Someone whispered to mama:

"How he's changed!"

I was like a short-course in the philosophy of the twentieth century. I didn't have enough to anchor me. Everything had become merely accidental. Only a brick falling on someone's head seemed to me to be a reliable phenomenon. I didn't know what to hang my morality on. My moral compass had collapsed. In the first year of university I went to the science library — and that was my first real university. With a coltish ecstasy, I discovered Russian philosophy, from Soloviev to Berdyaev. I drowned in Russian idealism. I liked its character as something that was to be applied, and the fact that it was open about this. In essence, it was pseudo-philosophy. It had to do with rescuing your own self. Dostoyevsky had done exactly the same thing. The vast outside world entered into me. But I still didn't have enough to anchor me — I didn't believe in it.

It may be that I had read too much Dostoevsky. His underground seemed more convincing than Alyosha Karamazov. He was indeed a child of the century of unbelief, and destroyed a great many Russian souls. His classic godforsakenness, emptiness, helpless way of the cross towards meaning was something that he hung around his readers' necks. He carried his cross but did not take it all the way — it came crashing down along the road. Releasing dense gases, he damaged the energy levels in Russia.

Rozanov complained about Gogol, who had led Russians into a dark forest of dead souls and abandoned them without leaving them the faintest glimmer of hope. But Gogol clung to his brilliant word like a swimmer adrift in the Dead Sea. Dostoevsky dragged everyone down to the bottom with him. Only the odd few managed to swim back up to the surface. For dessert I read Zamiatin and the rest of the verbal snowstorm that was the 1920s. And it was then that I was infected by the tragedy of youth. I discovered Nietzsche. It happened in Leningrad, where we used to spend the winter holidays with some friends of my parents. I would read Nietzsche by night, surrounded by the aroma of the new year fir-tree and a huge, disorganized home library, whilst they, behind a half-closed door, seeming very old and absurd to me, made love, breathing heavily. After reading Nietzsche, I broke away from time. Admittedly, I loved the poetry evenings of the poets of the sixties for a long time thereafter, and kept going to them as if in a dream. They seemed to me to be gods, such was their inertia. But godforsakenness had become the key theme. I had glimpsed the chasm between morality and the world. The accidental nature of the world had become my own accidental nature. The world had flown off into the absurd. I was nineteen years old.

I pulled out two lucky lottery tickets. The Marquis de Sade was going through a boom in popularity in France at that time. I threw myself on his works with X-rated intentions, but what I found was not a philosopher: in a coarse, dry, but very convincing form, he taught me the theory of impunity, which, when applied to the Soviet marasmus, opened my eyes to a lot of things. To this day I remain grateful to the marquis for this lesson. My second luck lottery ticket was Shestov. He was the one to tell me that Russian writers were like a wounded lion. This lion has an arrow sticking out of its side, but nevertheless it runs off to feed its young, pretending all is well. Shestov brought some relief to my competition with the world, proposing that I give in to coincidence and despair and approach meaning from the other side, recognizing the imperfection contained within the world. A little behind the times historically, as is often the case in Russia, I rushed after existentialism, which was fast going out of fashion. I felt like the hero of Sartre's *La Nausée*. People made me feel sick. Evil and good had been mixed up. I experienced some wild attacks of loneliness, and lost my motivation in life; nothing seemed nice any longer; I got as close to suicide as my atheist fear of death allowed me to get. I considered various forms of proud suicide, trying them out for size in my mind. It was love that saved me.

•

The critical mass of coincidences, however, which had accumulated in his young life, was caused by the games of fate. Fate was playing a game of hide-and-seek with him. He did not grasp this immediately. It all started with mere trifles. All he had to do was ponder about the fact that he hadn't got a speck of dust in his eye for a long time, and that same day he would have to go to the eye hospital in Blagoveschensky Sidestreet, next to our apartment block, where he sat in a queue of people with black eyes. On another occasion, involuntarily thinking that he had not been given a grade of 'two' for a long time, he found himself at the blackboard, utterly at a loss how to solve some geometrical problem. The same thing happened with his tonsillitis. Slowly but surely these examples began to come together to form a system. Fate seemed to be playing for the other side. Things would happen exactly when he was beginning to feel surprised that they had not yet happened, were slow in coming, or when he had begun to doubt they were even possible — as if on someone's orders. Fate always deviated from the task he had set himself. If he wanted to go to a camp to meet a new girl, or went up to a girl to ask her to dance, the result was always offensive, fate had prescribed rejection; when he had complete faith in some venture or other, he would be met by failure, but if he went into something without giving it a second thought fate would be more than generous towards him. And so, after spending the final years of school dreaming about having his work published in the fashionable journal *Youth*, in which his idols' works were published, with an anthology of his verses and a photograph (the way they added photos to the poetry page in the journal was particularly touching), he sent a selection of verses, which had been published in *Erika*, by post, literally across the street, and started waiting languorously, in something akin to an erotic experience, and...was rejected (even the form on which the curt rejection was printed evoked respect and joy in him, because they had at least bothered to respond; the poetry department of the *Young Guard* responded with a lengthy rejection letter, accusing him of writing verses that were "anti-national", in which he was clearly using rhyme the way Mayakovsky had done: "the street was banal...not in the style of Chagal" — and his grandma, who feared the consequences, forwarded the review to his parents in Africa — there was no feedback at all from them), but the moment he started having serious doubts about himself, a solution would come along out of the blue and cheer him up.

At first he concluded that he needed to be a bit more careful. He tried to resist even the idea of formulating the question of *why* it wasn't happening for him. He realized that instead of waiting in anticipation, he needed, on the contrary, to move away from the objective toward which he was headed. In the same way, a person who suffers from insomnia, waiting in vain for sleep to come, summoning it by monotonously counting sheep, or camels in the desert, eventually drifts off to sleep when they least expect it and no longer hold out any hope that sleep will come. He became particularly careful in his attitude to mother. In the fifth grade, in the children's public library in Tryokhprudny Side-street, the librarian recommended that he read a contemporary author of books for teenagers. The book contained a description of the young protagonist's mother, in the realist style. He found it hard to come to any conclusions about the literary merits of the author, whose name he soon forgot — in the same way that the general public never remembers the names of film directors, but the subject matter got stuck in his head like a splinter and could not be dislodged for years. He feared that his mother would die. Millions of different ways in which she might die popped into his head, each one more horrific than the next. He even forgot about the fear he had experienced in Paris that his parents might get a divorce. Already sensing, though not fully aware of this game of hide-and-seek that fate was playing on him, he was forced to construct the concept of defense, so as not to do any harm to mother. He was beginning to realize that if this was the case, he had become the custodian of his mother's life, but he never confessed to anyone, as he would have confessed even now, forcing him to change the third person pronoun to the first person, or even the second.

On the other hand, realizing that he could not ask about it directly, he tried to find the key to solving this game. All knowledge is at once insufficient and excessive. Moreover it can also be called into question. As he got older he intuited that the very fact that fate had an interest in this game of varying dimensions — from a mote in someone's eye to a plane crash, relieved him of the charge that his life was random, and told him the news that someone was watching over him. He understood the significance of this choice, and was prepared to match up to it, in such a way that he would not be suspected of machinations. In his defense he could have said that the choice concerned not just him alone, and was, in essence, no less a piece of good news than the text of the gospels, although here hope had been declared in relation to a very localized slice of consciousness. Not only did it have to be reckoned with. It could not be humiliated by a literary reception of any kind. It was not supposed to be a subject for interesting conversation, which might draw the listener in, but as a revelation it needed an apocryphal transmission for those in doubt or despair. Subsequently, seeing his most successful colleagues constructing aesthetically pleasing, inter-textual castles in prose and verse, amazing readers with their wit, powers of observation, and tracking of the transient life of language and style, and the invention of their imagery, from the outer appearance, dark glasses and outfits to the strategic tasks of a literary career, he realized that they were never blessed with that dangerous piece of knowledge about hope, which engenders humility and prompts you to ponder about the idea that any style that is in fashion must inevitably come up against a ceiling. But the coarseness of a Tolstoyan attitude to language, augmented by a scattering of details reminiscent of the cathedral in Toledo, and caused by the search for a worthy reconciliation with the inaccessible, was in no way something to imitate. Just like in the game of hide-and-seek that fate was playing with him, he realized that no images could be symbols of any kind, and that some modest hint at the truth might be hidden behind some accidental turn of events, ill-chosen word or wild scene. But for him, that was all still to come. Then, as he got older, he reasoned about the extent to which he could get into the fabric of events. He knew beyond doubt that he couldn't just order something and expect it to happen: the idea of the splinter that hadn't got in his eye for a long time was something that had occurred to him involuntarily; he would have to learn to halt this thought, but he realized that its involuntary nature was itself due to a complex web of circumstances, into which it might have been possible to sew one's own wishes and intentions. If he hadn't liked the US president Kennedy, for example — out of a sense of contrariness, let's say — because of the way he had conquered the world, and it was not about youthful jealousy but about his reasoning on global roles, although we cannot discount the sheer hooliganism of a hacker who was ahead of his time, and he spontaneously started thinking about the fact that no US presidents had met a violent end for a long time, then the events of November 22, 1963 might have been an answer to his involuntary thoughts. He would not have had time to prepare a conspiracy, but someone would have tried on his behalf. The most obvious case might have involved the state regime of his own country, yet he was intelligent enough not to break the rules of the game, which concerned far more important matters. Games of hide-and-seek were his guiding star — until, that is, he no longer noticed the algorithm between randomness and fatalism, which formed the basis of things in the world, and in which we currently find ourselves. However that may have been, he had no wish to kill Kennedy.

•

Mama was kind enough to help me with my books. Returning from Dakar via Paris, I picked up quite a lot myself from the YMCA press, making good use of my diplomatic passport. A big row broke out in our family. Mama sorted out the ones that were allowed (poetry, philosophy, Nabokov) from the ones that weren't (rude books, books about our life, defectors: l'antisovietisme primaire). The cut-off point in this (essentially liberal) ban ran between Orwell (permitted) and Beethoven (prohibited). With the purge of the books, a stand-off began. Our cultural union was destroyed by her fears over papa, though these were not expressed in detail, however, for liberal reasons.

MAMA: You'll do your father some damage. It's not allowed, end of story.

Papa feared losing his diplomatic passport more than anything in the world. Road accidents, burglaries, tropical fevers, the death of his friends — all these were mere trifles when set against losing his passport. To lose one's passport was tantamount to putting your head on the chopping block. Papa took his passport with him everywhere, and only trusted one person when he went bathing in the ocean at Ngor beach: my mother. We walked into the water, while mama stood looking after my brother and the passport. My brother wore glasses. With his glasses on he looked like a little boy from West Germany. In Dakar I found myself a girlfriend — the daughter of the ambassador of South Vietnam. The war was going on at the time — we were enemies. That made us incredibly close. We rode around in her 2CV at night on the wild beaches, and danced in the nightclubs to hits by the Beatles, who had already been to Paris. I would return home towards morning on a real high, but the security guard said nothing: I was untouchable. An ambassador is more senior than a president. The Ukrainian resident spy Telega hid under the roof of the *Soyuzexportfilm* building — he used to sell Soviet films. He could make life a misery for any Soviet citizen. But nobody, apart from me, was doing anything reprehensible. Early one morning, the Soviets were fishing on the pier, trying to save up enough money to buy a *Volga*, and by night they would take their trash out to the tip themselves, so as not to have to pay the Senegalese rubbish collectors to do it. The Africans used to lie in wait for the Soviet diplomats and give them a real beating. Mama and papa were scandalized. Papa called a party assembly on a remote beach. The thinking was that no-one would eavesdrop on them there. Telega invited us all round for dinner. My parents hesitated for a long time, but in the end decided to go. They went to see him with fastidious expressions on their faces. They fed us up for the slaughter. We talked about food. When mama mentioned the word 'melon', a melon was brought in; when she mentioned 'meat' some meat was brought in. The resident spy was content: we stuffed our faces and had loads to drink. In the morning I tried to catch a fish using a spinning-rod, missed and hooked a Frenchman by the ear. If he'd been Russian he'd have turned the air blue, but the Frenchman merely waited patiently while his ear was taken off the hook.

•

Papa was losing his understanding of the country he represented. It seemed to him to be the way he had seen it in the chalky albums of the Leningrad publishing house *Aurora*, which he used to give to foreigners. It was a country that gave gifts. It was a great country. It had everything: Lake Baikal, Kizhi, the Dnieper Hydroelectric Station, huge birds flying over the Kazakh steppes, palm trees, glaciers, parades on the Red Square, flooding on the Volga. All that remained to be done was to make one final push: to raise the population's living standards, but there were a thousand objective reasons that meant this task had to be put off year after year. Papa was prepared to bide his time.

The newspaper *Pravda* lived a life of its own — it was the most optimistic newspaper in the world, in which good conquered evil on a daily basis; it was a fairy-tale newspaper, which papa read after dinner, but as the years went by he would nod off over it more and more often, after getting tired in the course of the day. Every headline in *Pravda*, from the front page to the last page, sounded so upbeat that it looked like a sexual beckoning. This was something that we students found entertaining at university. When papa returned to Moscow, he didn't know how to pay for a ride on the trolleybus, or how much it cost (I'm not too sure myself either, as it happens). The half-empty shops made him feel puzzled, in a merry sort of way. He was willing to stand in line at the baker's, covered in filth from the wood chips which the cleaner spread all over the floor — the very same one who considered the French to be "very dirty people". To papa, the shortages of foodstuffs were a temporary problem, confined to one month's leave. Ambassador Vinogradov came to visit us. He lived on the floor below us. Vinogradov asked me, with a cunning look under those thick eyebrows of his:

"How are things going on the girl front?"

This was considered a sign of attention. My parents sat there looking switched on. The dinner was splendid: roast beef in its juices or chicken almandine. The *pièce de résistance* was mama's trademark lemon pie. The question was asked every time, year after year. I blushed. Then I came to the conclusion that Vinogradov was an idiot. I found out from someone that

Vinogradov had a lover: she worked as a cashier at a store, and he used to take gifts to her. I pictured the love between the cashier and ambassador Vinogradov. It was a thing of beauty. Grandma Sima, expressing the view of the people, could not understand why my parents did so much travelling.

SERAFIMA MIKHAILOVNA: A real man has everything contained within himself. He's got Europe, Africa and Rostov-on-Don inside him.

"What about New Zealand?" I asked, in all seriousness.

As ever, without asking, mama's third cousin from Tambov came over early in the morning to see us. He and mama sat in the kitchen drinking coffee. Dressed in her dark blue, fleece robe, mama was telling him how beautiful and diverse the world was. With the cunning, grubby face of a man on a business trip who had spent the night on a Russian train, Uncle Gelya spoke, giving the perspective of a typical Tambov resident.

UNCLE GELYA: They're building skyscrapers in Tambov, too. Two have gone up already. There are twelve floors in each of them.

"I'm ashamed to be Russian these days," my mother said to my father in August 1968. Papa said nothing in response. We walked down into the dark valleys created by the sunflowers, which had grown overripe in the sun. The sunflowers stood with their heads bowed.

"I know what's going on, but I'm not going to say anything," mama told me in those days.

It seemed to her that this was the wisest course of action. She was protecting her nest. Breaking through between lost hope, faith in non-existent reason and protecting father's interests, she had no idea that the path to freedom led through this shame. For many years I was disarmed by her naive egotism. This European level of comfort had to be paid for with the silence of the tanks. In the end I couldn't take any more, and I said:

"If you ask me it's just cowardice."

Between us there was now the silent enmity of people who

were close to one another in spirit but alien to one another in terms of the degree of their familial responsibility: an analogy from the world of politics would be Lenin and Trotsky. What did I push her into doing? Into going out onto the Red Square? Into complete schizophrenia? I found it much easier to talk to my father than to her. She and I were subconsciously longing for a break. It arrived in September 1973, because of Chile.

What has Chile got to do with me? But at that time my hatred of the system, in which I could see nothing other than an ideology, had attained such proportions that in my eyes, Allende was a utopian socialist who was screwed in advance, a man put in place by the Kremlin, and I was sent into raptures by Pinochet's junta and the CIA's triumph. I was pleased when Allende was killed. I enjoyed the way Moscow howled in response. It was the high point of my political irresponsibility: I was so left-wing that I had become right-wing in order to defend my leftist views. I would accept anything at all — as long as it wasn't Moscow. The discussion about Chile in that kitchen in Moscow, filled with the paraphernalia of everyday French life, was short-lived. Mama started shouting that I was a good-for-nothing. Papa was, as always, in Paris. Because of Pinochet we didn't celebrate my birthday — the only time that happened in my life.

•

The Soviet Union, which my father served so loyally, robbed him. Culture, however, never let go of my father. In 1970 papa was once again thrown into the world of culture. He was appointed vice-president of UNESCO. Let's go over the lesson one more time: a follower of Molotov, who used to play the violin in a restaurant, who had not allowed during his time as prime minister any dialogue with cultured people, papa instinctively sensed that culture was a dangerous quagmire which contained the bright flowers of poisonous water-lilies. All those at the apex of Soviet power who spouted nonsense about ballerinas, the

Bolshoi, and their artist friends — people like Kirov, Kalinin and Voroshilov — were either a hair's breadth from destruction, or had met their end. The salaries paid at UNESCO were huge. Papa gave three quarters of his salary to the Soviet embassy. Not only was his advisor earning more than papa, but so was his Israeli driver. One of father's American colleagues at UNESCO whilst he worked in Paris bought himself an eleven-meter square apartment on the Champs Elysees: the US administration paid him an extra 10% because he was working abroad. Father only received all of his salary when he went away on business trips. He struggled against Western influence at UNESCO and, from his position in charge of the staff, did all he could to turn UNESCO into an anti-American organization for the "third world".

At the same time, an unseen struggle was being waged on a different, internal front: inside the system of the Soviet colony in Paris, father had turned into a self-governing Republic. He was now an international civil servant of senior rank, officially independent from the Soviet state; he made his own decisions, and was sinking in this international environment: his subordinates and his boss were foreigners. He was drawn into a different style of work, one that was dynamic and genteel, joined a prestigious tennis club, where he played against Englishmen, and drove the very latest DS. He did not enjoy as flashy a lifestyle as his American colleague, but he lived a respectable life, in a bourgeois apartment, in a bourgeois building in the seventh arrondissement, on Place Francois Xavier. The light from the Eiffel Tower's search-lights glanced off his windows in the evenings. The USSR's new ambassador to France, Chervonenko, who referred to the chateaux of the Loire as the chateaux of Laura, inspired restrained scorn in him, and he tried his best not to show up at the embassy unless there was an urgent need for him to be there. Not only was all France accessible to him — the rest of the world was too. One could sense in him the inner peace of a large man in his fifties. Taking me to Roissy one Sunday, he and mama took me straight to Normandy, to the seaside and the mist-covered cliffs — to revel in the Impressionism in nature. He had fulfilled the dream of his youth: he had been to Spain; he had flown halfway around the world on an international inspection, fallen into a wasps' nest in Sri Lanka, and seen a passenger jet crashing into the runway in Irkutsk, an event which he talked about in a very matter-of-fact manner, as if it was an unavoidable fact of life. He had accomplished something, something that gave him this inner condition and spoke of his future development. When a colleague of his — a Frenchman of Russian descent, with the interesting name Alexander Blok — had a book about Mandelshtam published, using the transparent pseudonym of Blo, in Paris, where the Soviet authorities couldn't get to him, my father faced a dilemma: Blok had breached the UNESCO charter, which forbade employees from engaging in any form of business activity without first securing the consent of the organization — should he be punished or shown mercy? Mama, reading a book with a pencil in her hand, rejected the idea that it contained primitive anti-Soviet material, shed a tear for the poet's destiny and asked that he be shown mercy. Father suppressed the whole affair.

Father faced an even more complex dilemma when Leonid Ilyich Brezhnev, who was making an official visit to France, decided to award father with the medal of Friendship between Peoples. Under UNESCO's laws, international civil servants were not entitled to accept awards from any state, including their own. Father knew, however, that Leonid Ilyich was more important than UNESCO, and agreed to accept the medal behind closed doors, in the conspiratorial setting of the embassy. Brezhnev awarded father the medal and, as was his wont, leaned in to give him a kiss on the lips. Father told me genially that at the very last minute he managed to get out of an 'imperial kiss', by presenting Brezhnev with his cheek instead, with its aroma of French lotion.

When father retired, he gave the money that UNESCO had paid him to the Soviet treasury. It took me a considerable amount of effort to persuade him, in the late 1980s, to keep that money for himself, by sending it to my account in Paris. Father reluctantly agreed to this, thereby saving himself and mama from a semi-destitute post-Soviet existence, although he made the executive decision to cut off his UNESCO pension, without even suspecting that this would affect him. In his old age he is living on money that, in essence, is paid by his Western enemies, against whom he fought to brutally. His lack of practicality evokes mixed feelings in me. When began working in senior positions abroad, the Soviet authorities started to take an interest in him: he might be able to fix their children up with good jobs at international organizations. A woman, who was deputy to Promyslov, the mayor of Moscow, offered father some land in Barvikh. One little house had to be built for two old women, who didn't have any heirs, and another — for ourselves. Try as I might, I couldn't persuade father to agree to it: he said he had no wish to build two houses. That plot must be worth at least a million dollars by now. When father declined to take it, the deputy mayor, assuming that she was not offering enough, offered father an entire estate, with a hectare of land, near Nikolina Mountain. We went there along with father. It was a wonderful place, with a wood and a babbling stream that flowed through the grounds. The main house, which had a colonnade and sixteen rooms, dated from the first half of the nineteenth century. We left the car by the side of the road and walked up towards the building. Turning it down — the estate is probably worth two or three million dollars at least, nowadays — was something only a complete idiot would do. Father turned it down. And yet he found the deputy mayor's son a job within an international institution just like that. Was he too good to be true, or just a simpleton? Or a combination of the two? Papa was a devout communist. He bought his first car late in life, when he was already an ambassador; later still, he built the modest dacha, where he mows the lawn — luxury was not his style.

When Molotov had grown very tired of life and was preparing to die, he asked to see Shevardnadze, who was Foreign

Minister under Gorbachev, so that he could hear his report. Through the grimace of a rejected retiree, his true face — that of a boss — could be seen. I think my papa often dreamt that he was heading off to Molotov's office with some documents. When Molotov was in a good mood, he used to ask papa:

"So how are things, Yerofeyich?"

That is probably what he says in papa's dreams, too.

•

It was love that saved me. The committed love I felt for Europe found its embodiment. In the first year of university I fell in love with my future wife. She came from Warsaw. We were both attending a course on ancient Greek literature, in the 66th lecture hall. She was different from the Soviet girls. We used to smoke so elegantly on the Black stairway — with sheepskin coats, which looked incredibly fashionable at the time, thrown over our shoulders — that people thought of us as the most attractive couple at the university. It was probably true. She used to treat me to *Carmen* cigarettes from Poland, which contained an admixture of American tobacco. She drove around with her father and brother in a magical gray Mercedes 190 with red diplomatic license plates: her father worked at the Polish embassy.

I would stand on the corner of Aleksei Tolstoy Street, next to the black mass of the embassy with its splendid flag, huge, brightly lit windows, behind which a life of luxury was being led, and the proud eagle on a gilt tablet attached to the building, and wait until she came out wearing a tight-fitting blue dress, with a white sash around the waist which had gilded coins at each end, nodding politely at the policeman guarding the embassy. We used to kiss in entrances to buildings and in the foreign cars which her friends used to borrow from their parents. We used to buy anthologies of Polish poetry, their bindings wrapped in cellophane, at a shop called 'Friendship'. Her pronunciation was so soft and tender: *Gal-chin-sky*. Her Polish 'l' with a line over it was worth all the poetry in the world. The way she said *chut-chut*, 'a little bit', filled me with so much love that I was fit to burst. She used to tease me because I didn't cut my nails often enough, and I thought of this as the voice of Europe. Life is made up of a web of small and large complexes, and it is in the hopeless overcoming of these complexes that it is expended.

•

In his relations with women, father would always suddenly turn out to be more similar to me than might have been supposed. That was the mystery of him. My papa had one solitary passion: it went by the name of 'tennis'. Tennis was his life's calling. In winter he would play in an indoor court at the government building on the embankment, above the Variety Theatre. This was considered such a prestigious place to play that there was simply nowhere better. In Paris papa bought a special little case for his rackets and his tennis clothes: it was blue and very long, with a little silver padlock, which a Russian thief could have bitten through with a single tooth. The case caught the imagination of other Muscovites, who were unaware of the existence of such things. On Gorky Street, a man came up to papa and asked him whether he was willing to sell "his saxophone". Papa used to have a good old laugh when he told that story. I too used to walk along the street carrying the case sometimes, wearing papa's wine-colored 'Bologna' hat. For papa, playing tennis was a sacred time. He would drive off and disappear for ages. It was a trait of his, in fact — the capacity to disappear. After each game he would take a shower. His woolly white socks gave off an appetizing smell. He did not play very aggressively. It was probably on the tennis court that his male nature shone through the clearest. For him, the idea of tennis was more important than the tennis itself — you had to just accept this somehow. His serves were never very powerful, but they were accurate. There was never much of a difference between his first serve and his second serve. He wasn't afraid to come into the net. He didn't like rough, unprofessional play, but on the court he was always patient with whichever partner he was playing against, and praised others' successes.

PAPA: *Bien joué!*[*]

I climbed up into the umpire's chair, turning my head from side to side in time to the music, but papa liked to keep score himself, and he didn't like it if someone said, when the score was 30:30, 'all square', or, worse still, 'tie-town', or some other such nonsense. At the change of ends, he would go up to the bench on which he had put his case, and carefully wipe the sweat from his face with a special tennis towel. My wife and I were running late for a show at the Bolshoi. Father had decided to take us there, but had had to drop us at Manezh Square: he was running late for his tennis. Thanks to him, we spent the first act in the gallery. Tennis was his freedom. He knew no other freedom. Tennis was his magic ball, in which, if you tried hard enough, you could spot all manner of transparent outlines, vague female forms and strange positions, just like in Bosch's *Garden of delights*. It may be that it was this association with Bosch that prompted me to have a dream: I dreamt that papa and I had a shared lover. A blonde woman supplies me with paper, which was in short supply, for Erika, takes me into the forest in Chkalovskaya and, lying down on the pine needles, unbuttoned her imported body on the damp perineum. What she seeks is not satisfaction but a forbidden comparison: she likes her daring position in our lives, she wants to talk about my mother with a sense of alienated respect, which is like a sense of erotic superiority, and, because of my lack of ability, I lose out in this match.

Papa put me in the hands of a former tennis champion in the USSR, Chuvyrina, to have tennis lessons at Dinamo's stadium. I took my racket with me on the metro three times a week and hit the ball against the practice wall: I played in

---

* Well played! (*fr.*)

the Moscow boys' championship, but tennis did not become my magic ball. Mama treated papa's tennis as a fact of life. She didn't get jealous — she merely worried about him, sometimes to the extent that her eyes filled with tears: where had he got to? Mama cursed his tennis whenever he was late for Sunday lunch, which mama managed to put on a par with tennis thanks to the ritual nature of it and the delicious dishes she cooked (the transparent *shchee* with fresh cabbage, to which papa and I used to add loads of pepper, and then surreptitiously add a shot-glass of vodka). He usually came back from tennis in a cheerful mood, with a glint in his eye, but looking slightly thoughtful, with an expression that could not really be said to be that of a family man; over dinner, however, his face gradually assumed more familial features. I think my father and I are brought closer to one another not only by our physical resemblance, which at times is almost pathological, but also by the fact that we both told a lot of lies about one and the same thing during the course of our lives.

•

Any first love needs a dress rehearsal, and this in itself is an absurdity. I had fallen into the trap of sensuality, which is capable of tearing any great love to pieces. I burdened Veslava's fragile shoulders with the responsibility and honor of dealing with the matter of Europe, and, stupidly, was surprised to find that she did not managed to handle it very well. I was inattentive to her merits, and her innate musicality, yet too soon I was horrified by her flaws, her feminine triviality, her lack of impudence and her avant-garde decisiveness.

As it turned out, rather than Europe trying to stay on the bucking bronco, it was the other way round: the bucking bronco was trying to stay on Europe. Love — if Plato is to be believed — is the acquisition of your other half, but all too often that half is a poor fit, like a part taken from the wrong model of car, and, losing patience, instead of working on your love you feel like saying to hell with it all.

"Bonjour, mademoiselle," my father said, as he walked into the room and met Veslava. He was shy, and in his shyness had forgotten that there were other countries out there, as well as France. After three years, he made all the arrangements so that we could marry. That was quite a feat in those days. Poland was the limit of acceptability for the son of an ambassador. If I had married a girl from Yugoslavia, papa would have lost his job in a flash. Papa was not afraid of this Polish girl, who had raised the subject of private "relations with a foreign girl" in our family — potentially such a dangerous subject. On May 20, 1969, he went to Griboyedova Street to try and persuade the bull-shaped female director of the only registry office in Moscow that was prepared (reluctantly) to register marriages involving foreigners, so that our marriage could be registered exactly thirty days after we had submitted our application. Catching sight of the diplomatic passport of the ambassador excellent and plenipotentiary, the principal caved in obediently. The ceremony was due to take place so early that we surrounded ourselves with alarm clocks, so as not to sleep through Mendelssohn.

I spent my honeymoon in the Soviet Army, which had a severely upset stomach at the time because of Neil Armstrong and his moon-walk, in a swamp in the Tambov Region, near the village of Bolshaya Lyada, at a training camp, where the frogs were even louder than the officers. On my return, we spent the autumn in the Carpathians. Ever since then, Poland has been my third homeland.

Where France had been distant, Poland turned out to be an unruly neighbor. Its unruliness was sometimes directed against me. On one of my numerous trips to Warsaw I got stuck in a traffic jam on the Krakow Przedmesce in my yellow *vosmyorka* with its Soviet license plates and metallic, traffic cop-style SU sign. An incredibly elegant gentleman in a tweed three-piece suit, of the sort that you simply do not find in Russia, by definition, spat on the hood of my car as he walked past on the sidewalk, as a sign of dissidence. A minute later I caught up with him in the car, and signaled to him. He turned round and, when he saw me, looked a little scared. Through the open window I gave him a big thumbs-up sign, encouraging his attitude towards the Empire: I'm pretty sure he loved it.

I must admit that in Poland I was forever seeking traces of the West, went to see American thrillers, and read journals at the French cultural center, but in the end it turned out that I had fallen specifically for Poland. I loved her invisible freedom, and the proud ridge of her noble nature, in spite of the stinginess of her people. After getting over her Polish pronunciation of 'God', Veslava no longer spoke to me in Russian. I learned Polish without ever once using a dictionary. Russians' love of Poland often goes unrequited, although this was not the case with me: the Poles, it seemed, took a liking to me, openly admitting to me that I was not like most Russians.

The complexes mama had had in Novgorod were re-awoken. To her mind, the hegemony of the proletariat ended with Marxist theory, which was tangential evidence of how near we were to *perestroika*. She suddenly realized that her son was getting married to the daughter of a chef. It was a mismatch. This was one of the most repulsive incidents in my life. I too was experiencing a feeling of inequality, afraid of plunging into the mass culture of a different country. Pan Zygmunt Skura was a wonderful chef. He was probably the best chef in Poland. Gerek used to invite him to his villa on Sundays. His pork chops were outstanding. He used to chop up long cucumbers, for a family-size salad, faster than the speed of sound. He smoked the meat himself, and made smoked sausage. He was a true provider. But his lips used to quiver when he read *Zhiche Varshavy*. He disliked communism and used to wave his hand in disgust at the poor quality of socialist produce. On the other hand, he was also a typical Polish anti-semite. In Poland, where, beneath the blanket of communism everything was abuzz with the energy of resistance, and where young people made fun of the authorities, the smell of the incense of insubordination was in every church, and the Polish intellectuals not only earned the right to translate Joyce's *Ulysees* but also awarded the Polish translation a state prize, which was unthinkable in Moscow, my Polish family lived according to some sort of warped reason, which I couldn't fathom, by which going out to the cinema was seen as improper, buying foreign journals was referred to as squandering, and when we were at home we were all supposed to sit on the ottoman watching TV and comment on what the presenters were wearing. And yet, in spite of all this neurotic delirium, I loved my Polish family. In that little two-room apartment on Dynasy Street, a rough block of stone on the way up to the university, I heard a lot of stories: stories about their involvement in the resistance and the Warsaw revolt, and about how after the war, when the city was in ruins, Zygmunt had bought his wife some yellow narcissi.

I made a decision: in the spring of 1976 Veslava left for Warsaw to give birth to Oleg, so that he would be a Polish citizen. I am sure that Zygmunt and Elzhbeta lived a more honest life together than my parents. Zygmunt was sent to Paris to work as the chef at the Polish embassy: his eyes lit up when he saw how many different kinds of fish were on offer at the market next to Les Invalides, and he made friends with some of the stall-owners, without knowing a word of French — whilst my parents were flying high at UNESCO. Veslava's mother, Pani Elzhbeta, who had been born not far from Poznan, worked as a buffet attendant. Garrulous and always well-groomed, she loved telling us about how various dignitaries at receptions had taken shot-glasses of Polish vodka from her tray and said nice things to her:

"Pani Elzhbeta, the vodka on *your* tray is the best of the lot."

Veslava blushed with embarrassment. She even passed wind loudly when we found out, following a call from Warsaw, that her parents were on their way to Paris. They lived in the same town as my parents but never met them, because my mother considered them to be plebs. However, when the French cashier at the UNESCO duty-free shop, which was only supposed to be used by the elite, checked with her neighbor how much the Colgate toothpaste cost, mama thought they were poking fun at her for being a skinflint. She used to move in front of foreigners in the queue, making only one exception — for Poles. When she left for Moscow, papa came running over to his Polish relatives diplomatically, for dinner and a glass of *Yazhembyak*. Zygmunt's mushroom soup, at Christmas, was no less beautiful to me than the poetry of Pushkin.

•

My father didn't bring me up to be a dissident, of course — he would never have dreamt of doing such a thing, even in his worst nightmares — but he showed me the world; that was all it took. I never became a *soviet* person. The situation at home became more and more schizophrenic and paradoxical. Father and I were both idealists who defended our views in a similar way, and that was the very thing that divided us. At a human level we loved one another unconditionally, but as time passed our ideological conflict between us grew into a cold war that was never openly declared. We didn't know what to do about it. I involuntarily took advantage of the privileges of his position: I wore expensive French sweaters and suede coats; I looked like a Western playboy yet carried a Soviet diplomatic passport. Our open arguments were an infrequent affair, but were never less than stormy. They literally knew no bounds, and would crop up all over the map, wherever he was appointed. We began arguing under the mango trees and the baobabs, in Africa, and then picked up where we had left off in Europe. On one occasion (he was vice-president of UNESCO at the time, whilst I was a long-haired student in the philology department at Moscow State University) we had an argument in his expensive Citroën that lasted all the way from Paris to Amsterdam, as we crossed from France into Belgium and Holland along the fantastical motorways lit up by fog-lights, paying no heed to the spectral borders, becoming increasingly annoyed by one another, and unable to look one another in the eye. Late one evening, in Brussels, he was stopped by a policeman.

"Why haven't you dimmed your lights?"

Papa refrained from saying that it had slipped his mind because of our verbal jousting. He kept his composure, but his inner calm had disappeared entirely. Mama decided to stay out of it, but whenever I took things too far she would try to try to change the subject, diplomatically.

MAMA: Let's look for a toilet, instead!

But when we found a toilet at the next gas station, and heard classical music coming from it, the argument flared up once again. Father was trying to argue something that to me was patently absurd: that there were more freedoms in the USSR than in the West, and that the quality of life was no worse than in Europe. What really enraged me was that, though he admitted his motherland had "the odd shortcoming", he didn't want me to "generalize" (this word was the key division between our two positions; he ever ready to acknowledge "the odd shortcoming", and he used to mock these shortcomings himself), or, worse still, to "touch" his cherished treasure — Lenin. Amsterdam had a soothing effect on our rows over the weekend, but in Paris I broke ranks with etiquette and moved from mere words to action. I started befriending all sorts of dubious characters, mixing with both right-wingers and left-wingers: I hung around elderly émigrés, defectors, traitors and renegades, like Pierre Pascal, who was an authority on Dostoevsky; through Maurice Druon I was introduced to Gabriel Marcel; on the other hand, bored with the day-to-day bourgeois nature of Europe, of its petty bakers and the political rhetoric of the ruling classes, I was drawn to the students who had fought among the barricades in 1968, to artistic revolutionaries, to the ardent lesbians Jacqueline and Veronique, who had long since dressed in black (but with a bare mid-riff — streets ahead of the fashion of the day) just in case the revolution failed. I was prepared to go a long way with these pot-smoking revolutionaries, all the way to Maoism, but I stopped myself on the very edge of it, sensing the wise image of Stalin was looming up before me: hi there! Then I went to see the harmless Druon, to have breakfast in his apartment in the grounds of the Rodin museum. He had a wonderful puppy called Pupe. Druon told me that Pupe had once had breakfast with Pompidou's puppy. We smoked cigars.

Thanks to Druon I was cocooned — but I was cocooned in the Kremlin, rather than in Paris. During the festivities marking the 150th anniversary of Dostoevsky's death, Maurice Druon, who went on to be France's Minister of Culture, came to see us in Moscow with his wife — 'mon bijou'. Suchkov, who had completed a prison sentence, and who was at that time the director of the Institute for World Literature, where the core activity of the teaching staff was worrying about informers, ordered me to accompany Druon. Everything went well until they started to use me as a simultaneous interpreter — that was torture. But when I found out that Druon had been invited to meet Furtseva over lunch, I realized that my shame would be complete and lasting. As it happened, someone else was to get a complete shaming. We drove through the Spassky Gates into the Kremlin, under the flag of the French ambassador Seydou (my legs were shaking with fear) and went to have lunch with Furtseva.

Furtseva — it's odd to think that they never put up a monument to her — was a historic woman. She saved Khrushchev from defeat in an internal party dispute with Molotov, and managed to get abortion legalized in the Soviet Union. Short, energetic and elegantly coiffed, she immediately began showering Druon with affection and charm, and fixed me with a long, testing gaze that did not conform to protocol at all. Plisetskaya and my father's friend Dubinin were already there.

"I see you followed in your father's footsteps."

"Don't say such a thing!"

I complained to him pusillanimously that I was probably going to fail, but in response he pulled an imperturbable expression, as if I had asked him to do the interpreting instead of me. Before lunch we had our photo taken together. I wonder where that photo is now. The photographer was a short man with the distinctive features of a European face.

"Do you know who that man is?" said our hostess. "Lunacharsky's son!"

The rest of us, as one, said: O-o-o-oh! The photographer started taking pictures of us all, as if he could sense the might of father's People's Commissariat for Education behind him. But Furtseva soon chased him away like a pet that had outstayed its welcome.

FURTSEVA: Go on, be off with you...

We sat down to eat. The waiters gave us warm rolls. The guests spread caviar on them with short silver knives. I was about to be sent away from the table in disgrace at the first sound of my indistinct interpreting, but then, at the last second, Furtseva's personal interpreter appeared — a young man with sharp, Kremlin manners and a black case which he used to record conversations, and I was able to stay on as an observer, with that fragment of the mirror from Andersen's fairy-tale in my eye. Furtseva took hold of the conversation as if she were seizing a bull by the horns. One could sense that this was what she was good at, and what she loved. First of all she harangued the British, who at that time had chased an innumerable number of Soviet spies out of the country. Plisetskaya, interrupting the minister's diatribe, said, with her famous smile — that of a ballerina who finds herself in very high places — that she was quite upset by it, and would not be going on tour to London. The French did not intervene on London's behalf. Next Furtseva, building on her political success, hit out at Czechoslovakia. This was in 1971, and emotions were still running high. Furtseva spoke very convincingly about the benefits of sending tanks into Prague, putting forward Jesuit arguments, and I noticed in surprise that our great French friend was starting to nod in agreement with what Furtseva was saying, over his bullion and *pelmeni.* Furtseva did not seem to have been expecting this either. She kept glancing over at me from time to time, as if trying to work out what to do with me next. But the whole thing was spoilt by the ambassador.

"Allow me to disagree with you, Madame Minister," Seydou began, stooping over in his seat to the right of Furtseva.

"You never agree with me," said Furtseva, waving her napkin impatiently.

What had begun as an amicable lunch was ruined. If there is anyone who is of the opinion that people don't change over the course of their lives, Druon is the proof of this theory. At the beginning of the next century I met him in an official capacity again — this time at the residence of the French ambassador next to October Square. Druon was resplendent — he had just been treated to lunch by Putin. He was a strange choice.

My improper political ties in Paris came to their inevitable end. They had left someone displeased. Aksyonov, who by then had been transformed from an unattainable idol, someone who shook up the calm waters of literature, the author of *Ticket to the Stars*, to my older friend with the unforgettable face of a boxer and a merrily drinking thrill-seeker, who had expressed his respect for my 'talent' in the dedication to his book, as a form of advance payment, snorted, with a laugh and a wrinkling of his nose:

AKSYONOV: You find it easier to go to Paris than to Tula.

In 1972 my parents, after inviting me to Paris one last time, let an iron curtain descend in front of me.

•

Mama always said there were some wonderful people in the Russian provinces. Accustomed to travelling, I couldn't give it up: I started going "to Tula". I spent whole days at the Central Home of Writers — the short, malevolent administrator, Arkashka, didn't let me in, but I used to get through using a secret entrance through the kitchen, where liberals and KGB agents were simmering in tall boilers, and where Kiev-style cutlets and Suvorov-style beefsteaks were being fried; and yet mama told me, after returning from Paris, that there were wonderful people in the Russian countryside — sympathetic folk. I believed her. I tried searching for these wonderful people, but I barely had enough time: I had to write a dissertation entitled *Dostoevsky and French Existentialism*, take part in discussions with Aksyonov and Voznesensky at the Institute for World Literature about the problems of extreme aeronautics, and bring up my younger brother, whom my parents had given to me and my wife to look after for five years, no less. As a reward for looking after him we were sent parcels of fruit and a few stripeless vouchers for the store called Beryozka, which sold Danish beer, Kremlyovskiye smoked sausage and American cigarettes. We were like West Berlin, besieged inside a ring, and when my parents moved back from Paris for good, struck by how many friendships with foreigners we had struck up, and by the extent to which their younger son had been corrupted by liberalism, they chased us out of the house that very evening.

We started renting shoe-boxes. In one of these shoe-boxes, owned by a friend named Vasya Grebenyuk, on Zhdanov Street, where the trains leaving for the East used to thud beneath our windows, we conceived our son. My wife and I left to spend the summer in Poland: it had become my only Western outlet in many years. Whereas only about a third of the wonderful people in Russia shared the same views as me, in Poland the obverse was true. Before long father was sent to Vienna. My wife and I continued to rent shoe-boxes. We finally settled near the Vagankovsky cemetery. When my parents arrived in Moscow, our family lunches looked more and more like the theater of the absurd. Narym somehow came about all of a sudden, out of nowhere. It was late August. Narym was famous for being the place to which Stalin was exiled. There were raised wooden sidewalks with rotten supports, and an inscription on the tall, clay banks of the Ob: "Blossom, my homeland!"

The homeland had indeed blossomed. From above, it looked as empty as the Gobi desert. It occurred to me that Stalin must have been cold there: at night the August puddles were covered by a thin crust of ice.

STALIN: What shitty weather.

I sat on the window-sill in Grandma Valya's hut, picking Polish ham in gelatin out of a big jar which Veslava and I had brought over from Moscow. In the morning I went off to the Taiga, and in the evening — to a dance, where they were playing Salvatore Adamo. I looked so much like Adamo that his wife once mistook me for him in Leningrad, where she had joined the singer on tour. The kindly, welcoming Siberian people lived behind high fences. By night you could hear hunting rifles being fired — it was the men chasing their wives and daughters around their plot of land...no-one batted an eyelid. Sometimes condensed milk flowed along the sidewalks — it was said to be a gift from Stalin. I ate raw sterlet in the middle of the Obi, chasing it down with vodka, along with the fishermen.

"We ought to put a sign up along the banks of the Obi: warning, drunkards!" they joked.

I went hunting in the marshes for ducks, worried that I might run into a bear in the taiga, and went for saunas in a filthy bath-house. The wonderful people were all around me: strong-men, illegal workers, child-killers, gals with cedar nuts, the remains of Polish deportees, policemen and local oiks. The locals put on a production of *Three Sisters* at the Stalin Museum.

"Grandma Valya, about that condensed milk..."

"It's a gift from Stalin."

"I get that. But where does it come from?"

"God knows!"

Is there anyone in Russia who doesn't remember those blue metal cans of condensed milk? You could spread it on black bread, mix it into your coffee or simply eat it straight from the can with a teaspoon, like toffee — and no matter how careful you were, the inside of the can would always be covered in a white web of the stuff — and that was when you put your tongue inside. Condensed milk energized the country, restored the nation to health, and was loved by soldiers and children alike. But why on earth were there thick rivers of it flowing along the sidewalks of Narym? Where did it come from? Where was it going? Grandma Valya, who was sitting on the stove, drew in her lips as old ladies do, and said nothing; it occurred to me that coincidence, the good news of the modern-day West, had led to the absurd, whilst Russian fatalism had led to a puppet theatre. With fatalism it was as though I was not living my life, but others were living off me; as for coincidence, nothing at all came of that. The tale of the condensed milk took root in my mind, as I sought a miraculous reconciliation with Russian reality. Wiping my rented tarpaulin boots on the sidewalk in Narym, and skidding on the condensed milk, I was on the verge of a national recovery. Oh those dear little cans of condensed milk...

•

The end result was that in 1979, father, at the height of his career, as he awaited a new appointment as assistant to the minister of foreign affairs, was removed, amid great furore, from his position — the USSR's ambassador and representative within international organizations in Vienna — and called back to Moscow; he was left without work, and our family life was plunged into gloom.

Sigmund Freud — a distinguished son of Vienna, that crossroads for international espionage, necrophilia, pastries and music — would have been pleased with me: I had made my own personal contribution to his theory about the relationships between fathers and sons, which later became the guiding principle of a whole century. But if I did him this service, then I did so unintentionally, and without feeling any sympathy for him. No-one was less suited than I was for the role of a father-hater. I spent my entire childhood in panic-stricken fear of causing my parents any harm, as if it were within my power to do so. Now, when I see my son's glee when he beats me at table tennis, I remember the perverse habit I had of sparing my father's feelings even when his level of aptitude surpassed my own. I was afraid of accidentally beating him at chess, although he played like a master, and I never got beyond the level of a dilettante; I started to worry when the score had, by some accident, got to 40:15 in my favor.

However, my *murder* was inadvertent only to the extent that it was defined by my thoughtlessness, the fact that I had been spoilt, and my careless dislike of the customs of the country in which I lived. In other words, it was almost entirely predetermined by the role life in which life had cast me. It occurred in the brutal and sensitive dimension of Soviet life that went by the name of *politics,* but with the passing of time I find I can perceive in it, ever more clearly, nothing more than a localized case of a universal collision that is capable of unfolding anywhere at all, from South Africa to Japan and the USA.

Literature, of course, is to blame for all this. The *only* things father read were the newspapers and the 'white TASS' — the summaries of information for private use. (I read the same material, too, after pinching it. I loved reading the 'secret' news summaries from TASS. Father used to hide them inside the newspapers and in the drawers in his writing desk. Mama loved reading *L'Express* and *Le Nouvel Observateur* in bed, as if they gave her her weekly ration of truths about life. As for me, I was probably the most loyal fan of *Time* and *Newsweek* in the world). I never saw my father holding a novel, not to mention an anthology of verse, but mama, who translated Dreiser for a Russian anthology of his works, instilled in me a passion for the books of Jules Verne and Jack London at an early age. I grew up to be a writer without even noticing it, to the extent that, cut off as I was from literary anthologies, for a long time I thought of the over-exuberant imagination I had had as a child, and the soap operas milling about in my head, as the standard amount of imagination allotted to us all. Utterly unsuspecting of my own talent, I was nevertheless prepared to bestow talent on everyone else.

I only came to my senses when it was too late to take a step back; and my parents, right up until the political scandal took place, could not fathom how a writer could simply come into being *just like that*, and regarded me with growing suspicion. And sure enough I had already written goodness knew what: my stories were neither politically seditious, nor did they contain openly dissident material — but they were unquestionably *improper*, and turned the principles of life (as it seemed to me) on their head. By turns, I experienced strong bouts of self-doubt, and saw myself as a young Dostoevsky.

I wanted to get something published, like any writer, but my country manifestly was not ready for that to happen. I stocked up on patience: I wrote stories, but started to have literary essays published: they were successful (after my article about Shestov, Aksyonov's mother, Yevgeniya Semyonovna Ginsburg, said to her son: "We've got a new philosopher on our hands,"), and, despite the fact that they were dubious from an ideological point of view, I was accepted (reluctantly, but that's neither here nor there) by the Writers' Union. Whenever I did anything that was doubtful in the eyes of the authorities, mama had a ready-made question that she always asked:

"Whatever do you need to do that for?"

In this, her subconscious pragmatism was at work, as she calculated the true worth of the act. Mama had imbued herself with materialism, and the ability to explain intricate things using the basic instinct of the benefit that was to be derived. But of all the occasions when this question might have been appropriate, it was when I decided to join the Union. I still had my membership ticket from the Soviet era: red Morocco-leather crusts around a picture of the Order of Lenin medal, the award that had been given to the Union for its services to the party. Whatever would I want to join a Union like that for? The dissidents (referring specifically to the opinion of Nadezhda Yakovlena Mandelshtam, whose voice carried a lot of weight) considered this a disgraceful act of collaborationism. In theory they were right, of course, but I probably looked on the Union objectively as an appendage to my restaurant-style company at the Central House of Writers. The Oak hall was at that time still in the hands of the poets of the sixties. They enjoyed the sweet life of writers and a bohemian atmosphere. Lacking any genetic connection to it, I did not have any knowledge of the Union that had killed writers. I was of course bothered by the sign in the entrance hall to the CHW, written in white letters on a red background: 'Writers are the helpers of the party'. But by my day, slogans like that, which were hung up all over the country, had already lost their meaning and become merely a stamp imposed by Brezhnev. If I had to choose between two women who published books independently, I preferred the stance taken by Yevgeniya Semyonovna Ginsburg, who sometimes used to urge Aksyonov: "Go on then, write something for them!" Dissident self-isolationism led to sectarianism rather than free creativity. On top of that, it was forced. The fact that I joined the Union was a manifestation of my infantilism — that is to say, my self-assertion: if I'm in the Union, I must be a writer. Without giving the matter any thought, I was on the side of the moderate majority which assumed that the Union's main role was to give writers the chance to have books published and reach a wider readership, and thereby achieve glory. Does a writer have any need of glory? Rare is the writer who is able to withstand the test of glory with dignity, but there are even fewer writers capable of withstanding the absence of it. All the writers that mattered had joined the Union, including, at one time, Solzhenitsyn. Membership of it was a charter of immunity: you could have your work published without it, but the golden rule was that those who had been expelled from the party could not have their work published. The elderly secretary from the literary criticism section, sympathizing with me because of my youth, hugged me, in that same Oak hall:

"Well, this is something that lasts forever."

She was referring to the prestigious social status that the club bestowed: the pass granting access to the club's restaurant, famous throughout Moscow because of the celebrities who frequented it; the fish *hors d'oeuvres* and bagels; the permits to arts institutions; the special polyclinic; the special deliveries of food for festive occasions, including caviar, which was in short supply at the time; the lecture tours around the country, and even a bit of foreign travel. If you were stopped by a policeman for going over the speed limit, all you had to do was show him your writer's badge and he would let you go without having to pay a fine. Such was the esteem in which writers were held. The authorities had bought off writers, but the liberal ones among them were merely pretending that they had sold out. They preferred the Oak hall to ideological meetings, using their status to secure proper catering, interaction and secret resistance to the regime.

The secretary jinxed me. I set the record for the most short-lived membership of the Union in its entire history, going right back as far as 1934. I did not stay in it long enough either to experience what it was like to have a book published, or to enjoy the benefits of the House of creativity. I was expelled after seven months and thirteen days. What for, you might ask? Literature is no more than invention, but the Soviet Union was an Empire of the Word and the Image. Foreigners find it hard to understand that the main form of life in this country, to this day, in spite of the radical changes that have taken place, exists in our minds, in the self-belief of consciousness, in the figurative system of the word — and not in reality, as is the case in other countries. Language is the only argument in favor of Russia's existence. It was of vital importance to the party to have a monopoly on the word, just as it had a monopoly on vodka. Any encroachment on this monopoly whatsoever was seen as an *unsealing of power.* The crazy idea that entered my mind, in December 1977, was to build and arm a literary atomic bomb.

5

Funeral dirges came pouring discordantly through our windows every day. My wife and I were renting a minuscule apartment which had belonged to my father's chauffeur in Vienna, opposite the Vagankovsky cemetery. They had stopped burying people in the cemetery a long time ago, but allowed people to "sneak in" relatives, and moreover, as was always the way, you could get away with anything if it was done "by way of exception". There was a coffin-maker's shop next to the building. The freshly painted lids of the coffins propped up right there in the street, to dry. Our eighteen-month-old son reached out towards the lids from his stroller. They fell over, to the coffin-makers' annoyance. The atmosphere inspired by this cemetery enabled a diabolical plan to take root: I decided I wanted to bury Soviet literature.

Following the famous 'bulldozer exhibition', which was held outdoors, and which was forbidden and crushed by bulldozers (in 1974), artists, with the support of the global community, won themselves a highly enviable veneer of independence: socialist realism took a step back. Before my very eyes, by way of example, were the artists of the Moscow avant-garde. As for literature, the situation had become insane: all a poet had to do was use the word 'black' several times in a poem, and the poet would be accused of anti-state pessimism. The only liberal journal, *Novy mir*, was crushed at the end of the 1960s. From time to time I managed to take to the stage to read stories. At an evening of "creative debuts" at Moscow's House of the Actor on Pushkin Square, which was to burn down many years later, I took to the stage following a dance by a young ballerina, and read out, trembling with excitement, my short story *Edrena Fenya*, about graffiti in public toilets, and it left the audience in a state of shock. It is about a young cock that gets a woman drunk. But it wasn't the plot that caused such a stir. The story had now been put into the public domain. It was alive, and trembling like a human liver wrapped in cling-film; it was processing its own contents, its subject matter, and its own self, in terms of its style — it identified with its style. It was a story wrapped up in its own style. There was nothing else to prove. An elderly actor, seemingly illuminated by the projector, shouted out to the whole auditorium, in the voice of a well-trained artist from the Moscow Arts Theatre: "This is a dirty trick!"

In spite of the reversion toward Stalinism under Brezhnev, I managed to beat the censors on two occasions in the first half of the 1970s, by having the first essay in Russia on the Marquis de Sade published in the journal *Matters of literature* (following Tvardovsky's departure from *Novy mir*, the intelligentsia soon noticed these pale tongues of liberalism), followed by an article about Shestov. The authorities were on the alert. The Central Committee's department of culture declared that the article about Shestov (in the tenth edition in 1975, with a red cover) was an "ideological mistake" on the part of the journal. Father tried to get me a job as an interpreter at UNESCO (following his return from Paris) — the director of the Institute of World Literature, Barabash, rejected me on the grounds of the criteria and started to squeeze me out of the Institute.

What would have happened to me if I had not slipped up, without knowing it, on Shestov? Would I have stayed in Paris or decided or chosen a path that was conformed more closely to the times? What would I have managed to write — or would I have expended all my abilities in Parisian restaurants?

But I no longer had a choice. Unlike most of my colleagues, and the intelligentsia as a whole, my knowledge of the authorities did not come from mere hearsay. I was a *son of power*, and formally I belonged to Moscow's *jeunesse dorée*. This circle consisted of the children of the Politburo, of Brezhnev's advisors, and of ministers, ambassadors and military chiefs. These people usually married someone from among their own kind, became patrons of an ice hockey team, had nice apartments with Yugoslav furniture in the *Nest of the Gentry* that was Kuntsevo, went on safari in Africa, went water-skiing on the Moscow River, had picnics at government dachas, read pornographic magazines stolen from their fathers' writing desks, and screwed their mothers' hairdressers, with whom they were sometimes required to enter into shotgun weddings. They had conspiratorial nicknames, consisting of parts torn from surnames that were symbolic at the time, such as Kuzya or Kapa, which created an atmosphere of mysterious elitism, which masked their self-confidence, lewdness and idiocy. I rarely spoke to them but when I did so it was with curiosity: through them I was able to find out a few of the less significant secrets of power, and catching sight, in passing, of their fathers, who loved to play dominos in their own way when they were on holiday, and watch US action movies that the general public were banned from watching. I was on closer terms, though, with the family of the top party civil servant for culture, Vasily Shauro, a Belarussian with a sorrowful expression, who had suffocated *Novy mir*, but who for many years was secretly in love with one of his passionate readers — my mama — and even went so far as to keep some hairpins belonging to her in a secret place. Mama looked down on Shauro mercilessly as "mediocre", but let him into our home. As he sat on the sofa in our dining room, he studied a print of a painting by Salvador Dali, depicting his wife Galya, naked.

"How can anyone bring themselves to paint their wife naked!" Shauro complained, slamming the album shut.

It was clear that someone like Shauro — who had hinted to me, in no uncertain terms, that if I joined the party he would take me in his department, to deal with culture — would be able to help me get my stories published. Gazing at him with innocent, friendly eyes, I thought about the authorities' reaction to my bomb. I knew that I could only talk to them from a position of strength, and carefully sought out this lever. And I found it — it would be my almanac, 'rejected by literature', consisting of texts banned by the Soviet censors because of the principle: "Look what they're publishing! Look what the authorities are afraid of!" It was a desire to show the authorities in their naked state.

What I mean when I say 'censorship' is a generalized image. Any publication with a print-run of more than twenty copies was subjected to preliminary censorship. But the censors rarely banned publications. Manuscripts were "chopped up" while still at the editing stage, because the editors knew that if they let any "sedition" through they would lose their jobs. The editors looked at you with pleading eyes: "You don't want to take the food from out of my children's mouths, do you!" The Soviet authorities sure knew how to handle people.

In the 1970s, however, the authorities were already in a state of semi-collapse; it was a time of vagueness, and their demands were obtuse. When, at the age of 23, I took the manuscript of my article on Sade to *Questions of literature*, nobody knew who or what Sade was. The manuscript was rejected. A year later I brought the very same text along, without changing a single word of it. "It's a bit better now," I was told at the journal's staff, who had grown used to Sade — and then they asked me to write an article on the role of sadism in bourgeois culture. Once again, I brought the exact same text back a year later. "That's more like it," they nodded, "that will work." To show my loyalty, I inserted a quotation from Engels into the essay — it had nothing to do with either communism or Sade, incidentally — and the text was printed. The next morning I woke up to fame "in certain circles". And I realized something: I had a field of play to work with — a small one, granted, but a field of play nonetheless. My clever text on an unfamiliar subject knocked the editors off their stride. With this thought in mind I wrote a letter to Shestov. Later, in the late 1980s, I happened to meet some Western publishers, who have a strong market-focus, and had occasion to be persuaded that they did not look on me with probing eyes. "Our readers think of themselves as intelligent," the editor-in-chief of the 'smartest' New York journal said to me, as he rejected my article about Nabokov. "If they read your work and can't understand it, it won't be you they're disappointed in, it will be the journal, and they'll stop buying it."

•

As the inventor of this 'bomb', I saw its component parts in the explosive gas of liberal writers and dissident writers. To unite writers who were famous throughout the country and whom the authorities used "for export", like Voznesensky, with dissidents who had been given up on, and show their *common* protest, amounted to accusing the authorities of a conscious destruction of culture, and prompted them to make concessions. Wandering around the disorganized alleys of the Vagankovsky cemetery; scrutinizing the graves, which were protected from the living by little silver fences; and feeling anxious for those who had died young (why were there so many of them?), I thought about the preliminary list of writers, but realized that I would not be able to cope with this task on my own. I had neither enough connections, nor enough authority among writers.

The words from the foreword to *Metropol*, as the almanac was called, to the effect that he had been born against a background of toothache, were more than just a metaphor. Everyone knows writers have bad teeth. Aksyonov, the key "westerner" in the literature of the day, and I both had our teeth tended to at the dentist's on Vutechich Street. We were put in seats next door to one another. The interior of the room we were in was surreal: it was a huge, open-plan hall, filled with the sound of gnashing teeth. It was here that, assuming an indifferent air, I seduced my famous friend with the project I had been working on.

"Let's publish the almanac in the West," was Aksyonov's response.

"No. We'll publish it here," I insisted.

In Peredelkino, on the cold terrace of the House of creativity, which had not been refurbished for a long time, I persuaded the "high-brow" author of the novel *Pushkin House*, Andrei Bitov, to help compile the almanac. He and I became good friends. He considered me a sort of antidote to Lomonosov. The third person to be seduced was a contemporary of mine, the Siberian Yevgeny Popov, whose prosaic debut had attracted a lot of attention when it was published in *Novy mir* in 1976. Popov and I met that same year, in Peredelkino, at a meeting of young prose writers, and became friends, probably because we were unlike one another. When I told him about my idea for an almanac in our apartment at Vagankovsky, Popov, without saying a word, gave me a hug that was almost evangelical. Then, on Aksyonov's recommendation, the Faulkner of *Abkhazia*, whose name was known throughout Russia — Fazil Iskander — joined us. This was the nucleus of the plot — a strong team — and we were up and running.

•

During the course of 1978, we gathered together a "fat" volume: over twenty authors from *four* generations, none of them mere passengers: each of them, from the poet Semyon Lipkin, also known as Gorky, to the young prose-writer from Leningrad, Pyotr Kozhevnikov, was talented in their own way. *Metropol* did not become a manifesto for a school of any kind (as was usually the case with literary almanacs in Russia); we came up with the idea of aesthetic pluralism spontaneously, of our own accord. It was more than just an aesthetic innovation — it was a hint of what was to come. In the works published in *Metropol* there emerged an image of Russia that was *free of taboo*, an image of Russia, with its religious searches, sexual catastrophes, drunken fights, diverse intellectual potential, which was shrouded in smoke like a wheel, mentality, the very latest in risqué art and a traditional rigorous aesthetic. It was a formulaic model for Russia, which was striving tensely for self-knowledge.

Wealthy car-loving liberals smoked American cigarettes, which were hard to come by at the time, at our conspiratorial meetings; whilst the poor dissidents let out the smoke of foul-smelling, thin Soviet cigars. Discussions broke out. The poetesses argued amongst themselves poisonously: the idol of the young, Bella Akhmadulina, who could win over entire stadiums, and Inna Lisnyanskaya, with her chamber music style. We left some of them behind, such as Yevtushenko, who by that time was playing games with the authorities. The odd one or two took their manuscripts back. The novelist Yuri Trifonov explained his reasons for doing so by saying that he would be better off battling the censors with his books, whilst the poet Bulat Okudzhava said that he was the only party member among us. Lyudmila Petrushevskaya was on her guard too. The doorbell rang (the apartment on the ground floor, to the left of the lift, which had belonged to the late Yevgenia Semyonovna Ginsburg, was the headquarters of the conspiracy); and in response to the question "Who's there?" the country's most popular writer and a *Metropol* author, Vladimir Vysotsky (roughly speaking, the Soviet equivalent of Bob Dylan), said:

"Is this where the counterfeit currency's being made?"

The number of celebrities taking part began to swell. Vysotsky wrote a funny little ditty about *Metropol* and its 'scribblers', and on one occasion, putting his feet up on a chair as he recalled the lyrics he had just penned with a smile, he sang it to us, while playing along on the guitar (the song has not survived). We chuckled, aware that we were going to get a kick in the teeth for our handiwork, but it never occurred to us that the authorities were really going to fly off the handle.

Metropol had a lot of invisible assistants. They typed up reworked texts on the type-writer, and did some editing. We had to glue 12,000 type-written pages onto Whatman paper, with a view to our symbolic print run of twelve copies, which we later read until they were in tatters, as I can tell by looking at my own copy. Whatever happened to those twelve literary chairs? — it's up to the literary archeologists to answer that one. What did *Metropol* look like, in its prototype form? On each page there were four type-written pages. The mock-up was designed by David Borovsky, from the Theatre on the Taganka. It looked like some greenish gravestone. Another theatre director, Boris Messerer, came up with the frontispiece and company logo — an old-fashioned gramophone with 'pluralist' bell mouths on it. At first we intended to stick photographs of the writers on it. Gorenstein had brought two photos along, in advance: a head-on shot and one in profile. But we soon realized that when you leafed through the pages the photographs soon came unstuck, and decided against it.

After assembling the almanacs so that they looked like a manuscript, we intended to hand it over officially to the authorities so that it could be published in the Soviet Union and abroad. A note in the foreword stated: 'Not to be published in any other format. No supplements or notes permitted'. This requirement particularly maddened our opponents.

We were later charged with having dreamt up *Metropol* with the aim of publishing it illegally in the West. As it happened, this wasn't the case. We had secretly reached an agreement with some French and US diplomats whom we knew to take the almanac overseas — for safekeeping, rather than to print it — and this proved far-sighted of us. The 'French' copy, which I transferred from the trunk of my green Zhiguli to the trunk of a Renault in a sidestreet off Novy Arbat, was taken to Paris by a softly-spoken authority on orthodoxy, Yves Amant, an attaché at the French embassy; he took it with him to Sheremetevo in a cloth bag with long handles. The 'American' copy was handed over to the cultural attaché at the US embassy in Moscow, Ray Benson, who would later become a friend of mine, and who was now retired and living in Middlebury, Vermont.

The act of the 'unlawful', not to say 'criminal' (from the point of view of Soviet law) hand-over to Ray took place on one of the coldest January days in the history of Russia. The thermometer read minus 40 Celsius. The streets of Moscow were deserted — most of the cars' engines had frozen. Ray was quick to appreciate the significance of the 'bomb'. Smiling cunningly, and giving a sniff of his blocked-up nose, he put it under his arm after lunch and took it away from Aksyonov's dacha in Krasnaya Pakhra, across a thick layer of snow, to his diplomatic car. The next day, he handed it over to the ambassador in a secret room at the US embassy, and the ambassador, without saying a word, shook his fingers affirmatively — let's do it! The almanac flew to Washington in the diplomatic mail.

•

We had planned it like this: we would organize an open day for *Metropol*, so as to introduce the public to it. We rented the 'Rhythm' cafe, next to that same Miusskaya Square where my parents had studied before the war, and where their marriage was registered. For our celebration, after agreeing on some fairly garish treats (*kalach* with red caviar and champagne), we invited three hundred people: Soviet and Western journalists, directors, actors, singers, cosmonauts and foreign diplomats. By Soviet standards, it was a huge 'act of provocation'. What happened next was straight out of a detective thriller.

The KGB opted for a military response: its staff cordoned off the area, took up positions in payphones, closed cafes and sealed them with the help of doctors from the sanitary station, claiming falsely that cockroaches had been found in them; there was a notice hanging from the door: 'Sanitary day', and we were dragged off to be interrogated at the Union of writers, where we had handed in a copy in advance, so that they could familiarize themselves with it.

There was a ring at the door of my apartment on Leninsky prospekt. A very deliberate one. Sign upon receipt. A summons:

you are required to appear...in the event that you do not do so...on January 20, 1979, an extraordinary meeting of the secretariat was held along with the Party Committee, to which five composers were invited. The whole thing had been carefully stage-managed. One public figure after another stood up, voiced their concerns, and tried to intimidate us. One of those present even started weeping out of hatred. Around fifty loyal Soviet writers, who had taken it in turns to read the almanac, locked themselves into a room at the Central Home of Writers (when they had read it, they came out shaking their heads), got right in our faces and shouted at us, accusing us of being in league with the intelligence agencies from the West, 'literary Vlasovites' who ought to be either put up against the wall or exposed to the people. It was all so loathsome, so cruel, that all we could do was try to put a 'heroic' front on it. Sitting by the wall in the large, beautiful room containing neo-gothic elements from the beginning of the 20th century, where the Moscow Masons had once sat, we thought of ourselves as a live painting of anti-socialist realism, painted in oil, in coarse, anxious brush-strokes. Strangely, they were still yet to find a new Repin, so that it really could be painted. Or, perhaps, both Repin and Salvador Dali. As I close my eyes, twenty-five years on from that evening, I see the autumn flies alighting on our faces, and somewhere in the back rows the instructors from the party's city committee are just visible in the darkness, and the KGB envoys glimmer intermittently. Rubbing his eyes in puzzlement, Iskander suddenly said curtly, and to our surprise, that we were living in our own country as if under occupation. Right away I see a car on the Moscow metro, in which Popov, to the amazement of the other passengers that evening, rips the buttons off his white shirt and, as a sign of his love for some random American woman, after following us around, swallows them gleefully, one after the other, like pills. But Popov didn't swallow his buttons that day. This Siberian hooligan with an eternal black eye was the target of particular venom, because he had taken the minutes of the writers' appearances before the public prosecutor. Aksyonov referred to the Writers' Union as a jumped-up kindergarten. I announced — standing there with my long hair and stretched, transparent expression (like something from Nesterov's collection) — that our almanac was a breakthrough.

"A breakthrough towards the West!" someone shouted out spitefully.

Bulat Okudzhava, who had turned up at the meeting — it was unclear which side he was on — said nothing (we got angry with him). I went out to have a smoke in the corridor — I was accompanied by puzzled stares, as if I had walked out of an interrogation of my own accord — and bumped into a legendary individual, an uber-conformist from the Stalin years, the bald poet Gribachev.

"Whatever you say in there, guys," he said, as if risen from the grave, "you're done, regardless."

The chair of the meeting, Felix Kuznetsov — a man with a multi-faceted appearance, who was sweating profusely; he had once been a liberal critic in the 1960s before becoming chief executioner at *Metropol* — said, in summary, "I warn you that if that almanac is published in the West, we won't accept any repentance from you!"

"Publish it here!" we insisted, stubbornly.

•

I would probably have been less surprised if I had ended up 'through the looking glass': I found myself at the heart of a scandal, and was at the epicenter of attention: some people wanted me passionately (the mysterious Western journalists, who had materialized out of nowhere, had been transformed into tall American guys and French intellectuals such as Daniel Verne), whilst others hated me. I was by turns torn apart, wined and dined, detested, and torn to pieces. Popov and I were like brothers in those days, and were never apart. People tried to tear us away from one another in all manner of ways. They said that Aksyonov was out of our league — he had a million in the West! But in what currency? The anti-Semites used to poke fun at Lipkin, calling him Lipkin-Vlipkin. The literature of Tatiana Kudryavtseva (mama had studied with her and even befriended her) and Tamara Motyleva prompted some well-known counter-espionage agents to expressed concern in print about our "ideological clarity". "*Metropol* is trash, not literature!" the Moscow writers' organization wrote. "Pornography of the soul!" The Russian literary émigrés turned their backs on us too, suspecting us of working for the KGB.

Through the howl of the mufflers, Western radio-stations reported my own texts, which had been printed in *Metropol*, back to me. I felt like a turtle that had been flipped onto its shell and was waving its legs in the air. And then came an unexpected blow from the USA. The almanac had been sent to Carl Proffer, the owner of the Ardis publishing house in Ann Arbor, Michigan, who was friends with many of us, and who published uncensored Russian literature. At his own initiative he announced on 'Voice of America' that *Metropol* was in his hands and that he intended to publish it.

Carl and Ellendea: this was a colorful film about love, money, glory and the American accent in Russian literature. By their efforts hundreds of Russian books saw the light of day. I ruined my friendship with Carl for personal reasons (an Ellendea in fur, with red lips, perfume and jealousy) when the Ardis team arrived in Moscow (they were still letting them in back then) and remained forever outside the publishing house's circle — but that night the time had come to clarify some non-personal matters. Popov and I rushed to Aksyonov's apartment, sinking in the snow, to call Carl, in our bewilderment — but just try getting through to America in those days!

"What's the point anyway! It's late!" Aksyonov shrugged his shoulders tiredly, and glanced at us, letting go of his pipe.

There was nowhere we could retreat to. Following its bright-yellow publication in Ardis, the almanac was published in English by Norton and in French by Gallimard.

•

However much I despised the Soviet authorities, my conflict with them, in the days before *Metropol*, had always been theoretical in nature. Now I felt the chill of the GULAG: they eavesdropped on my telephone calls, impudently, and recorded them (the telephone switched itself off completely from time to time — this was clearly when the eavesdroppers had gone to the toilet); my male and female friends — including the 'Russian beauty', were called in to see the intelligence agencies, and talked out of befriending me, using talk of "unpleasantness"; and they broke into my car, to search it — I found it with all four doors open the next morning. Wild rumors circulated: "Aksyonov and Erofeyev are homosexuals — they decided to create *Metropol* to test the strength of their male friendship. Four secret agents trailed me for a whole year. My hapless KGB 'moderator', Boris Ivanovich, lost his job after letting *Metropol* slide under the radar (he owned up to it in the Gorbachev era, when I bumped into him by chance).

"Victor Vladimirovich? Can I talk to you for a minute?"

It was like something straight out of a movie. These banal words marked the start of my 'kidnapping' by KGB agents in broad daylight, from the little courtyard of the World Literature Institute, where I worked. Two men in dark suits and ties shoved me, with surprising speed and adeptness, into a *Volga* in which there sat a silent chauffeur; we drove out onto the Garden Ring in complete silence, then drove towards Smolensk Square in complete silence. I was taken to the tall hotel *Belgrade* (it is now the *Swiss Diamond*). We went up to the top floor and walked down the corridor; the duty maid watched me go past, looking frightened. I was taken into some sort of special room (apparently it belonged to the institute), and the door was locked for a long time. I sat down on a narrow single bed and stared at the painting on the opposite wall, over the second bed. In it, a famous church near Suzdal had been depicted playfully, like something out of a travel brochure. As if guessing their intentions, I quickly got up and glanced out of the window: if they threw me out, I'd have a long way to fall...I picked up the ivory-colored telephone receiver and put it to my ear. There was dead silence on the line. Or would they perhaps throw money at me? Or poison me with a gas of some kind? The key turned in the lock. The door opened. The same two men walked in. They sat down on the bed opposite. But they were just trying to intimidate me: they spoke coarsely, suggesting that I return the manuscripts "without any fuss", so that they weren't required to conduct a search; they wanted to "familiarize themselves more closely with my creative output", and threatened to launch criminal proceedings against me for "pornography".

●

Chance and law: this was their rhythm in life. Proust is all chance, plus feelings. What is it that gets transformed into law? According to Proust/Sartre/Kundera, and on the Russian front, according to Bunin — only art. It is a fixation of the imagination. At what point does life become fate?

See below.

Who chose me, pointed their finger at me, and said that I had to come to Russia if I wanted to discover the heart of it?

What?!

Or is all that mere chance, too?

What do I mean by everything?

What is my mission, when all's said and done?

My mission?

What would have become of me if I had been exiled, like Solzhenitsyn?

I don't know.

Why was I ordered to stay in Moscow?

I don't know.

Did I rise to the occasion?

No.

Did I piss away my role?

Yes.

Why was I punished with hatred?

I'll hazard a guess: for my metaphysical impudence.

How do you make chance and causality fit into the same rhyme scheme?

I don't know.

I fell under suspicion because of my dubious heritage — in cruelty and informing. Vitya Kiselyov, with whom I had travelled to Narym, was surprised when he found out from the KGB archives, during the Gorbachev era, that I was a genuine enemy of theirs. As strange as it seems, I was a knight, fearless and beyond reproach. Admittedly, I had 'conciliatory' dreams at a later stage. But no more than that. Moreover, "they" did not stretch out their hands. I fell into a pit for eight years. It was quiet in there: there were no interviews, and no television. I sat there and wrote — it was almost a happy position to be in (though it later grew turbid due to various glamorous accoutrements). It occurs to me now: when am I finally going to do something, realize that I am in this pit for good, and take a step in their direction, by asking for some indulgence? They had eternity on their sides, and I had just one life — but in the event everything turned out to be the exact opposite, as if in derision.

•

It was only a long time after these events, in Nepal, that I found out what the KGB had actually had in store for me. I travelled to Kathmandu in the mid-nineties. Boris Grebenshchikov had decided to acquaint me with the Orient, and with Buddhism. There was an element of semi-deceit in this, but the trip proved to be a revelation. Grebenshchikov knew the ambassador — he was going to have dinner with him, and wanted to take me along — but the ambassador didn't invite me. In the morning, Grebenshchikov told me that the ambassador wanted to have a one-to-one talk with me. I was surprised — but decided to go along with it. At the agreed time, the ambassador's gigantic red jeep, with a Russian flag sticking out of it, was waiting outside the hotel. The good-natured chauffeur (he later turned out to be a fervent communist and a restoration fanatic) opened the car door for me servilely and took me to the ambassador's residency, to the accompaniment of the latest Russian hits. We drove into a small tropical garden. The ambassador was standing outside the mansion, dressed in a light-colored suit and tie, and extended a greeting that was almost a military salute — as if I was a ranking officer, a distinguished visitor. We were soon left alone. Over dinner we drank half a ton of vodka, and we were soon addressing one another using the informal form of 'you'. I sat there at a loss as to what he was driving at. East — West — East: that was the pattern the conversation took — but there was something else. The sun came up. As we heard the wild cries of parrots, A.K. confessed to me that he had not dared...

"Go on?"

He fell silent, and remained so for a long time. It got to the point where I began to think the vodka had made him drift off to sleep. But then he began telling me a story, with a nervous smile; he had the intelligent face of a famous orientalist. He worked at Gromyko's secretariat, on the ties between the Ministry of Foreign Affairs and the KGB. It had been Andropov's idea. The document had been handed over by courier, and was addressed to the minister of foreign affairs. A.K. examined it: the KGB, he told me, had hatched a plan to exile me for my role as the protector of the almanac, along the same lines as Solzhenitsyn: they were going to lock me up in Lefortovo overnight, then put me on a plane bound for the West the next morning. Gromyko, without giving the matter much thought, added his signature —

and the document was sent back to the KGB (evidently so that it could be signed by the other members of the Politburo, then by Brezhnev, and then acted upon).

"Come on, let's have another drink!"

We downed some more vodka, and I sobered up completely. A.K. and I lived in the same cooperative apartment block, owned by the Ministry of Foreign Affairs, on Leninsky Prospekt. I didn't know him. He met me in the entrance hall when he came home from work. In spite of my anti-Soviet activity, which the whole apartment block knew about, I had a calm appearance. I used to walk around with my son, who by then was as seasoned a tricyclist as I had been in my own childhood. When he came from work that evening, aware of what was going to happen to me in the coming days, I called out to him as he stood waiting for the lift:

"Wait."

I had the tricycle in one hand. With my other hand I was holding onto Oleg. I looked ridiculous.

"Thank you. I need the eighth floor."

He already knew that. The lift started to rise. A.K. was agonizing over it, and thinking: I ought to tell him. To make sure he doesn't try anything stupid, try to resist. What if he's got a weapon stashed away somewhere? It will all be painless, and won't last long — just one night. And then they'll put him on a plane, take off the handcuffs, give him breakfast, and before he knows it he'll be in Frankfurt, where he'll have freedom and a new life. But what if he goes and throws himself out of the window? Who knew what might happen when someone was incarcerated. The lift stopped on the eighth floor.

"Goodbye," I smiled politely, pulling Oleg after me. The tricycle got stuck in the door. I pulled it towards me. "Damn it!"

A.K. nodded. I walked out.

"Forgive me."

"It's all right."

Outside, the parrots were shrieking. There were monkeys running along the rail of the balcony.

"You can't imagine how much I was suffering...I saw you and couldn't work out why you were still here, why you hadn't been exiled...

"Sasha, let's have a drink," I said, already feeling quite far gone.

•

As a traitor to my class, the KGB, unbeknownst to me, had given me the nickname Woland — what can I say: my belated thanks go out to them. The problems I had back then paled into insignificance compared to the suffering which befell Anatoly Marchenko, or Sakharov. I was never beaten at a camp or force-fed during a hunger strike. But during that *Metropol* year I gained a better understanding of the essence of the society in which I lived — the moral fiber of its people; the meanness and cowardice of some, and the noble nature of others — than I could have picked up in half a lifetime. "I no longer have anything to say about the stories of Erofeyev, for example," Grigory Baklanov, a fairly liberal writer who went on to become a supporter of perestroika, wrote in the newspaper, "which have nothing to do with literature whatsoever." Did the venerable writer really not appreciate that statements like that would lead to stern conclusions being taken by the intelligence agencies? The oppression began, affecting almost all of *Metropol's* writers: they banned our books (the libraries didn't let their readers take out the ones we had already published), they banned our plays, and they chased us out of our jobs. My own work as a member of the teaching staff at IMLI was first brought to an end by the KGB (there were horrific scenes in front of curly-haired teaching staff), and then I was chased out of there too. But not for long; they restored me to my position, having evidently decided not to turn me into a parasite. They whispered to me, outside: "Come to the institute," and I went; I was given a demotion, and they forbade me from working with French literature; the rest of the staff gave me distant looks, incidentally, some of them greeted me sympathetically, and even chatted to me — I was packed off, first on a sabbatical, then on special exile — to study Canadian literature.

Some time after the crushing of *Metropol*, the director of the Institute of World Literature called me in for a meeting. He told me gloomily that he was giving me the honor of taking part in the creation of a multi-volume history of world literature, as author of the chapters on Canada. "You must take this seriously." I thanked him and took my leave. I had to start from scratch. I went to the Foreign library. There was nothing there. I wanted to go the Canadian embassy, but I was warned against doing so. The clock was ticking. I realized that if I didn't hand in my chapter on the origins of Canadian literature on time, I would be kicked out of the Institute of World Literature again, but this time for a proper reason: for being unsuitable as a professor. There were two weeks left until I had to discuss my work — and I had done nothing. I went to the Foreign Library again, and pulled a Canadian encyclopedia off the shelf. There was a tiny bit about literature: a list of names, with dates of birth and death. In desperation, I copied all of this down into my exercise book. I couldn't get an overall sense of Canadian literature from it at all. When I arrived home, I admitted defeat. After this, I picked up my typewriter (not Erika — a different one) and began writing, inventing extravagant biographies for these Canadian writers, and describing the polemics between them, poisonous critical reviews, religious conflicts, the struggle to form a national literature, and, most importantly of all, the plots of novels. I dreamt them up one after the other, inventing characters for all the protagonists. The plots, which were disguised, revolved around what had happened to *Metropol*, and were interwoven with love stories. After printing four volumes of my academic work, I handed out the manuscript to the rest of the teaching staff, for review, and awaited the discussion. The only expert in Canadian literature in the USSR — some university lady — had been asked to attend it.

There was a surprise in store for me at the discussion. My fellow philologists told me they had to admit that they had not expected such color, such expression and such variety of genre of Canadian literature. The woman confirmed my competence, and made a few valuable observations. Thereafter I invented the whole of Canadian literature, from beginning to end. Not a single word of it was true. And it was published in an academic work. I felt as if I was the Stalin of Canadian literature, and had created a literary-historical fiction. Ultimately I found it entertaining. It was my retribution — against whom? against what? Against literary criticism itself, probably. All literary histories are fictions, because literature — if you can talk about it as an object at all — exists not only outside the framework of history, but also outside the framework of likelihood. In 1994, at a writer's festival in Toronto, at a packed theatre (Brodsky was giving a speech that evening), I publicly confessed to the Canadians. The Canadians started howling with glee, and demanded more details. I confessed open-heartedly that I could no longer remember either the stories I had invented or the actual names of the writers. This amnesia seemed to me to be the crown of mystification.

●

Metropol's biggest victim, however, was my father. Late one January evening, at their Vienna residence, when mama was reading in bed, as she was in the habit of doing, half-lying in bed, my father came into the bedroom, handed me a fresh edition of the French newspaper *Le Monde*, and said, in a gruff voice:

"Have a read of that. You might find it of interest."

She read it and was stunned. The newspaper's Moscow correspondent, Daniel Verne, was writing about the growing scandal at *Metropol*:

"*La suite depend de l'Union des ecrivains,*" the article ended. "*Passera-t-elle l'eponge sur une petite incartade, ou choisira-*

t–elle le scandale en prenant les sanctions contre des ecrivains dont le seul tort est de vouloir publier ce qu'ils ecrivent?[*]

"Will they call us back?" Mama looked up at father, who had sat down on the edge of the bed.

"We can't rule it out," father nodded. "But it would be better if you had the operation here."

The doctors were worried mama had breast cancer.

"Here, I am both Soviet power itself, and comrade Stalin, to you," a Soviet ambassador had once said to his subordinates, and this had gone on to become a symbol of Soviet diplomacy. Did I see my father as the hateful "comrade Stalin"? Had I thought up *Metropol* in order to get through to him via a row in front of the whole world, to explain to him his political misguidedness and incompetence, in spite of all his ambassadorial chic, his splendid gestures, and the dependency which his countless employees, chauffeurs and servants had, to see in me an accidental 'scribbler'? Just as, during a big row at home, the inkwell, vases and crockery services all come into play, had I thrown myself at him with all my talented, world-famous friends, my own intellectual baggage, and ultimately the texts of my stories, which he would never otherwise have read? All this remains outside the realm of the knowable, but my 'bomb' went off in his hands.

Just two weeks before Ray Benson took a copy of the almanac away with him, my parents were in Moscow for the new year holidays. We saw in the New year with oysters and French champagne. It was fun, and we didn't have any arguments about politics (that might have put my parents on alert). Mama said nothing about the fact that she might have breast cancer. I said nothing about my conspiratorial activities. I realized that my parents disapproved of it; yet I was naively counting on victory.

---

[*] What happens next will depend on the Writers' Union, the article ended. Will it overlook this little misdemeanor, or will it choose to stir up a scandal by taking measures against writers whose only crime is that they want to publish what they write.

Now that the KGB's secret documents on *Metropol* have been published, along with our enemies' memoirs, it is clear that there were people on both sides of the argument, and it was probably those same people (the then head of the fifth department of the KGB of the USSR, Bobkov, wrote in his memoirs in 1995: "We asked them not to inflame passions and publish this anthology" — can we take him at his word?) who had wanted to publish *Metropol* in the Soviet Union, i.e. in effect take away the monopoly on socialist realism. Perhaps we were short of two or three big names (the likes of Okudzhava and Trifonov) that might have helped us win. But as I saw it, we had a chance of winning — and I had no desire to involve my parents in all this. It was the other side that got them involved. The KGB quite rightly decided that my father was my weak spot, and that was where they struck out at me.

•

For the last time in my life, I saw my father whilst he was still seen as a Soviet VIP. A black limousine, which had been sent by the Ministry of Foreign Affairs to pick me up, took me to Sheremetevo International Airport. For the last time, as the barrier went up so that we could drive onto the runway, a soldier gave me a salute simply because of the fact I existed. The car taxied towards a blue-and-white Aeroflot TU-154 liner, which had just landed from Vienna. I climbed the stairs and walked through to the first-class area clutching an Astrakhan hat for my father — it truly was a freezing winter that year. Father kissed me, smelling of cognac; he put on the hat and, as he walked down the gangway, said:

"This time I came because of you."

And then straight away, without giving me time to respond, he uttered, for the first time in his life, a conspiratorial phrase that was directed not against the West, but against *his own side*:

"Don't talk about business in the car. While the driver's there."

Within a week of father's arrival, Galina Fyodorovna, a friend of my parents', came round to see me and asked, slightly over-eagerly:

"Are they going to call back Volodya?"

Galina Fyodorovna had altered her lifestyle dramatically. She had dumped the KGB agent Lodik, married a writer named Balter, and begun hanging around in liberal writers' circles, meeting celebrities and becoming something of a Decembrist. All this would have been fine, but paradoxically the KGB agent had always been liberal towards his wife, whilst the liberal writer behaved like a jealous dictator, beating her up when the mood took him. But Galina Fyodorovna bore this domestic terror bravely, now that she was able to listen to Okudzhava's songs and Voinovich's satire at home. It may be that women, with their innate intuition, had a better sense of the path Russia was to take in a few years. A close friend of hers, a beautiful woman named Maya, was already planning to dump the Stalinist documentary film-maker Roman Karmen, in order to bind her life to Aksyonov. Both women were now preoccupied with such concerns as whether or not the novel had died, and when Brezhnev was going to die.

"What does father have to do with any of this?" I shrugged my shoulders. I didn't want to believe the worst. I genuinely believed: he'll bear it. It seemed to me that what interested Galina Fyodorovna most was the juicy situation. Galina Fyodorovna looked at me in bewilderment.

My parents' maid, Klava, was sobbing loudly when she met us at my father's flat. She had thought the rumors that I had been "shot" to be true. Things were far, far worse than that. Mama had stayed in Vienna, with suspected breast cancer. Ahead was a black hole. When I woke up the next morning, I noticed that my hairs had turned gray overnight. I was thirty-one years old.

Four organizations got their hands on my father. He was called by turns to the MFA, the KGB, the CC CPSU and the Writers' Union. My opponents' idea was as follows: given that

I was one of the people who had put the almanac together, if I wrote a letter of repentance, which would be published in the 'Literary gazette', *Metropol* would lose its legal standing and we would be able to stop it being published in the West. The secretary of the party organization at the MFA, Stukalin, expressed his own personal view of the matter.

"If I were you I'd renounce a son like that," he said to my father, after calling him into his office.

The object of my father's diplomacy was not the USA, not the European democracies, but his own son. He was the person who was being asked to convince me to write a letter of repentance. Father continued to receive his ambassador's salary in foreign currency, "working" with me at the minister's behest. We had both fallen into a trap. Gromyko brought to his attention the price that would have to be paid for the failure of the operation.

GROMYKO: If we don't get that letter, you will be recalled from your post in Vienna.

In my view this was a Nazi-esque way of looking at the matter. Father rushed off to get help from his close friend Andrei Mikhilovich Alexandrov (Brezhnev's external political adviser), who was famous in Moscow and Washington as the architect of 'detente'. On one occasion I had managed, with his help, to send Aksyonov, who never went anywhere, to the USA. Aksyonov, on his return, gave me a really cool lighter, and by all accounts told his friends about the endless possibilities I could open up. In the Oak hall, the writers started tugging at my sleeve one after another, so that they could ask to have a trip fixed up for them as well, over lunch. Alexandrov, a smart man whom I called 'the spermatazoid' behind his back because of his predilection for sex, his resourcefulness and his slenderness, met his friend gloomily.

"And you thought you were going to spend your whole life abroad?" he said, already aware of the position Gromyko had taken.

At the KGB's offices he was shown a secret dossier about

me. It was an impressive three-hundred-page document: denunciations of external surveillance agents, records of telephone conversations, a list of meetings, lists of acquaintances, ties to foreigners ("Who's this Frenchwoman of yours?" "What Frenchwoman?" "The one you've been dating. Don't give me that!" "I'm not dating anyone," I played dumb. But what really shook father was the conversation he had at the Central Committee. The Politburo, the country's most senior executive body, discussed the issue of *Metropol* twice at its meetings, and came up with a plan to suppress it as an intellectual mutiny. Father was summoned by the CC's secretary of ideology, Mikhail Zimyanin:

"Do you realize that *Metropol* is the start of a new Czechoslovakia?"

Zimyanin spoke to my father using the familiar form of 'you'. This was not just a greeting adopted by a senior boss, but that of an acquaintance, with whom father had played tennis on several occasions.

"I hear your second son has shown signs of being a dissident, too."

"Where did you hear that?" was father said, in alarm.

"Simonov came to see me. He told me all about it."

An element of trust could be seen even in this revelation. Father realized that he had to come up with the perfect answer.

"How strange," he chuckled to himself softly. "I ran into Simonov recently. He proposed that my younger son marry his daughter Sasha."

"Well, you can sort that one out for yourselves," Zimyanin frowned.

Sasha was my brother's bride. The last time he came over to see in the new year, father had been invited round to Simonov's house to discuss the wedding. Papa came home in a jovial mood. Wait for me! Lower than Simonov in rank, he demonstrated his independence, by making it clear to this popular classic of Soviet literature that wedding dates were a matter for children.

The high-cheekboned Sasha used to come and see us almost every day. My mama used to be a bit afraid of her: she was eccentric and spoilt, and didn't wear any underwear. But she was Simonov's daughter! Simonov had the unique reputation of a Soviet liberal, without actually being a liberal. Sasha idolized him. My papa! My papa! She used to buzz in our ears about her papa. He stood at the very summit of her consciousness, the Elbrus of it, which not even mountain birds could attain. "She's too much," we decided amongst ourselves. But her papa really was a charismatic legend. I saw him a couple of times: he had the charm of a bon viveur, gourmet and literary prince. It seemed as though this prince had forced communism to work for him, in the interests of his intellectual and material possessions, like no-one else. Simonov had a protective sensibility for order outside the party, which protected him from the hail of criticism that came his way from the liberals. And then here he was betraying Sasha's betrothed to the party leadership. As for Simonov, he lost courage, and turned out to be a false prince: he showed himself to be on the same level as the people who had read the almanac in a locked room at the Central Home of Writers, and who had taken part in the 'Pornography of the soul' selection, published in the 'Moscow literary review', which I had laughed about with my brother — and with Sasha. When a father is funny, he is not a father. Moreover, Simonov ordered his daughter to cut off all communication with our family. He was beset by fearsome Stalinist visions. When he found out about the betrayal, Sasha at first refused to believe it. She sat on our sofa, her eyes wide with disbelief. She got into Simonov's study without him knowing, and looked in his writing desk. Simonov kept a daily diary. The diary contained a record of a conversation with Z., and my younger brother was referred to. Sasha broke off with her father. She refused to see him. She no longer even talked about him. Later, when the whiff of searches was in the air, she hid a stash of old copies of *Metropol* in her apartment.

After telling my father about Simonov, almost warning him

about the betrayal, his acquaintance Zimyanin thereafter (taking things seriously now) did not feel like talking to my father one-to-one, perceiving him henceforward to be not quite "one of us": the shadow of my heresy hung over my father. The head of the CC's Culture Department, none other than Vasily Shauro, was present during the conversation; he was quite partial to my mother, and my father had known him since his student days. Zimyanin pointed at my father:

"Do you two know each other?"

Shauro stretched out his hand and introduced himself drily: "Shauro."

Zimyanin read out loud to my father all the "juiciest" bits of the almanac (father didn't listen very attentively, and got distracted, inspecting, as was his wont, the tip of the man's polished boot, testing his secret superiority over his would-be love rival, who had leap-frogged him in his career), and then insulted Akhmadulina, calling her a "prostitute and drug addict" (father looked up at that), before singling me out for special criticism:

"Your son's the worst of the lot. From a political point of view."

Father fell silent. Gray-haired, with his hair in a quiff, Shauro wrinkled his brow.

Zimyanin frowned:

"Alexandrov proposed that we send your son on a business trip on the Baikal-Amur Mainline. To write an article about the construction site."

Father thought: "Ingenious," and in this thought there was a faint flicker of hope; Shauro livened up a little bit as well.

"Why not?" father said. "I think that's a pretty good idea."

"For him to write shit about BAM? All he's good at writing about is toilets."

The flicker of hope was extinguished. Zimyanin continued, insistently:

"What's more he was planning to emigrate."

"Where did you get that from?" father said cautiously.

"Kuznetsov told me about it. Your son admitted it to him himself."

It was pure slander.

ZIMYANIN: Tell your son that if he doesn't write that letter — we'll have him for breakfast.

•

This threat, coming from an influential figure within the party, was serious. They could do whatever they wanted with me: pack me off in the army (Zimyanin told my father about this in an open letter) and quietly deal with me behind the closed doors of the barracks, put me in prison and instigate an "unfortunate incident". I can't honestly say I was scared. Father had brought me up not to be a coward, and now that I was supposed to demonstrate my 'bravery', it had in effect turned against him.

I found myself torn. I saw how he agonized, coming home each evening looking as if he had been *killed* after all these meetings, I couldn't recognize him. He had probably begun to see for himself what it meant to go against a regime that he had served with faith and truth. I got the impression that if his career came crashing down, he wouldn't survive it. Before we started talking, father took the telephone into the other room and hid it under a pillow — he asked me to keep my voice down, and even resorted to using some French words: he didn't want his own government listening in on us.

On the other hand, I could not betray my friends. Me — the instigator of the undertaking, the great seducer with an ironic smile on my fat lips, the hero of our times from *Edrena Fenya*-surrender just like that! Never! I'd rather be killed! I'd rather never have been born! I could picture the faces of my friends and enemies *too well*:

"What is it, little ambassador's boy, have you covered yourself in shame?!"

A letter of repentance from me would signify not just the death of the undertaking, not just eternal disgrace for me: I knew, based on the fate suffered by Soviet writers, that the ones who were broken by the KGB were never able to start writing again. But in cases like that you always end up on your own: when my friends found out about the situation I was in from *Metropol*, they adopted the pose of observers. They didn't give me any advice. They simply had no more words to say. The political dissidents, however, said to me:

"If you've crawled out of the trench, you'd better run straight ahead!"

I didn't want to be a soldier in a helmet, with a bayonet by my side. I wanted to be a turtle, crawling towards the sea. Things reached the point where Veslava was afraid to hand our son over to the kindergarten: we imagined that the KGB might kidnap him, and then blackmail us. *Metropol* had turned into a ship that couldn't be steered. As I observed how heated passions had become, I thought by turns about the Zaporozhye Cossacks writing a letter to the Turkish sultan; the wandering gypsy camp (we often slept on top of one another at someone else's place, in bedrooms, in the bathroom, or under the kitchen table — fully clothed or undressed — wherever and however we ended up); and about Arthur Rimbaud's *'bateau ivre**. The more moderate members of the team tried to avoid a direct hit, but the more radical ones, who were battle-ready, and who had nothing to lose other than their own chains, were prepared to put on "helmets". I was up to my knees in condensed milk. But nobody surrendered — not a single one of us — nobody betrayed *Metropol*. In this regard Semyon Lipkin had some cheering words to say:

"In the history of the Soviet Union, the sailors who took part in the Kronshtadt anti-Communist uprising in 1921 who were the only ones who remained unbroken, refused to surrender and were shot — all the other acts of protest were successfully

---

* 'Drunken ship' (*fr.*).

suppressed in one way or another, with admissions of guilt forced out of the accused."

It seems to have turned out rather pompous. I wasn't writing down what he said and can't reproduce it word for word. I'll try to repeat it by appealing to the poetic essence of what he said. So then, Semyon Lipkin said some cheering words:

"Since the Kronshtadt uprising in 1921, there hasn't been a single collective act on the part of the opposition that the Soviet powers have not brought to the point of break-up, betrayal and disgrace.

That's a little better (if only a little). It's a pity those "sailors" have left us. Be that as it may, *Metropol* held firm. We can take pride in that. They all deserve to have their names mentioned. Those who are still alive and those who are no longer with us. I don't differentiate between them in this book — the characters in it are immortal. When the authorities threatened Lipkin with talk of the "secretariat", he said:

"I'll be appearing before that one soon enough," he said, glancing upwards, "before that other Secretariat."

He lived to a ripe old age. Pray silence. Boris Vakhtin, Vladimir Vysotsky, Yuri Karabchievsky, Henrich Sapgir, Friedrich Gorenshtein, Semyon Lipkin...

The history of literary almanacs in Russia is the story of the devastation of nests of authors. Who was first? Who will be last? It is an intriguing statistic. The dead cramp the living. It is a game involving only one set of goalposts. If you undertake a collective act of protest (extending to our participation in a collective amateur photo: here's Sasha Simonova...she died...young...), you always end up, as a result, facing the three dots of death. There's a reason why people stroll along the paths of the Vagankovsky cemetery.

•

I met my father almost every evening in his big apartment on Gorky Street. After taking off my coat in the cramped hallway, and changing out of my winter boots into traditional open-backed slippers, I walked down the hall, which had African masks hanging from the walls — father had collected them in Senegal — and straight into the kitchen, which was painted yellow and contained stylish French equipment. He had never been able to cook — he couldn't even manage fried eggs for breakfast, he was utterly helpless without mama and Klava, whom we had decided not to involve in our affairs. I peeled some potatoes and made some chips, mixed together a green salad and some tomatoes, and boiled some sausages, and we sat down to dinner at the round table in the dining room. Then we had tea and chocolate-coated *zefir* — his favorite dessert.

The objects in the bedroom — the chairs, the paintings, the sideboard — somehow looked completely different now: they looked alien and diseased. Not even the brightly-lit chandelier was capable of illuminating them and bringing them to life. I wouldn't say my father *pressured* me into writing the letter, or forced me to write it. That wasn't the case. He kept thinking up various alternatives that might do for the time being, but they fell away one after another because they didn't suit anyone. The row had escalated dramatically. *Metropol* was being talked about a lot on the airwaves, and written about in the foreign press. The newspaper Moscow Writer published the opinions of several Soviet writers about *Metropol* — they were very carefully selected, extremely hostile and hysterical. The almanac was officially declared "pornography of the soul". My father, on scrutinizing the newspaper, discovered to his dismay that some of his oldest friends were among the persecutors.

I awaited the outcome and, to be honest, was scared of it. What if father says we have to do it after all? For his sake, for mama's sake, for the sake of saving our family. "Look how his hands are shaking, look how he's aged!" I said to myself. "Who means more to you: him or 'Voice of America'?" "He's done nothing but good for you in life." I didn't believe in miracles. The case of Simonov came to mind. There were other examples too, all equally sad. My father's friends had gone into hiding. None of them called the apartment any more. Whenever the phone happened to ring, it caused alarm. And what evenings we had enjoyed there! What fine food we had served our guests! It had all been destroyed. The ground had been burnt. That was the difference between us: I received calls, I had a lot of people supporting me. Moreover, when our *Metropol* circle gathered, meeting first at one member's home, then at another's, we used to tell jokes all the time — some because they were young, some out of desperation — and I probably drank more champagne that year than at any other time in my life — we drowned our problems with champagne that we had bought using the last of our money.

•

On the fortieth day after his arrival in Moscow, my father invited me round for dinner again. I found him sluggish and pale, to such an extent that I howled with pity for him on the inside. He said nothing for a very long time, chewing the sausages that had become a ritual for us. At length, he said:

"There's already one corpse in our family. And that's me."

I said nothing, merely staring at him and trying to work out where this was going. He laid down and straightened out his crumpled napkin, mechanically.

"If you write that letter," father added, "there will be two."

•

There comes a time in a writer's life when you do something, the consequences of which cannot be foreseen. As the Russian proverb has it, 'it's all or nothing now'. If it's *all* — your life will be transformed and assume the shape of an artistic fate. Not necessarily a sweet fate — perhaps even a disgusting fate — but fate nonetheless. If it's *nothing* — you're left with nothing. But if you do not take that action, you cannot claim to be a writer at all. This was the role of *Metropol* in my life — a flight into the precipice... any second now I'm going to be smashed to pieces! — and a happy, almost miraculous deliverance, *thanks to my father's sacrifice.*

After killing my father politically, I ought to have gone about resurrecting him, and making his sacrifice comprehensible to me. What I needed to do was not take vengeance on the authorities, but write. My father had acknowledged that I was a writer — all I had to do was prove that was the case. I suddenly found I had a powerful motivation to write — it consisted of the antiquity of patricide and the modernity of my literary niche and destiny. All this was subordinate, however, only to an idle, superficial logic. In reality the pyramid had been turned upside down — or at any rate, that was how it seemed to me. It was destiny, nothing else, that secured my niche in modernity and was the guarantee of my patricide.

•

A few days later, Gromyko ordered father to return to Vienna, to host a farewell reception. He was given a KGB guard on his arrival. They were afraid lest the Soviet ambassador get into his big black Mercedes and try to tear off to Munich in search of freedom. But father didn't go tearing off anywhere — he merely said farewell to his colleagues. It must be said, however, that the ambassadors of the communist countries did not come to see their "disgraced" ally — whereas the Western "enemies" shook his hand amicably and asked him to send their regards to me, in hushed tones. The supply chiefs and maids from the Soviet representative office — who until recently had been so slavishly devoted to him — boycotted father as well. He and mama, who was still weak due to the surgery she had undergone (it was a success, thank God) had to pack all their belongings themselves. At the station, the Soviet staff stood in a big arc, wary of getting too close to their toppled boss. A Frenchwoman whom mama knew gave her some Chanel No. 5 as she stood on the steps of the moving car.

•

It suddenly transpired that the world was a place in which you could hear the tweeting of birds. It was noon on a sunny day in May.

"Get out here, you ancient fellow!"

"What is it?" came the sleepy voice of Popov from the car; he looked a little bit like Socrates.

As we sat on the freshly mown grass, munching sandwiches from a woven basket, lovingly prepared by Aksyonov's Maya and spread out on a tablecloth, we had sensed that the sun was shining more brightly than it did in Moscow — and had let go. Three hundred kilometers to the south, along the Kiev Highway (we had decided to go via Kaluga) we made our first stop on the hard-shoulder. As father packed his things in Vienna, the three of us (Aksyonov, Popov and I) had set off for the Crimea in Aksyonov's green Volga. Aksyonov had experienced a moment of enlightenment: the Crimea was an island. Popov, whom we had appointed chef, had spent the entire journey asleep on the back seat, thereby freeing himself from *Metropol*-induced stress.

Aksyonov and I had taken turns behind the wheel. Aksyonov crossed himself every time we passed a church — he was a neophyte. He had the feeling that the KGB wanted to destroy him physically. In order to save him, Maya was proposing that they leave the country. They had talked about this in Peredelkino, in the new dacha that the literary foundation had provided, when we were all drunk: they had gone to bed, but Popov and I had drunk two more bottles of rose wine without our hosts' permission (recently, while staying with Aksyonov in Biarritz, I finally paid back an old debt I owed him). In Kharkov we fixed his car at night, in the taxi depot. Before dawn, when it was still dark, Aksyonov, sitting behind the wheel, told me that he had given his consent for his novel *Burn* to be published in the USA. This came as quite a blow to me.

"But the KGB warned you you'd have to leave the country if *Burn* was published abroad."

"There were such threats, yes," Aksyonov agreed.

"So you're leaving?"

"What makes you say that?"

"You're in breach of your agreement with the security services."

"Everything was different after *Metropol*."

"But we told you — we're not doing *Metropol* only for it to collapse."

We had told the whole world about this. That was the strength of our position. We drove along in silence for a long time. To our left, the stormy rising of the Ukrainian sun was being played out; we were nearing Zaporozhye, and, as I fought off my early-morning sleepiness, I thought: "Fine, perhaps we'll be spared!"

In the Crimea, we met Iskander at the Koktebel House of Art.

"The sea's cold," Iskander complained. I wouldn't say he did a very good job of cheering us up.

Once we had downed a couple of shots of Calvados each, he suddenly recalled:

"I got an anonymous letter."

He showed us the anonymous letter: "Take that, you bastard! Two of those son-of-a-bitch writers have finally been kicked out of the Writers' Union."

"Who's been kicked out?" Popov said.

"It's all nonsense!" I said.

We drank some more Calvados, and the mood became Crimean once again.

•

A directive from the secretariat of the Writers' Union of the RSFSR:

"Taking account of the fact that the works by the writers Y. Popov and V. Erofeyev were assessed negatively by all concerned at the Moscow writers' organization, the secretariat of the Writers' Union of the RSFSR hereby withdraws its decision to admit Y. Popov and V. Erofeyev as members of the Writers' Union of the USSR."

•

Not a single official from the MFA met my parents when they arrived from Vienna at the Belarussky station. I was able to "cheer" my father up with the news that I had just been expelled from the Writers' Union, as I had learned in the newspapers. My father shook his head gloomily.

"Perhaps I ought to organize a press-conference for foreign journalists?" he asked me, when we were inside his parents' apartment.

By the standards of the day, this was a suicidal act of dissidence, the fast-track to the loony bin — I tried to talk him out of it. Expulsion from the Union amounted to literary death. I saw through the authorities' murderous approach: strike out at the young ones, so as to intimidate and spread discord among the others. But our comrades at *Metropol*, who were members of the Union, wrote a letter of protest: unless we are reinstated they will leave the Writers' Union — A. Aksyonov, A. Bitov, F. Iskander, I. Lisnyanskaya, S. Lipkin. A letter along similar lines, which consisted of several slanted, hand-written lines, was sent by Bella Akhmadulina as well. Voice of America wasted no time in reporting this. We had entered a new phase of our resistance.

On August 12, 1979, the front page of the New York Times featured a telegram sent by some American writers to the USSR's Writers' Union. Kurt Vonnegut, William Styron, John Updike (who, at Aksyonov's invitation, had been involved in *Metropol*, which had featured an extract from his novel *Overthrow*), A. Miller and A. Olby spoke up in our defense. They demanded that we be reinstated at the Union. It was clear that unless this happened, they would refuse to publish our work in the USSR. At the Writers' Union, they were terrified. Vague negotiations about our reinstatement began, and were to go on for many months.

Anyway, after the telegram from the US, a bigwig at the Writers' Union, Yuri Verchenko, who had already "done a number" on a fair few dissidents, began dealing with Popov and me. Majestic, fat and odious, Verchenko was like a powerful Chicago mobster. The top layer of the Union, as it seemed to me, consisted of a labyrinth of universal servility and groveling. The bosses, as a rule, were exaggeratedly polite to us — we were enemies — but treated out subordinates, including Kuznetsov, with extreme disdain. They did not let it upset them, however — they thought of it as a display of affection. Once, in Verchenko's office, in that same detached house on Povarskaya Street, where, legend had it, Natasha Rostova's first ball was set, Georgy Markov — the faceless boss of all Soviet writers — came in to have a look at us. Verchenko stretched and then started shouting.

VERCHENKO. "This is what I'm saying — that *Metropol* of yours is a pile of shit!"

Markov walked around, sniffed the air and left, without saying so much as 'hello' or 'goodbye'.

"Wait," Verchenko sniggered, turning back to our negotiations — "we'll take you back, you'll be put at the top — you know everyone at the top."

He wanted us to cut off all communication with the West.

"What's that bag you've got there?"

Verchenko was deeply afraid of the bag Popov was holding, assuming that there was a tape recorder hidden inside it.

•

My friends at *Metropol* failed to recognize my father's achievement. Akhmadulina, to be fair, paid attention to it, and Vysotsky took an interest (in the corridor of the Theatre on the

Taganka): as for the rest, they said nothing. They never asked how he was doing, or what he was doing.

But thanks are due to Sergei Petrovich Kapitsa. In this regard, he proved to be a worthy son of Pyotr Leonidovich, whom I had once spoken to about Shestov over lunch. After *Metropol*, Sergei Petrovich was forever inviting my parents to his dacha at Nikolina Mountain. Mama wrote about this in the nineties, in her book of memoirs, *A garden that was never dull*. Mama wrote openly about the food that was served at the MFA, but barely even once did she evoke her husband — the man who had been the engineer of her life. So mama, too, failed to recognize his achievement. What was he so guilty of?

Unloved October was raining down hard on Krasnaya Pakhra. I had gone to see Yuri Trifonov at his dacha. Despite the age difference between us and our differing tastes, he and I had become good friends. He was in the fashion industry at the time. Foreign translations of his novels lay on the coffee table. I couldn't understand how it was possible that he didn't like Platonov, but I felt a degree of empathy when he said that he liked soccer but couldn't bring himself to support the Soviet national team. It was a clear autumn day. We were planning to have some tea, but Aksyonov came round. Talking mainly to Trifonov, he said that he had met Kuznetsov the previous day. That's big news! A chance of reconciliation? Kuznetsov had agreed to let his whole family leave the country. It looked as if this was a victory for Aksyonov. They stood there on the terrace — big, grown-up writers, whilst I was a young and naive idealist.

"It's a victory for Kuznetsov," I said. "He went round telling everyone you'd leave."

"But if you get reinstated, I won't go."

"Why on earth would they reinstate us," I couldn't stop myself from saying, "if you..."

This subject became the predominant theme of the autumn. Maya taught me and Popov how to be courageous. I did not listen carefully enough to what she said. Meanwhile, the talks with the Writers' Union continued. Sergei Mikhalkov threw his hat into the ring. Within the structure of the Union, he was in charge of writers from Russia. It was on this republican level that people were either admitted to the Union or excluded from it. On the face of it, Mikhalkov behaved in an entirely liberal manner. In the hush of his huge office on Komsomolsky Prospekt, the man who had written the Soviet Union's national anthem said that what was required of us was a "bare minimum of political loyalty".

We wrote a short statement to the effect that we had been admitted to the Union.

•

December arrived. Popov and I were called in to the secretariat of the Russian Writers' Union. We decided not to go: seeing as they had expelled us without doing so face-to-face, let them reinstate us the same way. The previous day Verchenko assured us that everything had been agreed with the right people and that we were to appear for the sake of good form, or else our comrades from the provinces would get the wrong end of the stick. We met Aksyonov that same day. This is important, because to this day there are those who believe he only did *Metropol* so that he could escape to the West. Vasily said, once again:

"If you're reinstated, everything will be okay."

Then I suddenly remembered that he had told me how horrified he had once been on the Champs-Élysées, at the thought that they might not let him go back to Russia. We are all the children of that condensed milk. Aksyonov even intended to go to some meeting of the revision commission, which he was a member of, a day later.

The night before battle was joined, Popov and I pondered what might happen. We realized there was a battle ahead of us. We thought we were going to be humiliated, and forced to repent, so that our pitiful words could then be published in the *Literary Gazette*; we thoughht we were going to have shit smeared all over us. But ultimately they would take us, and that would mean the Union would have to alter its *Soviet essence*. We saw the reinstatement as a victory.

In the windows of the house a liquid December light could be seen. Popov and I were standing in the corridor smoking. His Socratic profile was adorned with a grimace of scorn for his fate. Kuznetsov was the last to arrive at the morning assembly. He came in noisily, dressed in a fur coat and looking overbearing, and went through to the hall without greeting us.

"Perhaps we ought to get out of here?" Popov winced.

But we stayed. We were forced to wait a long time, and then we were invited in, but one by one, rather than together. Popov was the first to go in: we saw him as a man of the people, a Siberian, and that therefore he might be able to defuse the situation to some extent. It's hard to say whether the outcome had been planned in advance. It may be that one order came through from their superiors first, and then another. The whole thing happened literally on the eve of the invasion of Afghanistan, and the people at the top could do without a load of liberal games at détente. However that may have been, one of the people there had spent time in high office. It must have been Kuznetsov, for it was he that began the meeting with an inflammatory speech decrying *Metropol*.

They were sitting at a long table and shuffling their hands indignantly: it was as if there was a load of snakes slithering around. Sitting at the chairman's table were Sergei Mikhalkov and Yuri Bondarev. Bondarev didn't utter a word, but expressed his irritation using showy mimes and gestures: one minute he grasped his forehead, the next he raised his hands. Valentin Rasputin, who knew Popov, left half-way through to go to another meeting. Mikhalkov was a picture of fairness and neutrality. When they began screaming: "We're done listening to them!" he exclaimed:

"No, comrades, we must get to the bottom of all this."

The fact that they had called us in to see them one by one had no bearing. We laughed afterwards: we had all given exactly the same answers. They wanted to blame everything on Aksyonov. Who induced you to do such a thing? Popov said that he was thirty-three years old, and that he could take responsibility for his own actions.

"I'm not a cupboard that can be moved around."

We agreed that when Zhenya came out, he would give me a sign to indicate how things had gone: good, bad or indifferent… Popov came out and merely waved his hand in frustration. When I went in they asked me straight away: do you consider that you took part in an anti-Soviet campaign? It wasn't hard to work out that we were being stitched up: participation in an anti-Soviet campaign — that was the 70th article of the Criminal Code of the RSFSR (five to seven years of strict regime), not a reception at the Writers' Union. Kuznetsov said:

"How on earth was it that as you wrote about all those Sartres and what not, you didn't realize you were being used as a pawn in a big political game!?"

Rasul Gamzatov, Mustai Karim and David Kugultinov behaved altogether differently. A moment arrived when Gamzatov stood up and said to Popov:

"I like your answers! Accept them, and there's an end to the matter!"

When Popov went out, Karim followed him and said:

"You said all the right things, but to *whom* were you saying them?!"

After we had spoken at the secretariat, one of the people involved came up to us and shook our hands. I later found out that they had voted unanimously. There was a very lengthy break. They were conferring. We stood in the corridor chatting. It was already getting dark. This time we were called in all together. We stood before the hall, to the left of Mikhalkov. The snakes started slithering around again. Some fellow named Shundik read out their decision. It had been edited by Daniil Granin, who became "Russia's conscience" during the perestroika years. The wording was unambiguous: expel them from the Writers' Union indefinitely. The tall young secretary at the side-table, who was keeping the minutes for the meeting, gave me a pitiful look. There were genuine tears in her eyes. She probably imagined that Popov and I would be sent straight to Siberia on leaving the hall. I smiled at her. Once everyone had gone their separate ways, Mikhalkov whispered to us:

"Guys, I did everything I could, but I was up against forty people."

Perhaps he really hadn't been the chief thug on that occasion?

All of this happened two days before the one hundredth anniversary of Stalin's birth.

•

"So that was how the Writers' Union marked its leader's anniversary," I sniggered to the New York Times's correspondent in Moscow at the time, Craig Whitney, who was standing guard on the doorstep of the Writers' Union. Craig started to write something down in a thin notepad.

"Now, by their standards, I'm an ex-writer," Popov said. "Let's go and drink to that."

"What about your friends?" asked Craig. He was wearing a Russian hat. You could see the breath coming out of his mouth. "Are they going to leave the Union, like they said they would?"

It was a good question. Recalling how Andrei Voznesensky, in the heat of battle, had disappeared off on an expedition to the North Pole, Popov and I took the precaution of calling on them, in a friendly letter drafted by me and containing a light touch of irony, to stay in the Union after being expelled, and not to leave the liberal flank unmanned.

Bitov, Iskander and Akhmadulina obeyed our instructions, circumspectly.

Lipkin and Lisnyanskaya, however, left the Union and faced years of poverty with dignity. They got it worse than anyone else: they had been deprived of their means of existence. Aksyonov left the Union too, but his brinkmanship had weakened our sense of unity. Before long he received an invitation from the American university, and he began by flying in style to Paris with his whole family, in first class on an Air France flight. We saw him off at Sheremetevo, as if we were at a crematorium: we thought we were never going to see each other again. He soon had his Soviet citizenship taken off him.

•

The idiocy of the dissidents was from time to time reflected in the idiocy of the authorities. Lev Kopelev, who was particularly popular in Germany, described my stories in *Metropol* back then as fascist. That meant that they were like the woman in charge of school No. 122. This reputation among Western slavophiles stayed with me for many years, and, when a dictionary of modern Russian writers was published, edited by Kazak, it didn't surprise me to see that there was not so much as a mention of my name. Iskander was predisposed not to like my stories, either. As he stood next to the long lunch table on which we had "sculpted" *Metropol*, he said openly, in that rolling, authoritative voice of his, that they had spoilt the almanac with their lack of moral clarity they had spoilt the almanac. I found myself in a strange situation, from which there seemed to be no way out: I had been ousted from my own almanac. I had fought so hard — and to what end? In the way I was reflected in the court of public opinion, I felt like a cat that had shat on the couch, and was being chided for doing so. I smiled guiltily, like a system error. When I started writing my story *The Parrot*, after *Metropol*, and brought it in to show my friends, Boris Messerer and Bella Akhmadulina, Boris secretly gave it back to me in the hallway of their dacha in Peredelkino, saying that when Akhmadulina read *that* she would definitely stop being friends with me. Bitov considered my prose the coldly calculated texts of a literary critic, as opposed to the work of my namesake, the literary gem. Unlike Popov, whose publication of a 'baker's dozen' of short stories in *Metropol* had made him the darling of the intelligentsia, I was unloved by both sides. Many years later, I realized how lucky I had been.

Aksyonov aside, Veniamin Alexandrovich Kaverin, who posthumously achieved worldwide fame for his musical *Nord-Ost*, was probably the only person who supported my first literary ventures: he was my own personal little bridge to the literary culture of the 1920s. But that's not really the point. Memory is like a corpse that is being gnawed at by your favorite dog. After meeting the Polish writer Tadeusz Konwicki, whom I had at one point planned to invite to take part in *Metropol*, but hadn't been able to find in Warsaw, I asked him why he hadn't written his memoirs.

"I can't remember anything," the Pole said.

"Then write a book about memory loss!

That would be much more interesting." I visited Kaverin at his dacha in Peredelkino so many times! What did we do there? We drank tea — I questioned him greedily about literary life in the twenties, about Pasternak, Fadeyev, Shklovsky, and Tynyanova, who was a relative of his. Before my eyes was a contemporary from a great literary era, and the author of the tale *The Barrel*. Kaverin, taking his time, told me all about it. He lived outdoors and was ruddy-cheeked — an honest old man. I listened carefully. I can't remember anything of what he said. Not a single word of it. With the exception of how he went quiet when asked about Nadezhda Mandelshtam's memoirs, but they were in the form of a text, rather than stories passed on by word of mouth. My memory has been drained, like water from a toilet tank, in order to wash off the dirt: a blood-stained Tampax floating in urine. Against this lifeless, earthenware backdrop, all I can see is my friend Masha, chilled to the bone, who was not allowed to get close to the great writer for obvious reasons, with her eyebrows raised in fury, who, throughout the endless hours I devoted to literature over tea, used to wander on her own down Gorky Street in Peredelkino, sniffing. I try to justify myself, as I crawl into a cold *Zhiguli*. I know what is going to happen next. Spring is coming. Veniamin Alexandrovich and I are wandering around his property. I am his last love. He stops next to a blossoming sapling of some sort, and whispers:

"Look, my memoirs are buried here. It's a secret — but just so you know."

I swear to him that I won't tell anyone. I feel proud. He has put his trust in me. I dig them up. I get them published abroad. We head off to have some tea.

A month later:

"Why don't we go out into the garden?"

Did he dig them up again and re-bury them, or something? We go up to the bright green sapling:

"Look, my memoirs are buried here. It's a secret — but just so you know."

He has put his trust in me. I dig them up. We head off to have some tea.

A month later:

"Why don't we go out into the garden?"

Here we go again. The sapling looks like it is about to bear fruit. It is an apple tree. Should I tell him, or not? In a conspiratorial whisper, he says:

"Look, my memoirs are buried here. It's a secret — but just so you know."

I swear to him I won't tell anyone. I feel proud. With any luck, this will be my future. There won't be another one. I love this three-act play: I always suspected that the possibilities afforded by the pure style were outside the memory of possibility (I find the Philistines of moral memory ridiculous). Veniamin Alexandrovich:

"How many times did you rewrite the text?"

"How many times did *you* rewrite it?"

"Me? A lot. I keep grinding away at it. What about you though?"

"Now and again."

After *Metropol*, Veniamin Alexandrovich gave me the opportunity to earn some money with TV scripts. I am up to my neck in condensed milk. I love the rawness of a first draft. A principled couple come to see me in my apartment. He is a writer, whilst she teaches family ideology. Both of them have close ties to Amnesty International. We are back in the days of *Metropol*. He declared that, as a CIA agent, I ought to know what was happening to my friend Popov.

"And what makes you think I work for the CIA?"

The dissident glanced at a folder of American magazines on my desk and smiled:

"All the American journalists in Moscow are subordinate to you. They quote you as if you're their boss."

I said nothing.

"Popov, on the other hand, works for the KGB."

I pictured what a pair we would make and gave a wild laugh, just as Stalin had done that time when my father said something funny. The writer waited for me to stop.

"I'm not joking," he said.

"Perhaps, as a CIA agent, I know best?"

He gave me a cautious look. In his eyes I had turned into an overseas commander.

"What makes you think he works for the KGB?"

"I was with him in Peredelkino the other day. We were sitting at the same table. I asked who was in favor of using violent means to topple the Soviet regime. There were a lot of people in favor. Popov said nothing at all."

"If he was a KGB agent," I said, "he would have been the first to speak in favor of overthrowing the Soviet regime."

There was an awkward pause. The writer thought of a response.

"Perhaps he's a cowardly agent," he suggested.

"Get out!" I said, getting to my feet.

That was the first time I had ever told anyone to get out of my house. Some semi-culturally aware girls, however (mostly Jews; Yesenin once said that his favorite admirers were all Jews) professed me to be their hero, and in the months when my parents and my wife were depressed by the genuine absence of a future, I put into effect a plan that would result in feast during a time of plague. Fame is a boundless field of freebies. Fame is when you grab your fat cock and start jerking off in front of girls, and instead of shouting out: "What the hell are you doing?!" they start yelling, in delight: "Go on, go on!" The millionaire is penniless in the face of the writer. I came home to Leninsky Prospect in the morning, smelling of perfume and semen. I put my key in the lock. My wife came out — the apartment was full of smoke. Where were you? There were two sisters doing somersaults in my dilated pupils. My wife, who had had a sleepless night worrying about me, and about whether or not the KGB had got me — hit me in the face, with tears in her eyes. I hit her back. She fell to the floor. The element of an inhuman game had become a part of my writer's nature.

·

Who stood to gain from my father becoming a victim, and from me — after losing my mind — rediscovering my senses sufficiently to be able to find myself? We are not talking about the historical Soviet powers. On the contrary, my father's sacrifice, which was echoed in the Gorbachev era, had some positive results. Even then they were *afraid* to push father to retire, with the same indifference with which ambassadors all over the world are sent packing with a letter, a call or a long drawn-out silence. Leaps in history such as this, however, had not become embedded in my consciousness, at least.

I was inclined instead to take a different view: the greatest paradox of Russian history, I thought, consists in the fact that, in spite of everything, Stalin remains a popular hero with a positive image. Love for Stalin is a good gauge of how archaic the Russian people are. And it's true: in the nineties he was not properly dealt with, despite all the things that came to light. He survived. And along with him — so did the dream.

Now I had to return to those thoughts again. We're at the start of the twenty-first century — and who's that giving us a friendly wave from way off in the distance?

All the bad things that crept out of my father stemmed from diplomacy, but he gave me the opportunity to catch a glimpse of the cyclical nature of Russian history. Stalin's impunity was absolute. What does that word 'absolute' mean? Russia was prepared to accommodate Stalin, yet ultimately could not cope with this task, and were left looking a little bit ashamed, whilst he parted form Russians in order to be understood in a perverse way.

Stalin today is the cult of power, nostalgia for the Empire, order, respect for brutality, and perfidy. Stalin was the birth of a new fear. Inside every Russian boss there is a miniature Stalin. I can feel Stalin inside myself, as well. He tosses and turns in my consciousness, restlessly. *My* Stalin is a great artist of life. A wave of his left hand — and the Chechens leave the Caucasus. A wave of his right hand — and half of Europe is building socialism. It almost seems as if, in the future, Stalin is going to enjoy the same reputation Napoleon has today. It almost seems as if Stalin is the apotheosis of the Russian people's dislike of democracy, their anti-European values, the 'kasha in their heads'. It is no mere coincidence that half the people in today's Russia do not see Stalin as a monster. Stalin was made in the Russian mold. Children stretch their hands out to him: Daddy! Daddy!

How can that be? Russians are suspicious even of 'half-bloods', refusing to acknowledge them as 'our own kind'. But in this case, not only did they acknowledge him — they lay prostrate before him. In reality, Stalin was colorless and simple, reserved and rancorous. He sits there cutting out pictures from the magazine *Ogonyok*. A strange insight stirs within me: this is a conspiracy. Why appear in such a blaze of glory? As it is, the blaze comes beating through these pictures with its rays. And what about the way he dressed? Two tunics, one ceremonial and one for everyday wear, and a single pair of boots. When he died, everyone was amazed by how miserly his wardrobe was. There is a conspiracy in that, too. And as for his nationality — that was a conspiracy, all the more so.

There are dozens of versions of Stalin in Russian literature: tyrant, sadist, genius, wit, leader, pervert, victor.

What were you, in reality?

Russian literature was unable to cope with Stalin. It turned a generalissimus into an executioner, and an executioner into a generalissimus. It turned the image over, and twisted it every which way, without finding any real meaning. It failed to notice that Stalin's appearance before the Russian people could be likened to that of Jesus, son of Joseph. Only Josef Vissarionovich appeared before a different chosen people, and called himself Antioch — receive your guest! — so that the guest would remain with this people forever. Russia deserves a good Stalin.

Russian literature failed to appreciate that this was the Russian God, pretending to be a Georgian for thirty years.

Stalin was a mask.

•

And what of my father? He was honored to have been noticed among the other young students, and perhaps even loved, by the all-seeing eye:

"Pour him some champagne!"

It is best to be a hero for no more than three days — just as a visitor ought not to stay longer than three days in a respectable household — any longer and the heroism will start to rot, like a fish. But my jobless father continued to stick it out: never once did he judge me, in spite of everything. Mama, though she often grumbled, did not judge him either. I heard my wife utter the words "unfortunate wretch", but she later took them back. Pan Zygmunt suggested that I move to Poland, forget about literature and open a hot-dog stand. My *Metropol* brotherhood ended in a bloody fight with Bitov late one night on old new year's eve in 1980, at Akhmadulina's dacha in Peredelkino. We failed to see eye to eye entirely over something, and almost ended up killing each other.

Metropol, in turn, killed Soviet literature. Dreamt up by me, but assembled by all the 'Metropolites' together, this bomb blew Soviet literature to pieces. A different form of literature emerged in its place. *Metropol* was a forerunner of Russian freedom.

In 1989, to mark its tenth anniversary, the first Moscow edition of the almanac was published, amid much fanfare and with a noisy presentation.

In 1999 there were wild celebrations to mark *Metropol's* twentieth anniversary in Messerer's studio, featuring champagne and dancing; a TV documentary about the almanac was filmed at the same time.

In January 2004, the newspapers, magazines, TV and radio all made haste to celebrate the historical significance of *Metropol*, which had just turned 25. But we did not hold a celebration of our own this time. There was no "us" any longer: it had dissolved and disappeared into legend. Bitov and I clinked glasses of tequila in my apartment, as we reminisced about the good old days — that was about the extent of it.

I will now return to that *annus Metropolis* one last time. My father once said to me, not without a little shyness:

"There's only one person who can save me. And that's you."

He asked me to write a letter to Brezhnev, but not a letter of repentance: rather, a letter to the effect that "the father is not responsible for the sins of the son". I wrote to the General Secretary of the CC CPSU ("Dear Leonid Ilyich,"), saying that I couldn't bear to see my father out of work, and that unless the situation changed I might do something stupid — i.e. hang myself.

In an attempt to make sure my letter reached him, I went to Staraya Square and called one of Brezhnev's colleagues, using my defunct contacts among the *jeunesse dorée*.

"I'd like you to pass on a letter for me," I said.

"Who's it for?"

I answered nervously, without wanting to, in the most dissident way I could think of:

"Leonid Brezhnev."

There was a cold, sustained silence on the other end of the line. "Leonid Brezhnev" was how he was referred to in the news items on foreign radio stations. I had no chance. But after getting to the end of his silence, my referent said:

"Bring the letter to the express postal service on Staraya Square."

He explained how to go about it.

"Thank you."

There was no response from the authorities. Time passed. I must admit I did not feel at all at ease. I had begun to have fits of strange absent-mindedness, and I couldn't drive my car — I would come over all dizzy. I genuinely didn't know *what* to do about my threat, about my own personal bit of blackmail: when should I hang myself: in a week? in a month? From time to time, as I gazed at my reflection in the mirror of a morning, I would touch my suicidal neck. Has the time come?

At last, the authorities dispelled my doubts. Gromyko, at Brezhnev's prompting, ordered that my father be given a job in the MFA's central administration on Smolensk Square. They made father sign a statement confirming that he (a diplomat!) was not going to meet up with any foreigners. He was given a unique, and in Kafkaesque terms, back-breaking job. He would arrive at his office by nine o'clock each morning to find nothing on his desk other than a fresh edition of the newspaper *Pravda*. The fact that he followed the same career trajectory as Molotov was a strange twist of fate. See above: "He sat at an empty desk, looking through nothing but Soviet newspapers and TASS

news updates. No other materials were sent through to him."
Incidentally, before he was *put out to pasture*, Molotov had had
exactly the same position as my father had had in Vienna. The
last time he met Molotov, in Zhukovka, Molotov said to him:

"So how are things, Yerofeyich?"

"I'm doing your old job."

"How so?"

But it was so. Father unhurriedly chewed away at the green
tablecloth that covered the oak desk of hemorrhoid-like clusters
of Party news. He was paid a decent wage.

"Vladimir Ivanovich, how about a little tea?"

He had his own personal secretary.

"Thank you, Asya."

And that was all he ever said. And it was like that for several
years in a row.

On weekends the two of us threw ourselves into games
of tennis, it must be said. Our ongoing contest was still going
strong — after all, we *now* lived in the same country. I wasn't
afraid of beating him, and the sound of the balls being struck, as
it echoed in the forest around the dacha, somehow inspired in
me the vague hope that change was in the air. I believed in those
balls, despite all the gloom surrounding us. I felt the shoves of
the future under the surface, as if I was pregnant with them. Life
had only just begun — and I wanted so much to live.

I had been transformed from a 'son of power' into a free
writer — in other words, I had essentially become a 'nobody',
just as I had promised Picasso I would, and in the long summer
nights I wrote my first novel — *Russian Beauty*. Fate had brought
its game of hide and seek to an end with a demonstration of
some altogether new capabilities. After completing the novel,
I woke up a new man. I now realize that this was so.

Glossary

Bals populaires – local dances (French).

Banya – the Russian bath-house.

Chekist – member of the Cheka (the Ch.K, the Emergency Commission), the first of a succession of Soviet state security organizations.

Elska min – 'my love' *(Icelandic)*.

Friedrichstrasse – a major street in central Berlin.

Katyusha – a Soviet rocket-launcher used during World War II.

Kalach – traditional East Slavic bread shaped like a padlock or wheel.

Krakow Przedmesce – literally 'Krakow Suburb', one of the most famous and prestigious streets in Warsaw.

Molotoshvili, Vyach – diminutive forms of the name Vyacheslav Molotov, used by Stalin to convey affection or scorn; by calling him 'Molotoshvili', Stalin has made his name sound Georgian by giving it a Georgian suffix.

Ogonyok – literally 'little flame'; one of the oldest weekly illustrated magazines in Russia, which reached the height of its popularity during the Perestroika years.

Oprichnina – the name of the secret police organization during a period in Russian history known as the 'oprichnina', between 1565 and 1572, when Ivan the Terrible introduced a policy of mass repression, secret police, public executions and confiscation of land from aristocrats.

Pastila – a Russian candy which is made using sour apples, honey or sugar and egg whites.

Pelmeni, pelmeshka – little meat dumplings made using thin dough and containing ground beef, pork or sometimes lamb. 'Pelmeshka' is a diminutive form of the word, used to refer to the dish affectionately.

Perestroika – a political movement for the reform and restructuring of the Communist Party of the

Soviet Union, instigated by,
and associated with, Mikhail
Gorbachev, in the 1980s.

Poireau pomme-de-terre –
a popular French leek and
potato soup recipe.

Politburo – a contraction of
the term Politicheskoye
Byuro, 'Political Bureau'; under
the Communist system, the
members of the Politburo
informally led the state.

Pravda – a Russian political
newspaper which was
launched before World War
I and became one of the
most prominent newspapers
in the Soviet Union after the
Revolution.

Shchee – cabbage soup.

Sots Art – short for 'Socialist Art',
a movement in Russian art that
is also referred to as Soviet
Pop Art, which emerged as a
reaction against the aesthetic
doctrine of Socialist Realism
favored by the authorities.

Soyuzexportfilm – an association
responsible for exports within
the Soviet film industry.

Stolichny salad – a salad made
using chicken or beef, popular
in Russia since the 19th
century.

Verst – an obsolete unit
of measuring distance in
Russia, roughly equal to
1.07 kilometers.

Vertushka – an internal
telephone system used at the
Kremlin; the name is derived
from the Russian word for
rotary dialers.

Vosmyorka – the Number 8
model of the Lada.

Zefir – a Russian candy made
using whipped fruit and purée,
sugar and egg-whites, plus
gelatin, and sometimes coated
with chocolate.

Zhiche Varshavy – a Polish
newspaper.

Zhiguli – the popular name for
the model of car produced by
the Volga Automobile Plant.

ZIS – the ZIS-110 was a
limousine made by the
Likhachev Factory (Zavod
imeni Likhacheva, or ZIS).

Dear Reader,

Thank you for purchasing this book.

We at Glagoslav Publications are glad to welcome you, and hope that you find our books to be a source of knowledge and inspiration.

We want to show the beauty and depth of the Slavic region to everyone looking to expand their horizon and learn something new about different cultures, different people, and we believe that with this book we have managed to do just that.

Now that you've got to know us, we want to get to know you. We value communication with our readers and want to hear from you! We offer several options:

-   Join our Book Club on Goodreads, Library Thing and Shelfari, and receive special offers and information about our giveaways;

-   Share your opinion about our books on Amazon, Barnes & Noble, Waterstones and other bookstores;

-   Join us on Facebook and Twitter for updates on our publications and news about our authors;

-   Visit our site www.glagoslav.com to check out our Catalogue and subscribe to our Newsletter.

Glagoslav Publications is getting ready to release a new collection and planning some interesting surprises — stay with us to find out!

Glagoslav Publications
Office 36, 88-90 Hatton Garden
EC1N 8PN London, UK
Tel: + 44 (0) 20 32 86 99 82
Email: contact@glagoslav.com

Glagoslav Publications Catalogue

- *The Time of Women* by Elena Chizhova

- *Sin* by Zakhar Prilepin

- *Hardly Ever Otherwise* by Maria Matios

- *The Lost Button* by Irene Rozdobudko

- *Khatyn* by Ales Adamovich

- *Christened with Crosses* by Eduard Kochergin

- *The Vital Needs of the Dead* by Igor Sakhnovsky

- *METRO 2033* (Dutch Edition) by Dmitry Glukhovsky

- *METRO 2034* (Dutch Edition) by Dmitry Glukhovsky

- *A Poet and Bin Laden* by Hamid Ismailov

- *Asystole* by Oleg Pavlov

- *Kobzar* by Taras Shevchenko

- *White Shanghai* by Elvira Baryakina

- *The Stone Bridge* by Alexander Terekhov

- *King Stakh's Wild Hunt* by Uladzimir Karatkevich

- *Depeche Mode* by Serhii Zhadan

- *Saraband Sarah's Band* by Larysa Denysenko

- *Herstories*, An Anthology of New Ukrainian Women Prose Writers

- *Watching The Russians* (Dutch Edition) by Maria Konyukova

- *The Hawks of Peace* by Dmitry Rogozin

- *The Grand Slam and Other Stories* (Dutch Edition) by Leonid Andreev

More coming soon...